# YOU CAN SCREAM

## Also by Rebecca Zanetti

**Laurel Snow Thrillers**
*You Can Run*
*You Can Hide*
*You Can Die*
*You Can Kill*

**The Dark Protectors: Witches**
*Wicked Ride*
*Wicked Edge*
*Wicked Burn*
*Wicked Kiss*
*Wicked Bite*

**Grimm Bargains**
*One Cursed Rose*
*One Dark Kiss*
*One Shattered Crown*

**The Scorpius Syndrome series**
*Scorpius Rising*
*Mercury Striking*
*Shadow Falling*
*Justice Ascending*

**The Dark Protectors series**
*Fated*
*Claimed*
*Tempted*
*Hunted*
*Consumed*
*Provoked*
*Twisted*
*Shadowed*
*Tamed*
*Marked*
*Talen*
*Vampire's Faith*
*Demon's Mercy*
*Alpha's Promise*
*Hero's Haven*
*Guardian's Grace*
*Rebel's Karma*
*Immortal's Honor*
*Garrett's Destiny*
*Warrior's Hope*
*Prince of Darkness*

**The Deep Ops series**
*Hidden*
*Taken* (e-novella)
*Fallen*
*Shaken* (e-novella)
*Broken*
*Driven*
*Unforgiven*
*Frostbitten*

# YOU CAN SCREAM

## REBECCA ZANETTI

KENSINGTON PUBLISHING CORP.
kensingtonbooks.com

KENSINGTON BOOKS are published by

Kensington Publishing Corp.
900 Third Avenue
New York, NY 10022



ISBN: 978-1-4967-6082-1

ISBN: 978-1-4201-5783-3 (eBook)

First Kensington Trade Paperback Printing: January 2026

10 9 8 7 6 5 4 3 2 1

Printed in the United States of America

The authorized representative in the EU for product safety and compliance
is eucomply OU, Parnu mnt 139b-14, Apt 123
Tallinn, Berlin 11317, hello@eucompliancepartner.com.

**For those who love without needing to be seen:**

You don't post it, parade it, or make it pretty for the world.
You live it—in quiet mornings, in long-held glances,
in the hand that always reaches back.
You are the steady heart,
the unshaken shield,
the one who stands between the world and those you love.
No fanfare. No audience. Just presence.
You are the proof that love doesn't need a platform to be real.

# Acknowledgments

There's nothing quite like plotting fictional murder to make you appreciate the people who keep your real life steady, sane, and relatively free of crime scene tape. I'm deeply grateful to everyone who helped bring this book to readers.

First, to Big Tone—thank you for being endlessly supportive, especially when I'm writing about suspicious deaths while we're on beach vacations. I appreciate that you never blink at the darker corners of my imagination or the random questions about golf-course weapons and body disposal.

To Gabe Zanetti and Karlina Zanetti, two of the most creative minds I know—you continue to impress me with your talent, your heart, and your unshakable sense of self. I can't wait to see what you take on next. I love you both more than I love a well-timed plot twist.

Thank you to my agent, Caitlin Blasdell, who can spot a plot hole from five miles out and close it with sniper-level precision. You handle contracts with the strategy of a chess grandmaster and the calm of a field operative. Thanks also to Liza Dawson and the entire Dawson group—your support means everything.

To my editor, Elizabeth May—thank you for keeping the timeline from unraveling and the plot from going off the rails. Your instincts are sharp, your notes sharper. This book is better (and deadlier) because of you.

To the rest of the incredible Kensington team: Alexandra Nicolajsen, Steven Zacharius, Adam Zacharius, Sarah Selim, Alicia Condon, Lynn Cully, Jackie Dinas, Jane Nutter, Vida Engstrand, Barbara Bennett, Justine Willis, Renee Rocco, Darla Freeman, Susanna Gruninger, Tami Kuras, Valeece Broadway-Smith, Andi Paris, Kristin McLaughlin, Shannon Gray-Winter, Kristen Vega, Carly Sommerstein, and

James Walsh—thank you all for the time, care, and sheer effort you put into making this series what it is.

To Anissa Beatty, for managing my social media life and leading Rebecca's Rebels, and to some wonderful Rebels: Kimberly Frost, Madison Fairbanks, Joan Lai, Heather Frost, Gabi Brockelsby, Karen Clementi, and Jessica Mobbs—thank you for the sharp eyes, clever suggestions, and relentless support. This team is a force.

Thanks to Kathleen Sweeney and the crew at Book Brush for giving authors the tools to make our books look as compelling as they read and to Writerspace for helping spread the word.

Finally, to the people who have my back no matter what: Gail and Jim English, Kathy and Herbie Zanetti, Debbie and Travis Smith, Stephanie and Don West, Jessica and Jonah Namson, and Chelli and Jason Younker—thank you for being the kind of crew anyone would want in their corner. No body-burying required.

# YOU CAN SCREAM

# Prologue

They were coming.

Shadows.

Ghosts.

Monsters.

His lungs burned like he was inhaling glass. He felt his brain swell inside his skull, making his eyes bulge. The pain threatened to take him to his knees, but he kept going. Kept running.

Branches tore at his bare arms, slicing welts into his skin, but he barely felt the sting. The relentless rain drilled into his scalp, failing to provide any relief.

What was happening?

Think.

God, just think.

But his thoughts wouldn't come, slipping through his mind like oil on water. Run. That was all he had left. That one command, overriding everything.

*Run.*

His body obeyed, feet pounding the earth in an uneven, desperate rhythm. His limbs were no longer his own. They were just separate, detached body parts propelling him forward. Warmth slid beneath his nose, thick and hot over his mouth.

Blood.

His stomach lurched. Frantically, he wiped his upper lip, fingers trembling. Red. So red. So warm. He stopped. Just for a second. Just long enough to look down at his hand.

Then silence. Not just quiet. True, absolute silence.

The forest was still moving. The trees swayed, the rain pelted the ground, and the wind surged. He could see it all, but he couldn't hear any of it.

Nothing.

Blissful. Terrifying. His heart pounded but his body had gone quiet. His mind had gone still. His eyelids sagged, the exhaustion pulling him down like a weight.

Wait. The blood. Why was he bleeding?

He swallowed hard, jerking his gaze to the side. The world kept tilting. The trees blurred and the earth dipped. He was standing still, but the ground rolled beneath him. The nausea hit him fast, bile burning up his throat.

A spiral of heat tore through his veins, curling up from his spine and bursting into his skull. His body jerked violently, like something inside him was fighting to get out.

Flashlights sliced through the forest behind him.

They were coming.

The bobbing lights swayed and dipped, bouncing through the trees. Not dark yet, but the forest swallowed the light, the wet leaves swallowing sound. Cover. Was he covered? Did he need cover?

A sudden dagger of pain pierced his skull.

His vision blurred.

*Run.*

His body reacted before his mind caught up. He turned, lurching forward, his arms scraping against rough bark. Blood. Monsters. Pain.

The world remained silent, eerie in its emptiness. His breath thundered in his chest, but he couldn't hear anything. They wanted to kill him. He knew that much. But he couldn't remember who they were.

His upper lip burned. More warmth. More blood. It dripped into his mouth, metallic and bitter, sliding down his chin.

He turned his head as he ran. Too fast. Dizziness slammed into him.

The lights were closer now. Too close.

Then impact.

The tree loomed out of nowhere, and he slammed into it, full force. The breath whooshed out of his lungs. He went down hard, knees slamming onto jagged rocks, hands catching in the snow, fingers crushing unforgiving ice.

He might've cried out.

Pain lashed through his legs. He forced himself to move, to get up, to keep going. His face felt like he'd shoved it into boiling water. The same water Grandpa Joe had used to power wash the deck. Grandpa Joe. He'd been a good man.

Pain enveloped him, swallowing him whole. He needed to do something. Something—what?

The lights came closer. The beams cut through the trees behind him, bouncing off slick branches.

*Run.*

That was it. That was the only thing left. He staggered forward, slapping away a tangle of bare bushes, grabbing onto frozen rock. He scrambled up, ice searing into his palms, his breath ragged. Rain and blood slid down his cheeks.

He coughed. More warmth. More blood. Why was his mouth bleeding? He couldn't think anymore.

They were coming. He had to beat them. The truth should win. His foot slipped. The world tilted. He windmilled his arms, skidding across an icy rock. Even gravity fucking hated him. His heart jackhammered as he teetered on the edge, his toes curling in an attempt to grip solid ground.

He looked down.

Way down.

A road twisted along the valley floor below, following the path of a rushing river. Cars crawled along the pavement, their headlights gleaming like tiny pinpricks against the dusk.

Too high up. He had to get down. Now. He turned around.

They emerged from the trees. Dressed in black. Lights in front of them. Hunting him. Shit. They'd found him. The one in front grinned, his crooked front tooth catching in the beam of a flashlight. He lifted a gloved hand, gesturing—a silent demand.

No. They couldn't have him. Not again.

Sound roared back in like a thunderclap. A shrieking, splitting explosion in his skull.

The man in front spoke. "Come on. Let's go." His voice was flat. Dead. As were his eyes.

"No." One simple word. The only thing he had left. He smiled, held out his arms, and fell back.

The men in black bellowed.

Air rushed around him, pulling at his clothes, whipping hair into his eyes. The rain hit like bullets. A sudden flash of pain stole his breath.

Horns honked. Brakes squealed.

Then—

Nothing.

"Grandpa Joe?" he whispered.

# Chapter 1

It had been exactly twenty-nine days since her half sister had brutally stabbed their father to death.

FBI Special Agent in Charge Laurel Snow sat in the back row of the courtroom, her suntan already fading after being home for three days from a much-needed vacation in Cabo. In Mexico, she'd done nothing but sit in the sun, stroll the beaches, and work through feelings with the hard-bodied Fish and Wildlife officer sitting next to her.

She wasn't accustomed to dealing with feelings, and neither was he. But they'd done their best, assisted along with too much tequila, to handle the loss of a baby they'd never met. Huck had been kind, open, and had wanted to cement their relationship for the future.

Her practical nature liked a plan. Of course, now they were home, sitting in this courtroom, waiting for a hearing that had yet to begin. She studied him from the corner of her eye, noting that the Cabo carefree Huck was gone. His face now appeared carved from stone.

Not granite. Not slate. But diamond—the strongest stone.

Though nothing about Huck Rivers sparkled. Not even his eyes right now. Now? They were a cop's eyes. Flat. Hard. Determined.

Did her eyes look like that?

Without moving his focus from the front of the courtroom, he reached over and took her hand in his.

She jolted and then allowed herself to appreciate the warmth of his touch.

Up front, an armed bailiff, a tall blond female with a sharp cut bob, walked through the door by the judge's bench, scanned the courtroom with light blue eyes, and then stood at post. Her uniform was so starchily pressed it could probably stand up without its wearer.

Laurel's shoulders tensed and she forced them down and back.

While the defense table remained vacant, the prosecuting attorney currently sat at her table, reading through a file folder. She had thick black hair and appeared to be in healthy shape, but she hadn't turned around yet. "Who's she?"

"Her name is Tamera Hornhart, and she's as ambitious as they come. She's won twice by a large margin and already announced her candidacy for governor. Taking down Abigail will be good for her career," Huck said.

Behind Laurel, the exterior door bisecting the benches opened and FBI Special Agent in Charge Wayne Norrs from the nearby Seattle office strode inside, his badge at his belt and his gun in a shoulder holster. He wore sharply tailored black slacks, a pristine white shirt, and a cobalt-colored tie. His bald head and compact, muscular frame projected an austere, almost formidable presence. He glanced at her, nodded at Huck, and walked to the front to sit in the first row, right behind the defendant's table.

"That answers that," Huck murmured.

"Abigail is keeping him close," Laurel said, her tone almost academic, "not out of trust, but utility. His endorsement confers legitimacy."

Huck glanced down at her, the different brown and golden hues in his irises sharpening. "Meaning it looks good to have him on her side? Believing in her?"

"That's what I said." It was the first time Laurel had said Abigail's name in more than two weeks. She and Huck had agreed not to speak of her half sister while they'd enjoyed their break from reality in Mexico. Although that hadn't kept Laurel from considering Abigail's next moves. Surely she'd plead not guilty to the murder, even though she'd been found holding the knife over the body, covered in blood.

The door opened again and the hair prickled down Laurel's arm. She automatically turned to see Abigail walk in wearing a blue skirt suit and white shell, with taupe-colored kitten heels. Her true auburn hair was down around her shoulders, and the suit jacket sleeves fell almost to her knuckles. Not quite.

She turned her heterochromatic eyes, the same as Laurel's, toward her. "Dear sister, it was so kind of you to come support me at my pretrial hearing." She glanced up at Agent Norrs in the front row of the other side. "Although you're sitting on the wrong side of the courtroom."

A man holding a shiny black briefcase and wearing a ten-thousand-dollar suit patted her arm. "Abigail? We need to go to the defense table." He had to be at least three or four inches taller than Abigail, who stood at about five-foot-nine in the heels.

She faltered and then gave him a tremulous smile. "Of course. Thank you, Henry. Laurel, we'll speak later." Her chin up, she maneuvered up the aisle with the male following her as another man, this one just as tall but probably twenty years younger than Henry, hustled inside with a stack of file folders in his hands.

He glanced at Laurel and then stilled, his gaze swiveling from her to Abigail and back to her. "You must be Abigail's sister."

"I must be," Laurel replied. Both she and Abigail had true reddish brown hair and one blue eye as well as one green eye, which was incredibly rare. Throw in the fact that they also had a star of green in their blue eye, a heterochromia in already-heterochromatic eyes, made them truly unique. And look-alikes, unfortunately. "You are?"

"Bud Thomas, one of the lawyers for your sister. I've been trying to get ahold of you?" His blond hair was mussed and his gray suit not worth ten thousand dollars. He probably worked as an associate at whatever law firm Abigail had hired. "I'd like to interview you."

Laurel was under no obligation to speak with the defense. "Captain Rivers and I were interviewed twice by the police regarding your case."

Thomas straightened, his eyes a deep green. "I can subpoena you for a pretrial deposition."

"Perhaps," Laurel said. "But you'd need permission from the judge as well as the DOJ first, and as I'm sure you know, depositions in criminal matters aren't often ordered in Washington State."

His brow furrowed. Showing confusion? "You don't want to help your sister?"

"No."

The judge walked through the doorway up front and moved behind his desk, followed by a court reporter and another woman who must be his scheduler. The judge had thick salt-and-pepper hair, sharp features, and dark brown eyes.

"All rise," the bailiff said.

Laurel stood, releasing Huck's hand. As soon as the judge sat, so did the spectators in the courtroom. The silence was blissful. Outside the building, cameras, news vans, and gawkers all created a frenzy of noise.

The judge slammed his gavel down and then reached into a pocket and drew out thin, black-rimmed glasses to perch on his nose. He flipped open the top of a file folder, read for a moment, and then looked up. "I'm Judge Warren Delaney. This is the matter of the state of Washington versus Abigail Caine." He read off the case number. "Who do we have here today?"

Abigail's attorneys, flanking her, both stood. "Henry Vexler from Vexler and Symons for the defense," said the obvious lead in his expensive suit. His voice was smooth and thick. Warm, even.

The prosecuting attorney also stood, wearing a deep red skirt suit with white shell and black pumps. "Tamera Hornhart for the state."

The judge nodded. "As you know, I cleared the courtroom today of press and other cases due to the lack of security, but the press will be allowed going forward." He glanced at Abigail. "Ms. Caine? Please stand."

"*Doctor* Caine," Vexler said quietly.

The judge's bushy eyebrows rose. "My apologies. Dr. Caine."

Abigail stood, looking diminutive between the two taller men.

Huck leaned toward Laurel. "Why is her suit too big?" He studied Abigail up front. "And not her usual style at all?"

Laurel lifted her chin. Her half sister favored black leather and high-end red dresses usually. "She looks vulnerable. Fragile. Defenseless." Frankly, it was a good look, and no doubt Abigail had come up with that herself. Like Laurel, she most likely ranked in the profoundly gifted IQ range and had attended college very young to earn multiple doctorates.

The judge stared at Abigail. "Dr. Caine? You are charged with murder in the second degree, for the death of Zeke Caine on April fifteenth. This is a Class A felony under RCW 9A.32.050. Do you understand the charge?"

"Yes, Your Honor," Abigail said.

"And how do you plead?" he asked.

Vexler gave her a brief nod.

"Not guilty," she answered. "It was self-defense, Judge."

An unnecessary addition to her plea, but now it was out there. In the judge's mind. Laurel studied him, wondering what he saw when he looked at Abigail. The woman was beautiful and often used men. Easily.

As if in tune with that thought, Abigail partially turned and looked at Special Agent Norrs, her lips trembling. They'd been dating since December, and Norrs was truly hooked. He couldn't see the malignant narcissist or psychopath or whatever deviant lay beneath Abigail's fragile looks. It would take years of meetings, tests, and studies to ever truly diagnose that woman.

Norrs leaned toward Abigail and said something, but Laurel couldn't hear the words.

Tears filled Abigail's eyes. She nodded and visibly steeled her shoulders, turning back around and facing the judge.

"Give me a fucking break," Huck muttered next to Laurel.

Judge Delaney looked to the prosecution table. "Ms. Hornhart, do you wish to be heard on release conditions?"

The prosecutor flipped open a blue file folder. "Yes, Your Honor. The state moves to revoke bond that was granted to the defendant during her probable cause hearing and remand the defendant into custody. Dr. Caine actively sought out the victim, who was avoiding contact and had gone into hiding from the authorities. She initiated a confrontation that resulted in the victim's death. She also holds substantial wealth and could relocate to another country easily. The facts of the case point to intent, not self-defense. Given the severity of the charge, we believe she poses a flight risk."

Vexler stood tall. "With respect, Your Honor, the state is attempting to dress speculation as fact. Dr. Caine has significant and verifiable ties to Tempest County. She's a tenured professor at Northern Washington Technical Institute, she owns multiple parcels of land through her business companies, and she has no prior criminal record. Her sister is a supervisory special agent with the FBI. She surrendered her passport and has complied with every condition of her release. There is no basis for revocation."

Hornhart leaned forward. "This was a brutal murder with multiple stabbings. The defendant had no reason to head out to that dive motel by herself that night when the authorities were already looking for Zeke Caine. She went there to kill him."

"Not true—" Vexler started.

Judge Delaney raised a hand before the argument could escalate further. "This court takes the charge seriously. However, the defendant's compliance and community ties are substantial. Bail will not be revoked at this time. Dr. Caine has surrendered her passport and will continue to abide by current conditions, including restricting her movements to remaining within the state of Washington. Any violation will result in immediate reconsideration."

Abigail didn't flinch. She simply exhaled.

"Next hearing is scheduled for May thirtieth. Discovery deadlines will be set by mutual agreement, or by court order if necessary. Anything further?" the judge asked.

Hornhart shook her head. Vexler remained silent, adjusting the cuff of his shirt with surgical precision.

"Then we are adjourned." The gavel fell, the judge stood and everyone else rose, and then he walked out, followed by the bailiff and his staff.

Laurel wanted to get out of there before Abigail could reach her, so she slid into the aisle and walked into the hallway, hurrying toward the two glass doors. Energy and movement sounded behind her as everyone exited the courtroom quickly.

"Agent Snow, wait a sec." The prosecuting attorney hustled up, her gaze darting to where Abigail and Agent Norrs stood against the far wall, talking animatedly.

Darn it. Laurel turned as the pretty lawyer rushed up. "Hi, Ms. Hornhart. What can I do for you?"

The woman took a deep breath. "Abigail's attorney just filed a motion for an expedited trial. I'm inclined to join the motion."

Laurel looked toward Abigail. Her attorney had acted fast. Since he wasn't currently with Abigail, she obviously knew it was happening. "I wonder what she's afraid we'll find out?"

Hornhart shrugged. "I don't know, but I'm going to put her away for good. The court has an opening the week after next." She blushed. "I have a friend in the scheduling department. I'll need to meet with you to go over your testimony and will have my scheduler call you later to get on our calendar."

Laurel clicked through her plans. "That's fine." She'd already given an interview, but she could brush up on testimonial strategy.

"Excellent." Hornhart's eyes gleamed.

"Let's go." Huck motioned toward the glass doors, leaning over to whisper when they were far enough away, "I can smell her ambition. While it's working for us now, I don't trust her."

Laurel didn't need to trust her. She needed the woman to do her job. She pushed open the doors with Huck at her side and then nearly fell back as the rush of reporters moved forward.

Huck instantly covered her, stepping in front of her and making a path through them. "Watch the steps," he said quietly.

Laurel nodded, keeping an eye on the hard marble steps as she made her way down them.

"Laurel?" Abigail called out amid the rapid snapping of cameras.

Laurel kept her head down and continued descending.

Huck stiffened in front of her and she ran into his back. "What?"

An odd ping whizzed through the air. "Gun!" Huck bellowed, pivoting and taking her down to the ground. Pain clicked through her shoulder as she landed between two hard steps. Her jacket tore.

Several people screamed.

Huck instantly bounded up, his weapon in his hand. "Stay down."

"No." Laurel pushed to her feet, drawing her gun from the holster at her thigh. "Who's down?" she yelled, looking around wildly.

People began picking themselves off the ground. Her gaze caught on Agent Norrs above the steps on the landing, who knelt by a prone Abigail. He lifted his hand off her, looking numbly at the blood covering his palm. His eyes widened. "She was shot. We need an ambulance. Now!"

# Chapter 2

Laurel paced back and forth in the hospital emergency waiting room, her shoulder aching and her suit jacket crumpled into a ball on a leather chair. The shooting had hit the news, and her mother had already phoned her from an island in the middle of the Caribbean. Laurel had strongly supported Deidre in taking a month on a sunny cruise with her new beau, Fish and Wildlife captain Monty Buckley, who was healing after successful cancer treatments. Having them both out of town while Abigail's legal proceedings continued was just a blessing. Period.

The outside glass doors opened and Viv Vuittron hustled inside, her wet tennis shoes squeaking on the tile. "Laurel?"

Laurel moved toward the girl. She was the eldest of the three of the Vuittron girls, whose mom, Kate, ran the local FBI office. "Viv? Are you back from softball camp already?" Time seemed to be flying.

"Yeah. I got back last night."

Wasn't today a teacher's work day? The girl should be sleeping. "What are you doing here?"

The girl pushed blond hair over her shoulder, her blue eyes wide. "I was on my way to my internship at Oakridge since there's no school today, and I heard about the shooting. The local news named you and said you'd headed to the hospital." She rushed Laurel into a fierce hug. "I was worried."

Laurel returned the hug and stepped back. "I'm fine, honey. The bullet hit Abigail, and I'm waiting to hear about her."

Viv exhaled slowly. "Okay. Good." She looked around the vacant waiting room. "Since you're here, I was wondering if you'd help me?"

"Always." Laurel focused more fully on the sixteen-year-old. "What do you need?"

Viv flushed. "My friend Larry died a week ago. The Seattle police are saying it was a suicide, but he didn't seem like he'd do that. He was always happy."

Laurel paused. "I didn't hear anything about one of your friends dying." Kate would've told her.

Viv stuck her hands in her light blue raincoat. "He's not from here. He's just a buddy who lives in Seattle named Larry Scott. I tried to talk to the Seattle detective, and she wasn't very nice. Would you please just call her?"

Just then, FBI agent Walter Smudgeon ran inside, his eyes wide. "Are you okay?" He skidded to a stop and touched Laurel's shoulder.

"Yeah, I'm fine," she said.

"You're bleeding."

She jolted and looked down at her torn blouse. It was white with tiny yellow tulips and had softened the blue suit, or so her mother had said when she'd gifted it to Laurel. "Oh, I'm fine. That's from hitting the ground." She rolled her shoulder and looked carefully. It was just a scrape.

He took a deep breath. "Okay, good. Hey, Viv. What are you doing here?"

"Hi, Walter." Viv glanced at the wall clock. "Crap. I have to get to my internship. We're seeing what yeast does to various materials today. Thanks for helping, Laurel." She patted Laurel's arm and jogged out of the hospital.

Laurel watched her go. Apparently she'd be making calls to the Seattle police department later today.

"What was that about?" Walter asked.

"She lost a friend." Laurel looked at her partner from the specialized

FBI office she'd opened in the small town. Walter had been shot months ago and yet appeared better than ever. He had lost weight and today wore jeans, a green T-shirt, and an overcoat. His belt appeared new, as did his shoes. Even his hair had thickened, noticeably so, and taken on a deeper, warmer shade, several degrees removed from its prior silvering. She suspected one of those color-depositing shampoos designed to mask age with just enough plausibility to escape casual scrutiny. "You appear markedly improved," she said.

His eyebrows rose over his brown eyes. "You're saying I look good?"

Wasn't that exactly what she'd just said? "Yes."

"Thanks. I've been making an effort at it." He gently took her elbow and led her over to the seats. "How about we take a load off, boss?"

"Sure." She sat.

He sat next to her and patted her hand. "I think you might be in shock."

She looked at him, her mind spinning. "I suppose it's possible. We were fired upon, and Huck slammed me into the marble steps with enough force to leave a mark, but I retained motor coordination, made rational decisions, and drove myself here. That doesn't align with clinical shock."

Walter winced. "You sure driving here was a good idea?"

"Perhaps not."

He looked around. "Speaking of Huck, where is he?"

"The captain remained at the scene," she said. Her vision wavered unexpectedly in an involuntary neurological response, most likely from fatigue or residual adrenaline. She gave her head a brief shake just as her phone buzzed. She retrieved it from her pocket with slightly uncoordinated fingers and lifted it to her ear. "Agent Snow."

"Hey, it's Huck. I'm checking on you. How are you feeling?"

"I'm functional," she said.

He snorted. "That you are, Snow. However, you hit the ground pretty hard. Sorry about that. I heard the shot and just reacted."

"I'm perfectly unharmed. Was anyone else hit?" So far there hadn't been anybody else brought in by ambulance, but that didn't mean they didn't have a body or two. She'd hurried away from the scene so quickly she hadn't taken stock. She thought most people were okay.

"Nope, just Abigail."

Laurel ran through the scene in her head. "Did anybody see the shooter?"

"No. The shot came from a distance."

She sat back in the chair. "You think we have a sniper?"

"I'm exploring that now. I just wanted to check on you. You sure you're good?"

"Yes," she repeated. "I'm fine. Walter's here with me. You must have been the one who notified him."

"Of course I called him. He's your partner." Huck added, "Well, when I'm not."

She couldn't be certain, but it sounded like there was a slight smile in the captain's voice. "Yes. You're both good partners."

His chuckle finally grounded her. Then the sound halted. "How's Abigail?"

"No update yet," Laurel said. "I'm waiting for the doctor to come out." The nurse had provided only a minimal data point in that Abigail had arrived alive.

"All right. Norrs is here breathing down my neck. As soon as you get an update, call it in."

"Okay, I will." She ended the call. It struck her as mildly unexpected that Agent Norrs hadn't accompanied Abigail to the hospital. But once he confirmed that Laurel would cover that front, he'd redirected his focus to locating the shooter. From one agent to another, she could respect the calculus.

A doctor emerged from the back wearing light green scrubs. He slowly pulled off his cap.

Laurel stood, along with Walter. "Doctor, hi."

He moved forward. "Are you family?"

Laurel bit back a wince. "I'm FBI Special Agent Laurel Snow, and this is Agent Smudgeon. The gunshot victim is my sister. Rather, my half sister," she amended.

"Dr. Bodie," he said. He looked to be in his early thirties with light green eyes and thick black hair. "Your sister's going to be all right and has already been moved to a room."

Laurel blinked, processing. "That's the entirety of your update?"

He smiled. "Yeah. She was wearing a bulletproof vest."

She glanced at Walter, then returned her focus to the doctor. "She was wearing a ballistic vest?"

"Yes. Saved her life. Even so, the bullet nicked the vest and her arm. You can go back and see her now if you want."

Laurel tried to get her bearings.

"Go ahead, boss. I'll wait here," Walter said.

Laurel hesitated and then followed the doctor through the county hospital until they reached patient room 212. She took a deep breath and walked inside.

"Why, Laurel. How nice of you to come see me," Abigail said, her tone slurred.

Laurel moved forward to see her sister in the bed with a bandage across her upper arm.

The room was dim and too warm, the lights set low to keep things calm. Pale green walls dulled the brightness of the late-morning light trying to push through the slats of the half-closed blinds. A faint scent of antiseptic clung to the air, mixed with something floral and artificial.

The machinery next to the bed made soft, rhythmic sounds, with a blood pressure cuff deflating every few minutes and a heart monitor pulsing steadily in the background. Abigail lay nestled under a thin blanket, one arm tucked awkwardly at her side, her IV line taped neatly into place.

"Why exactly were you wearing a ballistic vest?" Laurel lowered herself into the chair.

Abigail looked like the true wounded heroine in the hospital bed, her thick, reddish-brown hair spread across the pillow, her eyes slightly dulled by medication. "Wayne insisted upon it. Can you believe it? I thought it was the dumbest thing ever. I just put it on to appease him. To appear agreeable."

Laurel raised a brow. "To manipulate him?"

"No, to ease his mind. The same as I'm sure you do for the Huckalicious every single day."

"Excuse me?" Laurel said, momentarily unable to follow the thread. Perhaps she had hit her head.

Abigail smiled, catlike. "Oh, come on. You take precautions with the captain around. He always drives you. You always wear your seat belt. He makes sure you're safely in the vehicle before he drives away. All that kind of crap."

"That's just the captain being the captain," Laurel said.

"And I guess that's just Norrs being Norrs."

Laurel had to concede that point. "Why did Agent Norrs think you needed a vest in the first place?"

"I thought it was an absurd idea," Abigail muttered. "I've received a couple of anonymous death threats I figured were purely melodramatic."

Laurel tilted her head to the side. "Excuse me?"

"Yes, a couple of death threats. I assumed they were from some of those unhinged church loyalists." She paused, paling. "I surmise Wayne was correct. Somebody shot me. Someone from the congregation?"

That thought held merit. Their father, Zeke, had worked as a pastor at a local community church and had quite the following. Even though he'd taken off for some time, he'd returned recently, and apparently the church had welcomed him back with open arms. Then Abigail had brutally murdered him.

"Who do you think threatened you?"

"I have no idea. Why? Are you going to be my tough little sister and go arrest them?"

Laurel exhaled slowly, her voice measured. "Technically, I don't think it falls within my jurisdiction," she said thoughtfully. "You were shot on county courthouse property, with no other apparent targets."

Abigail's eyes widened. "Nobody?"

"No. And based on everything I've heard, there was only one shot," Laurel said, her voice dropping. "So, I have to ask. Did you set up this situation to garner sympathy?" Surely a prospective jury would see the media reports.

Abigail blinked. Once. "You honestly think I'd allow myself to be *shot*?"

Yes. Without question. "I believe so, if it helps with your defense."

"I don't need help with my defense. I did not orchestrate this fucking situation. I was shot, damn it."

Fair enough. "Which means this was a deliberate and precise sniper. Abigail, who wants to kill you?"

Abigail stared at her for a moment, her face unreadable, though Laurel had no doubt a flurry of neural calculations fired behind those eyes.

"Like I said, I really don't know," Abigail replied, her voice softening and her lips almost curving into a smile. "This is a bit of a surprise."

What was the woman planning now? Not for the first time—or even the thousandth—Laurel wished she possessed reliable instincts when it came to people. "Tell me about the threats."

"You just said you couldn't investigate."

Laurel exhaled again. "Tell me about the threats anyway."

"Fine." Abigail rolled her eyes. "They were from an anonymous email address. Wayne's trying to track them and hasn't had any luck."

So the Seattle FBI office was involved? Officially or not so much? "What exactly did the threats say?"

"I'll forward them to you," Abigail said. "As soon as I get my phone back. Why are you acting like you care?"

Laurel was both a witness and a trained FBI agent. "I care when people are shot on the county courthouse steps."

"Isn't it more than that?" Abigail asked. "I am your sister."

"Half sister," Laurel said evenly. "Let's not forget, I'm trying to put you in prison for killing Zeke Caine." She refused to refer to him as their father.

Pink dusted across Abigail's smooth cheekbones. "He killed you, Laurel. For a few moments, anyway."

A surprising pain clicked through Laurel. Their father had drowned her, and she had been dead for a second or two. "I'm aware of that fact. And yet I would like to know why you murdered him."

Abigail's eyes widened even further, which Laurel would have thought was impossible. But if anything, her sister had learned to perfectly mimic human emotions. Laurel could barely read them. "I was upset that he had tried to kill you and ended your pregnancy.

I was quite looking forward to meeting that baby. So were you. He attacked me and I fought back."

If that wasn't nonsense, Laurel didn't know what was. Abigail was relentlessly calculating; nothing she did lacked intent. Which meant there was a reason she killed Zeke. There had to be. "I will find out the truth."

Abigail plucked at the blanket covering her. "Oh, little sister, when are you going to learn?"

Laurel stood. "I'll let Agent Norrs know you're recuperating well. Apparently, he's quite worried. When are you going to stop manipulating him?"

"You think I'm using him?" Abigail pressed a hand to her chest. "You don't think it's true love?"

"We both know you're incapable of real love. You don't have the slightest idea what it means." With that, Laurel shoved out of the hospital room, shaking her head.

It was possible someone in the Genesis Valley Community Church congregation wanted revenge for Zeke's death. He'd been their spiritual leader for years, and some people didn't care if their messiah turned out to be a monster. They'd follow him straight into the fire and call it faith. But Laurel had no idea where he'd even been the past sixteen months. He'd disappeared without warning, and when he returned, he acted like nothing had changed.

He could've made enemies in that time. Dozens. But the real problem, the one Laurel couldn't ignore, was Abigail. The hobbies her sister had gotten involved in—misguided experiments, questionable medical research, people she manipulated for funding or data or who knows what—those had created their own kind of wake. One had even turned into a serial killer.

Those were just the possibilities Laurel knew about.

She pushed through the hallway doors back into the waiting room, mind still spinning. Walter sat in one of the hard vinyl chairs, hunched over his phone, the screen glowing blue across his pale face. He didn't look up. He didn't even blink.

"Walter." She slowed. "What's wrong?"

He exhaled sharply, staring down at the screen, his expression carefully controlled. Too controlled.

She stepped closer, her mind already cataloging the details like a micro-tightening at the corner of his mouth, a fractional delay in his blink rate, the way his shoulders squared just a little too precisely. Not shock. Not panic. Suspicion? Calculation? Her pulse ticked up. "Walter?"

His gaze lifted. A flicker of something passed over his face. A hesitation. One she couldn't track. "It looks like my brother's missing," he said, pushing to his feet. "I have to go, boss."

Brother? What brother?

# Chapter 3

A light rain began to mist the plaza as the crime scene tape flapped uselessly against a growing wall of press and bystanders.

Huck finished reading the text from Laurel and tucked his phone in his back pocket. Truth be told, he liked her safely away from this scene. "Norrs?"

Agent Norrs finished a phone call and strode toward him. "What?"

"Just received a text from Laurel, who's on her way to Elk Hollow for an unrelated case. Abigail is going to be fine and can probably go home later today. Bullet hit the vest and just sliced across her arm." He studied the able-bodied agent. "Why was Dr. Caine wearing a bulletproof vest?"

Norrs flushed. "She's had a couple of threats lately. I figured it might be somebody from her dad's congregation, or maybe someone who's against pot farming, so I made her wear it."

Huck doubted very seriously that anybody could make Abigail do anything. Sometimes he forgot the doctor also owned a successful marijuana farm. "You probably saved her life. Send me the threats."

Norrs's thick chin lifted. "I'm looking into it."

Huck sighed. "This isn't a federal matter, and you know it. I'll see what I can do to get assigned to it." In Washington State, Fish and

Wildlife officers were fully commissioned and could work on any case. However, an attempted murder case was a rare one for his department. Yet . . . he was a sniper. Or had been one in the army, anyway.

The shot earlier had cracked like the world had flinched.

Norrs looked toward the street. "I can't believe someone shot at my woman." Anger flushed red across his face. "Nobody saw a shooter? Not even a vehicle?"

Huck shook his head. "One shot, suppressed. Not random. Not close. The kind of shot that didn't come from panic. It came from planning."

Norrs's chin dropped. "You're saying a sniper shot her?"

"Yeah." The plaza was loud with working deputies, humming camera crews, and reporters shouting names over each other.

Huck crouched low by the point of impact and saw a small chip in the granite column just left of where Abigail had been standing. He pictured her again. Five-nine, squared off slightly at an angle. The round had hit the upper part of the vest and clipped her left arm. That meant the shot had come down, not across. A high trajectory. The shooter hadn't been on street level.

He turned slowly, scanning rooftops above the crowd and the press vans. The Tempest Grain Cooperative building loomed three blocks away and was made of red brick, twelve stories, busted windows, and no tenants. High enough. Dead-on line of sight. It was the only thing tall and vacant enough to work.

Boots approached fast on the sidewalk, heavy and irritated.

"Jesus Christ," Genesis Valley sheriff Upton York growled as he ducked under the tape, eyes scanning the chaos like it personally offended him. He wore his city uniform, his thin brown hair in a comb-over, and his pudgy face sharply shaven. "You turn your back for one second and killers are taking rounds on courthouse steps."

"Accused killer," Norrs snarled. "She's innocent."

York looked toward the reporters angling for position. "Sure she is. Jesus. You're blind, man."

Huck couldn't agree more. He didn't look at either of them. "Single round. Suppressed. Took the victim in the vest, hit her arm as well. Entry angle's too steep for ground level."

York frowned. "You're saying this came from a building?"

"Not just any building. That one." Huck pointed toward the old Co-Op tower. "Top floor. Angle matches. Nothing else has that line."

Norrs whistled. "That's what—six, seven hundred yards?"

"Closer to eight-fifty," Huck said, standing now. "Wind was low. Shooter had time. No panic in the shot."

York's mouth worked, but no sound came out. Around them, deputies pushed the press back toward the secondary perimeter, where two local news anchors were already reporting live from just beyond the tape.

Norrs appeared beside them, eyes following Huck's line. "You think this was a hit on Abigail? Just her?"

"If they wanted more bodies, they'd have fired again," Huck said. He turned from the courthouse, gaze still locked on the distant rooftop. "This was deliberate. Clean. Controlled."

York squinted up at the tower. "You think he's still up there?"

"No," Huck said, already moving. "I think he left exactly when he wanted to leave. Let's go find it."

York made the mistake of grabbing his arm. "This is my scene, Officer. The crime happened in Genesis Valley, and I'm the Chief of Police."

Huck didn't have time for this crap. "The state is taking over the investigation." He didn't want a pissing match over jurisdiction. "This was a sniper shot, and I once worked as a sniper. I'm happy to keep you in the loop, or we could investigate together, but I'm not messing around here."

Norrs cleared his throat. "You know, I believe the FBI would like concurrent jurisdiction. The victim has received threats via email, which triggers federal jurisdiction."

Rain matted York's thin hair to his head, giving his comb-over a thicker look. "Could've been somebody local, and you know it. That's not enough to give the FBI jurisdiction, and as the local, I'm not asking for it."

"In addition"—Norrs continued as if York hadn't spoken—"the victim is not only dating an FBI agent but is the sister of one. That proximity could give jurisdiction."

Doubtful. "Conflict of interest," Huck said firmly. "You've got it and you know it. Back off, Norrs. The state is taking this, and I will keep you and your office informed." Damn, he hoped he had the juice to take the case. "Let's go find this guy's perch."

They crossed under the tape with minimal words, Norrs matching Huck's pace while York huffed behind them, muttering about assholes.

"Huck." A willowy blonde ducked her head against the rain and hustled up to him, her phone out and pressed toward his mouth. "You heard the shot, right? You yelled 'gun' before most of us realized what had happened."

He kept his face expressionless. "No comment."

"Come on," Rachel Raprenzi said. "You were a sniper and you must've recognized the sound. Who do you think tried to kill Dr. Caine?"

"No comment." He could not believe he'd once been engaged to the ambitious journalist. She'd thrown him under the bus for a story once, and he'd never let her do it again.

She didn't move her phone away from his face. "I know about your time in the military, remember? You should talk to me so I get the facts right."

The woman didn't care about facts. She cared about ratings. Sure, she knew he'd been a sniper, but he'd never confided in her. Not once about that time in his life. "Watch out for slander this time," he murmured, not forgetting she'd accused him of being a serial killer just a month ago.

"I'm sorry about that, but when Zeke Caine kidnapped me, he made it seem like it was you. I was one of his victims, too." She pushed a strand of hair away from her smooth face.

Huck motioned for one of the county deputies, who ran up, eyes wide. "Make sure none of them follow us. Thanks." He ignored Rachel's sputtering and moved out into the street.

The three of them cut through the edge of the crowd, drawing a few camera lenses and more than one shouted question. Huck didn't break stride. He didn't even glance at the press.

The sidewalk shimmered with rainwater. Old brick storefronts blurred past in Huck's periphery as they moved toward the Co-Op tower. Half the top floor windows were punched out from storms or vagrants. A place like that, quiet and forgotten, made the perfect blind.

York pulled a key ring from his jacket as they approached. "The city gave me master access after the copper thefts last year." He grunted as he unlocked the rusting side entrance to shove open the door, its hinges squealing loud enough to echo off the buildings behind them.

The inside smelled like dust and waterlogged insulation. Graffiti crawled across the hallway walls like veins. Huck took the lead up the narrow stairwell, flashlight beam bouncing off cracked tile. His steps remained nearly silent.

"You think they stayed long?" Norrs asked from behind him.

"No," Huck said. "But long enough to get the shot right. And they weren't in a hurry on the way in."

Norrs sneezed twice. "How do you know?"

"They didn't go through the front entrance. No smashed lock. They had a key or a tool set."

York blew out a breath behind them. "So what, we're looking for someone with real estate access and a rifle habit?"

"We're looking for someone who understands patience," Huck said.

They reached the twelfth floor. The landing was wide, empty except for old office chairs and broken-down electrical panels. Puddles reflected the pale daylight slipping through shattered glass.

Huck scanned for footprints in the dust. Something more than the usual. Ten feet from the west-facing window, he stopped. "Here."

The gravel and dirt along the floor had been disturbed and flattened in a tight oval. Prone position. Elbows, belly, bipod legs. An old radiator beside it had been shifted just enough to offer cover. The shooter had created a nest. Clean. Temporary. Huck crouched and aimed his flashlight.

Brass glinted near the baseboard.

"Round was fired from here." He picked up the casing delicately in his gloved hand. "Seven-six-two. Could've been Lapua, maybe a custom load."

York stood behind him, arms crossed tight. "They leave a signature?"

"No," Huck said. "They left competence. That's worse."

"Any prints?"

"Not if they wore gloves. Which they did." Huck turned toward the window, kneeling at the spot where the shooter had lain. The angle was perfect. The courthouse steps lined up directly in the center of the broken glass frame. He imagined Abigail standing there. Head, shoulders, vest. The timing had been exact.

Norrs moved slowly around the space. "There's no second casing."

"Because there was no second shot," Huck replied. "One round. No wasted motion. They weren't here to make noise." But the sniper had failed.

York looked unconvinced. "Could've been a warning. Could've been meant to scare."

Huck stood and turned to face him. "He aimed for her chest and had no way of knowing she wore a vest. Shit. I watched her walk by me and didn't know. It's an aberration and not one I would've planned for in this case." He studied Norrs. "You're paranoid. I didn't read that in you."

Norrs looked around the dusty area. "Not paranoid. I just love her."

Well, shit. Abigail Caine was a predator, pure and deep. She had no problem using people and no hesitation when it came to killing. The farther Huck kept Norrs from this investigation, the better. "I need to interview you." Well, after he managed to get assigned the case. Somehow.

He and Laurel should've stayed in Cabo.

# Chapter 4

Laurel settled into the passenger seat of Walter's brand-new Volkswagen Tiguan and reached forward to turn on the seat heater. The small city of Elk Hollow was about twenty-six miles from Genesis Valley, closer to Everett. It would take them around forty minutes, give or take.

She waited until Walter had driven through town and merged onto Washington 530 before she cleared her throat. "You've never mentioned that you had a brother."

Walter flipped on the windshield wipers as a spring rain began to slash across the glass. "I know. Tyler and I aren't close. Never have been."

Okay. That was something she needed to unpack, as Huck would say. "Tell me about Tyler."

"He's actually my half brother," Walter said. "My father died from an aneurysm just after I turned five. So it was just me and my mom through all of my childhood. I went to college and she fell in love and got remarried my sophomore year. Then Tyler came along the next year. He was a surprise. Her new husband didn't really want me around, to be honest."

Laurel watched a logging truck slow down up ahead. "Why not?"

"I don't know," Walter said, lips twitching at the corners. "Maybe he had this idea of a perfect family, and some twenty-year-old stepson, who was honestly only fifteen years younger than him, didn't exactly fit the mold."

So his mother had married a younger man. Interesting.

"Then I graduated, joined the FBI, got married, started my own life. I don't know . . . we didn't even spend holidays together." He shifted slightly in his seat, adjusting his weight like the conversation itched somewhere under his skin.

They had never discussed his ex-wife in any meaningful way. When Walter joined her team, he'd been newly divorced and drinking more than was professionally acceptable. Since then, his behavior had stabilized. He showed no current indicators of emotional volatility or impaired judgment. There was no need to revisit the subject unless it became operationally relevant. "Please continue," she said.

He hit his blinker and shifted into the left lane to pass a truck. "That's about it. I mean, we've seen each other through the years a little bit, but honestly, the kid turned into this conspiracy nut—anti-government, anti-FBI. Last time we were even in the same vicinity, we got into an argument. It made my mother miserable, and we were both supposed to be there to comfort her. She'd just been diagnosed with stage four pancreatic cancer."

Laurel turned toward him. "I'm so sorry to hear that. When was this?"

"Three years ago." He exhaled slowly. "I'd like to say that's when things started going downhill with my wife and me, but our problems had started long before that. I guess I'm just not that good at interpersonal relationships."

Laurel disagreed. Walter was easy to be around, easy to work with. He'd embedded himself into her team like he'd always belonged there. Huck's crew had taken to him just as quickly. Maybe romantic relationships were different, or maybe Walter simply didn't give himself enough credit.

"Sometimes family is . . . difficult," she offered, aware that it was a thin and inadequate truth.

He gave a short, humorless laugh. "Difficult. Yeah. You're exactly right."

"You haven't seen your half brother for three years?"

Walter sighed. "Nope. After our big argument, we just saw each other once at her funeral. Didn't even talk."

That sounded sad. "I'm sorry, Walter."

He shrugged one shoulder. "Sometimes I catch his podcast just to see what he's up to."

"Podcast?"

"Yeah. It's called *Eyes Open with Tyler Griggs.* He mostly talks about conspiracy theories. Deep-state stuff, chemtrails, shadow governments. He's always chasing something weird. It's been a while since I tuned in, though."

Laurel raised an eyebrow. "Yet he lives in Elk Hollow?"

Red crept up Walter's neck, the flush sharp against the gray sky filtering through the windshield. "Apparently. I didn't know. I thought he was still down in San Diego, where my mom lived. According to the woman who called me, he moved to Seattle, then Everett, and now out to Elk Hollow. Cheaper rent, less overhead. Figures."

Laurel stared out the window, watching the rain trace diagonal lines down the glass. Empathy didn't come naturally to her. But grief? That she understood. Not just the sorrow, but the awkward fractures it left in its wake. She could picture Walter at that funeral, standing across a gravesite from someone who shared his blood but not his life.

She considered offering platitudes but didn't know which one to choose. She disliked platitudes. She liked facts. And the fact was, Walter had shown up. That counted.

She remained quiet and shifted her attention away from him. Creating more space sometimes led to greater clarity than pressing for answers. Proximity and silence often produced results that direct inquiry disrupted. Huck had proven that more than once.

Curious, she pulled out her phone and searched for Tyler Griggs, keeping the volume off. There he was. His podcast popped up almost instantly, and she skimmed through the recent episode titles: "The

Shadow Beneath Homeland Security"; "Operation Indigo Fog: What They're Not Telling You"; "The Census Chip Agenda"; and "FEMA Zones and the Quiet Takeover."

She clicked through the site and located a photo of Tyler. He appeared to be approximately twenty-five years old, with sandy blond hair that curled loosely around his ears. His brown eyes matched Walter's in both shape and color, but beyond that there were no strong physical similarities. The twenty-year age difference accounted for most of the distinction.

She continued reviewing the site. Tyler demonstrated a categorical distrust of governmental systems. He framed institutional authority as inherently corrupt and adversarial. His podcast content referenced surveillance programs, climate manipulation, falsified public records, and consumer-level tracking mechanisms. The repetition across episodes indicated a fixed ideological structure rather than impulsive speculation.

Outside, the rain continued in steady vertical sheets, obscuring long sight lines and muffling ambient sound. Walter pulled the Tiguan to the curb in front of a light gray six-plex, the kind of structure built for functionality rather than aesthetics. Darker gray shutters framed each window. A small strip of patchy lawn separated the building from the sidewalk, and the neighborhood looked older but maintained. Several houses nearby had security signs staked into the ground without visible camera systems to support them.

Across the street, in a small yellow painted home, a curtain shifted. A silhouette moved behind a set of vinyl blinds and paused. The slats closed again without further movement.

Walter glanced at his phone, then up at the building. "Okay," he said. "This is it. Bottom floor."

Laurel unbuckled and stepped out. Rain collected quickly in shallow dips along the narrow brick walkway leading to the building. The surface had poor drainage, and slick patches had already formed. She avoided a larger puddle and moved toward the row of exterior doors. Each unit bore a black, stenciled letter, A through F, applied with a template and no apparent concern for symmetry.

Walter approached Door A and knocked.

"Who's there?" a woman called from inside.

"Agent Walter Smudgeon. You called me." His voice rose just enough to carry.

The door opened a few inches, but the chain remained latched. A young woman peered out. She looked to be in her early twenties, with long red hair and pale blue eyes. "Badge?"

Walter frowned slightly but reached into his pocket and pulled out his badge. "Here." He slid it through the gap, the door held tight by the chain.

She took her time examining it. The door shut again, followed by the metallic rattle of the chain being unhooked. A moment later, she fully opened it. "Hi. Come in. I haven't touched anything."

Walter stepped inside first. "You're Sandra?"

"Yes. Sandra Plankton. Thank you for coming." The redhead pushed back a strand of her hair.

Laurel followed, her boots leaving a faint trail of water on the entry tile.

The apartment measured under eight hundred square feet and showed signs of violence. A living room led to a kitchen, separated only by a bar with two overturned stools. The leather sofa had been cut along a central seam, and its internal padding had been pulled out and scattered across the floor. One lamp was broken. A second had been knocked over but remained intact. A large television lay flattened with a fractured screen and visible impact points along the lower edge.

Walter stiffened. "You're sure no one else is here?"

"I'm sure," Sandra said. "I checked every room."

Laurel glanced at Sandra again. She showed no visible injuries. Her pale green sweater had a small snag at the hem, and the denim of her jeans showed patterning from repeated wear. The braid over her shoulder lacked tension and consistency, indicating it had been secured without the use of a mirror. She wore no makeup or visible jewelry. Her appearance suggested minimal preparation rather than deliberate presentation.

Laurel walked through the space with measured steps, hands in her coat pockets. "The scene shows signs of both a fight and a methodical search."

"Shit," Walter muttered.

Laurel stepped into the hallway. The carpet underfoot suffered from long-term wear, especially in the center. A bathroom stood at the end, door open, and she moved that way. "Sandra? Did you go through anything in here?" she asked, keeping her voice neutral.

"No," Sandra said from just behind her. "I looked in, but I didn't touch anything."

The medicine cabinet door hung open. The mirror had been shattered, with jagged remnants still clinging to the edges. A few shards had fallen into the sink and across the counter. All three vanity drawers had been removed and placed on the floor near the tub. The contents—personal items, toiletries, over-the-counter medications—had been dumped into the sink basin. A plastic cup lay on its side near the faucet.

The toilet tank lid had been removed and set on the floor beside the base. The shower curtain had been torn free from most of its hooks and now sagged, half inside the tub. A damp towel lay balled up in the corner.

Walter stepped into the doorway. "Whoever did this took their time."

Laurel said nothing. The evidence didn't suggest panic or urgency. The sequence had a rhythm. Methodical, not chaotic.

She exited the bathroom and entered the bedroom to the left. The mattress had been removed from the frame and now leaned against the far wall with the gray and blue bedspread crumpled beneath it. The dresser drawers had been pulled out and placed in a row on the floor. Clothing had been thrown about. The closet door stood open. Only one bent hanger remained, twisted sideways on the rod.

"Can you tell if anything is missing?" Laurel looked back at Sandra.

"No," Sandra whispered, her face pale. "I mean, I don't think so. Not from his bedroom."

No female clothing. "You don't live together?" Laurel asked.

Sandra shook her head. "No. We have keys to each other's apartments, though."

Across the hall, Laurel stepped into a smaller room. Foam acoustic panels covered most of the walls, though a few had been peeled off and now leaned against the baseboard. A condenser microphone lay on the floor beside a detached boom arm, and a metal-framed desk had been cleared. A desktop tower sat open, side panel removed. Several internal components were missing, but the remaining ones looked undamaged. A monitor leaned against the far wall, unplugged but intact.

The red vinyl chair sat pulled back slightly from the desk. No overturned furniture. No broken glass. No clutter on the floor.

She crouched and scanned beneath the desk. Dust marked where the tower had originally sat. No debris, no scattered screws.

Walter stood near the door. "I take it we're missing items here?"

"Yeah," Sandra said. "His hard drive obviously. Also, he keeps notebooks near his computer with his research. Three of them, and they're all gone."

Laurel studied the room.

Tyler could have staged this himself for his conspiracy podcast. Maybe this mess gave him material. Maybe it fed the narrative. Or maybe it was for marketing. The visual chaos played well into his themes.

Or someone else had searched the place and taken the computer and notebooks. She wanted to interview Sandra, but this couldn't be Laurel's case. She lacked jurisdiction. "Sandra, how long has he been living here?"

"About six months."

"He ever mention being worried about anyone local? Businesses? Neighbors?" Laurel asked.

Sandra shoved her hand in her pocket. "Tyler always thought people were watching. But he never mentioned names."

Laurel looked around. "Walter, what do you think?"

"Hell if I know."

She moved back to the hallway and paused from the new angle. "Walter?"

He stepped up beside her. "What is it?"

She pointed to the doorframe. A smear, about chest height. Dried. Red-brown in color, with irregular edges. "That looks like blood."

Walter leaned closer. "Yeah. Could've come from someone reaching out, maybe holding themselves up." He turned to Sandra, who hovered by the destroyed sofa. "Why didn't you call the police?"

She raised both hands. "Because they won't believe me. I know how that sounds, but I'm serious. I just saw the damage, looked around quickly, and called you. I didn't even see that blood." She wiped her eyes. "Seriously. I should have but just didn't. I feel like I'm in a fog. Something bad happened to Tyler. I just know it."

Laurel observed her speech pattern and body language. The response lacked defensiveness. Her cadence had slowed, and vocal tension had diminished. "Why do you believe the police would disregard your report?"

Sandra shifted her weight. "Tyler doesn't trust the government. He's had a few arguments with local officers, nothing violent, just a few conflicts. He talks about it on his podcast. They know who he is, and I think they've stopped taking him seriously."

Laurel flicked through her memory. There had been an episode listed on Tyler's site about the Elk Hollow Police Department. She'd have to listen to that later. "I think we need to call the local police, Sandra. This apartment appears as if a fight occurred either before or after a search."

Sandra turned to Walter, her eyes wide. "You think Tyler found somebody searching his home?"

Walter glanced at Laurel. "I don't know."

If Tyler had interrupted a robber, where was he? Laurel watched the young woman.

Sandra paled. "Tyler said if anything ever happened to him, if he disappeared, I should call you. That's how I had your number. He trusts you. Not them. You have to find him."

Laurel crouched and looked closer at the gray and blue carpet. Against the scratched baseboard, a series of dried red dots disrupted the uniform pattern. "There's more blood," she said. "It has soaked beneath the baseboard." She stood slowly, her gaze sweeping the space once more. No assumptions. Not yet. She cataloged what was visible, noted what wasn't. Mainly, more blood.

Walter sucked in air. "Just drops, though. No spray."

Sandra paled. "You're in the FBI. You can find him, right?"

Walter blanched. "I'll help as much as I can, but this isn't an FBI case." He angled his head and strode back into the living room, moving toward the door. He zeroed in on the bottom of the door. "More blood. Just drops, but definitely blood."

Laurel nodded. "It's time to call in the local police."

# Chapter 5

Walter Smudgeon had his fair share of regrets from this lifetime. One was probably not getting to know his kid brother any better than he had. Sure, Tyler's dad didn't like Walter and never had, but Walter could have made more of an effort. The fact that the kid hated the government made that even more difficult, and Walter's job with the FBI only cemented the divide.

He stood in the rain outside the squat, gray six-plex as two local police officers conducted a quick search of Tyler's apartment. The building looked neglected, its paint cracked and peeling, the gutters sagging under the weight of wet leaves.

Sandra hovered near Laurel, half behind the shorter woman, her hands fisted tightly at her sides. The kid looked young . . . and lost.

Laurel remained still, her gaze calm and steady, unbothered by the rain soaking into her thick hair.

Walter didn't know what he'd do without Laurel Snow. She'd given him a second chance at life, first by offering him a place on her team, and then by refusing to let him give up after he'd gotten himself shot. His chest still ached sometimes, a dull, persistent reminder of mistakes made and lessons learned. But he was alive, and that was because of her.

He had wanted to ask her on the drive over how she was doing, but Laurel was even worse than he was talking about feelings after the miscarriage. Plus, his mind had been locked on Tyler, the kid's disappearance gnawing at him even before he'd arrived at the apartment.

The officers emerged from the apartment, their boots thudding against the uneven cement. Rain plastered their hair to their heads, droplets clinging to their jackets. Officer Jillian Jackson, a stocky brunette with pale green eyes and a sharp jawline, crossed her arms as she approached. Her partner, Officer Diaz, stood at least six-five, his frame lean and stretched, like he hadn't quite filled out his height. He had cropped close black hair and dark eyes that gave nothing away.

Both cops glanced at Sandra before making their way over to Walter.

"You called it in?" Diaz asked.

"You know I did." Walter looked up the four or five inches to the younger officer's face. The man was seriously tall, built like a basketball player, and his expression held a flat neutrality. Walter took out his badge, the flash of metal catching what little light seeped through the overcast sky. "FBI."

Diaz's eyebrows rose. "Why is the FBI here?"

Walter held his gaze. "Tyler Griggs is my brother." The words tasted strange in his mouth. Raw. Like he hadn't said them out loud in years.

Jackson's eyes narrowed. "Your brother?"

"Half brother," Walter corrected. "He hasn't been answering his phone, and his apartment looks like it's been tossed."

"Yeah, we noticed," Officer Jackson said. She glanced toward the open door of Tyler's unit. "The place looks like somebody tore it apart, probably looking for something specific."

"Or Tyler staged the break-in," Diaz added, his gaze fixed on the doorway. "This could be a stunt. We know he's into conspiracy theories, and maybe he's trying to gain notoriety."

Walter kept his face neutral, but the idea clicked too easily. Tyler loved attention. Drawing an audience to whatever theory he'd latched onto that week would've been a temptation for him. A dramatic break-in might fit his agenda. But it didn't explain the blood.

"Any idea where he might be?" Jackson asked, her focus shifting to Sandra.

Sandra shook her head, her voice tight. "No. He's not answering my calls. He should be home. We were supposed to record a new podcast today."

"About what?" Walter studied Sandra's face.

She appeared exhausted with her pale skin and red-rimmed eyes. "All I know is that Tyler was on to something big. He said he had enough to go national with this one."

Of course. He'd probably found evidence that the government had not only hidden the existence of Bigfoot but created him in the first place. Walter sighed. "You must have more details than that?"

"I don't," she whispered.

Diaz folded his arms. "If this isn't your case, Agent, you might want to step back and let us handle it."

Walter didn't flinch. "Fine. As long as you're handling it."

Jackson's jaw tightened. Diaz's expression didn't change. Walter caught the edge of irritation in the air, but it didn't bother him.

Laurel remained silent, her attention locked on the officers. Walter knew that look. She was studying them, measuring their responses, and cataloging every inconsistency. The rain continued to fall, the rhythmic patter against the pavement the only sound for several long seconds.

"Can you do a missing person's report?" Sandra asked, staying close to Laurel, with the toes of her shoes nearly touching Laurel's heels.

The officers exchanged a glance. Diaz's mouth tightened, a muscle twitching along his jaw. Jackson pulled out a notepad, the paper already damp and curling at the corners. Her pen moved fast, the strokes deep and hard. "We'll take a missing person's report and put out a BOLO for Tyler."

Diaz rolled his eyes. "Come on, Jillian."

"There's blood in there," Jackson added, her voice flat but clipped. "If it turns out he staged it for the notoriety or his podcast, we'll arrest him."

Diaz's mouth twitched. "Okay, that sounds good."

"We didn't stage anything." Sandra's words shot out quick, her fists tight, knuckles pale. She glared at Diaz, but her gaze darted to Walter like she expected him to back her up.

Jackson kept writing. "When was the last time you saw Tyler?"

Sandra pulled in a breath, shoulders rising and falling fast. "Friday night. I was away all weekend on a girls' trip and got home this morning. When Tyler didn't answer my calls, I headed here and opened the door with my key. I saw the mess and called Tyler's brother. I didn't know what else to do." Her eyes shifted to Diaz. "I knew you wouldn't believe us."

Diaz's arms crossed. "I've arrested you twice."

Sandra's chin snapped up. "But you're still taking this seriously, right?"

Walter focused on Sandra before Diaz could answer. "Why were you arrested?"

Sandra's mouth flattened. "I like to protest." Her fingers dug into her sleeves. "Somebody has to do something about the corruption in this area."

Diaz let out a loud, exaggerated sigh. "Agent Smudgeon, what about you?"

Walter kept his voice flat. "I haven't seen Tyler in three years."

Jackson's pen stopped. "Three years?"

He nodded once. "We didn't speak three years ago at our mother's funeral. Haven't kept in touch. Sandra's the only one who thought to call me."

"Why?" Diaz's weight shifted, his feet planted wide. "You two haven't been in touch for years, but she calls you instead of us?"

"Tyler told me to call him if anything ever went wrong." Sandra shrugged. "He doesn't trust the cops. Especially not here."

Jackson's pen moved again. Diaz's gaze stayed hard on Walter, but the muscle near his jaw kept twitching. The air smelled like wet concrete and cigarette smoke, drifting in from somewhere farther down the six-plex.

"We'll take the report and put out a BOLO," Diaz said. "But if your brother's pulling a publicity stunt, we will arrest him."

Walter looked at Sandra. Her shoulders stayed hunched, fingers twisted into the cuffs of her sleeves. She hadn't stepped out from behind Laurel.

"He's not pulling a stunt." Sandra's fists tightened against her sides. "He wouldn't do that."

Walter glanced at the apartment door. Whose blood was in there?

Diaz pulled out his phone, his thumb moving fast as he sent a text. "I'll have our photographer come in and capture the scene. We'll need to call in the county department or maybe the state patrol to process it. We don't have anybody like that on hand." His gaze snapped to Sandra. "Any recent threats or confrontations with Tyler?"

"Nothing but the usual." Sandra's shoulders jerked in something close to a shrug. "We know the corrupt establishment hates us."

"The establishment doesn't know you exist," Diaz muttered.

Sandra's mouth pulled into a tight line, but she didn't respond.

"We'll get this assigned to a detective. You'll need to come in for an interview." Jackson's pen hovered over her notepad.

Sandra's arms folded across her chest, chin tipping up. "I'm not helping you out."

Laurel stepped to the side, turning fully to face Sandra. "Do you want assistance finding your boyfriend or not?"

Sandra's gaze dropped to her feet. "Yes." The word came out grudgingly, her shoulders curling inward.

"What do you do when you're not protesting?" Walter asked. He was careful to keep his voice level. This wasn't his case, but the question felt relevant.

She shrugged, eyes still down. "I work at the movie theater to make some money. Other than that, Tyler and I are both dedicated to his causes. I help him research all I can, and soon we'll be making enough money off the podcast that I can quit my other job."

"This will probably help cause a little intrigue," Diaz said, glancing over his shoulder at the apartment.

Sandra's frown deepened. "We didn't do this."

Walter wasn't so sure. He'd seen Tyler's work before and hadn't paid much attention to it until now, but he knew the kid had a knack for theatrics. Still, the blood in the apartment made the whole thing feel off. He needed to watch some of Tyler's most recent podcast episodes to see if anything stuck out.

Jackson tucked her notepad away. "I'll secure the scene. I've got crime scene tape in my car, and then I'll go door to door to see if anybody saw or heard anything." She peered out into the rainy street. "Maybe we'll find a Ring camera or two."

Walter nodded, eyes narrowing as he glanced back at the apartment. He'd seen the inside and knew the damage wasn't random. Someone had gone through Tyler's things with purpose. If it wasn't Tyler himself, then who?

Even though this wasn't his jurisdiction, he couldn't just let it go. Not when blood was involved. Not when his brother—his own blood—was missing.

Hopefully, Laurel would use her big brain and help him. Walter had a good gut, but Laurel had a mind built for putting puzzle pieces together. And right now, nothing fit.

# Chapter 6

Huck strode into the hospital room, steeling his shoulders and tucking his phone into his back pocket.

Abigail Caine looked up at him, one eyebrow arching. "Hucka-licious. This is a nice surprise."

He doubted that very much. "Dr. Caine, I've been assigned your case." He moved closer to the bed, forgoing the one orange chair to lean against the sterilized counter. "If you're up to it, I'd like to ask you a few questions."

"Only if I may ask you a few," she purred.

He kept his expression blank. Hearing the bullet whizz by him earlier had taken him back to a place he didn't want to visit. "This is an official inquiry, Dr. Caine."

She settled the soft-looking white blanket over herself. In the bed, she looked smaller than usual, and it was always fucking odd to see Laurel's stunning eyes and unreal auburn hair on another woman. One who was a predator, through and through.

She glanced down at the bandage partially peeking out from her hospital gown. "An attempted murder is a far cry from chasing poachers around and checking fishing licenses, Captain. Somebody tried to kill me. I'd like the best working on this. Where's my sister?"

Half sister. "The FBI doesn't have jurisdiction. Who wants to kill you?"

Abigail blinked once. "I can't imagine anybody wanting me harmed."

Ha. He could more than imagine it. "Hypothetically, say you experimented on sociopaths, or psychopaths, to get them to embrace their darker sides. I need a list of those people as well as an idea of which one or ones would come after you. Plus anybody with sniper or military experience."

Her eyes widened, showcasing the green star in the blue eye. "I've performed no such experiments."

Bullshit. She'd created a serial killer whom Huck was pretty sure she'd later murdered. Not that he could prove it. "Dr. Caine. Someone wants you dead. Work with me here."

Her tongue darted out to wet her bottom lip. "Hypothetically, if I had created such clinical trials, not one of my subjects would want to shoot me. I promise." She reached for a plastic cup on the tray next to her and took a sip before continuing. "Now. How was your trip to Cabo with my sister?"

"I'd like access to the records of your, ah, trials."

She rolled her eyes now. "You wouldn't understand a line of it. No offense."

"Will you turn them over?"

She lifted one delicate shoulder. "I'm sorry, but no. Even if I didn't consider those records confidential, and even if I didn't want to protect my subjects, my hard drive crashed and I lost all of my documentation for those trials."

Right. Huck kept her gaze. The woman stared back at him. Was there life in there? A soul? He'd faced psychopaths before, and they all had a stare that defied description. As did Abigail. Although hers also glinted with obvious intelligence. "That's unfortunate." Could he get a subpoena for a victim's records that no doubt included medical data? Probably not. He switched tracks. "Considering you've been charged with killing Zeke Caine, we need to explore who'd now want you dead."

She lifted both hands, showing neutral painted nails. Oh, she'd definitely toned down her style for her hearing earlier. "I'd look at his entire congregation. Some of those people followed him with terrifying devotion."

"Can you narrow it down?"

"Is Laurel over the loss of the baby?" Abigail's expression smoothed out. "Are you, Huck?" The capricious curiosity in her expression chilled down his spine.

He crossed his arms. "Stay away from Laurel." He'd never hurt a woman in his life, and he didn't want to harm this one. But if she ever came at Laurel, he'd protect her. How could two sisters, who looked so much alike, be so different? While Laurel led with her impressive brain, she had a kindness and softness to her that brought out a side of him he'd considered long buried. "I'm done messing around with you about that."

Abigail gasped and pressed a hand to her chest, looking like a damsel in an action movie. "Are you threatening me, Captain Rivers?"

Shit. "Of course not." If he gave her an inch, she'd get him kicked off this case. And he wanted in. Wanted to know who tried to kill her and if that put Laurel in the crosshairs. "I will find the person who fired upon you." Might've killed her without the vest.

Her chin lifted. "You were a sniper, no?" A slight British accent emerged with her question.

He'd forgotten she'd gone to school at a very early age in Great Britain. "Yes."

Her eyes glittered. "So you're alibied for this shooting. I guess it's lucky for you that you stood on the steps near me when the shot was fired."

"Lucky for *you*," he murmured.

"Why is that?"

He remained in his relaxed pose. "If I'd been the shooter, you'd be dead."

Pink bloomed in her smooth cheeks and she licked her lips again. Appraising him. Was that approval? "Fine. How about we forget the fact that you arrested me for killing my father, when I most certainly acted in self-defense, and work together to identify the sniper?"

He'd wondered what approach she'd take. If she wanted to pretend to cooperate with him, then great. "Sounds good. Does anybody come to mind?"

She tapped her finger against her bottom lip. "A couple of people. First, Uma Carrington, who I believe had an on-again and way-off-again relationship with my father. We've never gotten along, and when I visited Pastor John a couple of weeks ago, she hissed at me."

Huck reached for his phone and began taking notes. "Has she ever threatened you?"

"Not with obvious words, but she dislikes me. No question." Abigail shifted her weight. "You dislike me as much. I'd wager you have sniper friends?"

Ah. Interesting avenue to take. "If I wanted you dead, Dr. Caine, I'd take care of it myself." He was a big believer in each person carrying the stains on their own souls. He wouldn't darken anybody else's. "Who else from the congregation?"

"I'll get you a list. I did have an odd call from Tim Kohnex last week. He was crying about my father's death."

Huck had dealt with Kohnex during an earlier case, and the guy thought he was a psychic. "Did he threaten you?"

"It felt like a threat, but he didn't say the words."

A silver-haired doctor walked in wearing a white lab coat over purple scrubs, his eyebrows bushy. "Abigail, how are you feeling?"

"I'm ready to go home as soon as my boyfriend arrives. He's an FBI agent," Abigail said, her gaze remaining on Huck. "He's highly intelligent and very dedicated to me."

Why did that sound like a threat?

The doctor looked at Huck. "I need a moment with my patient."

"We're not done. I'll be back in a few," he warned Abigail, turning and striding out of the room. That woman gave him the creeps.

Abigail's lawyer instantly stood in his way. "Captain Rivers? I'd like a moment. I'm Henry Vexler, and I'm representing Dr. Caine." The man stood tall, his expensive cologne drifting between them.

"Sure," Huck said easily. "She's a psychopath who murdered her father for a reason I haven't found yet. It had nothing to do with Laurel. My guess is that he had something on Abigail, most likely the fact that she tried to kill him before. Or a couple other things. She's guilty as hell."

Vexler's hazel eyes narrowed. "You found her and arrested her right after her fight with her father?"

"Yep. She was covered in blood and fully aware of her surroundings and deeds." Huck wanted Abigail in prison and away from Laurel, and he spoke the absolute truth.

Vexler leaned in, his jaw hard. "That sounds personal. I'd like to interview you at length."

"Get a subpoena."

Vexler's chin lifted. "Abigail wants me to take it easy on your girlfriend on the stand, but you know I can't. She's had a tragedy lately, and I doubt she wants to go through a cross-examination by me."

Now Huck stepped in. "Are you threatening Laurel?"

Vexler's smile looked like a cobra's. "Of course not. Just stating facts."

"We're done." If Huck didn't leave, he'd hit the guy. He walked down the hallway. Wanting to check on Laurel, he saved his notes and called her.

"Hi, Huck," she said, her voice settling something inside of him. "Did you find the shooter?"

He moved down the hallway to pause and lean his back against the calming pastel green wall. "Not yet, but I'm working on it. How are you? I took you down pretty hard earlier."

"I'm well. You protected my head, which is what matters," she said. "We're driving back to Genesis Valley right now and should be there in about ten minutes."

Good. He liked her close. "Did you find Walter's brother?" She'd texted him an update earlier.

"No, and his apartment was disheveled. We found a bit of blood. Not much. Then the local police interviewed us, and they promised to keep Walter informed." She didn't sound certain about that.

"Do you want the state to look into the situation?" There was a time all he and his dog worked on was scaring bears and finding poachers. He liked that life. But it hadn't included Laurel, and he'd rather have her than quiet peace. "Did the locals put out a BOLO?"

Something rustled across the line. "Yes. I think we should allow them to investigate right now since they're sharing information with Walter. Nobody is quite certain that Tyler is actually missing."

A muffled "What the fuck?" came through the line from Walter.

Huck stiffened. "Everything good?"

"Shit," Walter snapped loud enough that Huck could hear him. "That bastard has been following us, but I didn't think anything of it. He's coming up fast."

"Laurel?" Huck pushed off the wall.

A crunch echoed.

"Black truck, lifted, two people in the cab," Laurel said calmly. "No license plate and they're wearing balaclavas. We just passed the abandoned Elephant Inn. The truck rammed us from the rear. I have my weapon."

Brakes squealed. "Damn it," Walter yelled. "Be careful, boss. They're speeding up again."

"Put me on speaker," Huck ordered, turning and jogging through the reception area and then outside. They were only about twenty miles outside of town. "Hold on a second." Fighting every instinct inside him, he clicked over to call it in. Hopefully, patrol cars were closer than he was right now. Then he clicked back to hear the sound of gunfire.

Loud.

"Status?" Huck barked, reaching his truck and jumping inside.

The line went dead.

"Put your seat belt back on," Walter snapped, his knuckles turning white on the steering wheel. "They're coming up fast again."

Laurel had tried to fire but her angle wasn't advantageous. Her phone had dropped to the floor. She partially turned and refastened her belt. "Reposition this side mirror fifteen degrees out."

Walter reached over and did so.

"Right there." Laurel pulled down the visor and slid open the mirror to see through the pounding rain. "They're both large and appear male." Her breath caught. "The passenger has a weapon. Appears to be an AK-47." Panic began to set in and she inhaled, filling her lungs and calming her central nervous system. "After they strike us again,

I'll turn on my knees and fire through the back hatch window." She'd aim for the driver. "Prepare for impact."

A pattering sound came and then the ping of bullets against the rear of the vehicle.

"Shit," Walter muttered, jerking the wheel to the right and swerving into the other lane. "Guess they decided to shoot first."

Laurel inhaled again. They were alone on a lonely stretch of road, which was a good thing. Her Glock felt solid in her hand, so she released her belt. The shooting had paused. Using the center console to balance herself, she swung around onto her knees, aimed, and fired through the back. The sound instantly deafened her.

Glass shattered and the truck jerked to the shoulder.

"You get him?" Walter yelled from what sounded like very far away.

Her ears rang. "Uncertain." The front window appeared intact as the truck barreled back into place behind them. "I don't believe so." Taking in another deep breath, she settled her elbows on either side of the headrest, lowered her chin, aimed, and fired at the shooter.

Her bullets hit along the truck's hood, sending up sparks of fire into the rain. The truck swerved, she fired again, and the front windshield shattered. The passenger fell back, blood sprayed, and the gun dropped out of sight. "Shooter down."

"Good," Walter said grimly, eyeing his rearview mirror. "Seat belt. He's still coming."

Laurel needed to reload. She dropped down, pivoted, and rapidly engaged her seat belt. "I'm out." Where was her bag? She had an extra clip in there.

"Here he comes," Walter yelled.

Laurel stiffened and then forced her body to relax to better take another impact. Stiffening would cause more injuries. "Try to go lax, Walter. It's better."

"Right." He shook his head. "I'd hit the brakes, but I think he'd run us over. I need room to be able to spin around so we can both shoot."

She fumbled for her bag.

The sound of an engine came closer. Too fast. Laurel calculated the time of impact based on the large truck's current trajectory. She forced her body to calm as adrenaline flooded her system. Then the impact hit. Harder than she expected, like a battering ram slamming into their vehicle. Her body jolted forward, and her seat belt bit into her shoulder and chest.

The roar of metal crunching against metal filled her ears, a violent symphony of shrieking steel and shattered glass. The world spun, a sickening tumble of sky and ground, and she cried out. The SUV pitched into the air, gravity relinquishing its hold for a heartbeat before yanking them back down with merciless force. It flipped once, twice. Maybe more. Orientation meant nothing. Laurel gasped and clutched the console with one hand and her Glock with the other.

Air rushed past as her hearing returned. Then the SUV slammed down onto the asphalt on its roof, metal crumpling with a sickening sound. The airbags detonated with precise fury, filling the cabin with choking powder. Laurel smashed backward into her seat, the recoil stealing her breath, her vision dimming as her brain scrambled to keep her calm.

The seat belt carved into her chest, the sensation of bruised ribs sinking deep. Then stillness. A haunting, hollow silence draped over the wreckage, disturbed only by the hiss of leaking fluids and the subtle pop of overheated metal. Gulping, she forced herself to turn her head.

"Walter?" Her own voice sounded distant, distorted.

"I'm good." Upside down, held in place by the seat belt, blood streamed down the side of his face, painting his pale skin crimson. His hands moved with a precision that belied the obvious pain, unbuckling his seat belt with a *clack* that echoed through the mangled space. He dropped and landed with a loud crunch.

Laurel did the same, landing on one hand and pivoting to her knees, her joints screaming in protest. The gun remained steady in her grip. "We have to get out of here." If the truck hit them again, they'd be crushed. Worse, now the driver had time to claim the weapon from his downed passenger. She tried to force open her door, and it groaned in protest, warped beyond function.

Sirens wailed in the distance. Walter kicked at his door, his face twisted with effort and fury.

Laurel eyed the glass-strewn ground, bits glinting with sharp edges.

“I’m going through the window.” She scrambled forward, ignoring the sting of glass shards slicing into her knees through her pants. Pain was a distraction she couldn’t afford. She ducked out and pushed to stand, her legs trembling but holding firm. The taillights of the truck were barely visible through the pounding rain as it sped back the way it’d come.

From the other direction, red and blue lights emerged from the murk, accompanied by the rumble of tires on wet pavement. As she watched, a Fish and Wildlife truck tore past the patrol cars racing toward her.

Walter shoved his way out of her window and stood, his gun hanging loose in his hand. Blood trickled down his face, but his eyes remained sharp and clear. “Looks like your boyfriend is coming.”

# Chapter 7

"I'm perfectly healthy," Laurel said for exactly the fifth time as she settled onto Huck's sofa with her feet on the coffee table and the soft Karelian Bear Dog cuddled against her side. "My vision is excellent, and other than bruising along my rib cage and a few cuts on my knees and hands, I'm remarkably well."

Huck piled two more logs on the crackling fire. "I still think we should have a doctor check you out." He stood and turned, his brow furrowed and his lips pressed together.

It remained fascinating learning about Huck. For some reason, he became angry whenever she was harmed. She could understand concern or even regret, but fury glimmered in his bourbon-colored eyes. As if fate had pissed him off. Or more likely, the cretins in the black truck. So far, the truck had not been identified nor found.

Experience told her that it might not be. Living in the Washington State mountains, she'd learned that making a vehicle disappear over a mountain edge or in a gully in the middle of nowhere often occurred.

Huck crossed around to sit next to her, stretching his legs out onto the coffee table before sliding an arm over her shoulders. "Is it too much of a coincidence that the half siblings of both you and Walter possibly have been attacked?"

She stretched her neck and tried not to wince as pain ticked down her spine. "Statistically? Coincidences happen. Just not this cleanly." She rubbed a knot in her shoulder, fingers itching to tap this all out into something more solid than thoughts pinging off each other like unruly particles. "We've got three events. Three variables. I'm trying to determine if they intersect or if they're all just swirling around like chaos theory on caffeine."

She ticked them off. "My half sister gets shot at by a sniper. That one's almost too easy to explain. She left a body count, including a pastor with a congregation that probably still lights candles in his honor. And that's just the obvious possibility. For all I know, she's made enemies so deep I'd need a submersible to reach them."

Huck snorted. "Including us."

"Then there's Walter's half brother, who's a conspiracy expert. Either he staged his disappearance to gain intrigue for his podcast, or he actually stumbled onto something and is truly in danger." She hesitated, annoyance bristling under her skin. "But then there's what happened to us. Someone shot at us and ran us off the road. Walter and me. Not my half sister. Not Walter's half brother. So either we're targets, or we were incidental casualties from the other two situations. That's where it gets tangled."

"I'm not liking any of this, but at least the FBI is investigating who tried to shoot you. For now, anyway," Huck said.

Her mind raced, overlaying theories like transparencies, one on top of another, until everything blurred. "Are the three attacks connected? Probability says no because the situations are too different."

Huck frowned, dragging his fingers through his hair. "I agree. The connections are so flimsy. Your half sister's enemies, if that's who's after her, wouldn't care about Walter's brother. And his conspiracy theories? They're sprawling, but not exactly shareable with a sniper good enough to hit Abigail from such a distance."

Laurel released her muscle and stretched her aching neck. "But then there's us. Someone shot at us and ran us off the road. Walter and I have made enemies through the years, and the people in that black truck were aiming for one of us. Who knows. They could've been following us for days."

Huck lifted her to cradle on his lap, her legs over one of his, offering warmth and comfort. He pressed a kiss to her temple. "That would make the most sense. We're dealing with three different investigations and should attack them that way. I'm on the courthouse shooting as a state officer, the Elk Hollow cops are on finding Tyler Griggs, who might not be actually missing, and the FBI is on the attack on two of its agents."

"Good summary."

"Let's talk specifically about the FBI case and that truck that ran you off the road." Huck's voice was calm. Too calm. Laurel's instincts pinged at the measured tone, the subtle flattening of his words. Huck was usually easygoing with a streak of smart-ass confidence. When he went deadpan like that, it meant something was stirring underneath.

Anger. Annoyance. Or maybe that cold sort of calculation he used when lining up a shot. She couldn't decide which.

She tried to read his expression, but his face remained neutral. The man was good at compartmentalizing. Dangerous when he wanted to be.

"The Seattle field office sent out a crime tech to gather the casings"—she hesitated, aware that he was listening to every nuance of her voice, just as she was dissecting his—"but I doubt we'll find anything in the system."

His arms tightened around her. He'd pulled her onto his lap without a word, maneuvering her easily with his impressive strength.

The intimacy should've felt off, but it didn't. Not after everything. His warmth seeped into her, pressing back the chill that had settled along her bones since the shooting. They had grown closer during their time away, the aftermath of loss building something new between them, raw but steady.

She appreciated Huck's steadiness more than she could ever say. It was one of the things she respected most about him. He didn't play games or leave her wondering where she stood. The man was a fortress of straightforwardness in a world full of double meanings and unspoken motives.

They had both mourned the loss of the baby, though Huck had been characteristically equitable about it. "Doesn't change anything between us," he'd said, his voice strong but quiet, as if daring her to challenge him.

She didn't. Not out loud. But deep down, she figured it had changed things. The pregnancy had forced them into a timeline neither of them had consciously agreed to, only to have that timeline snatched away. Now she felt like she was stranded somewhere between what could have been and what was. Or she was overthinking it all.

Huck's gaze stayed locked on her, his brown eyes sharp. "So, you're telling me Wayne Norrs is in charge of the investigation into the attack on you as the head of the field office in Seattle?"

"Yes. Considering Walter and I were fired upon, it makes sense to have an outside team investigate the attack."

The Pacific Northwest Violent Crimes Unit worked all over the region, headquartered out of Genesis Valley but often crossing jurisdiction with Seattle and other offices. Her unit was specifically tasked with violent crimes and serial killers, but cooperation with other agencies had always been a given.

For now, anyway.

Agent Norrs definitely had taken over the investigation. That hadn't surprised her. His expertise was solid, his presence commanding, but he had a tendency to bulldoze anyone who got in his way. Of course, the man's temperament wasn't her biggest concern. Abigail was. If she grew bored of dating Agent Norrs, which she inevitably would, things would become tricky.

Right now, everyone seemed to get along, but alliances had a way of crumbling under pressure.

"What about the truck?" Huck's voice rumbled against her, low and patient, though his fingers were drumming against her thigh with the restless precision of a man holding himself in check.

"They haven't found a thing, and they probably won't."

"Hell." Huck's frustration broke through, punctuated by a rough exhale. "I suppose both you and Walter are going through old cases of yours to look for an enemy."

"We are. There might be something relevant from one of our pasts."

Huck's mouth tightened. His fingers stopped their rhythmic tapping against her leg, settling there with a solid, possessive weight. "Or both," he said.

The possibility hung between them, thickening the air.

But instead of pressing the point, Huck's hold softened. His hand slid absently along her side, drawing warmth through the fabric of her shirt. The man's touch was a grounding force she didn't know she needed until it was there.

They weren't done talking, but for now, she let herself lean into him. And Huck, true to form, let her take the moment on her terms.

"I don't think anyone from my father's church would fire upon me, but that's definitely an angle we need to look at. Considering someone shot at Abigail as well . . . the connection could be the two of us," she mused.

The words tasted sour, thick with the bitterness of too many threads tangling into a knot she couldn't quite unravel. Theories and probabilities spun through her mind, refusing to settle.

She let out a sigh, the sound rawer than she intended. "I'm tired of thinking about it."

Huck barked out a laugh. "Laurel Snow is tired of thinking. Now, that's a headline."

She grinned, rolling her eyes. "Whatever."

He laughed again, the rich sound vibrating against her skin where his chest pressed into her back. "I've never heard you say 'whatever' like that. There's usually a long litany of words that come in front of it. Usually something about probability ratios or statistical anomalies."

Laurel leaned back into him, shaking her head. "I've been spending time with Kate's teenage daughters. I'm picking up on modern vernacular."

"There we go." His voice went dry, teasing. "A wonderful side effect of hanging around mere mortals." He kissed her temple, sending a spark of warmth racing down her spine. The firelight danced around them, warming her in a safety she was beginning to rely upon. Huck's heat was real, solid, the one constant she could actually rely on.

When his lips trailed from her temple to her jaw, the captain taking his time, she turned in his lap, using her knee as a lever to straddle him.

Her hands tunneled into his hair, enjoying feeling the thick and unruly strands between her fingers.

He raised an eyebrow, his gaze locked onto hers with the kind of intensity that should have made her nervous. But instead, it settled her. Centered her.

"You sure you aren't hurt?" he asked, his voice a low rumble.

"Positive." She leaned down and kissed him, letting herself sink into his heat.

His mouth was demanding, commanding even, as both of his hands clamped onto her hips, his fingers pressing into her skin.

The captain was all hard-cut muscle and unyielding strength, but his touch was careful. Measured. As if she were something breakable despite every bit of evidence to the contrary. She hummed her appreciation when he deepened the kiss, the world narrowing to the heat and pressure between them.

Huck pushed to his feet, his arms locked firmly around her. A startled laugh tore from her as her legs cinched around his waist.

"What are you doing?" she whispered.

"Taking you to the bed."

She murmured against his mouth, "I figured the couch."

"No." His words were firm, laced with that unyielding authority she'd come to rely on. "You're still bruised and probably going to ache a lot more than you think, come tomorrow."

Her heart warmed despite the sensible logic behind his words. As strong, intelligent, and well-trained as she was, Laurel could admit, just to herself, that she felt safe in the captain's arms. It wasn't about needing protection. It was about trusting someone to catch her when the world tilted off its axis.

He wouldn't let her down. Huck was a dangerous man, his instincts honed to lethal precision. He would never let anyone get to her if he could help it, and that kind of protection came with a confidence she hadn't realized she craved. She liked that . . . and him.

Growing up without her father around, not even knowing who he was, had been a blessing in disguise. She was quite unaccustomed to relying on the strength of a man, to leaning on someone and expecting them to hold their ground. Huck kept proving over and over again that he could be trusted. That he would be there.

And yet, they had jumped into a relationship far too soon. Without analyzing all the different angles, without mapping out the possibilities or properly assessing the variables. Even while on vacation, they hadn't talked about long-term wants, needs, or goals. They'd just tried to heal from the loss, from several physical injuries they had both sustained, letting themselves fall into each other rather than sorting through the messy reality of what that actually meant.

Huck reached the bedroom and kissed her, his mouth going deep and insistent, carefully removing her clothing with a patience she didn't expect. The captain could be both gentle and wildly rough when the occasion called for it. Tonight, apparently, called for gentle.

She tugged on his jeans, and he helped her remove them before tearing off his shirt. Then all of that hard, smooth muscle with several scars and scratches lay within reach. He covered her on the bed, but then rolled them over until she was on top of him, sprawled across his chest.

She laughed, breathless and feeling almost reckless, safely back on birth control. "I'm okay, Huck."

"Let's prove it," he murmured, his voice thick with challenge.

"All right." She kissed him, her body softening and arousal heightening, her thoughts slipping away with each brush of his lips.

He scratched his hands down her back to cup her butt. The foreplay was usually longer, but she wasn't in the mood to wait. Her body was already sparking, nerves firing under his touch. So she slowly, carefully, grasped him and lowered herself onto him.

He groaned as her weight settled on his thighs, his hands clenching against her hips. "Nice."

"I am gifted."

"That you are." He reached up and tweaked her nipples, his grin sharp and wicked. "I take it fast this time. Slow later."

"Agreed."

She pressed her hands onto his shoulders, muscles coiling as she lifted her hips and then drove them back down, their bodies colliding with a force that lit her up from the inside. He slammed her back down again, his fingers digging into her skin.

They set up a hard, unrelenting rhythm. When he powered inside her, her body went lax and loose, her muscles quivering under the intensity. She let herself sink into it, surrendering to the heat and hunger. Finally, her mind stilled. No more thoughts, only sensation. A truly rare occurrence. This was the kind of clarity she craved.

She reached the pinnacle, her body shuddering as she whispered his name, her climax tearing through her. Huck was seconds behind her, his hands gripping her hips hard enough to leave marks, his own release crashing over him as he jerked wildly inside her.

Gasping, slightly sweaty, she collapsed forward and nuzzled her face into his neck, letting the warmth of him soak into her skin. "You always make me feel better. Head to toe," she mumbled.

He chuckled, a deep, satisfied rumble as he rolled them over again, his big body bracketed above hers. "Good, because we're just getting started."

# Chapter 8

Morning brought a sharper wind as Laurel stepped out of Huck's truck and dodged through the rain toward their shared office building. The sturdy, two-story structure clung to the hillside, its facade solid. Rain dripped from the eaves, splashing onto the uneven pavement.

The middle suite on the ground floor housed Staggers Ice Creamery, its new neon sign glowing bright yellow, humming faintly in the misty air. The scent of fresh waffle cones and melted sugar seeped through the doorway every time a customer came or went, blending with the sharp bite of rain-soaked asphalt. The FBI offices took residence on the floor above the creamery.

To the right, the Washington State Fish and Wildlife offices took up both floors. The lower level buzzed with activity most days—radios crackling, heavy boots thudding against tile, the occasional bark of dogs. Metal desks, utilitarian chairs, and the constant hum of computers added to the underlying mechanical soundtrack.

Laurel's mother had leased a section of the ground floor to the left for her tea subscription business, but the space remained stubbornly empty. Rainwater streaked the glass, smudging the cursive *COMING SOON* sign that had been there a bit too long.

Above her mother's space sat Rachel Raprenzi's studio, Killing Hour Studios. From the outside, the narrow windows gleamed with freshly cleaned glass. Inside, Laurel imagined a mixture of high-end recording equipment and cluttered research boards.

Laurel stepped into the shared vestibule used by the FBI and Fish and Wildlife. To her right, Huck's office was marked by a hand-carved sign that read **FISH AND GAME**. The dark wood gleamed under the dim lights, grooves worn smooth from years of touch. She paused, having wondered but not asked. "Why do you have an incorrect sign above Fish and Wildlife?"

"A while back, a group of woodworkers—old, retired guys—made it for us," Huck murmured, grinning. "We didn't have the heart to change it. I like it. Adds charm."

"It adds confusion," she countered. But the quirk had grown on her, the sign's rustic look fitting the rough-edged nature of their work. "Although, I do like it. Charm is a good thing, right?"

"Exactly." He pressed a quick kiss to her head before opening his glass door. "Try not to get shot at today."

"Ditto." She moved to the scanner to the right of her door, its flat surface cold and slick beneath her fingertips. They'd finally had new security installed to better protect the office.

She swiped her ID over the plate, and the door clicked open. Inside, warmth replaced the rain's chill. The stairwell leading up was lined with garish wallpaper of cancan girls, bright skirts twirling against deep crimson backdrops. Laurel still hadn't replaced it, even though she'd meant to. The pattern appeared ridiculous and outdated, but it amused most of the agents and techs who walked through the door. Maybe that was enough reason to leave it alone.

As she climbed, her boots scuffed against the worn wood steps. The air grew cooler the higher she went, the scent of coffee thinning until only the faintest trace remained.

She reached the top landing where Kate Vuittron, her office manager, sat behind an old pastry glass display case repurposed as a desk. The glass still bore scratches from trays and dishes long since discarded. Beneath the polish, faint smudges remained, like ghosts of the sweets once displayed there.

Kate glanced up from her computer, her gaze searching. "Hey, how are you feeling?"

"Just fine. I have a few muscle aches and contusions, but nothing else to worry about." Laurel rolled her shoulders, fighting off a twinge of pain. "How's Viv doing? I haven't had a chance to check on her friend who died."

Kate blinked. "What friend?"

Laurel stilled. That was interesting. "I don't know. He's from Seattle, and I assumed she knew him from school sports."

"Huh." Kate cocked her head. "I guess I'd better get to the bottom of that one when I get home today. She has been attending many of the softball and baseball coed camps in Seattle, so I figured she'd made some new friends. If she found a new beau, she's probably stressed about her current boyfriend, Ryan. Maybe. Who knows."

Laurel chewed on her lip. She wouldn't have kept a secret from Kate, but she hoped Viv wouldn't be mad. Although, why hadn't Viv told her mother about the deceased kid from Seattle? Laurel would dig down more on that, as Walter would say. Speaking of whom . . . "Is Walter in yet?"

Kate nodded, her blond hair brushing her shoulders. "Yes, and I've already requisitioned him a new vehicle. He's in his office. The man is moving a little slow, like you."

"Thank you. Is there anything I need to focus immediately upon?"

"Not at the moment." Kate smiled, looking like her three daughters captured in the picture behind her on a small glass shelf. "But we both know that'll change somehow."

Laurel moved past Kate's desk and through the door that bisected the reception area into the hub of their operations. She walked past the conference room and the restrooms, and headed straight for Nester's lair.

The computer expert's office was a cluttered, buzzing mess of cables and monitors. Mangled snowboards decorated the walls, some splintered, some bent, all of them salvaged from Nester's hobby on the hills. They gave the room a reckless sort of character.

He glanced up from his monitors, his dark eyes cool and steady. His freshly shaved head gave him a harder look, and the overhead lights reflected off his smooth dark skin. He lifted a steaming cup from Staggers and took a deep gulp, the logo already faded from his grip. "Good morning. I'm glad you're okay after the wreck."

"Thanks. Your computers are all humming." Laurel scanned the bank of monitors he had lined up like a fortress.

"I've got a few things running at once." Nester set down his coffee, fingers already flying across the keyboard. "I know the Seattle FBI office is working the case, but I've been doing a deep dive on the truck that ran you and Walter off the road. I'm cross-referencing every traffic cam, drone image, even random social media posts. So far, nothing. The thing's a ghost."

"The ballistics report?"

"Yeah." Nester frowned, his fingers tapping against the keyboard. "The report came back with no match anywhere. The rounds were standard 7.62x39mm. The kind you'd use in an older AK-47. It's common and dirty. Easy to get, hard to trace."

A chill swept over her skin that had nothing to do with the rain outside. "And the shooters?"

"No record of the passenger seeking medical help. At least, not that I've found." Nester's gaze didn't leave his screens. "I've contacted every hospital, urgent care, emergency room, smaller doctor's offices, even a couple of veterinary clinics, just in case someone tried to patch him up under the radar. Nothing."

"They were both wearing balaclavas. It follows logic that they'd cover their tracks everywhere else, too," Laurel said.

"I'll keep working, boss," Nester said, his gaze never leaving the monitors.

As far as Laurel was concerned, Nester was the absolute best. Quiet, steady, relentless. He worked every angle until it snapped or twisted into something that made sense. "All right. Just try not to step on the toes, as they say, of the Seattle office too much."

"I'm being very careful," he admitted. "So far, they're working with us and seem happy to share info."

Laurel wondered how long that would last, but she'd take the good fortune while she could. The Seattle office had jurisdiction and didn't need to share information. They were playing nice, but everyone had their limits, and if Abigail ended her relationship with Agent Norrs, things might become difficult. "Do you have anything on the courthouse shooting?"

Nester shifted to another monitor. "The ballistics haven't come in from the state yet on the weapon used to shoot Dr. Caine. I have to be even more careful there because we really don't have jurisdiction, but Huck's office is keeping me informed as much as possible."

She'd figured as much. Huck would keep her updated whether it was technically under her jurisdiction or not. "Our focus has to be on whoever fired at Walter and me. That's an FBI case, but again, it's not ours. So I appreciate everything you're doing."

"No problem." He took another drink of his coffee. "I'm also in contact with the Elk Hollow City Police, and so far, they seem open to our help finding Tyler Griggs. Not much going on there, though."

Laurel frowned. Where was Walter's brother? "I'm sure Walter appreciates it."

Nester tossed his empty Staggers cup into the garbage. "Also, DC sent several files for you to review and render opinions on. They're in your inbox. One deals with a possible serial killer out of North Carolina, and there are two suspicious bombings in Michigan they want you to take a look at."

"All right." Laurel shifted her stance, already mentally sorting through her day. "I'll get to work." She turned away and moved farther down the hallway. Walter's office sat to the left of the small kitchen and hers to the right. She poked her head into Walter's office. "How are you feeling?"

He looked up, dark circles etched under his eyes, his face pale. "Like my SUV rolled over onto me. How about you?"

She smiled, though her own muscles protested at the movement. "About the same. It'll take a few weeks until we both feel better, statistically."

"Statistics matter." Walter's fingers drummed against his desk, his computer screen lighting up his tired face. "If you don't mind, I'm going to keep tracking my brother's disappearance. I still haven't found anything."

"I don't mind," she said. "Right now, I'm working on a couple of outside cases that don't involve legwork here. I'll let you know if anything comes up."

"Thanks, boss." He turned back to his screen.

She paused in the doorway, aware she should say something comforting but finding herself empty of platitudes. She didn't believe in them. Or in lying just to make someone feel better.

Walter glanced up again and managed a grin. "I got you. I appreciate the support."

She relaxed a little. "Oh, good. Thank you." Turning away, she walked down the hall to her office and paused at seeing the old door stretched across blocks that she used as a desk. She could requisition a new one, but she'd become accustomed to this one.

Once inside, she shrugged out of her raincoat and draped it over the back of a chair. She figured she'd be at the office all day, so she'd worn jeans and a light green sweater, something comfortable and practical. She moved behind her desk, her computer already awake with notifications blinking across the screen. Her phone buzzed from the desk. "Agent Snow," she answered.

"Hi. It's Rachel Raprenzi, and I'd like to interview you about the shooting of your sister on the courthouse steps."

"No comment." Laurel ended the call. She took a breath, settled into her chair, and logged into her account to begin working through the morning's emails. The room remained quiet, save for the soft hum of her computer and the patter of rain on her window.

She responded to the easy inquiries first, clearing out messages that required nothing more than polite acknowledgments or brief updates. The rhythm of work was comforting, anchoring her thoughts and keeping her from spiraling into frustration over their lack of progress on the shootings.

Once she'd thinned the clutter, she put in a call to the Seattle Police Department, spoke to several people, and finally found a Detective Laticia Trodd.

"Yeah, I pulled the Larry Scott case," Detective Trodd said. "Clear suicide. The guy slit his wrists in his bathtub."

Laurel tapped her pen on her desk. "Was there any other evidence?"

"Sure. His girlfriend had broken up with him a week before, he'd gone off his depression meds, and he had given a bunch of his stuff away." Papers rustled over the phone. "We cleared the guy, and his family came out here and had him cremated, before taking his ashes back to Michigan." More papers. "Oh, no. I meant, Missouri. Close enough."

Laurel sighed. "His family came out here? Did he live alone?"

"Yep."

Laurel turned to look out her window at the mountains still tipped with snow. "Was he in high school?"

"Nope. He was twenty-five."

Laurel paused. "I see." How in the world had Viv known him? "What was his place of employment?"

"Let's see." Detective Trodd coughed. "Sorry. Allergies." She was silent for a moment. "He worked at Oakridge Solutions as a lab technician. I interviewed his boss, a Sally Shermington, who confirmed that his work had slipped and that he had seemed really down lately. His family also noted that he was depressed."

Oakridge? The name had Laurel sitting straighter. It sounded like the detective had done her job. "All right. Thank you."

"No prob." The detective ended the call.

Laurel leaned to the side. "Kate? Isn't Viv's internship with Oakridge Solutions?" The place was one of many in the Seattle area conducting medical research.

"Yes. They recruited her right after Christmas, but it's been tough with her sports schedules. Why?"

"Larry Scott, her friend that died? He worked there apparently," Laurel called back.

Kate moved down the hallway to lean on the doorframe. "I see. She didn't tell me, but I'm thinking she had a crush. He had to be older, right?"

"Yes. He was in his twenties." Laurel frowned. What did that have to do with anything?

Kate sighed. "I sometimes forget you missed your teenage years. She probably had a crush, but currently has a boyfriend in high school, and she didn't want to talk about any of it with her old mom.

Especially since this Larry was too old for her. I'm glad she came to you with concerns, though."

As was Laurel. "It really does sound like her friend died from suicide. I'm so sorry."

"Thanks. I'll let her know tonight and make sure she does speak with me." Kate winked, then turned to head back up to her area.

That sounded like a good plan.

Laurel then pulled up the files DC had sent for her review. The North Carolina case had been presented as a possible serial killer, but it didn't look like one to her. The three murders felt disjointed, unrelated in method and motive. Different killers. Different circumstances. Laurel typed out her analysis, noting the inconsistencies and backing her conclusions with statistics and probability ratios. Then she sent the email off, her fingers moving with crisp efficiency.

The fire bombings were another matter. She scanned the details, her gaze catching on patterns that didn't quite fit. It was messy, but it held potential. After making several notes, she fired off inquiries to her contacts in the ATF, requesting additional data. She needed more than what she had to reach any sort of conclusion.

A glance at the clock told her it was nearing lunchtime, but she ignored the slight ache of hunger. Her mind was already shifting to the next task when Walter appeared in her doorway.

His skin had gone pale, several shades lighter than usual, and his eyes were wide, unfocused. Sweat clung to his forehead despite the cool air, and his hands trembled at his sides.

Laurel's body tensed. "Walter, what is it?"

He shook his head slowly. Too slowly. Like his brain was fighting to form words. His lips parted, but no sound came out at first. Finally, he managed to speak, his voice cracked and hollow. "It's my brother." The words seemed to scrape from his throat, raw and painful. "They found Tyler's body. He's dead."

Laurel's mind stuttered, her analytical side trying to grab hold of something solid. Something to make sense of the blunt finality of his words. "Where and how?" Her voice came out steadier than she expected.

"On a smaller roadway along the Widow's River. An hour or so outside of Elk Hollow." Walter's shoulders slumped. "It took the county time to identify him."

How terrible. "He was hit by a vehicle?"

Walter shrugged. "Don't know. The detective who called me wouldn't give me information. Just wants me to come back in for an interview."

"Walter, sit down." She gestured to the chair across from her desk, her tone more command than suggestion. The county coroner was the best, and she figured they might have reached a friendship level. If not, a good colleague level. "I'll start making calls. We'll figure out what happened."

He shook his head. "I promised to head to Elk Hollow. Can I borrow your rig?"

She reached for her raincoat. "As your supervisor, I'm going with you." She would call Dr. Ortega on the way.

How had Tyler died?

# Chapter 9

The Elk Hollow Police Department was nestled between a pawn shop with a tidy red awning and a malt shop painted in mint green and pink, both clean and inviting looking.

Laurel parked her Nissan Murano in the gravel-lined lot. Sunshine filtered through the windshield, a clear break from this morning's rain. Walter sat in the passenger seat, shoulders pulled tight.

During the drive, they'd both watched out for that black truck that had rammed them. Just in case.

Laurel called Dr. Ortega three times after leaving the office. Each attempt went straight to voicemail. Hopefully, he'd soon conclude Tyler's autopsy.

"Ready?" Laurel asked, keeping her tone neutral.

Walter nodded, the motion stiff.

Laurel stepped out of the SUV and waited for him to join her. The police station looked clean and bright, fresh white paint and blue trim gleaming in the sunlight. Brass letters above the door read ELK HOLLOW POLICE DEPARTMENT. Petunias and snapdragons lined the walkway in symmetrical rows.

She opened the sparkling clear glass door. Cool air drifted out, carrying scents of lemon cleaner, brewed coffee, and cinnamon. The floors gleamed with fresh polish, and sconces along the walls cast a soft glow over thick leather chairs in the waiting room. Buttery yellow paint covered the walls.

Framed photographs hung in tidy rows above the reception counter, highlighting officers posed with children at town events; others showed them accepting plaques or shaking hands with grinning officials.

An elderly woman looked up from a jigsaw puzzle spread across the mahogany counter. She'd twisted her silver hair into a precise bun, and her blue eyes appeared bright and alert. The vibrant pink pantsuit she wore added a splash of color against the muted tones of the lobby, matched by chunky gold jewelry at her ears and wrists. A daisy-shaped pin glinted from her lapel. "Can I help you?" she asked.

"I'm FBI Special Agent Laurel Snow accompanying Agent Walter Smudgeon." Laurel met the woman's gaze. "Detective Robertson asked him to come in."

The woman's attention shifted to Walter, her expression softening. "Yes, he mentioned you'd be here. Follow me."

Walter moved behind Laurel and the woman without a word.

They walked down a hallway painted in a calming sage green.

The woman opened a conference room door to reveal a polished oak table under a soft overhead light. Potted lilies and ferns with thick and vibrant leaves filled the corners, and a faint scent of vanilla lingered, likely from the candle flickering on a side table.

"Detective Robertson will be with you shortly," the woman said. "Can I get you anything to drink? Water, tea, coffee?"

"No, thank you." Walter dropped into a chair.

"I'm fine," Laurel said, her attention locked on Walter's stillness. Might he still be in shock?

The woman slipped out, closing the door quietly behind her.

They sat there quietly for almost fifteen minutes before Walter leaned forward, elbows on his knees. "I don't appreciate being kept waiting."

"I agree. I hope the detective isn't playing games." Treating Walter like a suspect was a mistake. Such a move didn't make sense to Laurel, but following other people's thoughts rarely did. Her mind moved along tracks most people didn't seem to see, and tracing their logic often felt like mapping fog.

The door opened, and a man who appeared to be in his early thirties walked in with brisk, purposeful steps. His dark brown hair had been neatly trimmed, and his hazel eyes scanned the room, flickering upon studying Laurel's face. His shoulders remained back and at attention.

"Hello. I'm so sorry to be late," he said, his voice even and professional. "We had a call about a wreck involving a couple of the high school kids." He shook his head, the motion sharp. "We also had two break-ins and a small fire, so all the deputies were out. I had to check on the kids myself."

Laurel stood, and Walter followed, his movements a little too careful, like his body hadn't caught up with his mind.

"Is everyone okay?" Walter asked, his voice steady and direct.

The man nodded. "Yes. Just bumps and bruises. The football team will still play this weekend." He flashed a brief, almost reflexive grin before his expression settled. "I'm Detective Joshua Robertson."

He offered his hand to Laurel first. She shook it, noting the firm grip and precise way he measured her with his gaze.

"Special Agent Laurel Snow, FBI."

Detective Robertson turned to Walter and extended his hand again. "You must be Agent Smudgeon. I'm very sorry for your loss." He gestured to the chairs. "Please, have a seat."

Laurel sat and tracked the detective's movements as he circled the table. He operated with the efficiency of someone used to handling emergencies, though his attention kept drifting back to Walter. Something more than professional curiosity edged his expression.

Walter lowered himself into the chair beside her. His shoulders looked tight, his posture almost rigid. "How did my brother die?"

Detective Robertson reached beneath the table and pressed a button. "I need to let you know this conversation is being recorded."

"Understood." Walter's gaze didn't waver. "How did he die?" His tone sounded harder than before, the words pressed through clenched teeth.

Detective Robertson kept his gaze steady on Walter. "Please let me do my job. I know you already spoke to Officers Diaz and Jackson, but I'd like you to walk me through the last time you saw your brother."

Walter blew out a breath. "Three years ago. At our mother's funeral. We didn't speak because we'd argued the week before about his conspiracy theories. I didn't know he'd moved to Elk Hollow. We hadn't been in touch since."

A knock sounded at the door.

"Come in," Detective Robertson called.

The door opened, and Officer Jackson stepped inside. Her dark hair spilled around her face in loose curls. "Maisie said to come on in." Her fingers fidgeted against the notepad in her hand.

"Yes, please have a seat." Detective Robertson gestured to the chair next to him.

Officer Jackson threw him a quick smile and settled into the chair, her posture tense. "Agents Snow. Smudgeon."

Detective Robertson nodded. "Jillian here is working on becoming a detective, so I asked her to help with this case. She conducted the initial interview with you both."

"That's fine," Walter said. "Now, could you please tell me how my brother died? I understand it was on a highway. Was he running from somebody? What happened? Did somebody hit him on purpose?"

Detective Robertson glanced at Officer Jackson, who seemed prepared to answer. "It looks like he fell off Frostline Peak," she said, her tone even.

Walter's eyebrows drew together. "Excuse me?"

Officer Jackson pressed her lips together before continuing. "We have several witnesses who were driving along the river road. I'm so sorry, but Tyler's body hit the road directly in front of them. At least two cars swerved to avoid hitting him, and another managed to brake just in time. One car ended up in a ditch. The driver called 911, and we've taken statements from all of them."

Laurel tracked the way Officer Jackson's fingers tightened around her notepad.

The officer's gaze flicked down and then back up to Walter. "Do you know if your brother was suicidal?"

"No. Not a chance," Walter snapped. "Tyler was obsessed with his investigations and theories. He was paranoid and restless, but he wasn't suicidal."

Detective Robertson maintained his neutral expression, though his focus on Walter sharpened. "You haven't spoken to him in three years." His voice remained calm, but the challenge threaded through it all the same.

"Maybe not, but I still knew the kid," Walter said. "He lived for his conspiracy theories. He wouldn't kill himself. Have you been up to the site?"

"Not yet." Detective Robertson's shoulders sagged slightly before he straightened. "The rain made the terrain nearly impossible to navigate, and we still don't know where he fell from. Frostline Peak isn't a single cliff; it's a series of ridges, ledges, and drop-offs. Without a clear point of origin, we're working blind."

Walter's jaw tightened. "Then you need to find out."

"We plan to. The problem is how extensive the area is. If we can't narrow down a location soon, we'll likely need to call in help from the state to conduct a proper search of the mountain and to look for Tyler's car." Detective Robertson paused, his eyes on Walter. "I understand your frustration. We're working as quickly as we can, but we're limited by the conditions and the lack of obvious evidence."

"Maybe somebody threw Tyler off one of those cliffs." Walter's voice dropped.

"That's a possibility," Detective Robertson acknowledged. "The coroner has your brother's body now. They identified him through fingerprints, but the autopsy isn't finished yet."

"How far has the coroner gotten?" Laurel asked.

Detective Robertson turned his attention to her. "Dr. Ortega only just began. The rain delayed recovery, and he's still working on the preliminary assessment. I know you want answers, but we don't have them yet."

At least the county coroner was the best Laurel had ever worked with. Dr. Ortega's meticulousness bordered on obsession, but that obsession translated to results. If Tyler had any other injuries beyond the obvious ones from the fall, Dr. Ortega would find them.

"Do you know what Tyler was working on recently?" Laurel asked.

The detective's mouth lifted in a smile that revealed twin dimples. "This is my case, Agent Snow. I'll ask the questions." He didn't wait for a response before shifting his attention to Walter. "Do you have any idea what investigations your brother was undertaking?"

"Not a damn thing," Walter said. "I listened to his podcast a few times, but it's been a while."

"What do you know about Sandra Plankton?" Detective Robertson asked.

Walter glanced at Laurel, his gaze sharp. "Nothing. She had my number, called me, and we showed up. Found the place trashed. Why? What do you know about her?"

"Ms. Plankton has been arrested multiple times for protesting," Officer Jackson said before Detective Robertson could respond. "And for vandalism and arson. She's a dangerous woman."

Laurel cataloged the statement, her thoughts shifting through her brief interactions with Sandra Plankton. The woman had seemed genuinely concerned about Tyler.

"Tell us more about her," Walter said.

"I don't think so," Detective Robertson cut in smoothly. "This is our case. You are witnesses only." He sat back and folded his hands on the table. "In fact, I didn't ask for your appearance here, Agent Snow."

"I'm aware of that," Laurel said. "But as Agent Smudgeon's direct supervisor, I intend to be present for any questioning."

Officer Jackson leaned back in her chair and crossed her arms over her chest. "You want to take the case away from us?"

"I would if I could," Laurel said. Walter needed answers, and she intended to help find them. "If we find there's any chance for federal jurisdiction, I'll take the case."

"You're definitely not a game player," Detective Robertson said, cocking his head as if studying her from a different angle.

Laurel remained still, her expression calm and focused. "No, I'm not." Hadn't she just made that obvious? "How many murder investigations have you handled?"

"We're not sure this is a murder," Detective Robertson returned instantly, the response so fast it sounded reflexive.

Walter planted his hand on the table. "I think it's a good question."

Detective Robertson hesitated for a moment. "This is my first one." His admission came out flat, matter-of-fact. "We're a small town, and we don't have many murders."

"Lucky you," Walter muttered. His fingers drummed once against the table before going still. "Have you personally had any run-ins with my brother?"

"No," the detective said shortly. The word snapped out with an edge that caught Laurel's attention. His voice sounded certain, but the flatness of it suggested something else. She couldn't quite pinpoint the discrepancy, but it registered like an error in a line of code.

"Have you met him?" Walter pressed.

"Again, I'm asking the questions," Detective Robertson replied.

Walter's eyes narrowed. "Who wanted my brother dead?"

"I have absolutely no idea. We'll investigate this matter thoroughly, I promise you," the detective said.

"Any chance that Frostline Peak is on federal land?" Walter glanced toward Laurel, his gaze expectant.

Laurel's mind scanned through her mental map of Washington State, the boundaries and jurisdictions she'd memorized long ago. "No. It's owned by the county." Walter's attempt to gain jurisdiction wasn't lost on her, and she admired the tactic.

"Agent Smudgeon, where were you the night before last?" Detective Robertson's question came out casual, but the tension around his eyes contradicted the tone.

Walter looked up at the ceiling, his eyes distant for a moment. "I was home. Worked all day, went home around five. Had dinner and went to bed."

"Can anybody verify that?" Officer Jackson asked, her arms still crossed over her chest.

"No. I was by myself."

Detective Robertson leaned back, adopting what appeared to be a relaxed pose. A muscle twitched in his jaw, the only sign of the tension beneath the surface. Laurel tried to read his expression, but his features remained frustratingly blank. Guesswork wouldn't help, and she had never been adept at drawing conclusions from people's faces alone.

She glanced at Walter, whose gaze had locked on Detective Robertson. "What is it you're not saying?" Walter asked.

Detective Robertson's shoulders rose and fell in a slight shrug, but his gaze never left Walter. "I spoke with Sandra, and she had some interesting information for us. Is it true that upon your brother's death, the entire residual of your mother's trust moves to you?"

Walter's posture shifted. "I don't care about that trust. I never have."

Laurel looked at him, her curiosity sharpening. "What's the corpus of the trust?"

"About five million dollars," Detective Robertson said smoothly. "The trust remains in place during the life of her latest husband, who's paid a set amount from it each month. Upon his death, the trust was supposed to be split evenly between the brothers." The way he delivered the figure sounded rehearsed, as if he'd prepared to deploy that piece of information at the right moment. "I guess that makes quite the motive, doesn't it?"

Walter's jaw tightened. "For someone, maybe. But not for me."

"Interesting," Detective Robertson said. "Your brother had quite a few enemies. But now, you're the one in the spotlight. You'd be surprised how often family plays a role when money's involved."

Walter snorted. "Maybe in your experience. But Tyler and I hadn't spoken in years. No bad blood, just different paths. That money doesn't mean anything to me."

Laurel studied the detective, her mind racing through the implications. "If you're going to imply Walter had something to do with his brother's death, then you'll need more than an inheritance to back up that theory. I'm assuming you haven't found anything to suggest foul play, correct?"

Detective Robertson hesitated, his eyes narrowing slightly before he answered. "Nothing definitive, but I'm not ruling anything out."

"I'd hope not," Walter snapped.

Should Laurel insist Walter obtain representation? Listening carefully, she allowed the questioning to continue. Finally, the detective wound down after also questioning Laurel about the scene at Tyler's house as well as the attack by the black truck.

Could it all be connected?

The detective walked them outside to a darkening day. "Rain's coming," he murmured, looking up at the bulbous clouds. "Be careful on the drive back. That black truck and AK-47 are still out there."

# Chapter 10

Miriam deserved this. The truth smacked her with a painful force, reverberating through her chest and pounding against her skull until her vision swam. Her brain felt swollen, thick and heavy, each tiny thought becoming sluggish. Painfully so. Karma was coming for her, damn it. She stumbled to her car and fumbled for the keys in her pocket.

Her eyes burned like she'd dunked her head in bleach. The pressure built behind her sockets like something sharp wanted to push through. Panic, fear—no, terror—twisted through her veins, coiling tight around her heart. Fuck. She collapsed into the driver's seat, slamming the door.

Driving was a mistake. She knew it. Hell, the rational part of her brain screamed it loud and clear, but that voice was buried beneath a raw, primal instinct to flee. But where should she go? There was nowhere to go.

Tears streaked hot down her face, stinging her chapped lips. She swiped them away with the back of her hand and tried to focus. She gulped air like her lungs had forgotten their job. Sobs clawed their way free, scraping her insides bloody, but she choked them down. There wasn't time for that. Not now.

She'd screwed up. Regret tasted bitter on her tongue, but she didn't have time to deal with it right now.

She didn't want to die. God, she didn't want to die.

Her mind raced, chaotic and jumbled. The car lurched as she threw it into drive, except she hadn't started the damn engine. A fresh surge of panic strangled her as she yanked the keys again, twisting them hard.

The engine sputtered to life, a harsh, growling sound that barely registered through the thunderous pulse in her ears. She jammed the gearshift into drive again, clutching the steering wheel and hunching over it as if trying to protect her vital organs. Animals did that. So did humans.

Seat belt. There was something she was supposed to do about a seat belt, but the thought slipped through her mind like smoke, impossible to grasp. She had to fucking get it together. She slammed her foot on the gas pedal, and the car launched forward with enough force to snap her head back against the seat.

They wouldn't want her to be found.

But she'd make damn sure someone found her.

She drove down the mountain, her fingers gripping the wheel, providing more pain for her. Did it center her? Maybe a little. The road wound and twisted, becoming narrow and treacherous beneath the beaming moonlight.

More tears burned their way down her cheeks, but they weren't the soft, salty warmth of fear or sadness. They scalded. Blood-hot.

Too late. She knew it with the kind of clarity that made her want to laugh, hysteria clawing at her throat. No one survived this. But she couldn't just lie down and quit. If she could just get to a safe place, she could figure this out. She had to save herself.

She floored the gas pedal, and the engine groaned as the car sped up, blurring the lines on the road into streaks of white and yellow. She swerved onto a busier road, disrupting traffic. Oncoming headlights burned her eyes, and several cars honked. A tire or two might've screeched from people hitting their brakes. Angry curses from pissed-off drivers echoed from half-rolled windows, and it should've infuriated her. It did, somewhere deep beneath the agony.

But her head hurt too much to express the fury that boiled under her skin. Not only at them. At herself.

What had she done? Why had she done it?

There had been good reasons, honorable ones to start with. But things never ended the way they began, did they?

Her vision swam, lines and colors bleeding together like wet paint dragged through mud. The darkness tunneled, narrowing her field of sight until all she could see was the wavering strip of road in front of her.

Headlights split her vision, blinding and brutal. She jerked the wheel, and her tires squealed when she clipped the edge of the road. Gravel sprayed, and she swerved wildly, nearly correcting before something, someone, flashed in front of her. Maybe just a shadow. Maybe a person. It didn't matter. She jerked too hard and barely caught sight of the tree before she smashed into it.

The world came apart in a shriek of twisting metal and the brutal shatter of glass. Her head jerked back, pain ripping through her like a live wire—sharp, sudden, and then . . . nothing. The pain was gone.

Finally, silence and . . . peace.

Laurel drove slowly away from the quaint town of Elk Hollow, the misting rain adding a dull sheen to the blacktop. Walter sat beside her, unnaturally silent, his body a tense mass of grief and something more. Guilt, maybe. She kept her hands steady on the wheel, but she routinely checked her mirrors, searching for that black truck or anyone else hunting them down. So far, nothing.

"I truly am sorry about your brother, Walter," Laurel murmured.

"Thanks, boss." Walter's voice came out gruff. "I just wish I'd kept in better touch. We just . . . didn't."

"Have you tried contacting Tyler's father?" Laurel kept her tone casual, probing without pressing. Walter wasn't the type to open up easily, especially about family, apparently.

He shrugged, the movement sluggish and heavy. "He and my mother divorced forever ago. Haven't spoken to him in years, so I called an old number and got his secretary. Had to tell her the news. She called back and said that they'd take care of the burial arrangements."

Walter coughed. "But I will find out how he died. It's the least I can do."

She flicked a glance at him. "This isn't our case. Not officially."

"I know." Walter sighed. "But if we can't get jurisdiction, I can't see what happened to Tyler through to the end."

"That Detective Robertson seems like he's got a good brain on his shoulders," Laurel said, navigating the wet curves out of Elk Hollow. "But I felt like he was holding something back. Did you catch that?"

Walter huffed out a short breath. "I'm not at a hundred percent here, and you don't go on instincts. What did you see?"

"There was something," Laurel continued, her fingers tightening on the wheel. "A twitch in his expression. His eyes darted away from mine a little too quickly. He knows something he didn't share."

Walter lifted a shoulder. "That makes sense. We never tell witnesses everything in our investigations either."

They drove on in silence for a while, and Laurel began to relax. Finally, she cleared her throat. "So . . . you enjoy wealth?"

Walter snorted out a laugh that was more pain than humor. "Not even close, Laurel."

"Five million dollars is a significant amount of money."

"Yeah, but neither Tyler nor I could touch that until Mom's latest husband dies, and that guy's fairly young. Figured I'd never see the money. Though, I guess if I have kids, they would."

Laurel blinked. "You're contemplating having children?"

"Yeah." Walter stared out the rain-dotted window. "Ena wants kids. And hell, so do I. Near-death experiences tend to put things into perspective."

He made a certain amount of sense. Laurel's chest tightened, memory flashing back to Walter laid out on a hospital bed, pale and gasping through tubes. That bullet to his chest had nearly killed him only a few months ago.

And yet here he was. Living. Moving forward.

She hadn't realized he and Ena had become so serious. "When I thought I was going to lose you, I swore I'd watch over the whole team better. But you, Walter . . . I should've made sure you had more time to heal."

"Boss." Walter shook his head. "You did everything right. I'm alive and healthier than ever because of this job, working with Nester, and even with falling for Ena. She's a bit of a health nut."

They drove for a few more minutes in silence, the rain turning heavier. Finally, Laurel pulled up to a square, two-story building near the county hospital.

Walter startled, like he hadn't been paying attention. "We're going to the coroner's office?"

"Yes." Laurel pushed open her door and jogged through the rain to the entrance. Walter followed, ducking his head against the rain.

Inside, they made their way down the antiseptic-smelling corridor to Dr. Ortega's office. He stepped out of the autopsy room as they approached, his white coat already discarded, leaving him in gray slacks and a light green polo shirt. His dark eyes took them in.

"Special Agent Snow. Agent Smudgeon." Ortega's voice was clipped but not unfriendly. He gestured them into his office.

Laurel followed him in, eyeing the neatly aligned photographs lining the walls in perfect symmetry. Ortega's tendency toward precision bordered on compulsive, but that attention to detail most likely made him excel.

"We're hoping you can give us information on Tyler Griggs's autopsy," Laurel said.

Dr. Ortega's eyebrows rose. "This is an Elk Hollow City case, isn't it?"

"It is," Laurel admitted. "But Tyler was Walter's brother."

Understanding flickered in Dr. Ortega's eyes. "Ah. Well, I can share what I've found so far, unofficially. But you know the locals have to request federal involvement. The fact that Walter is Tyler's brother complicates that even more."

"We understand," Laurel said.

Dr. Ortega leaned back, his hands clasped loosely in front of him. "The cause of death wasn't the fall. He was dead before he hit the ground."

Walter's fingers tightened against the chair's arms. "What killed him?"

"That's where things get . . . uncertain." Dr. Ortega's gaze sharpened. "There are lesions on his brain. Microscopic but extensive. Clusters of neural degradation."

"What kind of lesions?" Laurel asked.

"Mostly concentrated in the temporal lobes and cerebellum. But not exclusively. The pattern is uneven and erratic. Certain pathways show severe degradation, while others are untouched." Dr. Ortega rubbed his temple. "I've requested Tyler's medical records. Something genetic could cause degradation like this. Neurodegenerative conditions normally don't act this quickly, but it does happen."

Walter scratched his chin, his gaze somber. "So, you're not ruling out disease?"

"No. Viral, bacterial, even something fungal. Or a chemical agent. It could be environmental, something new or modified. I've sent samples to specialists in DC," Dr. Ortega replied. "Neurotoxicologists, geneticists, virologists. I'm not ruling anything out. But the rapid deterioration . . . that's what worries me."

Laurel breathed deep. "What does your gut say?"

"I don't go on my gut any more than you do on yours." Dr. Ortega's expression remained solemn. "The deceased could've had a genetic disease that has been affecting him for a while, and we haven't received his medical records yet. But you need to get Detective Robertson to request your involvement, officially."

"Understood," Laurel replied. She rarely relied on instincts, but none of this felt right.

# Chapter 11

Huck finished the last interview of the day so far, his voice scratchy from repeating the same questions over and over. He'd managed to speak personally with everyone present during the courthouse steps shooting, and he had his team tracking down anyone else in the vicinity. CCTV from the courthouse showed nothing except the bullet hitting Abigail. No hint of a muzzle flash, no stray figure lurking in the shadows. Whoever took the shot had done it clean. Professional.

CCTV along the routes the sniper probably took had so far revealed nothing of value. Not surprising. Huck was a trained sniper himself; he knew how to avoid cameras, how to blend into the landscape so thoroughly even the best digital eyes wouldn't pick him up. The shooter had likely used alleyways and pedestrian routes, maybe even public transportation. No car to trace, no license plates to run. He'd been good. Hell, if Abigail hadn't been wearing the vest, the shot would've been fatal.

Huck had put out feelers to old contacts from his military service, asking them to track down any signature or style that might match this shooter. But it was like fishing in an empty lake. No nibbles, no leads. Which meant the guy was good.

Obviously he was good if he'd hit Abigail from that distance, threading the needle between columns and across a windy square. It was skill, sure, but also a damn message.

A knock at his door pulled Huck's attention from the sprawling mess of files and notes carpeting his desk.

Laurel appeared in the doorway. "Hi," she said, her voice as steady as ever, even if the subtle lines at the corners of her eyes betrayed her weariness.

"Hi, come on in." He waved her toward the one chair that wasn't drowning under stacks of paper. How he'd gone from pretty much living alone with his dog to now not only being part of this office but running it, he still couldn't entirely grasp. It had happened gradually, then all at once, like falling asleep on guard duty.

Monty, the other captain in the office, was healing nicely from chemo, but the guy still needed frequent breaks. He was currently on a Bahamas cruise with Laurel's mother, Deidre. They seemed like a good pair, but if things went south, it'd get awkward for them all. So Huck was hoping for everybody that they ended up in love and married and all happy.

Laurel walked inside, her heels clicking softly against the floor. She looked pretty today, in a feminine green sweater and jeans. That was probably Deidre's influence. Her mother had an uncanny way of getting Laurel to wear whatever she thought best, whether it was comfortable or not.

Her earrings were dangly and pink, the necklace sparkling with tiny stones arranged like blossoms on a vine. Deidre had definitely given those to Laurel as a gift. And Laurel had worn them because his brainiac woman had a huge heart.

"You look like you've been living in here," Laurel said.

Huck scratched the back of his neck. "Feels like it. But we're not getting anything useful from the cameras. Whoever took that shot at Abigail was a pro."

"I figured as much." Laurel settled into the chair. "Abigail's bruised but still breathing, thanks to the vest. She's fortunate to be alive."

He tried not to let frustration bleed into his voice. The more he dug, the more dead ends he found. "I'm reaching out to some old contacts to see if there's any chatter about a sniper fitting the bill. So far, nothing."

"Maybe he's that accomplished," Laurel said, her voice thoughtful.

"Perhaps he's not working alone." Huck leaned back, folding his arms across his chest, studying the woman he'd do anything to protect.

When she'd been pregnant, they'd started making plans to move in together, maybe build a barndominium on her mother's property. Something rustic but solid, with thick logs and wide porches with enough room for them and whatever life they'd managed to piece together.

He knew Laurel still intended to build the place eventually. Rent it out, maybe, or use it as a safe house when one of her cases went sideways. She was pragmatic like that. Even in grief, she kept moving, eyes forward. But Cabo . . . Cabo had been different. They'd spent their time there like two people trying to escape the world. No badges, no crime scenes, no mixing themselves up in other people's pain. Just ocean and sun and late nights tangled up in each other's arms.

He wanted a future. Still did, even if she wouldn't quite look at him the same way since the miscarriage. Like she was afraid of asking too much, of hoping for anything other than the here and now.

"Any news about Walter's brother?" he asked.

"Yes," she murmured, her gaze dropping to her hands like she hadn't figured out how to frame the words yet. "There were . . . odd lesions on Tyler's brain. Like cancer."

"Cancer?"

She shook her head, her brow pinching. "Not exactly, but Dr. Ortega has sent samples to the lab, so we'll see. Dr. Ortega does not guess, which I appreciate. He wouldn't want to raise any alarms quite yet."

"Raise the alarms." Amusement caught Huck. "Look at you getting all into recent vernacular."

She almost smiled. Almost. But something in her gaze remained shadowed and distant.

He shifted, leaning against the cluttered edge of his desk. "How's Walter doing?"

"He says he's doing all right," she said, her lips pursing, the motion tight and troubled. "I don't know if he actually is. I'm not . . . great at reading people, but I'm getting better."

"You're getting good at it," Huck countered. "And Walter's probably just trying to keep himself from crumbling. He lost a brother he barely got the chance to know. Feels guilty about it, too, I imagine."

Laurel blinked, her eyes weary. "I imagine so."

"You manage to wrestle jurisdiction away from the locals?" Huck asked, already knowing the answer.

"No." Her lips turned down, and hell, if the expression didn't make her look adorable. Those unique eyes, all exasperated and stubborn. "So far, no luck. There's no federal case here. Dr. Ortega said the locals need to request our assistance before he'll tell us anything else about Tyler's death."

"At least Ortega had the decency to give you something." Huck glanced at her, cataloging the faint lines of tension in her shoulders, the way she kept tucking her hair behind her ears. She had truly glorious hair. Thick and gorgeous in a deep, rich reddish-brown that reminded him of fall leaves and firelight. He loved tunneling his hands through it, feeling it spill through his fingers like silk.

She tilted her head in that analytical way of hers. "Did you interview Abigail?"

"Sure did," Huck muttered.

"She likes you." Laurel held up a hand before Huck could scoff. "Well, that's not true. She doesn't like anybody. But you intrigue her, and she very much wants to impress you. You can use that when you interview her again."

Huck leaned back, and the office chair creaked under his weight. "I'd think she wouldn't want to end up dead. So you think she'll work with me?"

"You never know what Abigail's going to do." Laurel's tone was as dry as a Montana summer before a storm rolled in. "I don't even know, and we share DNA."

He nodded. "I'm headed out tomorrow to interview everybody at the church. I called Pastor John, and he arranged for me to speak with people he thought were most disturbed by Pastor Zeke's death tomorrow. I'm also going to see that Tim Kohnex."

"Good luck with him. I believe he truly thinks he's psychic."

Huck would worry about the odd man tomorrow. "How about we grab a pizza, head home, and you stay the night with me?"

She smiled, and damn, if the sight didn't punch him straight in the chest. The kind of smile she only gave him when they weren't in the middle of a murder investigation or tangled up in half-truths and bitter memories. It was warm, real, something like peace. "I think I'd like that very much."

"Good."

They were on the same page at least when it came to that. Which was something, considering how much of their lives felt like one wrong turn after another, all roads leading back to Abigail's troubles and Laurel's too-sharp focus. For some reason, everything bad that touched Abigail seemed to come for Laurel as well. Like their shared blood marked them for some kind of twisted fate neither of them had asked for.

Not this time.

Huck was going to find the bastard who wanted Abigail dead. Not just because it was his job, but because he couldn't stomach the idea of Laurel in danger again. She had too many scars already. He'd lock this case down, track every lead, interview every suspect until he got the truth. And if it meant ruffling feathers or kicking down doors, then fine. He'd do it with a damn smile on his face.

Because whatever storm was building, Huck wasn't about to let it take Laurel down. Not now.

Not ever.

# Chapter 12

More spring weather arrived in the morning as Laurel hopped out of Huck's truck, a light rain drizzling the earth and releasing the fresh, sharp scent of pine and damp soil. The snow in town had finally melted, although the jagged peaks surrounding them remained dusted with white. Higher in the mountains, winter clung stubbornly, refusing to relinquish its hold. Maybe it never would. And that was fine by her. She liked the view. Something about the distant frost made the world feel clean, untouched by the messes she spent most of her days sorting out.

Huck shut his door and crossed around to meet her in front of Staggers Ice Creamery, his steps sure despite the slick ground.

They'd had a quiet night together, and she'd slept well. "Thanks for inviting me to stay last night," she said, meaning it.

He looked down at her, his gaze steady, expression softening. Today, he appeared strong and broad, wrapped in a flannel shirt that stretched over shoulders built for endurance and hard work. The gray mist hanging in the air framed him, making the bourbon color of his eyes appear calm and mellow. His facial muscles were relaxed, and his thick, dark hair had grown out a little longer than usual. She wondered how often he remembered to get it cut, if at all.

He'd shaved the sharp, rugged line of his jaw, but she knew from experience that by midafternoon he'd have a five o'clock shadow, stubborn stubble determined to reassert itself by three o'clock. The thought amused her.

"What do you think about moving in with me?" he asked, his voice gruff as he opened the door for them.

She blinked, caught off guard by the question, her brain still groggy from the warmth of his bed and the rare luxury of sleep uninterrupted by nightmares or phone calls.

She'd been moving forward on her plans to build the barndominium on her mother's property. The blueprints were rough but coming together—something small but solid, efficient and functional. She enjoyed living with Deidre, even if her mother's brand of nosiness tended to veer into interrogation territory. Still, her own space sounded nice. A place that was hers, maybe theirs, but that was a different sort of commitment.

"I don't know," she admitted, because honesty was easier than trying to wrap the answer up in polite evasion.

Huck swallowed. "We were making plans to move in together just a month ago."

"Yes, but I was pregnant with your child. We both decided that was the best path for the baby."

He looked away, a flicker passing through his eyes before he met hers again. "I understand that. But I think we should still make plans to move forward. With the two of us."

She held his gaze, thinking through every scenario. It wasn't stubbornness; it was survival. She'd never lived with a man before. Not really. Her last boyfriend had been, as Kate would put it, a jackass. The sort of man who couldn't understand her dedication to her job.

But Huck was different. He understood the long hours, the unpredictability. He wasn't threatened by her work because he had his own life, his own duties, his own frustrations to wrestle with. But he wanted something solid with her. That much was clear.

Often, their cases did cross paths, which could create a sort of conflict. More logistical than personal, though it could still scrape raw if left unchecked. But that had paled in comparison to what was best for the baby and the family they had been trying to form.

Now, there was no baby and no family. Just two people trying to pick up the pieces of what they'd been building.

She saw the hope in his eyes, a quiet determination that refused to be brushed aside. Huck didn't do halfway. Not with his work, not with his feelings. And not with her.

The realization tightened her chest, but she forced herself to breathe through it. Focus. Process. Evaluate. The same methodical approach she applied to everything else, even when her emotions wanted to claw their way into the equation.

She'd made her life about duty and loyalty. To her job, her family, her principles. But Huck was asking her for something more. And maybe it was time she started figuring out what she really wanted.

"Just think about it. All right?" Huck's voice remained steady.

"Of course I will." Thinking about everything was what she did best. Weighing probabilities, considering angles, analyzing risk. But it was different when the subject of examination was her own life.

She left him in the vestibule, scanned her ID against the plate with a quick swipe, the small beep confirming access. As Huck disappeared into his office, probably planning to pore over the stacks of files he kept like an unintentional barricade against the rest of the world, the outside door swung open behind her.

"Oh, wait, wait. Agent Snow, wait a second."

The voice was familiar. She turned partially, keeping her hand on the open door to shut it at any moment.

Tim Kohnex strolled inside, his dog trailing behind him. Kohnex was an ex-basketball player in his fifties, tall enough to make her feel like a kid. His frame was wiry now, the kind of lean that spoke more of obsessive running than the muscle he'd once built on the court. His gaze fixed on her with the sort of intensity that made most people back away.

"I think you're here to see Captain Rivers at Fish and Wildlife." Laurel's hand remained on the door, fingers tight against the cool metal.

"No, I'm meeting him later at the church," Kohnex said, his words quick, jumbled, as if he'd been rehearsing them. "But I wanted to talk to you. I need to warn you."

It took effort not to roll her eyes, but the urge still flared. She'd picked up that unfortunate habit from Kate's girls, sassy teenagers who weren't shy about expressing their disdain. Not that they aimed it at her, but it was impossible not to absorb some of that attitude when she spent time with them.

"I appreciate the thought, but I don't want to speak with you."

He threw up his hands. "I am psychic, you know. Whether you believe me or not."

"I do not," Laurel said flatly. She'd dealt with enough con artists and self-proclaimed prophets to know the signs. Kohnex wore his madness with pride, like some kind of badge that excused his lack of boundaries.

He continued undeterred, his words tumbling out faster. "I had a dream about you the other night." His eyes were wide, too bright. "It's imperative that I speak with you."

Laurel pivoted fully, planting her feet and putting her body between him and the door. No way was she allowing him up into her office. "Mr. Kohnex, I've asked you not to contact me."

"I haven't." He spread his hands like a preacher delivering a sermon. "I'm running into you. That's all."

She glanced at her watch. "You have thirty seconds."

He took a breath, relief flooding his expression. "The shooting the other day at the courthouse. I think that bullet was meant for you. Not Abigail."

Laurel's spine stiffened, her body instantly on alert. "That was a trained sniper."

"Yes, but you look so much alike. Don't you understand?" Kohnex's voice rose, his hands gesturing wildly like he could somehow shape the air between them into something coherent. "From a distance, someone who didn't know could mistake her for you. I can feel the danger coming. Somebody wants you dead. It's a dark, oily, desperate anger that's coiled and coming for you."

A thread of unease curled in her stomach, tight and unwelcome. Not because she believed him, but because there was a logic buried somewhere in the manic pitch of his words. From a distance, the resemblance between her and Abigail could be striking, especially to someone who hadn't spent time around either of them.

"Your thirty seconds are up," she said. She wasn't about to let him see the doubt working its way through her mind.

"Just . . . be careful." His shoulders slumped. "Please."

Laurel glanced at her watch. "Don't bother me again."

Kohnex hesitated, a flicker of hesitation passing across his face before his features settled into something she almost wanted to label as pity. The sudden shift made her stomach clench, not with fear but with irritation.

"I also had a dream about the two of you," Kohnex said, his voice dropping to a conspiratorial whisper. "He wants something from you that you can't give."

"Excuse me?"

"He needs more." Kohnex's gaze bore into her, all fervor and sincerity. "He'll always be unfulfilled with you. I'm so sorry to say that, but the wind never lies to me. Please, listen to me."

She stared at him, her eyes narrowing. The gall of the man, to presume he knew anything about her relationship with Huck. About what either of them needed. And yet, his words needled her, probing old insecurities she'd kept buried under layers of professionalism and cool detachment.

Laurel had read about con artists who specialized in cold reading—spotting micro expressions, seizing on the smallest hint of hesitation, and spinning it into something that felt like truth. It was an art form, really. A twisted, manipulative art form. But it worked. Maybe Kohnex was better at it than she'd given him credit for.

The thing was, he'd hit on something real. Huck had asked her to move in with him. Asked her to build something with him beyond a night here and there or the tangled mess of cases that too often dictated their lives. She didn't know if she could give him what he wanted.

But there was no way Kohnex could've known that.

"I just want what's best for you," Kohnex insisted, his voice lilting into something that might have sounded poetic to the right audience. "When the wind talks, one must listen."

She gave him a short, curt nod. "Let me know if the wind says anything about the upcoming game between the Mariners and the Dodgers. I'd like to wager a bet on that." Before he could retort, she turned on her heel and shut the door behind her. The heavy click of the latch was more satisfying than it should've been.

The stairs up to her office creaked underfoot, their groan a familiar sound that did little to chase away the unease prickling at the back of her neck. Kohnex's words were ridiculous. Complete nonsense. Yet they itched at her skin like a rash she couldn't quite ignore.

The idea that someone could be gunning for her instead of Abigail wasn't out of the realm of possibility. That sort of mistake happened. The shooter might've hit the wrong target. But Abigail had enemies. Not Laurel. Not the kind that aimed snipers at courthouse steps in broad daylight.

And that other comment, about Huck . . . Laurel shoved the thought aside before it could take root. Huck was solid. Steady. The kind of man who didn't need games or manipulation to say what he meant.

But Kohnex had managed to find the concern that lurked in her mind when she was awake at three a.m., staring at the ceiling and doubting herself, like any human. Kohnex had been trying to bother her, and she wouldn't let him.

That didn't mean he was wrong.

# Chapter 13

Laurel continued up to the office, her boots echoing lightly against the stairs. The hallway smelled like cheap coffee and lemon cleaner, while Kate's desk looked like a riot of papers and sticky notes, all crammed into a system that probably only made sense to Kate. A half-eaten muffin sat next to her keyboard.

"Hi, Kate. How are you?" Laurel paused to take in her assistant's frazzled appearance. Kate's hair was askew, blond strands frizzing out in the humid air, her eyes slightly wild from whatever mini-crisis she'd been wrestling with that morning.

"Hectic," Kate replied, blowing out a breath. "One kid home with the flu, one cranky about somebody named Tysen, one stressing about batting order on the softball team. Which means, of course, that the healthy one left her mitt at home and I had to turn around and go back for it."

Laurel couldn't help but smile. "Head home. You can go home with the kids. You don't have to stay here."

"I do." Kate's tone was adamant, but there was an exhausted sort of resignation in her gaze. "Agent Norrs from Seattle has called twice."

Laurel glanced at her watch. "It's only eight-thirty. What's his emergency?"

"He apparently wants to send a case your way," Kate said.

"Okay," Laurel said. "Did you speak with Viv about her friend?"

Kate's brow wrinkled. "Yeah, and she didn't want to talk about him. They just worked together, and I'm giving her some space right now. She'll talk when she's ready."

"She's a smart girl and is probably just processing her feelings. Please let me know if I can do anything to help." Laurel walked past Kate's desk, her attention already shifting toward the tasks ahead. As she passed the computer room, she nodded at Nester, who was hunched over his monitor and muttering softly to himself. His computer room was a disorganized labyrinth of cables and monitors, the glow of multiple screens casting harsh light across his unshaven face.

He barely looked up, a grunt of acknowledgment his only greeting. Whatever case he was working on had him hooked.

"Good morning," Laurel murmured, continuing down the hall. She appreciated his dedication every day.

Her own office was quiet and cool, the air heated just enough to make her shoulders relax. The rough door that served as her desk was mostly clear, save for a stack of reports and an empty coffee mug. She needed caffeine. Now. "Kate?" she called, her voice echoing down the hallway. "Hey, you didn't have a coffee in your hand when you came in, and I forgot one earlier."

"I'll go grab goodies from Staggers. Be right back," Kate called.

"Thanks." Laurel slipped off her jacket and tossed it over the back of her chair, hoping a double shot would help her to focus.

She pulled her phone from her pocket, flipping through messages until she found Agent Norrs's number. She pressed the button, lifting the phone to her ear and glancing out the rain-speckled window. Spring might be inching its way into the mountains, but the chill in the air felt more like November than May.

"Norrs," he answered, his voice clipped.

"Hi, Special Agent Norrs. It's Agent Snow. Kate said to give you a call."

"Oh, yeah. Hey, Laurel." His voice carried a hint of strain. "We are swamped right now with the attack on you and Walter, two RICO cases out of Seattle, plus the O'Malley trafficking bust, a cartel double-homicide, and a couple of missing kid searches we're coordinating with local law enforcement. And that's just the crap on my desk. I need to call in a quick favor but only if you have time."

"I do," Laurel said. So far, the jurisdiction for Abigail's shooting had remained with the state, and Tyler's death with the Elk Hollow police. Her frustration with the lack of progress sat heavy in her chest, but she pushed it aside. "What do you have for me?"

"I'm emailing you all the documentation." Agent Norrs's voice crackled with static for a moment before leveling out. "The body of Dr. Miriam Liu was found and identified late last night by the county coroner."

"Dr. Liu?" Laurel repeated, her mind already cataloging the name and filing it away.

"Yes. Miriam was married to one of my buddies from the service who died a year ago from cancer, and I promised to kind of check in on her. She doesn't have any other family, and it looks like she might've died just in a car accident, but she was always so careful. Meticulous. It doesn't feel right, but it's not really an FBI situation, and I don't have a lick of time right now. Plus, her body is with Dr. Ortega for the autopsy, and I know he's your buddy. Will you just check in with him?"

Laurel seemed to be checking on people left and right. "Of course. Can you tell me anything else about her?"

"Miriam was a biomedical researcher, one of the best. Under contract with the federal government."

Laurel booted up her computer. "So we might be able to gain jurisdiction if necessary."

"It's possible. She worked with Oakridge Solutions. I thought maybe you could poke around there and just make sure she didn't have any enemies. Her boss was a guy named Dr. Sandoval."

Laurel's fingers hovered over her keyboard and then paused. "Oakridge Solutions?"

"Yeah. Why?"

"Your friend is the second person who's died from there lately. The first was a lab tech whose death was ruled a suicide." Sometimes coincidences did happen, but still. She might have to call Viv that night.

Agent Norrs took a deep breath. "That's odd, but the causes of death seem different. Yet I wouldn't mind if you checked it out. You have time?"

"Yes." Curiosity would propel her forward, regardless. If for no other reason than to assure Viv that the truth had been found about her friend. "Do you know anything about Oakridge other than they have governmental contracts?"

"No. Oakridge is one of many research firms in the Seattle area, and I've never heard anything interesting about them."

Laurel really needed coffee. "Okay. I'll be in touch."

"Also," Norrs added quickly, his words coming out in a rush like he'd been holding them back, "your sister's really thrown by the shooting on the steps. If you could give her a call, I'd really appreciate it."

Laurel stiffened, her gaze cutting to the rain-splattered window. "Nothing throws Abigail, Agent Norrs. She killed our father, and she's been charged. This thing is going to trial, and apparently sooner than anticipated. Why would she want that?"

"To get it over with. She's innocent, Laurel. It was clear self-defense."

The guy had no clue. "I hope you're not a witness," Laurel said slowly.

"I wasn't there," Agent Norrs replied, irritation sharpening his words. "But I do know how much she feared your father. You'll need to tell the truth on the stand as well, Laurel."

"Of course I'll tell the truth." Laurel's words came out clipped, and she didn't bother trying to soften them. "But I think Abigail killed Zeke to hide something."

Agent Norrs huffed a breath. "Like what?"

That was the problem. Laurel didn't have a concrete answer, just a tangled knot of suspicion and instinct. Abigail was too composed, too calculating. Every move she made seemed deliberate and strategic.

"I don't know," Laurel admitted, relying on facts and not emotion. "I believe that she tried to kill Zeke once before, but he refused to confirm that fact before dying. I also suspect her in other deaths.

Perhaps he had proof about those murders. All I know is that she isn't who you think she is."

Agent Norrs snorted. "Give her a chance. Good Lord. She was so upset that you lost your baby, she went and challenged a man who then tried to kill her. It was self-defense."

"Was it?" Laurel's temper flared. It wasn't like her to lose her cool, but she was starting to like Agent Norrs, and Abigail would hurt him in the best of circumstances. In the worst, who knew what she'd do.

"Yes—definitely self-defense." Norrs's tone rose. "Your father was a monster, and Abigail had every right to defend herself."

Laurel shook her head. "I don't trust her, and you shouldn't either." How in the world could she convince him to protect himself?

"There wasn't a lot your father did except hurt her," Norrs said, his voice losing some of its edge. "You don't know her the way you think you do, and whatever your differences, she's still your sister."

"Abigail and I are not close. You need to realize that now," Laurel said. Why wouldn't he see what was right in front of him? "If you're not going to see the truth regarding her, someday she'll show it to you."

"Oh, yeah? You think she'll dump me?" Agent Norrs chuckled.

"I certainly do. That's her pattern."

A chair creaked through the line. "Does her pattern include getting engaged?"

Laurel sat back, her breath catching. Before she could reply, Kate appeared in the doorway, holding a latte with a pink sleeve wrapped protectively around it. "Thank you," Laurel mouthed, offering Kate a smile as she accepted the cup. "Did you say *engaged*, Agent Norrs?"

"Yes." His voice now lowered and softened. "I asked Abigail to marry me, and she said yes."

Laurel paused with the coffee in her hand. Abigail was taking this one further than she would've guessed. "Wow." The woman moved quickly, but this was outright sprinting. "Agent Norrs, I've given you all the warnings I can. Let's just keep our relationship professional and worry about what happens to Abigail later."

"I worry about what's going to happen to Abigail every second." His words came fast. "She needs you in her corner, and it's the right place for you to be. That man was evil. Don't you agree?"

Laurel let the warmth from the drink seep into her palm. "I do think he was evil. But one doesn't preclude the other. Abigail could be just as evil. Open your eyes."

"I will, if you will," Agent Norrs fired back.

"Of course. It was nice speaking with you." Laurel ended the call.

Abigail was planning to marry Agent Norrs? The man was too stubborn to see anything beyond what Abigail wanted him to see. His loyalty was commendable but also blinding.

But she'd made a promise to help him, so she'd do her job. Laurel reached for the phone again and dialed the main line for Oakridge Solutions. The receptionist answered on the second ring.

"Hello, this is FBI Special Agent Laurel Snow. I'd like to meet with Dr. Sandoval," Laurel said, her mouth watering for that latte.

"Oh, I'm sorry," the receptionist replied. "Dr. Sandoval is unavailable right now, but I can make you an appointment for a bit later today."

Laurel placed her coffee on the desk. "All right. I'll be there in less than an hour." She tossed the phone down and took a sip of her latte, enjoying the sugar.

Walter walked down the hallway and stopped just outside her door, his posture stiff, his eyes dark-rimmed with exhaustion. His gait still carried a slight limp from the accident.

"Hi, Walter," Laurel said, studying him. "How would you like to take a drive with me?"

His eyes snapped up. "Of course. What's the situation?"

"Probably nothing, but it beats just sitting around here."

Walter nodded. "I'm with you."

"Maybe we can grab lunch afterward," Laurel said, already reaching for her jacket. "Let's go."

# Chapter 14

Huck tossed a biscuit across the office, the arc lazy and unhurried, landing with a soft clatter near the plush, overpadded dog bed Ena had supplied. Another one. Seemed like every few weeks, a fresh monstrosity of fluff and orthopedic foam appeared, courtesy of her insistence that Aeneas deserved comfort, too. Huck was convinced the woman had stock in a dog bed company.

Aeneas lounged on the latest addition to his growing collection, a broad rectangle of memory foam covered in something Ena called durable fabric. It was already fraying at the corners, courtesy of Aeneas's industrious teeth. Chew, tear, destroy, and the game continued with a fresh bed. Huck half smiled.

The dog was striking. A Karelian Bear Dog with a coat of pure black and white, the contrast sharp and clean. His chest was broad, head narrow and intelligent, with pointed ears that twitched at the slightest noise. His dark eyes glinted with an almost human awareness. All muscle and instinct, he was built to charge straight at a bear instead of away from it.

Aeneas had the nerve for it, too. No hesitation, no second-guessing. Pure adrenaline and drive.

"It'll be bear time soon, buddy," Huck promised.

Aeneas's core function was to scare bears off before they even thought about wandering into town. Sure, he was one of the few breeds in the world that didn't go jelly-legged at the sight of a grizzly, but he was just as damn effective at search and rescue. Huck had relied on him more times than he could count. Between tracking down lost hikers and keeping wildlife at bay, the dog had earned his keep ten times over.

Huck's phone rang, the shrill tone jolting against the quiet. He snagged it off the desk. "Rivers."

"Hey, it's Agent Norrs." The man on the other end sounded as ragged as Huck felt. "Is this a good time?"

"Sure." Huck settled deeper into his chair, eyes flicking back to Aeneas, who had curled himself into a tight coil of muscle and fur on the torn-up bed. "What do you have on the attack against Laurel and Walter?"

"Not a whole hell of a lot," Norrs admitted, his voice slipping into a flat tone of frustration. "We're combing through old case files of Laurel's as well as Walter's. Trying to see if anyone's recently out of prison or if any past cases have flared up. We're also checking more recent cases, seeing if there's any connection."

Huck's gaze drifted to the window, the bleak stretch of gray sky outside offering nothing but another dismal reminder that the world wasn't in a mood to make things easy. "And the black truck?"

"Nothing. Not even on CCTV."

Huck straightened. "So you think it was just waiting out there on that deserted highway for them?"

"Looks like it." Norrs's tone was clipped. "Can't find it in town, not in Elk Hollow. We're running scans of the CCTV in Genesis Valley, too. Still coming up empty. And your office building? Nothing from the security footage there either."

Huck's jaw tightened. Whoever was behind the attack had been thorough, clean. If there was one thing he hated, it was hunting a ghost. "Damn it."

"I always think there's some crazy out there causing trouble," Norrs replied. "Or, what if there's a slim chance that the attack on Laurel and the shooting of Abigail could be related?"

Huck leaned back in his chair even more. It creaked in protest. "How so?"

"Abigail killed Zeke, and it's well-known Laurel didn't like the guy. She wanted to put him away. I wonder if this is some sort of revenge on the whole family."

"It's possible," Huck murmured, figuring that since Norrs had given up the goods, he might as well do the same, just in case the investigations were related. "I'm headed out to the church later to interview a few people Pastor John thinks could be involved in the shooting of Abigail. He doesn't believe anyone there would do such a thing, and he claims he doesn't know any snipers, but you never know. We're also running deep dives here in the office on some of the congregation members. So far, we haven't found anybody with a sniper's background."

"Doesn't mean somebody didn't hire him," Norrs said.

The guy was quick. "That's my thinking as well. I need more probable cause before I can get search warrants for any bank records, but I'd like to go see who catches my attention at the church. Keep in mind, the attack on Abigail might not be from a church member." Huck rubbed his chin. "I also have state officers checking at the Tech Institute where Abigail works, in case she has any enemies there. Right now, we're looking into backgrounds, just in case."

"Sounds good. I appreciate you keeping me apprised."

"Ditto," Huck said. They might as well work together, at least as long as they could.

Norrs cleared his throat. "Abby's coming in to speak with you again today. She wasn't calm when you visited her in the hospital. She should be there any minute."

Huck grunted. "Okay."

"Be nice to her, would you?"

Huck snorted. "I'm always nice."

"Getting shot really shook her balance. She desperately wants to have a relationship with your girlfriend," Norrs said.

"Sure." That wouldn't happen. Laurel could take care of herself, and Abigail Caine had the survival instincts of a cornered rattlesnake.

"I'll catch you later." Norrs hung up, abrupt as usual.

Right on cue, Ena poked her head in the door. Her long black hair was braided today, tight and neat, and her Fish and Wildlife uniform was so freshly pressed it looked like she'd ironed it while wearing it. Huck noticed she seemed happier lately. No doubt because she was dating Walter Smudgeon. "Hi, Huck. Dr. Abigail Caine is here to see you."

He shoved a stack of file folders aside, barely clearing enough space. "Send her in."

Abigail strolled through the doorway, moving like she had all the time in the world. Today she wore a black leather skirt, black boots, and a deep red sweater that hugged her curves. Jewelry glittered at her ears and throat, diamonds and rubies, flashing under the overhead lights. A small white bandage showed along her clavicle that disappeared beneath the sweater.

Two uniformed Genesis Valley police officers hovered outside, their eyes darting inside before they took position on either side of the door. Abigail closed it behind her, shutting them out.

"Have a seat." Huck nodded toward the one chair that wasn't buried under gear or stacks of clutter.

"Thank you, Captain." Her voice was a purr, the kind some people might mistake for civility. Her hair was down, curled just enough to look effortless. Laurel wore hers like that sometimes, but on Abigail, it appeared like armor. "Are you any closer to finding the person who shot at me?" She slid into the chair, all elegance. "I'm growing very tired of Lurch and Dumbass flanking my every move."

Huck let one eyebrow lift. "I'm sure Genesis City would take the bodyguards off if you wanted. Though considering somebody's trying to shoot you, I'd think twice."

"Somebody could get at me from long distance and you know it." Her voice was clipped, eyes sharp. "I feel like there's a bull's-eye on me at all times."

"There very well might be." Huck kept his gaze steady on her, watching her like he'd watch a bear trying to decide whether to charge or bolt. Abigail's fingers drummed on the arm of the chair, too controlled to be nervous. The woman was pissed. She should be scared.

Huck took out a notepad and reached into his drawer, his very messy, disorganized drawer, to find a pen buried in the back. He fished it out and popped the cap off. It was one of those cheap ballpoint pens he liked best. Reliable. Disposable. Nothing fancy.

Abigail glanced at it and smirked. "You need something a little more official than that."

"I really don't," he murmured, eyes on her face, which looked way too much like Laurel's. "Do you have any idea who'd want you dead?"

"Besides you?"

For fuck's sake. "I don't want you dead, Abigail. I just want you out of Laurel's life."

"There's only one way that's going to happen, Captain," she said easily, crossing her legs and revealing toned thighs. It was too damn chilly to be wearing a short skirt, considering it was only spring in the Washington mountains.

Huck deliberately kept his gaze on her eyes and not lower. "Besides the threat from Tim Kohnex and your father's girlfriend, whom I'm going to meet today, who else do you believe wants you dead?"

"Nobody." She lifted both hands. "Honestly, I have a few ex-boyfriends, and I brought you a list." She reached into her bag and pulled out a folded sheet of paper. "But not one of them wants me dead. I ended things amicably, including with Pastor John. You know he has former military experience, right?"

Huck hadn't known that. He was still waiting for the background checks from the state. "Was he a sniper?"

"I have absolutely no idea," Abigail murmured, her eyes glinting as if she found the question amusing or irritating. "Maybe both."

"I want to tell you really quickly, since we have a moment, how sorry I am about the baby."

"Thanks. We're all sorry," Huck said curtly. "Let's stay with your case."

Abigail held up one hand, revealing nails painted bright red—a far cry from the polished, restrained look she'd donned for the courtroom.

"No, I'm worried about my sister. It's a good time for you to make a clean break."

"Excuse me?" Huck said, ice skittering down his back.

"Oh, please. Laurel needs somebody as intellectual as her to keep her interested. She shouldn't have to dumb herself down every second. You two started a formal life because of the baby, and the baby no longer exists. You need to let her find someone who can challenge her and keep her entertained. While you're good-looking and no doubt fit, those attributes don't last forever."

There was enough truth in her statement that his temper began to spiral, and he forced it down. Ruthlessly. "Dr. Caine, the last person in the world I'd seek dating advice from is you. Let's stick to who wants you dead. Is there anybody in your past besides these men?" He took a quick glance at the sheet of paper and noticed a notation. "You were married. Very briefly."

"It was a bit of a fling," she said with a careless shrug.

Huck read the name again and then whistled. The guy was a venture capitalist, well-known, probably worth a few billion dollars.

"Yes. Let's just say my divorce settlement was rather lovely," Abigail said with a smug tilt of her chin.

"Unbelievable." Huck shook his head. "Well, he could afford a sniper."

She waved a dismissive hand. "Oh, he doesn't want me dead. He'd love to get back together."

Huck almost believed her. The kind of man with that much money didn't need to hire a sniper to make his problems disappear and would probably just bury them under piles of cash. "Do you have any known enemies at the church?"

"Not really." Abigail reached into her bag and pulled out several more pieces of paper. "Here are the death threats I've received via email. I'm sure Laurel could trace the IP addresses."

"So can the state," Huck said. "We're keeping the cases separate."

Her eyes widened, voice pitching up with genuine disbelief. "Why? Both my sister and I were attacked within a day of each other."

"If so," Huck said, "that leads to the only real connection between you, and that's the church and your father. Did he have any close friends? Anybody who would kill for him?"

"Not to my knowledge."

There had to be more victims out there. "How about women other than Uma Carrington?"

"He dated many," Abigail said, shaking her head. "Several in the church, but Pastor John would know more about that than I would."

Zeke Caine had taken off on some supposed sabbatical, and nobody had been able to trace him except to a small community in Arizona. "Where has he been this last year?" Huck asked.

"I truly don't know," Abigail admitted. "But it's not something I cared about. As you know, I did not want him to return home, especially once I discovered Laurel."

Huck had other state officers digging into Zeke Caine. They were working angles Huck couldn't cover himself, reaching out to local precincts, running Caine's name through databases, tracking anything from cheap motel receipts to social media pings.

He'd also obtained a warrant for Zeke Caine's financial and phone records, making sure it would be executed by Washington State authorities, wherever the trail led. The report probably wouldn't come in for a few days, but Huck had patience. Sort of.

"I don't suppose you want to talk about the night you killed your father?" Huck kept his tone casual.

Her smile was catlike. "I don't suppose I do. I'm fully willing to cooperate to figure out who shot at me. However, since you're trying to put me in prison for defending myself, I'll not discuss that other matter with you. Besides, you know I can't without my attorney present."

"I'm surprised your attorney isn't here." Huck eyed her closely. Abigail Caine was a true narcissist and probably didn't think she needed her lawyer.

"Oh, no. I wasn't going to pay him nine hundred dollars an hour to sit here and try to protect me from you. I'm perfectly capable of doing that myself."

Yeah, that's exactly what he thought.

She stood and stretched, the movement deliberate, drawing the material of her deep red sweater tight across her high breasts. Huck kept his gaze above her neck. Abigail played games. He didn't.

She turned, gaze flicking toward the corner of the room. "Oh, I didn't even see him. Cute little puppy sleeping there."

Of course she had. Huck knew without a doubt that Abigail Caine missed nothing. Aeneas looked up, his sharp, dark eyes locking on her for a long moment before lowering back to his bed. There were very few people he wouldn't stand and greet. She was one of them.

Huck fought down a smile. He had learned long ago to trust his dog's instincts. Aeneas rarely misjudged people. If the dog didn't like Abigail, there was probably a good reason. "What about your farming operation?" Huck asked. "Any enemies there?"

She tapped her lips thoughtfully, that calculated smile still in place. "I really haven't been all that involved in it for quite a while, but I can see if we've received any threats. I guess a lot of people don't like pot farming, even in Washington State."

"I can ask Pastor John when I interview him later today as well," Huck said. Abigail and the pastor owned a successful marijuana growing operation together, one of the more surprising facts he'd uncovered. It was also where she made much of her income. "I know you've conducted experiments on participants that have pushed them to violence. I'm not looking to arrest you for that . . . yet. But I need a list of every single one of your subjects."

Her smile didn't so much as flicker. "I'm afraid I can't do that, Captain. As you know, patient confidentiality is paramount, even if the files weren't destroyed, which they were."

Huck's eyes narrowed. "All right. Then give me the name of anyone who would possibly want you dead."

"I would if there were any." She sounded cheerful, almost playful. "You have to remember, Jason Abbott didn't want me dead."

"Not until the very end when he unraveled," Huck countered. She'd really fucked with that guy's head until he started killing women. "For too long, he wanted to kill everybody except you."

"Well, he certainly came around on that point," Abigail said with a wry smile. "And now he's dead."

"If you have other enemies out there, you need to tell me who they are."

Abigail straightened and moved toward the door, her chin tilted in that superior way Huck had come to associate with her worst moods. "Captain, the biggest enemy I have in this life right now is you."

# Chapter 15

Oakridge Solutions rose from the edge of a hillside like a modern puzzle box with three stories of glass, polished steel, and black metal panels arranged in clean, sharp lines. The reflective windows were dark, designed to block out glare while preserving energy.

Laurel Snow drove her SUV along the paved road toward the main gate. The asphalt was pristine, with no cracks or uneven patches. Shrubs lined the drive, clipped with precision and spaced at even intervals. Pine and fresh-cut grass mingled in the air, clean and sharp. She reached a guard booth and rolled down her window.

The guard was young and clean-cut with an easy smile. "Good morning, ma'am. I'll just check you in." He had a slight Pacific Northwest accent that was clipped but friendly. He glanced at Walter and took his badge as well. "We've got you both on the schedule. Welcome to Oakridge Solutions."

Laurel nodded. She'd asked Kate to call ahead with their information. "Thank you." She handed over her ID, noting how quickly and smoothly the guard entered their information. Professional, but polite.

The guard double-checked their names, glanced at his screen, and returned their badges along with two visitor lanyards and a bright green parking pass. "Park in the structure and take the elevator to the main floor."

"Thank you." Laurel accepted the lanyards and passed one to Walter before driving forward.

The road curved through trimmed hedges and past fountains, water running over polished stones. The landscaping was deliberate, designed with symmetry and clear lines. The parking garage entrance was marked with illuminated signs, bright and clear.

The garage itself was cool and dim, the lights placed evenly without dark spots. Laurel followed the arrows to the guest section and parked. The air held a faint lemon scent, likely artificial and pushed through the ventilation system.

"This place is efficient," Walter said, glancing around. His fingers tapped lightly against his thigh, a habit he didn't always notice.

Laurel stepped out of the SUV and adjusted her lanyard over her head. "The setup is organized, maintained, and rather pretty."

Walter nodded, his gaze already moving to the nearest exit. "They've put a lot of money into it."

They walked toward the elevator, where Laurel stepped inside with Walter close behind her. The elevator doors closed with a soft hiss when she pushed the correct button. The walls were brushed steel, polished and clean.

The elevator moved smoothly, the air inside filtered and cool. The doors opened onto a third-floor lobby painted in pale gray with glossy white trim. The floor was polished stone, the pattern subtle but precise. Modern art hung at regular intervals in bright, geometric pieces that likely cost a fortune.

A woman approached them, her heels striking the floor with measured steps.

"Hello," she said with a polite, open smile. "I'm Dr. Bertra Yannish, and please call me Bertra. Welcome to Oakridge Solutions. We've been expecting you." She held out her hand, shaking both of theirs with a firm grip. Her hand was cool, her shake quick and efficient. She appeared to be in her mid to late forties, with sandy blond hair pulled into a smooth, low twist. She wore gold-rimmed glasses over brown eyes.

"I was Dr. Liu's assistant," she said. "Please, come this way." She led them down a wide hallway past several glass-walled offices. Each office contained a sleek desk, computer monitors, and chairs arranged with precision. The surfaces were clear of clutter. No loose papers, cords, or personal items in sight. Potted plants—broad-leafed, healthy, and real—stood at regular intervals along the hallway.

Bertra stopped at a corner office near the rear of the building, opened the door, and gestured for them to enter. "This was Miriam's office."

Laurel stepped inside. The office was large, with dark wood furniture and a polished desk. A closed laptop sat at the center. Several framed certificates and degrees hung on the wall, their labels clean and legible. Bookshelves lined one side of the room, filled with medical texts and neatly labeled binders. The air here was slightly warmer than the hallway.

"What projects was she working on at the time of her death?" Laurel asked.

Bertra stood near the door, hands clasped in front of her. "Just one. We're working on a clinical combination aimed at preventing Alzheimer's and certain dementias, as well as potentially curing them. Dr. Liu was heavily involved in the project."

Laurel walked over to the glass windows and looked out at the rolling hill leading to a mountain. "How many floors do you have in this building?"

"Three above ground. Four below." Bertra remained by the doorway. "Most of our research and anything involving chemicals is documented and protected. Neither of you have clearance to enter the laboratories, but if you obtain it, I'd be happy to give you a tour."

"Was Dr. Liu working exclusively on this trial?" Laurel asked, turning her attention back to Bertra.

"Yes. We have contracts with several pharmaceutical companies, private investors, and government agencies."

Footsteps sounded from the hallway, and a man entered without knocking. He appeared to be in his early fifties, with brown hair streaked with silver. His eyes were brown, and he wore a dark suit with no tie over a lean body.

"Matteo," Bertra said. "These are the agents from the FBI."

The man nodded once, his gaze clear behind wire-rimmed glasses. "Dr. Matteo Sandoval. Chief of Operations. Bertra, I'm sorry to have kept you waiting. I had another call." His voice was smooth and even. He stepped into the office, reaching out a hand. "I worked closely with Dr. Liu."

He shook Laurel's hand first in a firm grip. Then Walter's. Afterward, he moved around the polished desk and settled into the high-backed leather chair.

Bertra shifted her feet, her lips pressing together.

Walter lifted an eyebrow, his expression sharpening in that way it always did when he noticed something off. "I take it you got the new office."

Dr. Sandoval nodded. "Yes. This has a better view than my previous one, and since Dr. Liu and I shared resources, the files are already here." He gestured toward the two leather chairs facing the desk. "Please, have a seat."

Laurel sat. The chair was firm but comfortable. Walter lowered himself into the other chair, his shoulders loose but his gaze steady.

Bertra remained standing, her skin noticeably paler than when they'd entered the building.

"Dr. Yannish, I'd like to speak with you alone after this interview, if you don't mind," Laurel said.

"Again, please call me Bertra, and of course I'll speak with you." The woman looked directly at Dr. Sandoval. "I'll go move my belongings into your former office, Matteo." She turned on her high heels and strode gracefully from the room.

Walter cocked his head, his eyes on Dr. Sandoval. "She's pissed. You're taking over her boss's office."

Dr. Sandoval leaned back in his chair, folding his hands on the desk. "She's not mad at me. She's mad at the world. They were close, and Miriam's death is a tragedy. I heard she might have been drinking again after being sober for over a decade. Do you have the autopsy results yet?"

"No," Laurel said, noting a slight tension in his posture.

Dr. Sandoval pushed his glasses up his nose, the silver frames catching the light. The wooden desk in front of him was sleek and minimalist, with clean lines and no drawers. A matching credenza behind him appeared to be the only storage unit, its doors closed and precisely aligned. "We're shocked about Miriam's death. Just shocked."

Laurel observed the tidy efficiency of the office. Everything in place. Everything controlled. "Is there any chance her death wasn't an accident?"

Dr. Sandoval adjusted his glasses again. Was that a nervous habit? "Of course not. She was a nice woman who worked on cures for the elderly. I can't imagine anybody wanting to harm her."

Walter cocked his head to the side. What had he noticed? Laurel couldn't see it.

She cleared her throat. "What about Larry Scott?"

Dr. Sandoval sat back. "Scott? That poor kid? He killed himself."

So the doctor had heard of him. "Did you know him?"

"Not at all," Dr. Sandoval said. "But when one of the young techs dies, we all hear about it. What a tragedy."

Laurel couldn't read him. "Isn't that odd? That there have been two deaths of your employees?"

Dr. Sandoval slowly nodded. "I suppose so, but hundreds of people work here. So maybe not? I truly don't know."

Laurel switched tactics. "What was Dr. Liu doing driving erratically in Tempest County? This facility is in King County. That's over sixty miles away."

"I don't know," Dr. Sandoval said. "I believe she may have had a cabin somewhere, or perhaps she rented a place. Dr. Liu enjoyed taking time away from the city to work or relax. We knew each other professionally, but not personally."

Walter leaned forward. "Have there been any other recent deaths? Of your many employees, I mean."

Dr. Sandoval paled. He cleared his throat.

Laurel measured his breathing and blink rate. Both had increased. "Doctor?"

"Yes." Dr. Sandoval swallowed. "A young financial analyst named Melissa Palmtree died a few days ago. She was efficient and detail oriented, and she handled our budgets and funding streams."

"How did she die?" Walter asked slowly.

The doctor shuddered. "She died falling down stairs at a bar in Seattle. Such a damn tragedy."

Laurel tried to click the three deaths into a pattern, but didn't see it based on causation. "You've had three deaths in six weeks—in a facility that contracts with the defense department. You know, Walter? I think we *do* have jurisdiction here."

"Same here, boss," Walter drawled.

"I understand your concerns," Dr. Sandoval replied. "But I haven't seen any indication of foul play. If you have specific questions, I'll do my best to answer them." He pushed his glasses up his nose again. "Larry heard voices sometimes. Geniuses often do. Plus, his girlfriend of five years broke up with him, and he didn't take it well."

"So you don't find it odd that three people, all of them working with a governmental contractor, are dead within weeks of each other?" Laurel asked.

Dr. Sandoval glanced away briefly. "They weren't all working on the same projects."

"Did all three of them work on the Alzheimer's project?" Laurel asked.

"Yes." Sandoval's gaze settled back on her. "They all contributed to it in different ways. Larry focused on biochemical modeling. Melissa handled the financials. And Dr. Liu was involved in the formulation process itself."

"Well, that's a definite coincidence," Walter said, his voice dry.

"I don't see how," Dr. Sandoval replied. "We have many contracts with the government, so we're monitored constantly. Sometimes people die. It's tragic but not indicative of anything sinister."

Laurel narrowed her eyes. "Wait a minute. Why is the government contracting with you to cure Alzheimer's? That doesn't make sense."

Dr. Sandoval's jaw tightened. "The contract is actually with Daisy Pharmaceuticals. But yes, it has governmental clearance."

Laurel nodded. "You receive grants from the government."

"Yes. Daisy Pharmaceuticals receives the funding, and they subcontract to us."

Walter looked at Laurel, his gaze sharp.

Laurel didn't rely on feelings or instinct. She focused on facts, evidence, and patterns. "Are there any other applications for Dr. Liu's research? Anything defense based?"

"No," Dr. Sandoval sighed. "Miriam just wanted to cure dementia. She lost her mother to the disease young and was very determined. I'm so sorry she's dead." His brow furrowed into what Laurel had learned was the grief muscle.

She stood. "Thank you for your time. I'm going to apply for a warrant for your records, all of them, so you might want to start compiling them."

Dr. Sandoval rose from his chair, his gaze sharpening slightly. "You don't have probable cause and you know it."

That was probably true. She needed to speak with Dr. Bertra Yannish. "I'd like to interview everyone working on the dementia and Alzheimer's study. Anyone working with Dr. Liu."

"Get a warrant." Dr. Sandoval handed her a business card. "However, Ms. Snow, you can call me anytime you want. Did you know there's a documented link between heterochromatic eyes and higher intelligence?"

"I did, and it's Agent Snow," Laurel replied. "There's also a link to an increased risk of certain genetic disorders."

Walter stood. "We'd like a brief tour of your facility—of what we can see. If you don't mind."

"That would be fine," Sandoval said. "I'll have Bertra give you the tour while I get settled into my new office."

Laurel tilted her head. "Where were you the night Dr. Liu died?"

"Here at the office," Dr. Sandoval replied easily, his tone smooth and practiced. "I'm always here at the office. I have no knowledge of her death. I am very sorry that she's gone because she was an absolutely brilliant biochemist. And we need her."

Walter's eyes narrowed. "Did you have a personal relationship with her?"

Dr. Sandoval's expression didn't change, but Laurel noted his blink rate increase as well as a subtle shift in his breathing, with his chest rising slightly faster.

"No. Not at all," the doctor said.

"Interesting. What about with Melissa Palmtree?" Walter asked.

Dr. Sandoval gulped. "No."

Walter snorted. "You do know that it's a crime to lie to federal agents, correct?"

Dr. Sandoval's gaze dropped to the floor, his shoulders tightening before he lifted his eyes again. "All right. Yes, Melissa and I had a relationship. But we both only lived for work. That was it. We didn't have outside relationships, and we didn't have time to form any. So, yes, once in a while we . . . we had sex in the supply closet."

"All right." Walter's tone remained even. "Did you want her dead?"

Dr. Sandoval shook his head, his gaze steady again. "No. I didn't love her, but I liked her a lot. When I'd heard she died falling down the stairs of a bar in Seattle, it broke my heart."

Walter nodded. "All right, let's go talk to Bertra and get a tour of this place. And our clearance is higher than you think, buddy, so we want to see some of the labs."

Dr. Sandoval's expression remained neutral. "Like I said, we'll show you what we can. But there are clean rooms you can't visit. The security protocols are strict." He moved around the desk and took Laurel's arm in a gentle grasp.

A sharp ping echoed through the office. Glass shattered.

Dr. Sandoval's head snapped backward as a bullet tore through his temple and exited the other side, glass fragments scattering to the floor. His body crumpled, collapsing to the polished wood in an unnatural sprawl. Blood pooled quickly, seeping across the flawless surface.

"Down!" Walter tackled Laurel to the ground, his shoulder slamming into her ribs as they hit the carpet.

Laurel twisted, her mind already processing angles, distance, entry points. She scrambled for her purse, yanking out her phone to call for help. "FBI. Possible sniper in the vicinity of Oakridge Solutions. We need all units and immediate surveillance on nearby buildings. Check CCTV now."

She crawled forward, keeping low, and reached for Dr. Sandoval's wrist. But she didn't need to check for a pulse. The exit wound was wide, blood and tissue staining the white wall behind him. His eyes, still open, were already unfocused and dimming.

"Another sniper," Walter muttered, his voice tight. "Would that have hit you if Sandoval hadn't moved right then and taken your arm?"

Laurel kept her gaze on the shattered window, searching for the origin of the shot. "I don't know. We need to track the trajectory."

Walter's breathing was steady, but his fingers flexed against the floor, ready to move. "You okay?"

"Yes." Laurel's phone crackled with dispatch confirming units en route and surveillance being pulled. She kept her eyes on the window. "Do you think the hit on Abigail was actually meant for me?"

"Two sniper hits in one week on what we considered to be different investigations?" Walter's gaze swept the room. "What are the odds of that?"

# Chapter 16

Huck clicked off the phone call with Abigail's ex-husband, who had a rock solid alibi considering he'd been in Tokyo for the last six months. The guy had sounded truly concerned about the woman and seemed to still be in love with her.

How did she fool so many people?

Shaking his head, Huck strode out of his office and crossed the reception area, his boots thumping against the well-worn floor. Aeneas followed him quietly. Ena stood behind the counter, organizing folders. She'd gone still, eyes locked on a piece of paper, her cheekbones darkened with a pink flush that didn't bode well.

He stopped, his gaze narrowing. "I'm heading out to Genesis Community Church to talk to suspects and witnesses about the courthouse shooting."

She snapped her head up, shoulders tight, almost vibrating with indignation. "You are not going to believe this." She pushed away from the desk, the movement sharp. "Absolutely not going to believe this."

Huck folded his arms, noting the way she gripped the paper as if she wanted to crumple it. "What happened?"

"The yew grove up around Stony Mountain. The one Fish and Wildlife has been monitoring for years?" Her voice cracked with anger.

"Someone's gone through it. Cut down trees, hauled them out. Even took some mushrooms."

Huck's fingers curled into fists. "They're clearing out the yews?"

"Craken McGregor was hiking out there a couple of days ago. It's only a mile or so from his cabin, and he said the grove looks like a war zone. Trees hacked down, brush trampled. The whole area's torn up."

Huck's jaw tightened. That grove held Pacific yew trees, which were rare enough to warrant special attention. Their bark and needles produced taxanes, which were essential compounds for chemotherapy drugs like Taxol. Poachers sometimes targeted the trees for that reason, especially in well-established groves like the one near Stony Mountain.

"Damn it." Huck ground his teeth and tried to shove down irritation. "Why would anyone risk poaching out there? It's posted with warning signs."

Ena grabbed her purse, her movements stiff and clipped. "Because they don't care."

"Take Officer Jordan, and both of you arm yourselves."

"Not a problem." Ena's eyes remained hard, determination etched across her face.

Huck shook his head, his mind already cataloging the mess. Plenty of people knew better than to mess with the yews. Fish and Wildlife kept tabs on those groves for a reason, and while the trees themselves didn't hold value for standard logging, their medicinal potential brought in poachers from all over. Still, the grove up by Stony Mountain hadn't been targeted before. "Be careful out there."

"We will. I'll go grab Officer Jordan." Ena shot him a glare before heading toward the bullpen in the back of the office.

Huck strode outside and to his truck through the misting rain, water clinging to his jacket. He secured the dog in the crate in back, his thoughts still turning over what Ena had told him. Rare yew trees uprooted and stolen.

He fired up the truck and pulled out, tires crunching over wet gravel. The drive to Genesis Valley Community Church took about ten minutes, winding along the river and past the outskirts of town. Rain continued to fall, soft but steady, painting the world in shades of gray and green.

The church rose ahead, its steeple cutting into the low clouds. Two stories of pale stone and painted clapboards by forest and open grass. Stained-glass windows gleamed even under the dull sky, their blues and greens depicting mountains and rivers with a craftsmanship that spoke of dedication. Beyond the building, the river swelled, its currents churning from the rain.

Huck parked near the front of the gravel lot, tires crunching over the uneven surface. The rain had turned the dirt to mud in patches, but most of the lot held firm. He jumped out, opened the back door to unlatch the dog crate before whistling for Aeneas to follow. The dog hopped down, his ears perked and eyes sharp, already scanning the area.

Huck clipped on Aeneas's leash, though the dog rarely needed it. They'd let him inside before, especially when Huck only planned to visit the offices and not the actual church. The air smelled of wet earth and cedar. Rain continued to fall in a soft drizzle, muffling sounds and making the world feel smaller, more contained. Huck stepped up to the church's entrance, his boots leaving muddy prints on the stone walkway.

Pastor John met him at the door, holding it open with one hand. "Huck," he said, his voice deep and welcoming.

"Pastor." Huck gave him a nod, eyeing the man's casual jeans and black sweatshirt. The outfit was a far cry from his usual robes, but it fit the rainy day.

They'd crossed paths on several cases before, and Huck had learned a few things about the man. Helpful when he wanted to be. Not exactly a saint. The pastor's habit of dating younger members of his congregation, married or otherwise, had stirred trouble before. Scandal had rocked the church not too far back, but since Pastor Zeke's death, Pastor John was the last one standing. As far as Huck could tell, the man did his job well enough, other than his weakness for risky relationships.

"Come this way," Pastor John said, already turning toward his office. In his midthirties, the pastor had deep brown skin, curly brown hair, and light brown eyes, and he was about Huck's height.

Huck followed, Aeneas trotting beside him with his nose twitching at every new scent. The dog's claws clicked against the tile floor, announcing their arrival.

The office looked different. Huck noted the changes immediately. A framed Seahawks poster hung on one wall, bold and bright, dominating the space. Photographs lined the credenza with shots of Pastor John with congregation members, smiling and shaking hands, mixed with fishing trips where he held up silver-scaled catches, beaming at the camera.

"You've redecorated." Huck's gaze lingered on the sports memorabilia before drifting to the photographs.

"Yeah. I packed up all of Pastor Zeke's belongings." Pastor John's voice held a note of finality. His gaze lingered on the shelves before shifting back to Huck. "I don't suppose Agent Snow would want any of them."

"Absolutely not." Huck shook his head.

Pastor John sank into his chair, eyes narrowing. "I've called Abigail a couple of times. Haven't heard back. Can't believe someone shot her right on the courthouse steps. It's insane." His brows drew down, deep lines creasing his forehead. "Unbelievable violence."

"That's what I wanted to ask you about." Huck remained standing, arms folded, his stance steady. Aeneas sat beside him, head tilted slightly, listening as if he understood every word. "You did date Abigail, and she did dump you. Correct?"

Pastor John leaned back, a slow smile spreading across his face. "I believe the breakup was more mutual. But yes, we did date." He paused, gaze steady. "I certainly don't want her dead."

Huck watched the man's expression, the way his shoulders remained relaxed despite the pointed question. "Do you own an AK-47?"

"I do not." Pastor John shook his head, his smile fading. "Nor would I know how to shoot anyone from a distance."

The response sounded plausible enough. Still, Huck planned to run a deeper dive on the pastor's history, just to be sure. "I heard that you served in the military."

"As a chaplain. Briefly. That was it."

"Is there anybody in the congregation who might want Abigail dead?" Huck shifted his weight, glancing briefly at Aeneas who had settled beside the desk.

Pastor John shrugged. "Not really. A lot of people are upset she killed Zeke Caine. That doesn't just go away." He paused, the lines around his eyes deepening. "And there are people who never liked her because she's not the warmest of women. Abigail's brilliant, but she's blunt and rubs people the wrong way. But I can't imagine anyone shooting her like that."

"Are you aware of anybody with the skill to pull off that kind of shot?" Huck pressed, his gaze never leaving the pastor's face.

"No." Pastor John spread his hands, palms up. "This isn't exactly a congregation full of sharpshooters. Although, weren't you a sniper?"

Huck's brow lifted. "I was," he said, wondering how the man had uncovered that detail. "But I was on the courthouse steps when Abigail was shot. So it couldn't have been me."

"I didn't think it was." Pastor John adjusted some papers on his desk. "You might not know this, but Tim Kohnex served in the military after his basketball years."

The revelation landed with weight. "He did?" Huck's mind churned through everything he'd uncovered about Kohnex during the last investigation. That piece of information had never surfaced.

"Yes." Pastor John leaned back in his chair. "I don't know what he did exactly, but you might want to ask him."

"Is there anybody else worth questioning?"

The pastor's gaze drifted to the window, his shoulders rising and falling with a slow breath. "Zeke's girlfriend is especially distraught. I've tried to counsel her, but she's in pain. They seemed to be casually dating, but apparently she was in deeper than she realized. As you requested, she's here waiting to see you."

"Thanks."

Pastor John rose from his desk and handed over a pink flyer. "We're having our annual Spring Worship Day next Thursday to kick off the better weather and outside activities. I'd love it if you and Agent Snow would come."

Huck took the flyer, folded it, and stuck it in his pocket. "I'll ask

Laurel, but I don't see her wanting to spend time in her father's old church. No offense."

"None taken." Pastor John smiled. "Just think about it. For now, I'll go get Uma for you. Unless you have any other questions for me?"

Huck did have one. "Has anyone confessed anything to you about Abigail's shooting?"

Pastor John's eyebrows rose. "If someone had, you certainly know I couldn't tell you."

"Could you give me a hint?"

"Absolutely not."

Huck let out a slow breath. "I understand."

Pastor John left the office and returned a few minutes later with a young woman who looked like she'd spent the last several nights wide-awake.

"This is Uma." Pastor John gestured her inside. "She was dating Zeke."

"Yes, I'm aware." Huck offered his hand. They'd met once before. "Would you please have a seat?"

Uma dropped into the chair, her fingers twitching against the strap of her purse. She had long brown hair and eyes and seemed much more intense than last time he'd met her. She looked everywhere but at him.

Huck shifted his own chair so he faced her directly. "Have you threatened Abigail Caine?"

Her cheeks flushed. "Define 'threatened.'"

"Did you say you were going to kill her?"

"No." Uma picked at a nail, the sharp movement betraying her nerves. "I ran into her in the parking lot at the grocery store. Told her she deserved to die."

"But you didn't shoot at her?"

"No." Uma's shoulders stiffened. "I didn't shoot her. Didn't hire anyone to do it either."

"I have a warrant for your home and bank records," Huck said, his tone flat.

Uma's chin lifted defiantly. "Feel free. I don't have any money. If I did, I wouldn't waste it hiring a sniper. But Abigail Caine will get hers. There's not a doubt in my mind."

"That sounded like a threat."

"I don't care." Her eyes narrowed, expression hardening. "I loved Zeke. We were going to get married."

When had she gone off the rails? "After dating a month?"

"When love happens, it happens fast." Uma shot to her feet, eyes blazing. "I don't have to talk to you."

"No, you don't." Huck's voice remained calm. "But you should tell me everything right now."

"Screw you." She stormed out, the door slamming hard enough to make the photographs rattle on the walls.

"That wasn't very churchly," Huck muttered.

Pastor John reappeared in the doorway, concern etched across his face. "That looked rough, but the love of her life was murdered by his own daughter."

"He wasn't a good man." Huck kept his arms folded, his gaze unwavering.

"I don't judge." Pastor John shrugged, but the gesture seemed forced. "If the rumors are true, then he'll face judgment. One way or another."

Huck rarely thought much about heaven or hell, but if anyone deserved to rot in hell, it was Zeke Caine.

The pastor cleared his throat. "Tim Kohnex is here waiting to speak with you. He wants me to convince you that he's telling the truth. I think he is."

Tim Kohnex strode inside, his mutt trailing at his heels. Aeneas lifted his head, sniffed the air, then rested his chin back on his paws. Kohnex took the chair Uma had vacated. "I didn't shoot Abigail," he said, voice rough and low. "But I warned her evil was coming for her. It is. She deserves it for murdering our beloved Pastor Zeke."

"Tell me about your military record," Huck said.

"It was brief. Worked as a mechanic. Didn't like the structure. Got out." Tim shrugged. "I'm not military. But I can shoot. Grew up hunting, fishing, shooting. It's what I do."

The man's twitchy gaze didn't match the nonchalance in his voice. Huck watched him carefully. "So you do want Abigail dead?"

"No." Tim shook his head. "I want her behind bars. But Captain, you need to protect yours."

"My what?"

Kohnex threw up both hands. "Your woman. She's in more danger than you can imagine."

"Is that a threat?"

"No." Tim tipped his head back, eyes unfocused. "The wind speaks to me. It tells me when there's danger. I know it's coming for Laurel Snow. I tried to warn her and she wouldn't listen. The nightmares won't stop. I have to get through to her."

Huck stiffened. "Really?"

Tim's eyes widened, the blue darkening. "Yes. I don't know how or why. But it's coming from a distance. Like a bullet."

Huck's phone vibrated in his pocket, cutting through the tension. He pulled it out and glanced at the screen. A text from Laurel.

Another sniper. Shots fired, and the doctor next to me died.

Everything inside Huck went cold.

Tim's lips curved into a slow, almost satisfied smile. "I am not sure what you just read, but I feel like the wind is happy. You believe me now, don't you?"

# Chapter 17

Laurel sank into Huck's sofa, her body angled toward the warmth of the roaring fire. They'd eaten dinner not long ago—chicken cacciatore, Huck's latest culinary experiment. The captain had a talent in the kitchen he didn't share with many people.

Fred Lacassagne, her cat, lay sprawled across her lap and part of the couch, his rumbling purr a constant vibration against her thigh. She absently rubbed him behind the ears, her fingers finding the soft fur at the base of his neck where he liked it most. She hadn't expected to bond so deeply with the little guy. He'd been a stray she found in a decrepit old barn on her family's property, looking half-starved and matted. Now, he was an affectionate fixture in her life. She hadn't planned to keep him; that would've been impractical, especially with her job pulling her all over the place. But something about his stubborn persistence to survive had hit her hard.

Usually, her mother took care of Fred when Laurel's work kept her away for extended periods. In Deidre's absence, Dolores, a family friend, had been watching Fred. Dolores had an affinity for animals, her house full of them, and she didn't seem to mind having Fred around. Laurel had fetched him on the way home, preferring the cat to be with her when possible. It was good to have him here, especially now. He gave her something normal to focus on.

Huck returned from stacking another log on the fire, settling down on the couch beside her, though he kept a respectful distance from the cat. Fred tended to be selective about his affection, and Huck wasn't always on the approved list. Huck stretched his legs out, propping them on the table with an ease that spoke of exhaustion.

Her phone rang, shattering the quiet moment. The caller ID showed Special Agent in Charge Norrs calling. Laurel pressed the speaker button, her gaze still on the fire as she spoke. "Hi, Agent Norrs," she said.

"Hi, Laurel," Agent Norrs replied, his tone clipped and all business. "We think we found the location the sniper shot Dr. Sandoval from. It was about seven hundred yards away up in a tree blind. We're pulling all CCTV from the area, but nothing useful has shown up yet. I've got everyone keeping an eye out for that black truck, too. I'm starting to think these situations are related."

"That is certainly a possibility," Laurel responded. Had Dr. Sandoval been killed instead of her? Her stomach rolled over.

"I've requested all of your case files from DC and we're putting together a team here in the Seattle office dedicated to this," Agent Norrs continued. "When somebody shoots at one of ours, we take it seriously."

"I appreciate that," Laurel said, her gaze finally shifting from the fire to the window where the night pressed in. "I can help you go through those."

"That would be great. For now, have you ever dealt with a sniper as a suspect?"

Laurel scratched Fred's chin, her mind pivoting neatly to the question at hand. "No." The certainty of her answer matched the clean, organized catalog of her memory. "None of my cases in DC or in any of the other jurisdictions where I've consulted have centered around a sniper." She mentally categorized former investigations. "I've caught a few serial killers, and people who committed violent crimes involving guns, but never a sniper like this. The level of precision and distance involved . . . it's different."

The fire popped, a sudden burst of sparks flaring before settling again. Huck stretched his legs farther onto the table, his fingers tapping absently against his knee.

"How about a case that this reminds you about?" Agent Norrs asked.

Laurel mentally sorted through the cases she'd worked over the years. Her thoughts moved in straight lines, each file opening cleanly and closing just as neatly. "I can't even think of any ancillary suspects or witnesses who may have had sniper experience. We don't usually conduct deep background checks unless someone stands out for a specific reason. Maybe military experience, but even then, we focus on what's relevant to the crime."

"Is there any direction in which you can point me?"

She shifted Fred's weight on her lap and his claws kneaded the fabric of her jeans. She didn't deal in maybes or vague hunches. Every observation had to be grounded in something real.

"There was one case in Kentucky," she said, filtering through the details. "We caught a serial killer who kidnapped women, abused them for several days, and then shot them. Execution-style." The memory came back with clinical clarity, her brain slotting each fact into place. "His name was Henry Jones Phillips. He came from a family of four boys, and I believe two of them may have had military experience."

"That case was about five years ago, right?" Agent Norrs asked.

"Yes. I'd zeroed in on him early. He ended up confessing and is serving a life sentence now." Laurel adjusted Fred again, her fingers brushing against the thick fur along his spine. "His brothers were interviewed as part of the investigation, but only in passing. They weren't considered suspects because they hadn't been in contact with him for years. From what I gathered, the family had splintered."

The fire crackled again, and Huck's gaze fixed on some point beyond the dancing flames.

"The brothers weren't close?" Agent Norrs prompted.

"Not from what I found. Sporadic contact, maybe a Christmas card here or there. That was all." She shrugged, the movement more for herself than Norrs. "But I can't rule it out. Just . . . none of them ever registered as a serious possibility."

"Got it." The click of keys on Agent Norrs's end had stopped. Now there was only the low hum of his breathing, his focus probably every bit as exacting as hers. "I'll need to bring you in for a formal interview soon. I know you've already given me everything you have, but protocol's protocol."

"Understood." Laurel watched the flames lick over the logs with restless precision. *Protocol.* The word made sense to her. Structure. Organization. A clean process meant to wring out the truth. She would go through the steps, give her statements, answer their questions, and hope the right details fell into place. "Have you looked into Dr. Sandoval or his family?"

"Yes. He didn't have family. No close relatives, anyway. So . . . there was no one to notify or investigate."

Well, that was just sad. The clean detachment in Agent Norrs's voice only sharpened the reality. Dr. Sandoval had died without anyone to mourn him. Without anyone but the government's official notice to mark his passing.

Sometimes Laurel wondered if, without Deidre's influence, soft and kind to a fault, she would've been more like that. Alone. No attachments. No one to consider her absence a true loss.

Huck's arm slid over her shoulders, his fingers brushing lightly against her hair in a touch so casual she almost dismissed it. But there was something deliberate in the way he played with her hair, like he understood the weight of her thoughts even when she hadn't voiced them. She would never understand how he did that.

"All right." Agent Norrs's voice cut through her musings. "If anything else comes to mind, please let me know. We're in agreement, right? That the shooter on the courthouse steps was aiming for you and hit Abigail. Then that same sniper accidentally hit Dr. Sandoval instead of you."

"That makes the most sense," Laurel said, a headache thrumming behind her eyes. Was anybody close to her a target at all times now? "We have Nester creating a computer scenario of Abigail's shooting that we'll look at tomorrow. Considering there was a sniper in my vicinity twice and somebody else was shot, I think that's a fairly easy conclusion to reach. But we'll see what Nester discovers."

"Okay. Sounds good. I'll head your way first thing in the morning and interview you as well."

"Of course," Laurel replied.

The line went quiet for a beat, just the low murmur of someone shuffling papers or maybe shifting positions. Then another voice cut in, bright and familiar. "Laurel, I'm so sorry to hear you almost got shot. Again." Abigail's voice, smooth and overly cheerful, carried a note of something too close to amusement for Laurel's comfort.

"Thank you, Abigail," Laurel said. "If the shooter on the courthouse steps was aiming for me and not you, I'm sorry that you took a bullet for me."

"Oh, I'd always take a bullet for you, dear sister." Abigail's response was gleeful, the kind of high-pitched delight Laurel had never really learned to decipher. "Don't worry about it."

Laurel shook her head, feeling the muscles in her neck tighten. "Just in case, you need to stay safe. This appears to be aimed at me, but we don't know that for sure. You were shot, so I would keep the Genesis Valley protection detail as long as you can."

"Oh, they've already waved off," Abigail replied breezily. "The sheriff decided you were the target and I didn't need protection. But don't worry, my sweet Wayne Norrs is keeping me safe."

"I'm sure he is," Laurel replied. "I'm glad to hear that. Have a good night, Abigail." She clicked off, placing her phone on the table. Fred shifted in her lap, his whiskers twitching as he adjusted to a more comfortable position.

"This is an odd one, Laurel Snow." Huck's voice was low and measured, his expression thoughtful. "I know you have no idea who would want you dead."

She shook her head again, her gaze on the fire but her focus inward. "Statistically, it's somebody connected to one of the cases I've already worked. That's the most probable explanation." Her fingers kept a steady rhythm rubbing along Fred's back, the familiar texture of fur under her fingertips an unconscious comfort. "But I can't pinpoint anyone. Nothing and nobody's coming to mind. It's frustrating."

Huck leaned over and pressed a kiss to her cheek.

Her phone buzzed again. Laurel sighed and reached for it. The number on the screen was familiar. "Agent Snow."

"Hi, Agent Snow. It's Dr. Ortega at the county coroner's office."

"Hi, Dr. Ortega." Laurel adjusted her grip on the phone. "It's good to hear from you. You're working late."

"I'm always working late," Dr. Ortega replied, his voice very slightly slurred, indicating exhaustion. "But I wanted to call you because . . . well, this is an odd one."

Laurel stilled. "What is odd?"

"I just finished the autopsy on Dr. Liu. She didn't die from the car crash."

Laurel frowned, her fingers pausing midstroke along Fred's back. "What was the cause of death?"

"The cause of death was from blunt force trauma due to the car crash," Ortega clarified, his words slow and deliberate. "But I believe she was in some sort of manic episode at the same time."

"I don't understand. Please clarify." Laurel's mind parsed the words like a computer processing data, isolating relevant details and discarding anything extraneous.

"That's the odd part," Dr. Ortega continued, the hesitation in his voice breaking through his usual clinical professionalism. "Dr. Liu's brain showed the same lesions, growth, and abnormalities as the ones I found on Tyler Griggs."

Laurel's hand stopped completely as her brain locked onto the name. Her thoughts realigned, recalculating. "Wait. What?"

"Tyler Griggs," Dr. Ortega confirmed. "The podcaster. Walter's brother."

"Yes." Laurel's reply was immediate. "I remember the case. But . . . the same lesions?"

"I've never seen anything like it." Dr. Ortega's voice shifted. "I'm still waiting for details from the state lab. Trying to get a clearer picture. I don't even have the bloodwork back yet."

Laurel leaned back, her shoulders hitting the couch cushions with more force than she intended. "How in the world was Tyler Griggs's death related to Dr. Liu's? I need to see those autopsy results as soon as possible." The two lived in different worlds.

"Of course. I called you because Dr. Liu is your case," Dr. Ortega replied. "I haven't contacted the city police about it yet."

"If somehow those two deaths are related, Tyler Griggs's investigation was just transferred to the FBI." Wait a minute. What about the other two deceased employees from Dr. Liu's lab? Was there any connection? Larry Scott had been cremated already. What about Melissa Palmtree?

Huck's gaze remained on her, unwavering and direct. His stillness made her hyperaware of her own agitation, her body tense beneath his steady focus. The fire's warmth felt distant, muffled by the sudden chill of what she'd just learned.

"What in the world could Tyler Griggs have in common with Dr. Miriam Liu?" Laurel murmured, her thoughts racing. "Except for those odd lesions on the brain. Could there be some new virus out there?"

"Let's not speculate. I'll see if I can put a rush on the chemical analysis, bloodwork, and histology," Dr. Ortega said. "Now, I have to go. I'll be in touch."

"Thank you." Laurel ended the call, her thumb hovering over the phone for an extra second before setting it down. She quickly rang up Nester. "Sorry if it's too late."

Nester laughed. "It's just after dinnertime. I'm still in my twenties, boss. So are you, by the way."

Sometimes she felt older. "I need you to officially get the Tyler Griggs murder transferred to the FBI. Fill out a warrant for Griggs's computer, apartment, and car. See if you can find a judge to sign off, and then take a couple of city officers with you to Elk Hollow to obtain the evidence. Keep the chain of evidence clear."

Huck rolled his neck. "Nester can take Tso from my office. He's itching to be back in the field." Both Tso and Jordan had been shot in a previous case, but both had recovered nicely.

Laurel relayed the information. "Thanks." She clicked off.

The quiet that followed felt too thick, the fire's crackle suddenly intrusive. Huck's eyes remained fixed on her. "What's going on?"

She glanced back at him, the intensity of his gaze offering something steady to hold on to. His honey-bourbon eyes reflected the firelight, familiar and grounding. Somehow, without explanation, she found an unexpected comfort there. "The truth is, I really have no idea."

# Chapter 18

Laurel had to admit she felt decidedly better the next morning. The tension in her shoulders had eased, though she wasn't entirely sure if it was because the FBI had taken over the Tyler Griggs case or the fact that Huck had been especially . . . energetic that morning. She looked through file folders with her office blinds closed tightly behind her, pleased that Nester had succeeded in obtaining warrants and now they had jurisdiction of the Tyler Griggs case. They needed to search his residence again.

"Hi, Laurel." Viv Vuittron strode into the room. She wore ripped jeans and a crop top, her curly blond hair around her shoulders. "I have my FBI internship application and was hoping you'd take a look at it." She placed a neatly stapled stack of papers onto the old door desk.

"Of course." Laurel had already written her letter of recommendation. "Hopefully you'll be assigned here." That is, if they caught the sniper trying to kill Laurel and made the office safe again.

Viv grinned. "That would be awesome." At sixteen years old, she seemed bright and ambitious. She sobered. "Thanks for checking on Larry for me. We worked together sometimes at Oakridge, and I really liked him. He treated me as an equal and not just like a dumb high school student." Her eyes glimmered.

Laurel nodded. "I'm sorry about his death." She wished he hadn't been cremated so she could order an autopsy. "Did you know either Dr. Liu or Melissa Palmtree?"

Viv frowned. "Yeah, kind of. Why did you just use past tense?"

Laurel sucked in a breath. "They're both deceased."

Viv blinked. "Oh, no." Her eyebrows slashed down. "By suicide like Larry?"

"No," Laurel said. "I can't tell you anything else, but I think you should end your internship at Oakridge now. Just in case. Okay?"

Viv gulped. "I understand." She glanced at her watch. "I have to go. We're working on double plays today for the next game." Her head down, she hurried from the office.

Laurel watched her go. Had she handled that correctly? Hopefully. She turned back to her desk and read through several reports for a while.

At some point, Huck poked his head in. "We're in the conference room ready for the presentation." His eyes held a hard focus. Apparently, having her in danger brought out the animalistic side of him. Not that she was complaining. There was something reassuring about Huck's intensity, the way his concern translated into action rather than empty reassurances. She could work with that.

She stood and hustled around the desk to sit in the conference room with Huck, Agent Norrs, Nester, and Walter in an unofficial task force. The air smelled of coffee and stale paper, the usual scents of long, relentless investigations. Their copper-and-glass table had been broken a couple of weeks previous, and Kate had somehow found a fifties-style teal-colored table to use for now.

"All right," Huck said, his voice steady and direct. "I've scouted the area in front of our offices. Checked all the surrounding buildings and rooftops for possible sniper points. We've identified eight locations within range."

Laurel noted the tightness around his eyes, the way his shoulders remained tense even as he tried to project calm. Huck wasn't one to trust easily, and the fact that someone had targeted her clearly had him on edge. She couldn't blame him.

"We'll keep the blinds all shut in the office," Huck continued. "No one can see in, but that only matters when you're inside." He glanced at her, eyes narrowed. "The more dangerous time for you is going to or from vehicles. My place is secure," he added. "I've got multiple floodlights and security cameras set up. I don't think you should go back to your mom's home. Not until we've got this under control."

"I agree." Laurel kept her voice steady, but her mind was already spinning through scenarios. Possible vantage points, attack vectors, methods of evasion. "You've done everything right so far."

Agent Norrs grunted his agreement, his arms folded tightly across his chest. "We'll have extra agents posted around the building for the time being. But I've seen what Huck's set up at his place. You're better off staying there."

"In addition," Huck said, his gaze boring into her with that familiar, stubborn intensity, "how do you feel about wearing a bulletproof vest?"

Laurel hesitated, the idea settling uneasily in her mind. Bulletproof vests were bulky, restrictive. More important, they sent a message she didn't want to project—fear. "I don't like the idea," she admitted. Her fingers drummed lightly on the edge of the conference table, a steady rhythm that helped her think. "They're cumbersome and can limit movement."

Huck's expression tightened, his eyes narrowing as if preparing to argue. The room had gone silent, all eyes fixed on her. She understood their concern, but that didn't change her dislike for the idea.

Walter shifted uncomfortably in his seat, his gaze darting between Laurel and Huck. The man's fingers twitched against his coffee cup, his usual nervous energy amplified by the tension in the room. "It's just a precaution, right?" he offered, his voice unsteady. "Doesn't mean you're expecting trouble. Just . . . being careful."

Laurel considered his words, her mind filtering them through her own pragmatic lens. Precaution made sense. But strapping herself into body armor still felt like admitting she couldn't control the situation. Huck wasn't going to let it go. She could see that in the firm line of his jaw, the way his arms folded over his chest like he was bracing himself for a fight.

"Consider it," Huck said, his voice low but forceful. "At least when you're outside. No point taking risks you don't have to."

Laurel met his gaze, her mind already calculating probabilities and outcomes. "I'll think about it."

"So we just need to be careful until we figure out who wants you dead." Huck's voice held a gruff finality, as if the solution were as straightforward as just waiting out the storm. His shoulders remained taut, every muscle telegraphing vigilance.

Agent Norrs nodded, his expression all business, mouth set in a grim line. "We're still going through all the applicable and relevant cases. The one with the four brothers—you know, Henry Jones Phillips? The killer's still in prison, as is one of the brothers. Another brother went to prison on unrelated charges and died there about two years ago. The final brother died in a bar fight about a year ago." The agent cracked his knuckles. "There are no other living relatives in that situation. At least, none that we've been able to locate."

Laurel nodded, her gaze fixed on the table as if the teal hue held answers. "So I need to think of who else might want to kill me."

"That's right," Norrs said. "Keep thinking through past cases."

"I definitely am," Laurel replied, though her focus had already splintered, her mind following two tracks at once. She forced herself to focus on the sniper and not her other investigations. "Nester?" she asked, her voice cutting through the silence.

Nester slid his laptop across the table, his eyes bright with the eagerness of someone who loved his work. "Yeah, here you go, boss." He tapped a few keys and a simulation bloomed to life on the screen. "If you look here"—Nester gestured at the display—"from where the sniper was positioned the day of the courthouse shooting, the bullet did go right by you and hit Abigail. Huck said he heard the bullet. So that actually makes some sense."

"So you think he was aiming for me?" Laurel asked.

"I don't know." Nester shrugged one shoulder. "I can just show you the trajectory."

On the screen, the simulation played out with meticulous precision.

It showed the shooter's position, the bullet slicing through the air, whizzing past Laurel's shoulder and colliding with Abigail's chest. Abigail crumpled backward, the image pausing just before she hit the ground.

It was an impressive simulation. Clean. Methodical. Exactly how Laurel liked things to be.

"So this guy isn't as good as we thought he was?" Walter asked.

Huck nodded, his eyes still on the screen. "Yeah. He thinks he's better than he is. He missed you both times. Unfortunately, someone else was hit."

"Unfortunately." Laurel echoed the word under her breath, her gaze fixed on the frozen image of Abigail collapsing. The simulation made the event feel sterile, mechanical, but that didn't change the reality of it. While Abigail survived, Dr. Sandoval had not.

Agent Norrs's gaze shifted to Huck, his expression expectant. "I know you interviewed witnesses out at the church about who'd want to shoot Abigail, but Laurel may have enemies there as well. She wanted to put their father in prison."

"I seriously doubt anybody at the church wants me dead because of Zeke Caine," Laurel replied. "In that case, Abigail would've been the target. She's the one who killed him." The memory of that day was clean and crisp in her mind, the image of Abigail holding that knife dripping with blood unassailable. "I believe the most effective way to figure out who tried to kill me is to continue the focus on my past cases. Whoever's targeting me likely has some connection to one of them."

"What about current cases?" Agent Norrs asked, his brows drawn tight.

Laurel considered the question, her mind cataloging her recent work with her usual efficiency. "I've only consulted on two cases recently, both of them just through email exchanges. I can send those files to you, but it'd be surprising if a sniper tried to murder me just because of something so impersonal. There wasn't much detail exchanged. Nothing sensitive."

"Agreed," Agent Norrs said, his fingers tapping lightly against the file he held. "But I don't want to leave any stone unturned."

Nester cocked his head with a curiosity that seemed genuine rather than idle. "Where does that expression come from, anyway?" His fingers danced over his keyboard, already searching for the answer.

"Well," Laurel said, the corner of her mouth twitching slightly, "it comes from a Greek legend. A general named Polycrates hid his treasure before being defeated in battle. To find it, his enemies were told to 'leave no stone unturned.' It's just a metaphor for thoroughness."

Nester nodded, his eyes flicking from his laptop to her. "Fitting. We're definitely not leaving anything unexamined."

"In the meantime," Laurel said, "keep all the blinds shut in the office. No one comes or goes unless absolutely necessary. When I leave, I leave alone."

"Bullshit," Huck snapped.

Laurel turned to him, her mind already running through potential arguments. Huck's determination wasn't something she could easily counter, and if she were being honest, she didn't particularly want to.

"I'm with Huck," Agent Norrs said, his tone firm. "Nobody's letting you go anywhere alone. Not until we have a better idea of who's behind this. I've already heard from DC, and I have no doubt our boss will be calling you soon."

Laurel already had a note to return the call of the deputy director.

Huck's gaze stayed locked on her, unflinching. "I'll know if a sniper has a gun trained on us. I'll feel it."

She didn't understand how that was possible. The idea of sensing something so precise without evidence seemed improbable, but Huck's instincts were far sharper than most. And considering his background, she couldn't dismiss his confidence as arrogance. Huck had been a sniper himself. If instincts like the ones he claimed to have were real, he would be the one to recognize them. He didn't overstate his abilities. If anything, he underestimated them.

"So that leaves the Dr. Liu and now Tyler Griggs investigations for me to work," Laurel said, forcing herself back on track. Whatever had been found in their brains wasn't just an anomaly. It was a pattern. One that might include the other two deaths from Oakridge. Maybe. "Walter, this afternoon, let's go through Tyler's most recent podcasts and see if there's anything that ties Dr. Liu and him together."

"Sounds good, boss," Walter replied, his shoulders relaxing a fraction. "I'd also like to bring Sandra in for questioning again. See if his girlfriend has anything else to add."

"As would I," Laurel agreed, her gaze shifting toward the whiteboard cluttered with hastily written notes and diagrams. The patterns weren't forming, and the disarray gnawed at her. "Maybe she remembers something she didn't realize was important."

Nester looked up. "She has some interesting arrests for protesting. Hates the government. Became violent several times."

"Please call her in for an interview this afternoon," Laurel said.

Nester nodded. "You've got it."

Huck glanced at his watch, the movement quick and efficient. "I have two Zoom meetings in a few minutes. We've had a bear sighting up in Northridge, and I need to go set up a trap afterward. Also need to check out the yew infiltration."

"The what?" Nester asked, his eyebrows drawing together.

"The yew," Huck clarified. "The Pacific yew tree. It's not endangered, but it is protected. Somebody's been razing them like crazy. Cutting them down or damaging them beyond repair."

Laurel frowned. "Why would they do that?"

"Not sure," Huck admitted, his eyes narrowing thoughtfully. "But I'll ask them when I find them."

"People are idiots," Nester muttered, his fingers tapping at his laptop like he was about to look up something about the trees.

Huck rose to his feet. "I'll be back in time to escort you home, Laurel."

"That's fine." Laurel stood. "Thank you, everyone."

Agent Norrs gave a tight nod. "I'm heading out, too. There's got to be CCTV of the sniper somewhere in town." He grabbed his coat with a sharp motion and strode out, his steps echoing down the hallway.

Walter cleared his throat, glancing toward Laurel. "I guess you'll conduct all your work here in this nice, safe conference room, huh?" His attempt at humor didn't quite land, but she appreciated the effort.

"I guess so," Laurel replied. She had to start thinking clearly.

Kate strode down the hallway and poked her head in the door.

"Um, Rachel Raprenzi called and said that she's interviewing Abigail and her attorney tomorrow night on *The Killing Hour*. She wants to know if you'd like to join them."

Laurel tried to breathe evenly through her nose to calm her central nervous system. "Tell her that the FBI has no comment."

Kate faltered. "Rachel said to make sure I told you that she's contacting you as Abigail's sister and not as an FBI agent."

The measured breathing wasn't working. "Then tell her to fuck off," Laurel said.

Kate's eyebrows rose and she burst out laughing at the same time as Walter. His guffaws filled the conference room.

Heat filtered into Laurel's cheeks. "Also, no comment."

# Chapter 19

The crash was a flash of metal and noise, a scream of rubber against wet pavement. Mark had taken the corner too fast in his beautiful black truck, eyes fixed on the mirror instead of the road. His truck spun out, tires catching mud, gravel spraying like shrapnel. Now the sweet truck had bullet holes in it from that FBI agent shooting back at him.

The impact sounded like a thunderclap. Steel met oak with a violence that shuddered through his bones, snapping his head forward hard enough to split his lip against the steering wheel. His chest hit the seat belt, the force like a sledgehammer to his ribs.

Then silence.

He woke with blood in his mouth and a thunderstorm pounding inside his skull. The airbag had deployed but deflated to a useless heap of nylon and powder. The windshield was a kaleidoscope of cracks, a dark vein of blood smeared across it from his forehead.

He'd gotten away, but they had to be coming for him. Tying up loose ends. He had to run. Now.

The taste of iron thickened on his tongue. Blood dripped from his nose, slow and steady, painting his upper lip with a warmth that shouldn't have been comforting. His hands shook as he fumbled for the seat belt release, fingers slipping off the latch twice before it finally clicked free.

He shoved the door open with his shoulder. It gave with a groan of metal, and a fresh lance of pain stabbed through his ribs. He stumbled out, his boots sinking into mud. The night was thick with rain, the air a cold bite that clung to his skin.

Something in his ankle twisted wrong as he moved, a sharp, splintering pain that nearly sent him to his knees. But he didn't fall. Couldn't.

He had to keep moving. Before they caught up to him.

His brain hurt like fingernails scraped across the delicate tissues. Like something alive had dug into his skull and was making room for itself.

Pain. Agony. Life.

He wiped the blood from his nose, but the streaks only smeared across his skin. His vision tilted, edges blurring in and out, but he forced his legs to move. Tripping over roots, he scraped his palms against bark slick with rain.

No sounds echoed from behind him. No engines. No voices. But they'd been there. He'd seen the headlights—too close, too deliberate. Or had he? Was he imagining things again?

The trees closed in, branches clawing at his face, leaves slapping against his shoulders. The world around him pulsed in shades of black and gray, shadows deepening with each uneven step.

And then, through the rain, a shape.

He stumbled to a halt, chest heaving, the air a knife scraping against his throat.

The figure was there, between two pines. Cloaked in darkness, its head tilted as if studying him. For a moment, it had shape, lines, and angles that should've made sense. But the longer he stared, the less real it became.

He blinked, and it was gone.

Just rain and shadows and the whisper of the wind remained.

His hands trembled. His mind spun excuses, some of them almost convincing. Blood loss. Exhaustion. A trick of the dark.

He'd done worse than hallucinate before. He'd drowned himself in whiskey until the world blurred around him, broken the wrong man's bones just to prove he could. Lived too long thinking rage was the same as strength.

He pressed forward, his breath sawing in and out of his lungs. The pain was a constant throb now, swelling through his skull until his teeth ached.

The ground sloped downward, slick with mud. He slid more than walked, his body twisting to catch his balance. Every jolt shot fresh agony through his ankle.

And still, the thought of stopping terrified him more than the pain.

Regret pooled beneath his thoughts, a dark, creeping thing he'd buried too deep for too long. No one would mourn him if he didn't make it out of these woods. That was the truth. Not his fault, not really. Just the way he'd built his life. He'd burned every bridge until the smoke blackened the sky.

But there was something worse than dying alone. Something worse than dying in this godforsaken stretch of trees with his own blood soaking into the dirt.

His brain felt too big for his skull, swelling until the pressure forced more blood from his nose. It dripped down his chin, hot against the chill in the air. He tripped into a clearing, his knees buckling as he collapsed to the ground. The cold seeped through his shirt, his chest heaving with every shallow breath.

That's when he saw it again.

Not twenty feet away, between the twisted trunks of the pines.

The Reaper. Just a suggestion of a figure, its outline shimmering with the kind of darkness that had weight. Solid enough to be real, but wrong in the way it moved. The way it waited.

He blinked, and it was gone.

His hands fisted in the mud, fingers clenching tight enough to make his knuckles ache. Another hallucination. Had to be. Maybe the crash had cracked something in his head. Maybe the blood dripping from his nose wasn't the worst of it.

But that didn't explain the certainty crawling along his skin, raising the hair on the back of his neck. He'd lived a bad life. Made decisions with the kind of casual cruelty that had come so easy, back when strength meant something different.

No apologies. No atonement. Just violence and vengeance.

And now, this.

He forced himself upright, his legs threatening to buckle. The pain was relentless, his vision a blur of shapes and shadows. But he kept moving. Because if he stopped, whatever lurked between the trees would catch him.

He was sure of that, even if he couldn't explain why.

Another step. Then another. The ache in his chest sharpened with every breath.

The ground dipped, slick earth stealing his balance. He slid down a short slope, his shoulder smashing against something solid. Bark tore at his skin, and his fresh blood mingled with the rain.

The Reaper waited at the bottom of the hill. Watching.

Mark let out a shuddering breath, the sound raw and broken. "Get the hell away from me." His voice was shredded, rasping through the rain. The apparition didn't answer and just stood there, a shadow with eyes he couldn't quite see.

He blinked again. Gone.

His head swam, pain twisting through his skull like hot wire. His body felt too heavy, his limbs leaden and cold.

But he kept moving. Because something was out there, stalking him with the kind of patience that suggested it had been waiting for a long, long time.

Regret boiled up again, bitter and sharp. Maybe it wasn't just the Reaper. Maybe it was every damn thing he'd left undone, every grudge and grift he'd run from. Maybe he'd spent so long escaping that he'd finally run himself down.

He wiped blood from his face, his fingers trembling. The darkness thickened, swallowing the world until nothing was left but pain and rain and the certainty that something was closing in.

He took another step.

And then another.

Because death wasn't going to take him without a fight. Yet as he fell between a couple of thick trees, unable to move, a hysterical humor took him. It wasn't the first fight he'd lost . . . but apparently it would be the last.

In her conference room, Laurel finished straightening the pictures and connected lines on the case board. So far, she had Dr. Miriam Liu, Larry Scott, and Melissa Palmtree from Oakridge Solutions on one board with Dr. Liu connected to Tyler Griggs because of the lesions on their brains. Off to the side, she taped a picture of Dr. Sandoval, even though he'd been killed by the sniper. She'd obtained a picture of Dr. Bertra Yannish from social media and taped her picture up as well. Perhaps she'd earned a promotion from the death of Dr. Liu.

The next board showed Laurel's face with sniper eyelines, a description of the truck, and a list of former cases she needed to examine closer.

The final board had Abigail's case on it, usually flipped over so Norrs couldn't see it.

Laurel sat on the Formica table and stared at the Oakridge Solutions board. "Nester? Have you found out anything about Melissa Palmtree?" Hopefully she hadn't been cremated like Larry Scott had. Not that Laurel had any proof their deaths were related to Dr. Liu's.

"Yeah. She was buried outside of Bellevue." Nester crossed into view, leaning against the doorjamb. Today he wore black slacks and a white button-down shirt rolled up at the sleeves, revealing dark and muscled forearms.

Laurel blew out air. "Start an application to have her body exhumed, would you? It's a long shot, I know. I'll create my own affidavit, but we'll need one from Dr. Ortega as well. Thanks."

"Sure." Nester turned and headed back to his computer room.

Kate called down the hallway. "Sandra Plankton is here to see you." She led the way down the hallway and gestured the young woman into the conference room.

"Thanks, Kate." Laurel hopped off the table, flipped the boards over to reveal the clear sides, and gestured for Sandra to sit.

Sandra dropped into the chair across from Laurel, her posture more defiant than polite. She couldn't have been more than twenty, her hair wild and tangled around her shoulders. There was a washed-out T-shirt stretched over her slight frame, the graphic faded but still readable: **STOP KILLING THE PLANET!** The lettering was half-obscured by her threadbare flannel shirt, sleeves rolled up unevenly. "Nice table."

"Thanks. It's temporary." Laurel pulled out a chair and sat.

Ripped jeans and scuffed hiking boots completed Sandra's look. Her skin was pale, her eyes rimmed red, like sleep hadn't found her in days. She didn't wear any makeup, but her expression appeared fierce.

Walter stepped into the conference room and tugged a chair his way to sit.

"Ms. Plankton," Laurel said. "Thank you for coming in."

Sandra huffed out a breath. "I didn't have much of a choice, did I?" Her voice had a rough, scratchy edge, like she'd been yelling recently or maybe just not speaking at all. She dropped a battered messenger bag onto the table and dug inside it. A moment later, she slapped a flash drive down on the table, its plastic case scratched and dirty. "I was gonna try to find you, anyway."

"What's this?" Walter eyed the light blue drive.

"I went through Tyler's fishing gear," Sandra said. "He kept stuff everywhere. Like, everywhere. I found this hidden in the pocket of his tackle box."

Laurel took the drive. "You didn't give it to the police?"

"No." Sandra's chin lifted. "The local cops are on the recordings. I didn't know who I could trust."

"What exactly is on there?" Laurel asked, her interest piqued.

Sandra swallowed, her shoulders hunching just slightly. "There are several unreleased podcasts. One about gasoline pipelines, a couple about conspiracies, and one about corrupt cops."

Walter's mouth tightened, but he didn't speak.

"The final one . . ." Sandra hesitated. "He sounded scared but determined to find answers about some possible attack coming soon. Tyler believed that true evil was around us and that we're all in danger. He was still looking for evidence. I don't know, man."

Walter eyed her. "What kind of attack?"

She shrugged. "I have no idea, but I can tell you he was really scared."

Walter leaned forward. "Why didn't you come forward with this sooner?"

Sandra's gaze shot to him. "I just found this yesterday, and like I said, the next podcast that was supposed to drop was almost finished, and it was about those cops. But the last one? That one I could tell. Tyler was seriously freaked out." Tears filled her eyes. "I miss him so much."

"I'm sorry about his death," Walter said gently. "But we need to ask you a few questions about your arrests. What were you doing?"

"Protesting," Sandra shot back. "The clear-cutting of old-growth forests. Pollution from corporations nobody bothers to hold accountable. You know. Basic stuff that shouldn't be controversial but somehow is."

Laurel grimaced. She'd had Nester dig up a couple of the reports. "You have quite the record."

Sandra's shoulders tensed. "I know. I chained myself to logging equipment to keep them from bulldozing an entire grove of ancient trees. They slapped me with trespassing and destruction of property. The cops acted like I'd burned the place down."

Walter's eyes narrowed. "What about the corporate protest downtown? The one where your group caused thousands of dollars in damages?"

"That was an exaggeration," Sandra snapped. "We walked through the lobby with signs. We chanted. We forced them to face us instead of hiding behind their security. They dragged us out and tore a banner, and somehow that turned into property destruction. Not my fault their fragile egos can't handle criticism."

"Tyler shared your beliefs?" Laurel kept her voice congenial.

Sandra's gaze dropped to the table. "Sort of. He was more into exposing corruption than saving the environment. He thought he could force people to care about both by throwing the truth in their faces, and he loved being a detective."

"And you?" Laurel asked.

"I just wanted the world to stop being so messed up," Sandra admitted. "Tyler wanted to blow it all wide open. I wanted to protect the things that matter." She shifted uneasily on her seat. "I'm going to stay with my aunt in Billings and away from here. I'll leave the info for you, but don't tell the Elk Hollow cops." She wiped a shaking hand across her brow. "I'm pretty sure they killed Tyler." She gagged and then sniffed loudly. "Or whoever the last podcast was about did. Something big is supposed to happen and Tyler was gonna stop it."

Laurel thought through what she knew about Tyler. "You have no idea what or who?"

"Nope. Just that he was terrified."

Laurel kept her voice calm. "Is there any place Tyler would hide something? More info?"

Sandra fiddled with her earring. "Dunno. I went through his fishing stuff. He liked to fish the Red River, right off the Salty Campground? Just fly-fishin'. He didn't have a boat or anything."

Walter shoved his hand in his pocket. "We need a list of his friends and their numbers before you go. Is there anybody he trusted more than others?"

"Just me," Sandra whispered.

Just wonderful. "Did he have any illnesses?" Laurel asked.

Sandra shrugged. "He had bad allergies, and he got a lot of migraines. I think he was stressed."

Migraines? Ones from lesions? "How long has he had migraines?" Laurel asked.

Sandra picked at a cuticle. "As long as I've known him. He said he's had them for years."

Long enough for lesions to form on his brain? Laurel pushed a tablet of paper toward the woman. "Please list all of his friends, acquaintances, even sources. As well as places he'd frequent. Does his vehicle have GPS?"

Sandra snorted. "No. He had a beat-up compact from the seventies."

Unfortunately, his computer and phone had been taken, and according to Nester, never turned back on. His car was still missing as well. "So he told you nothing about this new podcast investigation?"

Sandra took a pen and started a list. "No. All he said was that if he didn't stop them, a lot of people were gonna die."

# Chapter 20

After making a quick phone call to DC where the deputy director had not only warned her to stay alive but had then questioned her about how many people she'd seen in the last week who'd worn emeralds, just to entertain himself with her memory skills, Laurel sat back in her chair as Walter ambled into the conference room with two buckets of popcorn. He set them down on the conference table before sinking into one of the too-sleek, white chairs that looked out of place around the scuffed, fifties-era table.

He handed her one of the buckets. "Ena popped it. Fish and Wildlife has a better microwave."

"Thank you." Laurel took the popcorn, her stomach growling from the scent of melted butter. "We could get a new microwave."

"We definitely should." Walter pointed the remote at the wall screen and hit the button.

The monitor snapped to life, spilling Tyler Griggs's first of two unaired podcasts into the room. His jittery voice filled the air, his pitch too high, his energy twisted and erratic.

Laurel slipped a piece of popcorn onto her tongue. It was warm, buttery, and properly salted.

Tyler's face appeared on the screen, eyes darting with a fevered energy that seemed to vibrate just beneath his skin. "Hi, folks," he began, his smile jagged and off-balance. "I've been watching the Elk Hollow Police Department, and let me tell you, the stench of corruption is so thick you could cut it with a chain saw."

Walter muttered something low and indistinct.

Laurel looked at him and swallowed. "Walter, this is too much for you. I can take care of it."

"No. The least I can do for the kid is figure out who might've wanted him dead."

"All right," Tyler's voice piped up from the screen, almost giddy. "Now, here's the evidence I have, and let me tell you, the corruption goes deeper than this." His grin widened. "Not only are these two having an affair, and keep in mind they're both married to somebody else, but they're taking bribes."

The screen cut to a series of grainy photos of Detective Robertson and Officer Jackson entering motels at all hours, their bodies angled close. One of Officer Jackson's hands brushing Detective Robertson's arm as they walked into a run-down building off Route 8, and one of Detective Robertson's hands on her lower back as they crossed a parking lot together.

They weren't looking over their shoulders, but as cops, surely they became suspicious?

"It seems like they prefer motels with bad lighting and nobody asking questions," Tyler said, his voice a strained whisper. "But they should've been asking themselves some questions. Like who's been recording their little meetings."

The screen flickered again. More clips, all marked with time stamps Tyler had added himself. The kind of meticulous, obsessive detail that suggested he'd spent hours combing through footage, stringing it all together.

There was footage showing Detective Robertson and Officer Jackson laughing together in a diner parking lot. Of them walking out of a bar just after midnight, heads bent close, Officer Jackson's fingers tangled in Detective Robertson's sleeve. Then several more clips of the two kissing passionately in Officer Jackson's patrol car.

Tyler's voice slid into something darker. "Detective Robertson and

Officer Jackson. Always sneaking around, always keeping it quiet. Maybe they're just screwing around. But what if it's more than that?"

The screen shifted to poorly framed footage of Detective Robertson meeting with men Laurel didn't recognize. One man had greasy black hair and a twitchy, nervous stance. Another older, heavyset man had sharp eyes that scanned his surroundings before he handed the detective a tightly wrapped package.

"Detective Robertson meets these guys all over town, and every time, there's something exchanged. Packages. Envelopes. Information." Tyler's voice rose. "Not once does he report it."

Tyler cut between images quickly, slamming together proof of the affair with clips of the detective accepting packages and passing envelopes to the unknown men. Laurel's eyes narrowed as she tracked the pattern Tyler had clumsily mapped.

"Whatever they're into," Tyler continued, his voice crackling, "it's bigger than an affair. This is corruption. Dirty money. Information leaks. And I'm going to prove it."

Laurel glanced at Walter. "We need to identify those people."

Walter grunted. "And figure out what's in those packages." His voice had gone rough, his attention locked on the screen. "I told Tyler's dad's secretary that I'd like to attend a funeral if there is one, and she said that she'd get back to me. I'm not counting on it."

"I'm sorry, Walter." Laurel returned her attention to the screen.

Walter scrolled through more of the scattered recordings.

Tyler's voice came through again, frenzied but deliberate. "It's not just Robertson and Jackson having their dirty little fling. They're part of something bigger. So much bigger. I almost have the evidence. There's an attack coming, my friends."

Walter paused the recording, his hand steady on the remote. "An attack."

Laurel didn't like guesswork. "That's what Sandra was talking about."

"Yep." Walter shut off the video, the sudden silence thick and heavy. "Remember that he was dramatic."

Laurel scribbled a quick note. "I know."

"But he also was pretty good at his job," Walter muttered. "What attack was he talking about?"

"I don't know." Laurel's pen hovered over her notepad. "But Tyler thought he was onto something, and if he was right, it might've gotten him killed. Also, I'd have to guess Detective Robertson and Officer Jackson weren't exactly happy with him."

"It's odd they didn't mention this," Walter said. "Robertson and Jackson. Tyler was tracking them, harassing them. How in the world did they not notice? They're both cops."

"I agree," Laurel said, reaching for the remote for the wide-screen plasma on the far wall. "Let's look at the last few of Tyler's posted podcasts." She hit play.

The footage rolled, Tyler rattling off about crop dustings in farming areas close to Everett. His excitement bled through his words as he described strange patterns appearing in the fields after the planes passed over. "Aliens, folks. They're here, and they're blending in." Tyler's grin was wide, eyes gleaming. "They're posing as policemen. Enforcers of the law. And one of them is none other than Seattle Councilman Eric Swelter."

Walter snorted. "If anybody's an alien, it's that jackass."

Laurel tried not to smile, but she couldn't help it. She'd dealt with Swelter in a previous case, and the term *jackass* truly did fit. "I always figured if we were visited by other life forms, they'd be a lot smarter than us since they could get here somehow."

"Good point." Walter's eyes narrowed. "Swelter's too dumb to be from a planet smart enough to create a warp drive that would get here."

Laurel's eyebrows lifted. "Warp drive, huh?"

"Well, sure. Isn't that how they'd get here?"

"Actually," Laurel said, leaning forward, "if they did come here, it's more likely they'd have found a way to manipulate space itself by using quantum drive, or something along those lines. It wouldn't be about speed. It would be about bending space, making two points touch for just a moment. Like folding paper so the ends meet. It would require incredible amounts of negative energy or something even more advanced—possibly by manipulating dark matter. Theoretically, it's possible."

Walter grunted. "That's not warp drive."

"Exactly." Laurel's focus remained on the screen.

Walter moved to the next podcast. Tyler's voice continued with its erratic rhythm, but his topic had shifted.

"This one's all about the conspiracy," Tyler said, his tone dropping into something almost gleeful. "Big oil, folks. Gas prices are just one piece of it. They control the supply, they control the demand, and they control the narrative. And nobody is asking the right questions."

Walter shook his head. "He's losing it."

"Maybe, but he's trying to make connections," Laurel said. "Even if they're the wrong ones."

Walter clicked to another clip, his jaw tight. Tyler's voice filled the room again, but the pacing was different. Slower, as he interviewed somebody.

"Is it that Tim Kohnex?" Laurel asked, her hand frozen midway to her mouth, popcorn forgotten.

"It is," Walter said, turning the volume up.

Tyler sounded oddly restrained, his curiosity tempered by something that almost resembled respect.

"So, I am psychic, and I can prove it," Kohnex said, his voice smooth and confident.

"How so?" Tyler asked, his tone carrying both skepticism and excitement.

"You have a brother." Kohnex's voice was calm. Unnervingly so. "He's in the FBI. Correct?"

Tyler's jaw dropped, his eyes wide. "How did you know that?"

"You're all but broadcasting it," Kohnex said, his smile faint but sharp.

Walter's head snapped toward Laurel. "How did he know that? You didn't even know that."

"My guess is he researched all of us." Laurel's voice was tight, her gaze fixed on the screen. "His interest in our little team is much deeper than I suspected."

"Our team? You mean you?" Walter's tone had a sharper edge now.

Laurel didn't argue.

Walter clicked to the next podcast, where a pale Tyler said he'd found the biggest story of his life. It was one that could involve a lot of people and danger. He leaned in close to the camera and said that an attack was coming and he'd have proof soon.

The screen went black.

Walter groaned. "That's it? The kid didn't have any more information?"

"Hey, you two." Nester's voice cut through the quiet. He jogged down the hallway and burst into the conference room, his phone clutched tightly in one hand. "I just got a camera hit on the black truck that rammed into you. The front end is all warped, and I can see bullet holes on the hood from where you returned fire."

Laurel's attention snapped to him. "Where?"

Nester sucked in a breath. "The footage is from the traffic cam at the base of Stony Mountain. It's only about a half hour away from here. I've notified Agent Norrs in Seattle, but he's a good two hours away."

Walter's gaze sharpened. "Then we can't wait for him. I'll go and report back in to you."

"No." Laurel stood. "This is my case, too. They shot at both of us."

"They shot at you." Walter's eyes narrowed, his tone dropping. "Wear a vest."

She didn't have time for this. "You wear a vest, too." She spun on her heel and rushed into the back room, her steps rapid and precise. Her fingers trembled slightly as she yanked open the cabinet, grabbing two Kevlar vests. She shrugged one on over her sweater, the cold, heavy weight pressing against her chest. The fabric was stiff, resistant, but she forced it into place and zipped her jacket over it.

Walter took the other vest without a word, yanking it over his broad shoulders and fastening the straps with the efficiency of someone who'd done it a thousand times before.

Laurel clipped her weapon into a leg harness, her fingers moving quickly and surely. She double-checked the fit before strapping a backup pistol to her ankle. The weight of the weapons sharpened her focus.

"You good?" Walter asked, his eyes already darting toward the exit.

"I'm good."

Nester hustled up, his arms full of printouts. "I'll let Norrs know you're both en route and you'll probably beat him there. I'm sending these to your phones, but I thought you'd want to see." He slapped the pages on the table and pointed to a highlighted map. "This mountain only goes up so far and then winds around toward Genesis Valley, going down the other side. He could head into Canada, but right now, he's closer rather than farther away."

Walter's gaze traced the routes, his jaw set. "He could be coming right here."

"You both need to keep your heads down." Nester's expression was tense, his eyes glancing from Walter to Laurel.

"Understood," Laurel said. "Let's go."

Nester cleared his throat. "Rachel Raprenzi called again about her interview with Abigail tomorrow night on *The Killing Hour*. She really wants you to join."

Laurel gritted her back teeth together.

Nester held up a hand. "That's pretty much what I told her."

Laurel nodded and then hurried out of the office and down the stairs, her boots echoing against the steps as she and Walter descended to the vestibule.

Huck was waiting for them, already armed and practically vibrating with impatience. Aeneas sat expectantly next to him, his ears twitching. "My Zoom meetings went long and I was just leaving when Nester called." Huck crossed his arms over his chest, his expression grim. "I'm armed. If I can't stop you from going, which I know I can't, I'm going with you." His voice was firm. "I know that area like the back of my hand. Aeneas and I have spent plenty of time on that mountain."

Laurel gave a single, terse nod.

"All right, let's go." Huck's gaze swept the parking lot before he pulled the door open. He glanced around, his phone in his hand. "I don't feel anybody out here, but let's make sure." His thumb scrolled through the camera feeds, the screen's glow reflecting off his tense expression. "Okay. We're good. Let's get to the truck."

Outside, a light spring rain had started to fall, the drizzle cool against Laurel's face as they strode toward the truck. The parking lot was a mix of shadows and dim lights, the air thick with dampness. She climbed into the front passenger seat, her eyes constantly scanning their surroundings as Walter took the back seat. Huck placed Aeneas in his crate and then jumped into the driver's seat, igniting the engine and backing out of his parking spot.

Her phone buzzed. She glanced down at the screen and then answered. "Agent Norrs. It's Agent Snow, and we're on our way out to Stony Mountain and the pass toward Canada. Or Genesis Valley, I suppose. We're about an hour and a half ahead of you," Laurel said, her voice clipped but steady. "I have Agent Smudgeon and Captain Rivers with me."

"Good. Isn't that Fish and Wildlife territory?" Norrs asked, his voice tinny through the speaker.

"Yes." Huck kept his gaze on the rainy road ahead. "If the guy hasn't headed into Canada, we'll get him."

"Keep me updated." Norrs's voice was sharp before the line cut out.

Huck's hands gripped the steering wheel as he pulled out of the parking lot. His gaze never strayed from the road, but his shoulders appeared wound tight.

"Drive fast," Walter growled.

"I intend to." Huck's eyes flicked to the mirror before settling back on the road.

The truck's tires splashed through shallow puddles as they sped toward the mountain, the rain thickening as the terrain grew steeper.

Laurel's phone buzzed again with another message from Nester that included updated coordinates with real-time tracking. She read through the data, her fingers gripping the phone a little too tightly.

If the suspect was heading into Canada, their window was closing. They drove up the mountain, high enough that drifts of snow still showed through the trees. Laurel stiffened and pointed. "Is that—"

"Black truck," Huck confirmed, slowing his vehicle. "It looks like it slammed into that pine." He angled the truck so his door faced the crumpled wreck. "Go out your side. Guns out. Stay sharp."

# Chapter 21

Huck opened his door and dropped behind it, pulling his Glock from its thigh holster, his eyes locked on the mangled black truck. Its front end had folded inward, the grill twisted and cracked. Steam hissed from somewhere beneath the wreckage, mingling with the spring chill.

Laurel moved around the back of Huck's rig, her weapon already drawn, her expression set. "That's the truck that rammed into us the other day."

Bullet holes dotted the hood, clean and vicious, a reminder of Laurel's encounter. Holes had been punched through the metal like angry exclamation points.

Huck levered back and opened his rear door, reaching in to let Aeneas loose from his crate. The dog jumped out, heeling instantly.

Walter came around the front of the truck, his shoulders hunched.

Huck approached the black truck slowly, Aeneas trotting at his side with a low growl rumbling in his throat. The dog's fur bristled, his ears pinned back.

The driver's door hung half-open, the metal warped where it had slammed against the tree. Huck moved to it, his gun held firmly. He leaned in, breath steady despite the chill prickling his skin.

Blood.

Smears of it across the seat, bright and wet. Not just a trickle. Someone had lost a lot of blood. It soaked into the cracked leather and streaked across the steering wheel like the driver had tried to haul himself out but couldn't manage it cleanly.

Huck glanced over the dash to see the keys still in the ignition. The engine had died with the impact. The air smelled of gasoline, blood, and cold metal.

There was no sign of a body. Just the red trail splashed along the console and pooling on the floor mat. Whoever had been driving was alive when they crawled out of the wreck. Alive and running.

"Laurel. Walter. No body." Huck kept his voice low so it didn't carry far. "Driver's injured. Badly."

Walter stepped closer, his gun trained on the truck's cab as if expecting something to lunge out of the shadows. "You're sure?"

"Enough blood here to knock someone out cold." Huck gave a nod toward the mess. "But the door's open and it's smeared. He crawled out. Crawled or fell."

Aeneas whined, nose to the ground. The dog sniffed furiously, his tail twitching in quick, anxious bursts.

"You've got something, boy?" Huck murmured, his tone low and encouraging. Aeneas barked once, short and urgent, then dipped his head back to the ground. "Let's see where he went." Huck moved to Aeneas's side, his eyes following the dog's trail.

Aeneas padded forward, his nose low, tail flicking as he wound through the wreckage. Blood drops spattered the ground, forming a thin but visible trail that led away from the truck and into the tree line.

"Blood trail," Huck said over his shoulder. "Fresh. Headed north."

The forest closed in quickly, the trees thick and dark, their branches heavy with moisture and dripping icy droplets. Huck followed Aeneas at a careful pace, scanning the ground for prints or signs of passage.

Then he caught himself. They stood in the middle of the yew stand. Signs of harvested timber lay to the right of him. The trail went to the left. Had Ena placed cameras around here?

His breath quickened. He'd call her after he found the driver. He might actually have the guy on video.

The blood trail skipped and splattered, sometimes thick and clear, other times barely more than a hint of crimson against the earth. Whoever was running was hurt bad. And bleeding worse.

Aeneas let out a short, clipped bark. His nose pointed left, then right, before he bolted forward.

"Easy, boy." Huck pushed through low-hanging branches, and sharp needles scratched at his arms and snagged his coat. His boots dug into the mud, the ground soft from the fairly gentle rain. He kept his senses tuned to the forest around them and the woman behind him. A quick glance confirmed that Walter flanked Laurel from behind.

Good.

Huck spotted the occasional streak of red along the bark of a tree or splashed across mossy rocks. The driver was stumbling, falling, slamming into things as he tried to escape. "I just see one track. Nobody was chasing this guy." He must've hit his head in the crash. Why else would he stumble away from safety?

"Doesn't make sense." Walter's voice cut in. "If he's hurt that bad, he should've gone downhill. Away from the mountain."

"He's panicking." Huck scanned the forest, eyes narrowing at a fresh smear of blood along a tree trunk. "He's not thinking straight. Or maybe he has a hiding place." In the yew stand? Huck let the dog guide him, his own instincts kicking in. He spotted a half boot print pressed into the mud, the edges blurred by rain but still clear enough to make out. "Blood's thinning out," Huck murmured.

Aeneas darted left, then right, his paws making quick work of the uneven terrain. The dog's tail lashed back and forth, his focus absolute.

Huck pressed on, gaze sweeping the forest as he moved. Pine needles crunched beneath his boots, and his breath fogged in the chill air.

Aeneas let out another bark, this one deeper, more urgent. Huck's pulse quickened. "We're getting close," he whispered. "Remember, this guy is probably armed." The dog surged forward, his paws tearing through the underbrush like he'd caught a stronger scent. Huck kept pace, his legs working hard to keep from tangling in the twisted roots and low-hanging branches that clawed at him like skeletal hands.

Blood. The trail was getting thicker now. Darker.

"Easy, boy," Huck murmured, though his own voice carried an edge of urgency he couldn't quite suppress. His eyes swept the forest floor, catching the telltale spatter of red against the frost-laced ground.

Aeneas barked, his voice sharp and triumphant. Then he stopped so suddenly Huck almost tripped over him.

"What is it?" Huck moved around the dog, his own instincts prickling. He'd tracked too many bodies over the years not to recognize the weight of death in the air.

The man lay face down, his body half-splayed across the uneven ground, one arm twisted beneath him at a brutal angle.

Laurel stepped up to his side.

Walter swept the area with his gun.

Laurel took in the entire scene, her head moving while her body remained still. "This area has been recently logged."

Huck nodded. "This is a yew stand. Nobody has the right to harvest here." Was it just a coincidence this guy ended up in the yew stand?

Laurel crouched, head angled, looking at the body. "There's an injury on his forehead, probably from hitting the tree." She turned her head, looking up at Huck. "Why would he run away from the road and into the woods while injured?"

He reached for her arm and gently tugged her to stand. "Bad head injury?" He glanced to the side and stiffened at seeing a mound of dirt between two still-standing yew trees. "What the hell?"

Laurel followed his gaze. "That appears recent."

"Agreed." Huck strode over to the freshly covered mound with steady, deliberate steps, his eyes narrowing as he assessed the scene. The earth had been disturbed recently, the soil dark and loose, clinging to patches of grass like wet clumps of ash.

The edges of the mound were uneven, like the ground had been shoved and scraped rather than properly smoothed. The pine needles scattered across the surface were too few and too deliberately placed to have fallen naturally. They clung to the moist soil like someone had attempted to camouflage the disturbance but hadn't cared enough to make it convincing.

"Looks like it was done in the last few days," Huck muttered.

Laurel stayed several feet behind him, her eyes locked on the disturbed ground with a precision Huck recognized. She was already processing, her mind making connections while his instincts continued to bellow that something was wrong. "The truck is the same one that smashed into us the other day, and I know I hit the passenger." She swallowed twice in an uncharacteristic show of emotion.

"You returned fire and protected your partner," Huck said quietly.

"Agreed," Walter said, holstering his weapon.

Had the driver buried his buddy right here? In the middle of the yew field? "I'm betting this isn't very deep," Huck murmured.

Aeneas whined, his gaze locked on the mound.

"It's okay, boy." Huck backed away from the mound. "We don't have service this far up. Let's head back to the truck and call this in. We need to secure the scene and have the crime techs head out here."

"Tell 'em to bring shovels," Walter said grimly.

The skies opened up to pummel them with rain. A more fanciful woman would've thought the gods were angry at them. Laurel, on the other hand, figured it was just springtime. She had donned one of Huck's Fish and Wildlife baseball caps to protect her face and had ditched the bulletproof vest to better tuck her jacket around herself.

She kept her arms folded against the creeping chill, her back straight as she watched the techs work. The yew trees around her smelled like damp earth and not nearly as strong as pine. The several techs tromping about had smashed the yew's red berries all over the trail, and they gave off a slightly sweet smell.

Never before in her life had she even thought about the yew tree.

The body of the driver had already been secured in the back of a forensic response van after the techs had collected evidence around it.

They were still processing the scene of the buried body. Two blue tarps had been spread over the worst of the mud, their edges pinned down by rocks and stakes to keep the slick material from sliding.

Another tarp had been propped up above the body, secured to tree branches and poles the techs had hammered into the ground. Water pattered against the tarp's surface, creating a soft, rhythmic sound that seemed both natural and wrong.

"Careful with that," FBI Agent Bill O'Connor muttered, his voice clipped but not harsh. He and another tech, Julie Evans, were kneeling beside the body. They were meticulous, brushing away soil from the man's clothing and photographing every angle before attempting to move him. Agent Norrs stood over them, watching carefully.

"Balaclava still on," Norrs noted. "Looks like he died wearing it."

Laurel nodded, her eyes sweeping over the scene. The body lay twisted, half-crushed against the dirt, as if the man had been dragged and then dropped in haste. The dark material of his jacket was soaked through, streaked with blood and clinging mud.

She shifted her attention to the other agents circling the area, their flashlights cutting through the growing darkness. The portable floodlights they'd set up created harsh, angular shadows that danced across the trees.

"Is Huck still trying to find a camera?" Walter's voice cut through the murmurs of the techs.

"Affirmative. Ena has given him directions, but I don't think they were very helpful," Laurel replied. She motioned Walter toward her, waiting until he strode gracefully over the crushed red berries. There had been a time she'd worried about him in the elements, but he worked out often now and appeared to be in good shape. Even so, water sluiced off his hair and down his face. "Let's go assist Huck."

Walter nodded. "Sounds good. Did you call Dr. Ortega?"

"Yes. He's waiting for both bodies. The Seattle FBI is processing the scene, but Norrs agreed to let Dr. Ortega perform the autopsies."

Laurel moved out of the trees and past the black truck to see Huck across the road. "Did you find a camera?"

"Finally. I had Ena guide me step by step from the damn road." Huck pointed upward, toward a thick-limbed pine a good twenty feet from where they'd found the body. "Up there. I'll climb up and retrieve it."

He didn't wait for a response before he grabbed a branch and swung himself into the tree, graceful and strong.

Agent Norrs strode out of the forest, an FBI ball cap protecting his head from the rain. "Thought you should know. They're still processing the buried body. The guy's got a bullet wound in his upper arm—clean through. Not fatal, but it would've hurt like hell."

Laurel straightened. "Probable cause of death?"

"Not the bullet." Even wearing the cap, rain dotted Agent Norrs's bulldog jawline. "He was stabbed. Deep. Looks like a hunting knife or something similar. Bled out fast."

Walter wiped rain off his face. "So his buddy stabbed him and then buried him? So much for honor among thieves."

Laurel's fingers tapped against her notebook, her mind processing the details. So she hadn't killed him. Sure, she'd been doing her job, but she was glad she hadn't ended someone's life. But why had he been killed? She turned her attention back to Huck. He was already halfway up the tree, climbing with practiced efficiency.

It wasn't long before he reached the camera. Laurel watched him cut it free, his body moving with the steady confidence of someone who'd spent years scaling worse obstacles.

"Got it," Huck called down.

He descended just as quickly, his boots hitting the ground with a crunch of wet leaves. He made his way to his truck, where Aeneas soundly slept back in his warm crate.

Laurel climbed into the passenger seat, leaving the door open for Walter to lean in to see. Huck slipped into the driver's side and pulled his laptop from its case. He plugged the camera into the port and waited for the files to load.

The rain drummed harder against the tarps, the sound an incessant, maddening patter. Walter hovered near Laurel, curiosity in his gaze.

The files finally loaded. Huck clicked on the most recent video, his eyes narrowing as the footage flickered to life. A series of still pictures came up from the last couple of days, since Ena had placed the cameras. "There," Huck said, clicking on a still of the black truck.

Laurel watched as it smashed into the tree. Then the driver fell out, bounding up, looking over his shoulder. Blood flowed down his face, even in the grainy recording. He stumbled several times, trying to run, every movement frantic. Twice, he grabbed his head as if in horrendous pain.

Then he ran out of the range.

Laurel took a deep breath.

Agent Norrs strode up with a plastic bag in his hand. "We found the truck driver's wallet in a bramble bush. He was named Mark Bitterson. Have you heard of him?"

Laurel mentally clicked through her earlier cases. "No."

"No," Walter said.

Huck shook his head. "Never heard of the guy."

Keeping the wallet in the bag, Agent Norrs maneuvered the driver's license out. "Guy was thirty and lived in Everett. I'm running a background check on him now."

Huck reached for a flashlight in the back and pointed it at the bag.

Laurel went cold. "Walter?"

"Yeah." Walter leaned closer. "I didn't recognize him with all the blood. But that's him."

"Who?" Agent Norrs asked.

Laurel studied the man's facial features. "We saw him on Tyler Griggs's podcast. He met several times with Elk Hollow police detective Robertson." She felt like she was running in circles when she needed a straight line. "Walter—"

"Oh, I'm calling them right now," Walter said grimly, his phone already to his ear. "Any bets they lawyer up and fast?"

Yet another bet Laurel refused to take.

# Chapter 22

Enjoying the weekend, Laurel finished replenishing the cat's water bowl, double-checked Aeneas's food, then returned to Huck's breakfast nook, where her notebook lay sprawled open across the table. She balanced her phone in one hand, the other already flipping through her scribbled notes.

"Yes, I'm taking today off, Mom," she said, a small lie sneaking through her smile. "Please tell me you're enjoying the sun."

"Oh, we are," Deidre gushed. "We haven't done much but sit in the sun, hop in the pool, and eat delicious food. But if you need me at home, I'll head right back."

"Nope. You're not needed at all." Laurel kept her tone breezy, gaze darting over her notes, seeking patterns or threads she hadn't yet pulled. "Everything is going smoothly."

Which wasn't entirely untrue. Despite the growing tension of Abigail's expedited trial, everything was under control. For now. Abigail's attorney would undoubtedly call Deidre to the stand, eager to force her to relive the nightmare of being raped by Zeke Caine more than two decades ago in the attack that had resulted in Laurel's birth. But with Deidre lounging in the Caribbean, far from the harsh scrutiny of the courtroom, Laurel could keep her mother protected.

"You stay there, nice and safe, enjoying the sunshine," Laurel insisted. "I hope you and Monty have a wonderful rest of your vacation."

"All right, hon. Thanks. We're about to go do water aerobics. I'll call you later."

"Sounds good." Laurel ended the call, her gaze lingering on the phone before settling on the notes strewn across the table. Her handwriting was sharp and precise with each line showing her mind's relentless push for control and clarity.

Through the wide kitchen window, she could see Huck outside, tinkering with the grill while Aeneas trotted around him. She wished they could just relax and not worry about Rachel's upcoming interview with Abigail.

But they'd have to watch.

The fire in the living room crackled merrily, filling the cabin with cozy warmth. It had a way of easing into her bones, making her believe that she could fit here. That she could belong.

She could see herself living here. The thought was as startling as it was comforting. But was it too soon? Probably. She'd never been proficient at pursuing relationships, her social skills stunted by the simple fact that she'd skipped most of childhood and all of her teenage years. College at eleven didn't leave much room for sleepovers and first dates.

She glanced back at her notes. What she wanted from Huck . . . it was terrifying. But so was everything else in her life. And she'd survived plenty of that.

Interpersonal relationships were most certainly not her strong suit. Her phone buzzed again, the vibration sharp against the wood of the table. She snatched it up, pushing her hair behind one ear. "Agent Snow."

"Hi, Agent. It's Dr. Ortega." His voice was rich and steady, like the hum of an old engine. "I was sure you were working on this fine Saturday, just like me."

She settled more comfortably in the wooden chair. Huck needed new cushions. "Yes, but I'm doing so by a cozy fire." She glanced toward the living room where the flames danced over split logs, their crackling song both soothing and distracting. "I take it you're in the office?"

"I am." Dr. Ortega sighed, the sound heavy and weary, like a man who hadn't slept enough nights in a row. "Though I need to get going in a few minutes because my niece has a soccer game."

"Wish her well," Laurel said, though her mind was already clicking into business mode. "What have you found?"

The sound of paper shuffling came over the line, a rustling reminder of the mountain of files they were both buried under. "I received the toxicology screenings and histology results regarding both Dr. Liu and Tyler Griggs."

"Excellent." Laurel's fingers drummed lightly on the table, matching the rhythm of her pulse. "Tell me about the toxicology."

"It's interesting," Dr. Ortega said, his voice sharpening. "The lab detected alkaloids present in both the brain and blood tissue that don't match any known synthetic drugs or standard poisons. So I've flagged them for further testing and a deeper analysis."

Laurel's eyes narrowed as she reached for her notebook, scribbling shorthand so fast the ink threatened to smear. She'd counted on Dr. Ortega sending the brain tissue for histology. "Please tell me about unidentified alkaloids."

"They're problematic because of their unknown chemical structures." Papers rustled again, quicker this time. Did that show frustration? "I don't know what we found, but I'm willing to bet it's whatever caused the lesions in both brains."

"Do you think it's a toxin of some kind?" Laurel prompted.

"Most likely. The chemical compounds are far from anything we've cataloged before. I stayed up most of the night and finished the autopsy on Mark Bitterson."

Laurel straightened, pen poised over the notebook. The driver of the black truck. "And?"

"It's consistent with what we found in the others," Dr. Ortega said grimly. "Same lesions, but the body buried by him was stabbed, no ID yet, and no lesions."

Her fingers pressed harder into the pen. "What's our next step?"

"More tests. I'll be pushing the lab to fast-track the analysis, and I've put a rush on Bitterson's toxicology and histology tests."

Laurel tapped a finger against her lips, her eyes narrowing as her mind churned through possibilities. "This is a long shot," she murmured. She quite enjoyed the vernacular. It felt like a puzzle piece fitting into place. "However, is there a way for you to test for the presence of derivatives from the yew tree?"

"The yew tree?" Dr. Ortega echoed. "May I ask why?"

"I'm trying to draw connections between situations." Laurel pushed her hair back, her fingers lingering against her scalp as if the pressure might force the pieces together. "Bitterson was found in a stand of illegally harvested yew trees. I seem to recall something about the yew tree having a therapeutic use."

A chair creaked across the phone line. "Sure, sure," Dr. Ortega said, his voice sharpening as if he'd sat up straighter. "The yew tree is most famous for producing paclitaxel, which is a chemotherapy drug."

"That's right." Laurel's pen scratched against her notebook, the ink bleeding into shorthand she would decipher later. "I believe some of the taxane derivatives could have anti-inflammatory or neuroregenerative properties."

"Exactly."

Laurel pressed her pen against the paper. "Dr. Liu was conducting research aimed at developing a treatment for dementia and Alzheimer's disease."

"Oh, fascinating." Ortega spoke faster. "I suppose the polyphenols and flavonoids present in yew trees could potentially protect neuronal cells from oxidative stress, which, as you know, is a key factor in dementia."

"And the anti-inflammatory properties?" Laurel prompted.

"They might reduce microglial activation, which is a key contributor to Alzheimer's disease progression."

Laurel sat back, the notebook resting against her thigh. The flames twisted in the hearth, licking at charred wood with an almost hypnotic rhythm. "Would any of that explain the lesions?"

"Well . . . I don't know," Ortega admitted. "Any compound could create brain lesions under the right, or wrong, conditions. And the yew tree is notorious for its toxicity. All parts of it except the arils—the fleshy red parts surrounding the seeds—contain toxic alkaloids and taxanes."

"Toxic alkaloids," Laurel echoed, her voice a whisper. Her fingers tightened around the pen, her knuckles pale. "Just like what the lab found in the blood."

"Yes," Ortega confirmed, his voice steady but grim. "If these alkaloids are involved, whether accidentally or intentionally introduced . . . we're looking at something lethal. And something new."

Laurel gazed out the window where Huck and Aeneas had vanished beyond her line of sight. "So you're telling me they could be a lethal toxin?"

"They could be concentrated into one, yes," Dr. Ortega replied. "I'll fire off an email to the lab and have them look specifically for derivatives from the yew tree."

Laurel recorded the note with precision, underlining *yew tree derivatives* twice. "Please inform me as soon as you acquire results. If any findings are linked to Dr. Liu, it will facilitate obtaining a warrant to search her former laboratory."

"Understood," Ortega said, the clatter of keys audible through the line.

Laurel tugged her laptop across the table and navigated through her inbox, her finger gliding methodically down the list. "Additionally, a judge has approved my motion to exhume the body of a woman who was employed at the same laboratory. Her name was Melissa Palmtree, and her cause of death was thought to be blunt force trauma to the head after falling down stairs. We'll coordinate the scheduling, and I'll have the cemetery contact you about when the body will arrive at your lab."

"Excellent." Ortega's enthusiasm sharpened his voice. "Let me know, and I will definitely put that autopsy at the top of my list."

"Thank you, Dr. Ortega. And good luck to your niece."

He clicked off first.

Laurel set her phone down, the cold surface jolting her fingers as she reclined into the chair. Her mind drew connections upon connections, threads winding tighter until her temples throbbed.

Mark Bitterson. Tyler Griggs. Dr. Liu. All three had lesions on their brains. The Elk Hollow police officials—and Oakridge Solutions outside of town toward Everett. Everything wove together in a tangled mess.

She pressed her fingers against her temples, willing the thoughts to align, to slot into place with the cool precision of a puzzle snapping together. She could tie Mark Bitterson to the Elk Hollow police officials. She could tie *them* to Tyler Griggs. The same officials had investigated Dr. Liu's death, and the lab hovered in their shadow like a ghost she couldn't shake.

But none of that explained why Mark Bitterson had tried to run her off the road.

Why was there a sniper after her?

She leaned back, eyes fixating on the flickering fire, its flames curling like questions she couldn't quite extinguish. The heat seeped into her, but her blood remained icy, her thoughts darting from one possibility to the next.

Nothing added up. She was still missing something. The connections were there, hidden beneath layers of secrets and agendas she hadn't yet unraveled.

But she would. So far, two people had been shot just standing too close to her. As she looked again outside, not seeing Huck, her heart rate increased. She couldn't get him killed.

Hands curled over her shoulders, and she jumped, yelping.

Laurel startled at the sudden pressure of Huck's hands on her shoulders, his grip firm, unyielding. His heat seeped through her shirt, rough fingers on her skin as he leaned down, his breath warm against her ear.

"Enough, Laurel." His voice was a low tenor that sent her nerves sparking. "You've been tearing yourself up all day. Let's give that big brain of yours a break."

She stiffened, her fingers frozen midtype over her laptop. "I can't just stop, Huck. You know that."

He made a sound, something between a grunt and a growl. "Yeah, well. Challenge accepted." His grip shifted, hands sliding under her arms and pulling her to her feet with one swift, graceful motion. The world tilted as he lifted her out of the chair, her body colliding with his chest.

"What are you—"

"Taking care of you." Huck's eyes were dark, wild, his mouth forming a smile. "You need to get out of your own head, and we're doing this my way."

Her pulse kicked up, a heady mix of intrigue and excitement buzzing through her veins. She should've pushed him away. Should've snapped something sharp and cutting. "You have a way?" But his hands were already on her waist, hot and demanding.

"Yeah. I think I do." His mouth crashed down on hers, his lips rough, searing. All the frustration, the tension that had been gnawing at her bones melted away under the force of his kiss.

"Huck—"

He kissed her harder, swallowing her protest. Her fists clenched in his shirt, and the fabric twisted between her fingers as his tongue slid against hers, hot and demanding.

"What are you doing?" she gasped, her lungs seizing when he finally let her pull back for air.

"What I should've done hours ago." His hands slid to her hips, his grin turning wicked. "Dragging you out of your mind."

His fingers dug into her waist, and then she was moving, stumbling backward as he guided her to the couch. Her knees hit the edge, and he didn't give her a chance to protest before he pushed her down, his weight following her like an avalanche.

"You think you can just—"

"Yeah." His mouth found hers again, unbelievably tempting. "I can."

Her head spun and the world narrowed to nothing but the heat of Huck's body pressing into her, his hands roaming over her like he couldn't decide where to touch first. "Well, all right," she whispered.

His fingers slipped beneath her shirt, dragging the material up over her head with a single, smooth motion. The fabric hit the floor, forgotten. "Laurel, you drive me insane."

"Good," she shot back, her voice ragged, her hands yanking at his shirt. "I like you slightly off-kilter."

His laugh was a rough, broken sound, his eyes blazing as she pushed his shirt over his head. Then his skin was against hers, hot and hard and everything she could ever want. "Off-kilter, huh?" he ground out, his mouth trailing down her neck, his stubble scraping against her skin in a way that made her entire body clench.

"You seem to be concentrating just fine," she managed, her fingers digging into his shoulders.

"I'm doing my best." His mouth moved lower, his lips closing over her collarbone. "I love having you right here. At my place. Safe and within touching distance." His hands slid to her jeans, popping the button with a rough flick.

She sucked in a sharp breath, her hips lifting involuntarily as he tugged her jeans down, his eyes locked on hers with that predatory gleam that always left her pulse thrumming. "You're incredibly sexy."

His grin flashed then. "You're a sweetheart, Snow." He tested her with two fingers.

Yes, she was wet and ready for him. The captain knew how to get her breathless. His hands were already sliding over her thighs, his mouth descending on hers again, hot and demanding.

He kissed her like he wanted both of them to forget the world, his hands moving with the same kind of reckless hunger. Every touch burned, every brush of his skin against hers left her gasping. Slowly, he eased inside her, taking his time.

"Huck," she whispered.

"You keep saying my name like that, and I'll make sure you can't say anything at all," he growled, his fingers digging into her hips, dragging her closer.

She liked this side of him. Maybe too much. Her legs wrapped around him on instinct, her body arching against his. "Is that a promise?"

He laughed, the sound dark and dangerous. "I'll give you any promise you want." Then he started to move. Slowly at first and then with strength.

She didn't care that the couch was old and creaky. Didn't care that their clothes were tangled around their legs like some kind of twisted snare. She only cared about the way Huck's hands were on her, his mouth tracing fire along her skin.

She clung to him, her fingers clawing at his back as he moved against her, the pressure building with a brutal intensity she hadn't even known she was craving. How did he bring this out of her?

"There you go," Huck rasped against her ear. "Forget everything but this."

"I'm trying." Her voice broke, the words splintering as he thrust deeper, his mouth hot against her throat.

"No trying." His teeth scraped along her skin, his voice a feral growl. "Just doing."

Her entire body arched, the world tilting as the sensation slammed into her. She cried out, her fingers digging into his shoulders as the tension snapped, white-hot pleasure crashing over her in waves.

"Laurel . . ." His own voice was rough, strained, his body locking up as he followed her over the edge.

They collapsed together, Huck's weight pressing her into the cushions, his breath ragged against her neck. For a moment, there was nothing but the sound of their breathing, harsh and uneven.

Finally, Huck lifted his head, his eyes glittering. "You back with me now?"

Laurel blinked, her mind still struggling to catch up. "What?"

His grin was lazy, satisfied. "I told you I'd pull you out of that head of yours. You're welcome."

She laughed, her body feeling lighter. "You're a dangerous man."

"Not to you, Laurel Snow."

Laurel didn't argue. Because he was right.

# Chapter 23

Hours after he'd taken her on the sofa, Huck crossed his living room and handed Laurel a glass of cabernet. His fingers brushed hers, and he was glad he'd taken her out of her head for a short time. She was so damned focused, her eyes remaining narrowed and distant even as she took the glass.

"We'll probably need it." He dropped down beside her on the old leather couch. It groaned beneath his weight, same as it always did. He kicked off his boots and stretched his legs out, crossing them at the ankles, and caught Laurel's glance dropping to his socks. She had that half-exasperated, half-amused look she always got when she noticed the holes near his toes. What was he supposed to do? Buy new socks every time a toe popped through? Hell, they were still good. Mostly.

He reached for the remote and turned up the volume. The damn show's theme song blared through the room, all dramatic synth and overly sharp violins meant to set the mood. Huck rolled his shoulders, the tension already curling up his spine like barbed wire.

Rachel Raprenzi's *The Killing Hour*. The title flashed across the screen, stark and bold, making sure everyone knew this was meant to be important.

Rachel appeared, perfectly coiffed and styled, draped in a navy blue suit with silver jewelry that glittered too much under the studio lights. Everything about her was calculated—from her soft blond hair to the way she widened her eyes to feign sincerity. To anyone else, she probably looked polished and genuine. To Huck, she looked like a vulture.

But the star of tonight's show was Abigail Caine.

She sat beside Rachel, posture flawless, hair swept up into a messy bun that was anything but casual. Her green dress softened her appearance and made her look delicate and even breakable. Huck noted the details immediately. The muted color scheme, the soft pink of her nails instead of her usual dark polish. It was a costume, and she wore it well.

But the eyes were the tell. Always were. Abigail's eyes were too sharp, too calculating. One blue, one green, and both trained like loaded weapons. She was playing everyone in that studio.

"Interesting," he muttered, taking a hefty swallow of his wine. It tasted expensive, rich and smooth, but he couldn't appreciate it. His jaw had already started clenching from the instinctive reaction to smelling bullshit. "This is going to suck. At least your mom and Monty are out of range. How many miles between Genesis Valley and St. Thomas?"

Laurel snorted. "Six thousand, one hundred, and fifteen kilometers."

"What's that in miles?" he drawled.

"Thirty-eight hundred," she murmured absently.

He needed to get her out of her head. "How many people in the last week did you see who wore both purple and blue?"

She blinked. "I'm fine, Huck."

"So answer the question, Ms. Genius."

She rolled those spectacular eyes. "Twenty-seven."

He paused. "That's a lot."

"Not really. Blue and purple are the school colors for the middle school, and I saw the soccer team on the field the other day preparing for a match."

Of course she had. He grinned and focused back on the television.

Rachel launched into her opener, her smile locked in place with the same professionalism as a news anchor covering a devastating tragedy. "As I've hinted at all week, we have Dr. Abigail Caine and her attorney, Henry Vexler, from Vexler and Symons."

Vexler looked polished. Hell, the man probably cost more per hour than Huck made in a week. Black suit, green-and-silver tie perfectly chosen to complement Abigail's dress. Staged unity. Huck's fingers twitched. Abigail hadn't left a single detail to chance.

"Let's start with a little history," Rachel said, leaning forward just enough to seem engaged. "You grew up in Genesis Valley, correct?"

"I lived in Genesis Valley until . . . maybe I was eleven." Abigail's voice lifted, just the slightest tremor at the end, her gaze pleading for understanding. Huck scoffed. She was laying it on thick. "Then my mother unfortunately died, and my father shipped me off to college. Overseas."

Huck noted how her shoulders dropped slightly to show the supposed vulnerability of a young girl sent away. Manipulation. She was damn good at it, but he saw the glint in her eyes. The intelligence and careful engineering of every syllable she spoke.

"What degrees do you have, just out of curiosity?" Rachel asked, as if the question hadn't been rehearsed and cleared by Abigail's team.

"Oh, I have a few doctorates," Abigail said, waving a hand like it was nothing. She'd painted her nails a demure pink. Too innocent. Too unlike her. "Computational neuroscience, social and decision neuroscience, game theory, biochemistry, and philosophy with a practical ethics emphasis."

Huck made a low sound under his breath. Impressive, sure. But the woman's talent wasn't in academia. It was in manipulation.

Rachel feigned surprise like a pro. "My goodness. All you have is a Juris Doctor, right?" she tossed at the lawyer.

Vexler laughed, smooth and easy. "Yes. I'm feeling a little undereducated here."

"The philosophy with the practical ethics emphasis is intriguing to me," Rachel continued, homing in on what she thought was the most accessible angle. "Compared to all the . . . well, sciences."

Abigail slid closer to her attorney, her shoulders subtly hunched as if seeking protection. Huck almost rolled his eyes. "Well, I believe we should be ethical in our approach to the world," Abigail murmured, her voice like honey. "Surely you've studied ethics in your journalism pursuits."

"Of course." Rachel puckered her mouth in her serious look.

"That woman wouldn't know ethics if it bit her on the ass," Huck grumbled.

Laurel stayed quiet, gaze locked on the screen. Her version of patience. But Huck was already seeing how Abigail was twisting the narrative. She was setting up the audience, priming them to accept her victimhood.

Rachel's voice came out smooth and soft, her tone set to "sympathetic journalist" mode. "So I know there's only so much you can discuss, but you were arrested for murdering your father, Pastor Zeke Caine, from the Genesis Valley Community Church. I'm sorry you had to go through that."

"I guess there's no question whose side she's on," Laurel murmured.

Huck shook his head. "There never was." Rachel was too slick, too eager, to plaster herself on the right side of the story. Abigail had probably handpicked her for that very reason.

On screen, Abigail flushed like she'd been caught off guard, but Huck could see the calculation behind her eyes: Always working, always thinking. She glanced at her attorney, waiting for the subtle nod of approval before speaking. "Yes, unfortunately, it was a rough day." Abigail's voice quivered just right, her gaze lowering with practiced vulnerability. "He tried to kill my sister. In fact, he did. She was dead for a few moments, we believe."

"That's horrible," Rachel cooed, her own eyes going misty in solidarity. "Why did he do that?"

Abigail shrugged, her shoulders drawn up like she was carrying the world's sorrow. "I really don't know. He was a terrible man, and I know he was a pastor, but . . . I believe that during my upcoming trial, quite a few women are going to come forward and tell us about him taking advantage of them. Possibly even drugging and raping them." She glanced at her attorney, eyes wide like a child asking if they'd said something wrong. "Allegedly."

Huck felt the low burn of anger uncoiling in his gut. Abigail was playing Rachel. "She's full of it."

Laurel made a noise of agreement. "I'm terrible at reading expressions, but even I can see she's putting on a facade."

Huck drained the rest of his wine in a single gulp, the alcohol scorching his throat in a way he welcomed.

On screen, Rachel's eyes glowed with eagerness. "So, after the pastor hurt your sister, you went to her bedside in the hospital, correct?"

"Of course," Abigail answered, her voice perfectly pitched to sound sincere.

Rachel faced the camera, shifting to the real meat of the story. "Just so everybody's in the know here, Dr. Caine's sister is local heroine FBI Special Agent in Charge Laurel Snow. She's the woman who solved both the Snowblood Peak and Witch Creek murders. She caught two serial killers all by herself." Rachel's smile widened. "Well, with the help of her steady boyfriend, Fish and Wildlife officer Huck Rivers."

Huck noted the instant change in Abigail's eyes. She didn't like that.

Abigail leaned forward, eyes bright and sharp like she was smelling blood in the water. "Didn't you also date Huck Rivers?"

"There she is," Huck muttered, reaching for the bottle and pouring himself another glass. Abigail's claws were out.

"Yes," Rachel said smoothly, not missing a beat. "We dated a long time ago, but unfortunately the captain doesn't give me any tips of stories in the area."

Vexler chimed in, his tone rich and polished. "That's professionalism, right there."

Abigail nodded. "Agreed. Of course, Ms. Raprenzi, didn't you accuse Huck Rivers of murder last month?"

Huck chuckled, not feeling amused. "It's like watching two cougars locked in a burlap sack."

Rachel recovered quickly. "I was kidnapped and Huck was framed, briefly. The truth came out soon enough, and we're good friends again."

"Huh," Huck muttered. Good friends, his ass. He swirled the wine in his glass, the deep red liquid catching the firelight as he watched Rachel shift forward in her chair. Her eyes were bright, hungry. She was closing in, aiming to hit Abigail with the hard questions now. About damn time.

"So the question really on everyone's mind, Dr. Caine," Rachel said, her spine straightening with that false air of professionalism, "is why you left the safety of the hospital with your sister and drove out to that dilapidated motel to confront the man who just nearly murdered her. Why would you put yourself in danger like that?"

Huck's gaze flicked to Laurel. She was leaning forward now, her shoulders tense, fingers curled tight around her glass. Her breath had quickened, and her pulse thrummed visibly in the light vein in her temple. She stiffened as she must've sensed the shift, just like he did. Abigail was about to deliver her big, dramatic explanation.

Abigail's gaze dipped, and she let out a carefully timed sigh, her shoulders slumping as if the weight of the world pressed down on her delicate frame. Huck could almost see the act click into place, like a stage prop lowered for maximum effect.

"Our father was missing for about a year," Abigail said, her voice trembling, just enough to convey pain but not hysteria. "I discovered that during that time, he was involved with human trafficking across the Canadian border." Her gaze shifted to Rachel, her expression bleak. "Which you know is near here."

Rachel's mouth fell open. "What?"

"Yes." Abigail nodded, like it pained her to admit it. She reached into her bag and pulled out a folded piece of paper, handing it to Rachel with trembling fingers. Huck's eyes narrowed. Everything Abigail did was deliberate. This was no exception.

Rachel was practically salivating at the supposed evidence she'd been handed.

"He confessed to me just a day before all this happened," Abigail continued, her voice dropping to a near whisper. "I was trying to imagine what to do, but I knew he still had one young victim secured somewhere, and I couldn't let her die." Her words came out rushed, her eyes wet as if the tears had been simmering just below the surface, waiting for this exact moment. Huck had seen skilled liars before, but Abigail was putting on a master class.

"We've finally found her defense," Laurel murmured. "It's good. The Tempest County jury pool is no doubt watching."

"Our father called me after he attacked Laurel," Abigail said, her voice breaking. "He told me to bring him money or he'd kill the girl. Said that if I told anybody, he'd kill her and disappear. I believed him." She paused, eyes shimmering with perfectly timed tears. "Her name was Joley McNalley. She was seventeen years old. From Seattle."

Huck grunted, his grip tightening on his glass. She was good. Too damn good.

"So of course I went," Abigail added, her voice thick with emotion.

"Of course you did," Rachel crooned, nodding like they were best friends. "You went to help this girl with no regard to your own safety."

Abigail shook her head, her features crumpling into what Huck guessed was supposed to be raw vulnerability. "I didn't care about my safety. I cared about that poor child."

Laurel reached for her phone and sent a text. "I'm having Nester conduct a background check on a Joley McNalley."

But Huck wasn't done watching. Abigail's performance wasn't over yet.

Rachel's voice dropped, all grave concern. "But the girl wasn't there, was she?"

Abigail shook her head, her shoulders slumping as if finally breaking under the weight of her own helplessness. "No. I tried to find out where he was keeping her, and he said she'd been dead for weeks." Abigail continued, her voice cracked and strained. "Then he attacked me, and I grabbed the knife off the counter . . ."

"That's enough," Vexler cut in, his voice low and smooth. The lawyer leaned forward, placing a firm hand on Abigail's arm like a father scolding his child. "We definitely have a self-defense situation here, but my client is done talking about it."

Abigail nodded, her lower lip trembling. With a delicate motion, she dabbed at her eyes, wiping away what was likely a carefully coaxed tear. "Zeke Caine was a monster, but I still pray to God every day for forgiveness for killing him. I didn't mean to. He hurt so many women. He hurt my sister, and she lost her baby." Abigail's breath hitched, her eyes glistening. "Honestly, I was just heartbroken and, of course, terrified."

"Of course," Rachel said, her tone syrupy and warm. She turned to the camera with the same gravity she probably used to report a national tragedy. "*The Killing Hour* is trying to secure an interview with FBI Agent Laurel Snow, as well as Fish and Wildlife captain Huck Rivers, because they were the ones who arrived on the scene first. I believe Captain Rivers actually arrested you."

"He did." Abigail let another tear fall. "And Laurel won't speak to me. She's so confused about all of this, and she didn't know what a monster our father was. Not really."

Huck wanted to puke.

Rachel reached out and patted Abigail's hand, her own smile settling into the perfect blend of concern and optimism. "I certainly hope you reconcile soon." She held the moment for several beats, milking it like a pro before turning back to the camera, her face hardening into concerned, resolute lines. "Wait for a preview for our upcoming episode Monday night featuring Sandra Plankton, the girlfriend of slain podcaster Tyler Griggs. She believes the police are involved in his death, and you just won't believe who's investigating his case."

Huck clicked off the TV, the remote dropping onto the couch beside him. His jaw ached from clenching. "I can't believe she has the Griggs story."

"It sounds as if Sandra contacted Rachel. Right now, I need to deal with Abigail's plans," Laurel said.

Abigail's plans. Words Huck never wanted to issue. "I'm sorry she wants to use you in her defense."

Laurel didn't respond immediately, her gaze still locked on the blank screen, her expression calm, too calm. Huck recognized that look. She was picking apart Abigail's words, rearranging them in her mind, searching for the thread Abigail was trying to tie around her neck. "We knew she would bring that entire situation up in her defense," Laurel finally noted. "I'm not entirely shocked she's done it publicly. The jury pool in Genesis Valley and Tampa County is small enough. It's a strategic move. A good one."

Huck watched her take two big swallows of wine, her throat working as she drained the glass. He followed suit, the cabernet searing down his throat, its quality wasted on his growing frustration. "Let's not worry about this."

"I'm not." Laurel's gaze flicked to him, concern and sizzling intelligence in her eyes. "I'm worried about her next move."

No shit.

# Chapter 24

On Monday morning, the bulletproof vest felt heavy. Too hot. Too tight. But Laurel kept her expression neutral as she entered the interrogation room at the Elk Hollow police station. Walter's shoulder brushed hers as he followed her inside.

Detective Joshua Robertson sat hunched at the table, fingers laced so tight his knuckles blanched. He kept his eyes on the chipped surface, shoulders curled forward like he could shield himself from whatever was coming. The sweat gleaming along his forehead had nothing to do with the chill outside.

But it was the man sitting next to him who caught Laurel's attention.

Henry Vexler.

Laurel stopped short, her gaze locking onto the polished attorney. He sat with the precise poise of a man comfortable at the table. His expression betrayed nothing.

"Agent Snow." Vexler's voice was smooth, measured. "Agent Smudgeon."

"This is a surprise," Laurel noted. What was Abigail's high-priced attorney doing there?

He offered a mild smile. "While on *The Killing Hour,* I heard Rachel Raprenzi mention her upcoming interview with Sandra Plankton, so I asked her to fill me in, and she quite happily did so. I, of course, followed up by calling the officers involved."

Laurel tilted her head. "Why?"

"Why not?"

So wait a minute. Her eyebrows rose. "The officers told you that I requested interviews with them, so you took their cases?" Just to get to her?

He tightened his jaw, and truly, he didn't have the jawline of Captain Rivers. In fact, his jaw looked a little . . . weak. "I plan to see a lot of you, Agent Snow. Either you come and talk to me about your sister's case, or I'll make it my mission to be on the opposite side of every single one of your investigations."

"That's a threat," Walter muttered.

"Actually, it's extortion," Laurel noted.

Detective Robertson finally focused. "Wait a minute. You're here just because of her? Not to represent me?"

Vexler didn't even look at his client. "I'm one of the best defense attorneys in the country. Take the gift horse and just be quiet." He inclined his head, his expression unreadable. "I assume you have questions for my client."

How did Abigail get these men, of all ages, to go to such great lengths to protect her? That was a puzzle for another day. "Many," Laurel said, taking a seat across from Detective Robertson. "Detective, I'd like you to explain your relationship with Mark Bitterson."

Detective Robertson's gaze snapped up, alarm flaring before he caught it. His fingers tightened around each other. "I don't have a relationship with him."

"Except you do." Laurel noted the pace of his breathing, which was rather even so far. "You've met with him. Repeatedly."

"I've met a lot of people." Detective Robertson's lips compressed. "Bitterson was a small-time hustler. A nuisance. If you've investigated him at all, you'd know that."

"I know he's dead," Laurel countered. "And so is Tyler Griggs, the podcaster who documented you meeting Bitterson on multiple occasions."

Detective Robertson's eyes widened, then narrowed. "I was investigating Griggs's death before the FBI stole the case from me, and I have no idea what you're talking about. There's no documentation because it did not happen."

"I see. Then it might shock you to learn that Tyler Griggs recorded you, very often, and documented not only your relationship with Officer Jackson but your meetings with the very deceased Mark Bitterson. Your attorney might want to explain to you that it's a felony to lie to a federal agent," Laurel said.

Detective Robertson's gaze flicked to Vexler, who remained impassive, his hands folded neatly on the table.

"I told you," Detective Robertson grunted. "I didn't have anything to do with Bitterson. He might've approached me a couple of times, but that's all. Nothing major." His expression cleared. "He was an informant for me."

Laurel paused. "Then you'll have a record of every meeting as well as documentation of his reports and any payments you might've made?"

Vexler sighed heavily. Yeah, his client appeared to be a moron.

"No." The word was too quick, too sharp from Detective Robertson. "I didn't, ah, document it."

Walter snorted. "Want me to arrest and charge him with lying to a federal agent?"

"I don't have to listen to this." Detective Robertson's chin lifted, but it was a weak attempt at defiance.

"You do if you want this to end." Laurel stared him down. "Mark Bitterson and you exchanged packages several times, and we've obtained footage of these meetings."

Detective Robertson flinched, the truth slamming through whatever defense he'd tried to build. "Footage?"

"Tyler Griggs documented your interactions. Every exchange, every whispered conversation. He was meticulous," Laurel said.

Detective Robertson sagged, his eyes darting to Vexler and finding no support. "It's not what you think."

"Then explain the situation to me," Laurel said.

Detective Robertson looked down, his fingers digging into his palms. The silence ticked around the conference room until he finally spoke. "Bitterson was blackmailing me."

"About what?" Laurel asked, her tone flat.

Detective Robertson's mouth twisted. "My relationship with Jillian Jackson. He said he'd make it public. Ruin me and both of our marriages. So I gave him . . . favors."

"What kind of favors?"

Detective Robertson's shoulders hunched. "We just exchanged manila envelopes. Not thick ones. Not big enough to hold any drugs, so I figured, whatever. Right?"

Now they were getting to what Laurel needed. "Your cooperation is appreciated. Who was on the other end of this exchange?"

Detective Robertson looked at the door as if he wanted to run for it.

Laurel waited him out.

"Answer the question," Vexler said quietly, his expression unreadable.

"Melissa Palmtree." The name tumbled from Detective Robertson's mouth, his shoulders slumping as if relieved to finally release the truth. "I just gave her what Bitterson handed me. I don't even know what was in the envelopes."

Laurel's mind raced. "Melissa Palmtree. The Oakridge Solutions lab tech who died in Seattle." She fell down stairs, and her body should be arriving at Dr. Ortega's lab any second. Yet one more connection to Oakridge Solutions.

"Yeah." Detective Robertson swallowed. "I read about her death in the news since it's out of our jurisdiction. Thought it was a coincidence. I figured . . . I figured when she died, my part was over."

Walter leaned toward him. "What was Bitterson passing to her?"

"I told you. I don't know." Detective Robertson looked sick, his skin pale and slick with sweat. "He just said she was the contact. My guess is that she was paying him, because he bought that sweet black truck that I heard he later wrapped around a tree. Suddenly, he was flush. But I didn't ask questions. My wife would kill me if she found out about Jillian." He looked up. "You don't have to tell her, right?"

Laurel couldn't believe this man. "Why would Melissa Palmtree pay Mark Bitterson?"

"I didn't ask. I didn't want to know. Bitterson said she was working on something at Oakridge Solutions, something valuable, and if I helped him, he'd leave me alone," the detective said.

"What about Dr. Liu?" Laurel asked quickly.

Detective Robertson's brows drew together. His mouth parted, lips slack. True confusion? "Who?"

Laurel tried to read his expression. "Dr. Miriam Liu. One of the lead researchers at Oakridge Solutions. She died in Tempest County in a car accident." Which also took her out of Detective Robertson's jurisdiction.

"I've never heard of her," he said.

Laurel measured his breath rate. Fast and from the chest. He was definitely stressed. "How did you exchange envelopes with Melissa Palmtree?"

"I pick up extra shifts as a security guard at Oakridge Solutions." Detective Robertson's expression crumpled. "Just on my off days. It's extra cash. I just walk the perimeter, make sure no one's breaking in. I didn't even know Melissa worked there until Bitterson told me, and then one day, there she was in the break room waiting for me."

Laurel's fingers tightened around her pen. "Was Bitterson harvesting yew trees? We found his body in a strand of them."

"*You* trees? What the hell is that?" Detective Robertson shoved back to stand. "I've told you everything I know. I'm done here."

Vexler rose smoothly, his expression polite but firm. "Unless you intend to charge my client, I believe this conversation is over."

"Why would Mark Bitterson have rammed our vehicle with his truck and fired upon Agent Smudgeon and me the first time we left Elk Hollow?" Laurel asked.

The detective's brow furrowed. "I have no fucking clue, lady. I'm out of here."

"For now," Laurel replied. "I suggest you stay in town, Detective Robertson. One more question. Did you have anything to do with the deaths of Tyler Griggs, Dr. Miriam Liu, Melissa Palmtree, or Mark Bitterson?"

Detective Robertson stumbled back. "God, no. Wait a minute. Are you saying—"

Walter palmed the table. "You might want to watch your six, Detective. It appears that people in your orbit are ending up . . . dead."

Detective Robertson fled the room.

Vexler trailed him with calm grace. He glanced back over his shoulder. "I'll get Officer Jackson for you. I'm representing her as well." He shut the door behind him.

Walter let out a low breath. "That lawyer is a definite shark. He's pretty much working for free just to mess with you."

"He's studying me," Laurel said. "Trying to learn how I think, how I work, and how I'll respond on the stand during Abigail's trial. This is the only way he can get close."

"Now, that's dedication."

Laurel had no idea how Abigail inspired it. Unless Vexler was just that dedicated. Laurel would need days with him to accurately diagnose him, but she'd bet he was a narcissist. Many successful people had narcissistic traits.

Walter hitched his belt up. Had he lost more weight? "Do we have enough to arrest Detective Robertson? For anything but being a dumbass courier of something that might not be illegal as well as being a cheating asshole?"

"Not at the moment, but we'll give a copy of our report to the police chief here. I bet Detective Robertson doesn't keep his job for long."

Even with his hotshot attorney.

"So, you and Detective Robertson kept your relationship quiet," Laurel said. They'd been interviewing Officer Jillian Jackson for almost forty minutes, and the woman was starting to wilt.

"Yes," Jackson admitted, her gaze flicking toward the door, desperation fraying her composure. "We were careful."

Walter's pen scratched against his notepad, his expression unreadable. He hadn't said much, letting Laurel take the lead.

"Careful," Laurel echoed. "That's one way to put it. You're married, Officer Jackson, and so is Detective Robertson."

Jackson's mouth tightened, her shoulders hunching defensively. "I'm aware. It was . . . complicated. It's not like we planned it."

"And Mark Bitterson planned to use that against you," Walter said.

She flinched. "I told you, I didn't know Bitterson. He never contacted me. Whatever happened, it was between him and Josh."

"But you knew that Detective Robertson was meeting him," Laurel pressed.

Officer Jackson hesitated. "He told me . . . he told me Bitterson was trying to dig up dirt on him. That he was being followed. But he said he had it under control."

"Except he didn't," Walter cut in. "Bitterson had him running errands, passing packages. And you had no idea?"

Officer Jackson's eyes widened, her voice growing sharper. "No. Why would I? Josh never told me anything like that. He said it was just . . . I don't know, him trying to deal with Bitterson's threats. I tried to get him to go to Internal Affairs, but he said it would only make things worse."

"What kind of threats?" Laurel asked.

Officer Jackson's gaze dropped to the table. "He said Bitterson would ruin us. That he had proof of the affair. That if Josh didn't cooperate, he'd leak everything."

"So he cooperated," Laurel said. "Even when it meant meeting a known criminal in dark alleys."

"I didn't know that was happening." Officer Jackson's voice cracked. "I swear. Josh told me he was handling it, and I believed him. I thought . . . I thought if we were careful, it would all blow over."

"'Careful' isn't how I'd describe what's been happening." Laurel's gaze bored into her. "You didn't ask why Mark Bitterson was targeting Detective Robertson? Why a man like that would go to so much trouble just to extort him over an affair?"

Officer Jackson's hands twisted together. "No. I thought it was about me. About . . . about us. I never imagined it was more than that."

"And when you heard Bitterson was dead?"

"Relieved." The word came out harsh and unfiltered. "I know that sounds horrible, but I thought it meant Josh could finally breathe again. That we could be . . . I don't know, something normal."

Walter's pen stilled. "You didn't ask him about the packages?"

"No." Officer Jackson's shoulders trembled. "He never mentioned that."

Laurel kept her gaze on the woman while her attorney remained silent next to her. So far, she hadn't admitted to anything other than having an improper relationship with a superior officer, which probably kept her somewhat safe. "Did you ever meet Melissa Palmtree?"

"No. Never heard of her," Officer Jackson said.

Walter stopped writing. "Do you pick up extra work at Oakridge Solutions?"

Officer Jackson shook her head. "No. My husband is the football coach for the high school, so my weekends are busy with games."

"When you're not cheating on him?" Walter asked.

Officer Jackson paled. "I fell in love with Josh. Didn't mean to, but it happened."

Laurel wasn't getting anything helpful from the woman. "Tell me right now if you know anything about the deaths of Tyler Griggs, Miriam Liu, Melissa Palmtree, Larry Scott, or Mark Bitterson."

Officer Jackson blinked rapidly. "I don't. Do you think they're related?" She pressed a hand to her throat. "Is Josh in danger? Am I?"

Laurel glanced at Walter and then back. "I'm sharing my report with the police chief, so you might want to speak to him first. You're free to go."

Officer Jackson shot out of her chair like it had caught fire. She hesitated, her gaze darting between them before she fled through the door and down the hallway.

Walter stretched his shoulders. "Well, that was a bust."

"Not entirely." Laurel's gaze flicked to Vexler, who remained seated, his hands folded neatly in front of him. "But we're not finished."

Vexler's smile was slow and measured. "No, I imagine we're not."

Walter stood. "I need a minute."

"Take your time," Laurel replied, her focus now solely on Vexler. Walter slipped out of the room, his shoulders tense.

Laurel leaned back in her chair. "Did you get what you needed today?"

"Not yet, but Abigail has accurately described you. You're data driven, calm, and rather unemotional. Very different from her."

Laurel barely kept from shaking her head. "You don't read people as well as you believe if you think Abigail is emotional. She can mimic emotion, and she knows how to manipulate people."

"Look who's talking," Vexler drawled. "From what I understand, you've made sure your mother is safely out of the country, somewhere she can't be subpoenaed in time for Abigail's trial. So I can't ask her about being raped by the evil Pastor Caine so many years ago."

Laurel's pulse kicked, but she kept her expression calm. "My mother's on vacation."

"An extended vacation." Vexler's eyes glinted. "Very convenient timing."

"Convenient for her." Yes, Laurel had seen the expedited trial request coming from Abigail. She'd protect her mother, no matter what.

Vexler chuckled, the sound low and cold. "You're a fascinating woman, Agent Snow. Always two steps ahead. But what happens when you're dragged back? You'll be testifying in Abigail's case, after all."

"I'm only interested in facts," Laurel said, keeping her emotions in check. "You want my testimony? You'll get it. Every fact, every detail, and not a word more."

"Not even for the woman you sent halfway across the world?" Vexler's smile held no warmth. "It must be comforting, knowing she's safe. Untouchable."

"Is there a point to this?"

Vexler rose, his movements fluid. "Just that your determination to protect certain individuals is as strong as mine. And maybe . . . just as misguided."

"I'm here for the truth," Laurel replied. "Not your version of it."

Vexler's gaze lingered on her, assessing. "You're going to make this very interesting, Agent Snow." And then he was gone, leaving the room colder than it had been when she entered earlier.

Walter poked his head in. "Nester just texted. His deep dive on Joley McNalley revealed a teenaged runaway arrested twice in Seattle for prostitution. Nothing else. The kid is from Oregon but has no family around. So there's no way to confirm or negate Abigail's big story on the podcast Saturday night."

"Wonderful," Laurel muttered.

Walter nodded. "Also, the warrant for Tyler's apartment just came through. Want to go search?"

"Absolutely. Please ask Nester to draft a warrant for Oakridge Solutions. I'll type up my affidavit to show cause when we return to the office, and hopefully we can get it signed tonight. We'll head out there first thing in the morning."

She was getting closer on this. The vest weighed her down and she lifted her head. "Keep an eye out, Walter." She could not get him shot. Again.

"Always," he replied grimly.

# Chapter 25

Pulling into the parking lot of her building, Laurel could not wait to get out of the bulletproof vest. The search of Tyler Griggs's apartment had led to nothing. She had Nester trying to track Tyler's last week, but there weren't many CCTV cameras in the smaller town of Elk Hollow. She pulled to a stop to the right of the Staggers Creamery door.

Walter angled his head, looking at the cloudy sky and trees around them. "Hold on, boss. I'm having Nester check the outlying cameras. He says there haven't been any disturbances, but let's just make sure." His phone dinged. "All right. Run from the vehicle into the vestibule. Ready? Go."

Laurel jumped out and jogged to open the door, not surprised that Walter flanked her back, his gun out and pointed at the trees. "We'd know if a sniper had climbed a tree. Huck and Nester have more cameras out there than we do in all of Seattle." She moved inside, already reaching for the Velcro beneath her sweater before stopping cold. "Abigail."

Her half sister leaned against the far wall, scrolling through her phone. "There you are. I've been waiting forever." She cast a glance around the quiet vestibule. "If you're going to have security on the door, you should at least provide somewhere to sit out here."

Walter walked in behind Laurel. "Ah, shit," he muttered beneath his breath.

Laurel strode forward and scanned her ID. The door clicked open. "Come up to my office."

"Happily," Abigail said, turning to follow her with a graceful hop.

Since it was after five, Laurel didn't expect Kate to be at her post, and a quick glance into Nester's computer hub showed him on the phone with somebody about CCTV. She nodded, waited for a chin jerk from him, and then continued down the hallway toward her office. "Walter, you can take off," she called back. "I'll head home with Huck."

"I'll wait until you go," Walter barked, heading into the conference room.

Laurel pulled the Velcro free as she walked into her office, loosening the vest before taking a seat across the rough door she used as a desk. The blinds were closed, but she could hear the rain pattering outside. "What do you need, Abigail?"

Abigail gracefully sat on one of the two white leather chairs and crossed her legs. Back to form today, she wore black slacks, a deep red sweater, and a Van Cleef necklace with matching earrings. Somehow, the red never competed with her natural auburn hair, which fell to her shoulders. Like Laurel's. "I merely wanted to make sure you were all right after my interview with Rachel Raprenzi. I'm trying to save my life, you know."

"I'm sure it amused you," Laurel murmured, studying the woman who looked so much like her.

One of Abigail's brows arched. "Being interviewed?"

"Yes, by the woman you once attacked and threatened to kill." Laurel couldn't prove it, but she knew that Abigail had done so a while back just to mess with one of Laurel's cases. "She has no clue, does she?"

Abigail smiled, showing perfect white teeth. "I'm sure I don't know what you're talking about." She brushed invisible lint off her pressed pants. "She is a twit, though, don't you think? Much better suited to the mouth breather you're dating than are you. They probably made a fine couple. I mean, if she wasn't such a useless bitch."

Laurel rolled her neck, really wanting to rip off her sweater and then the damn vest. "I had a run-in with your attorney today."

Abigail pursed her lips. "That's interesting. Tell me more."

So he hadn't cleared his plan with his client. "How do you do it?" Laurel stretched out her legs beneath the desk.

"Do what?"

How did she even ask? Why would she? "Get these men so devoted to you? To believing what you say instead of what the evidence shows? Get them so inspired?"

"Oh. That." Abigail waved a hand in the air, showing newly painted red nails. "Men are easy. The key is making them think everything is their idea."

All right. "How long do you plan to dangle Agent Norrs on the hook?" She liked the metaphor but not the reality.

Abigail's eyes widened. "On the hook? But I love him, Laurel. He's so big and strong." She wrinkled her nose. "He keeps me safe, you know? Just like your Huck does for you. We really should double-date once in a while. I mean, after this whole murder charge goes away." Her tongue darted out to lick her bottom lip. "We're so much alike, you and me. Both dating tough, by-the-book badasses. Right?"

Except Laurel truly cared for Huck. Abigail only cared for herself. "Do you ever wonder about it?" she mused.

Abigail's gaze sharpened. "Wonder about what?"

"What the rest of us actually feel. You mimic emotions but don't truly feel them. Are you curious?" She couldn't help but be intrigued.

"That's just mean." Abigail pouted. "I feel everything. More than you could even imagine."

Perhaps. Not love or empathy, but definitely something. Laurel shrugged. "Agent Norrs is a good man, I believe. Stop using him." But he would certainly help with Abigail's trial.

Abigail flashed her left hand with a two-carat diamond solitaire. "But we're engaged. He went all out. Isn't it pretty?"

Laurel lifted her chin. "He's not like the others you've manipulated. When you dump him, he'll be angry."

Abigail laughed now. "They all get angry. Men are barely a step up from children. Please, Laurel. I do know what I'm doing." She leaned in, her voice dropping conspiratorially low. "As do you. Nice move getting your mother out of the country on a long vacation. My attorney would've eviscerated her on the stand."

Laurel kept her emotions under control, slowly placing her phone on the desk and then pulling a notebook and pen toward her. She pressed the recording button. "Interview with Dr. Abigail Caine." She gave the time and date.

Abigail's lips twitched. "What are you doing?"

Laurel lowered her chin. "Dr. Caine, you alleged on *The Killing Hour* Saturday night that you have pertinent information regarding a trafficking ring here in Washington State. How did you come by such information?"

Realization dawned across Abigail's face and her cheek creased. "My fiancé should be here in a few moments to pick me up. Stop being silly."

Laurel angled her head to the side to call down the hallway. "Nester? I need you to prepare an emergency warrant for us to hold and secure Dr. Caine as a material witness. Please do so now."

Abigail's chin slowly lowered, and her eyes gleamed. "You're making a mistake."

Laurel kept her expression blank. "Dr. Caine, you said you have information. Either you lied on the podcast, or you need to start talking now. Who is Joley McNalley?"

"All right." Abigail crossed her legs. "She's a girl our father said he had secured somewhere, and when I arrived at his motel room, he said she'd died weeks ago from an overdose. He would not tell me where her body lay, so I have no idea."

"You gave a list to Rachel Raprenzi during the podcast. What was on it?" Laurel asked.

Abigail lifted a shoulder. "It was a list of missing teenagers from the Seattle area that I found online. I'm not an investigator like you, but I felt like I should at least perform a Google Search."

How annoying. "So you have no real information about a trafficking ring?"

"No. Just that our father said he made a bunch of money recently by assisting with a ring and saying he had that girl hidden. That's all. I certainly wish I could provide more information to you." Abigail uncrossed her legs. "It's your job to figure out where dear old Dad played the last year."

The man had certainly hidden himself well. He had spent time down in an artist co-op in Arizona, so perhaps he'd just been wandering. Abigail had probably made up the entire situation as a defense for herself. There was no way to prove it, however. Laurel clicked off the recording app.

Abigail lounged across from her, looking far too pleased with herself. "You're so cute to tag me as a material witness. My attorney would've chewed you up and spit you out so quickly. But I'm glad I could help on this investigation." Her voice was light, almost smug.

Laurel tapped a staccato rhythm against the desktop. "If you do have any information regarding Joley McNalley, be a decent human being and—"

A sharp ping echoed through the office, metallic and faint. Laurel's head snapped up. Abigail's smile slipped, her brow furrowing.

The next sound was louder. Violent. Glass exploded inward, shards spraying across the desk and scattering over the floor. Metal clattered as the blinds jerked and twisted, punctured by a bullet that ripped through with vicious precision.

Laurel's brain registered the gunfire a split second after her body was already moving. She lunged across the desk, slamming into Abigail and driving her hard to the floor.

"Get down!" Laurel's shout was guttural, the adrenaline twisting her voice.

Abigail hit the floor with a gasp, limbs tangled awkwardly beneath her. "Laurel, what the—"

Another shot cracked through the room, tearing into the wall behind them. The blinds shredded, their metal slats flailing like loose wire. Rain blew in through the ruptured glass, icy and stinging.

"Shots fired," Laurel yelled, flattening herself against the floor, her arm slung over Abigail's shoulders to keep her pinned. Abigail's heart beat steadily against her. Too calm. "Stay down," Laurel growled.

"I am down." Abigail's voice was muffled, pressed against the hardwood. "Is this your idea of hospitality?"

"Shut up." Laurel's fingers were already at her holster, her sidearm cool and solid in her grip. The laptop was thrown askew, its screen cracked from where it had slammed against the edge of the desk. Papers drifted like leaves caught in a storm.

Another bullet tore through the window, punching through the broken glass and embedding itself in the opposite wall. Laurel's mind raced, calculating angles, positions. North side—behind the building somewhere in the trees? They didn't have security back there. She'd kept the blinds drawn. Had the shooter just guessed?

She angled her head to see Walter and Nester headed up the hallway, guns out, crouched low.

Walter caught her gaze. "Laurel? Report. Are you hit?"

"Negative. We're both fine. But we have a sniper outside, north ridge." She pressed a warning hand on Abigail's arm and then rolled to the other side of her desk, coming up and shooting into the tree line and into the forest. To where she could loosely calculate the sniper might be.

Walter edged around the desk on the other side, still low.

Another bullet tore through the air, the blinds jerking violently before falling to the floor in a tangled mess.

Laurel twisted, her eyes narrowing as she aimed toward the shattered window. She couldn't see anything. The rain outside was a solid sheet of gray, masking whatever vantage point the shooter was using. "Now—higher to the north."

She and Walter rose at once, firing toward the northern tree line while Nester grabbed Abigail's shoulders and pulled her out of the office toward the conference room.

A truck coughed from the tree line. Then an engine gunned. Two other trucks zipped around the building, lights bright, pointed toward the trees. Laurel's phone buzzed from the floor and she dropped back down, noting it was Huck calling. She pressed the speaker. "We're fine. Nobody hit."

"Good. Stay covered." He clicked off.

Laurel levered up to see Huck leap out of one truck, his gun out.

Then he pulled Aeneas out of the back. Agent Norrs barreled out of the other truck, and they both headed into the forest toward the mountain, their flashlights bobbing in the rain.

"Laurel?" Nester called out. "Report?"

Laurel watched the moving flashlights. Her heartbeat thundered in her ears, and her vision wavered as the adrenaline started to ebb in her body. Her hands began to shake. "Captain Rivers and Agent Norrs are in the woods, but I heard a truck engine before they arrived. I think we're secure."

"Huck and Wayne?" Abigail called out with a small chuckle. "How sweet. Our big, bad men are protecting us, Laurel. Don't you just love it?"

Walter, back to the wall on the other side of the window with rain and wind blowing in, looked at her, his eyes narrowed and his chest heaving. "That chick is batshit crazy, boss," he whispered.

# Chapter 26

The rain pounded against the windows of the Fish and Wildlife office in a relentless, feral downpour. The storm had swept in from the north, thick and punishing, drenching the world outside with icy precision.

In their conference room, Laurel cupped her hands around the mug of coffee cooling in front of her. She preferred her own office to the Fish and Wildlife conference room—less cluttered, more secure. But with her own window currently a twisted, shattered mess thanks to the sniper's attack, Walter had insisted she use this space instead. Away from open sight lines, with walls thick enough to provide some degree of protection.

Across from her, Agent Norrs shifted in his chair, his shirt still wet from the storm. The dark fabric clung to his shoulders, highlighting the compact, muscular build of a man who looked like he could break through concrete. With his bald head and flat, dark eyes, he looked even tougher than usual.

The speakerphone in the middle of the table crackled, and Deputy Director McCromby's voice cut through the static.

"So you didn't find the shooter," McCromby growled, his voice clipped and irritable, the fatigue of late-night duty evident. It was nearly three hours later in DC.

"No, sir," Norrs said, running a hand over his scalp, the wetness glistening under the harsh lights. "We swept the forest. There's an old logging road that cuts toward the mountain. He was gone by the time we got there. It's raining heavily, and I doubt there'll be any evidence when the techs go back out tomorrow morning."

Laurel took a deep breath and tightened her hold around the coffee mug. The chill from her damp jacket hadn't fully left her bones, and the uneven temperature in the conference room wasn't helping her warm up. "We've swept the entire building," she said, her voice even. "The only shots fired went through my window."

"So the shooter knows which office is yours," McCromby interjected, the line crackling.

"Possibly." Laurel's mind clicked through the facts, fitting them into place like puzzle pieces—most of them still wrong, the edges ragged and frayed. "But it was after hours. I walked into the building, and Walter hadn't gone to his office. Even though we had the blinds drawn, my office was probably the only one with illumination seeping through."

"So this asshole felt fine firing into an FBI office, not caring who he hit?" McCromby snapped, his irritation palpable.

Agent Norrs wiped wetness off his face. "Apparently. We're still looking through Laurel's previous cases, but nothing stands out. Nobody's been recently released, and so far every lead we've tracked down hasn't panned out."

Laurel leaned back, her shoulders stiff. The incongruity gnawed at her like a dull ache. "Regarding my case, the real outlier is Mark Bitterson, the petty criminal found dead in the woods days after he rammed his truck into Walter and me, his passenger firing at us. Neither of them were snipers. They were different attackers than the sniper who hit Abigail and Dr. Sandoval."

"So, in other words, somebody has a hit out on you," Agent Norrs said grimly. His gaze cut to her, his expression more concerned than she'd expected.

Laurel cleared her throat. "Bitterson has lesions on his brain, which connects him to the Dr. Liu case. Nothing in his past shows he'd take a contract killing. This just isn't adding up for me."

"Why not?" McCromby barked.

She was still missing something. "What if the two situations aren't related? What if two people want me dead? It seems unlikely, but . . ."

"You're onto something, but you're not sure what," McCromby growled. "I need certainty, Snow."

"I don't have it. Yet."

McCromby cleared his throat, the sound thick and irritated. "What's the plan?"

Norrs glanced at Laurel before looking down at the speakerphone. "I'm thinking Agent Snow should take a leave of absence."

Laurel's muscles tensed. She turned sharply to face him, eyes narrowed. "Absolutely not."

McCromby was silent for several beats, the line crackling with faint interference. "It might not be a bad idea," he said finally. "You've been shot at several times, Snow. Maybe it's time to step back and reassess."

"I'm an FBI agent, Deputy Director McCromby." Laurel would not go into hiding. "If someone shoots at me, I don't run and hide. Otherwise, we'd all be running all the time."

"You get shot at all the time," Norrs burst out, throwing his arms up.

Laurel fought an inappropriate smile. Now that the adrenaline had fled her body, she was getting loopy. But he did look humorous. "I agree," she said, her tone level. "But the only way to find out who's doing this is to keep doing my job. Running and hiding won't get us anywhere."

McCromby's sigh sounded heavy. "It's your call, Snow. But figure out who's gunning for you, and do it fast."

"Yes, sir," Laurel and Agent Norrs said in unison.

The line went dead with a sharp click.

Agent Norrs shoved back in his chair. "I'm sorry," he said lamely. "It would just be easier to figure out who's trying to kill you if I wasn't worried about you actually ending up dead."

Were they becoming friends? That wouldn't end well. "I've been careful," Laurel said, her voice softer now. "Nobody thought this guy would shoot from the mountain into an office. Snipers aren't usually so careless. But this idiot has missed three times. I think we've been giving him too much credit."

"Agreed." Agent Norrs stood. "I should warn you that Rivers is pretty pissed off about the entire situation."

Laurel frowned. "What's the logic in that?"

"The logic?" Agent Norrs echoed, his brows drawn.

"Yes," Laurel said. "There's a sniper. We will find him. Getting angry doesn't serve anything."

Agent Norrs stared at her for a long moment, his eyes assessing. "You're an interesting one, Snow. I'll give you that."

"Thank you?" Being thought of as interesting or even odd wasn't anything new to her.

"Anytime." Agent Norrs exhaled and adjusted his stance. "I think we should put a protective detail on you. Two agents from Seattle. Your office is too small to handle this."

"No." Laurel held up a hand. "I don't want a detail. I have a job to do, and so do you. Find him."

Agent Norrs nodded, his mouth tight. "I won't stop until I do. I promise."

Laurel stood, pushing back from the table and heading toward the door. As she shoved through the heavy wooden door and into the narrow hallway, the storm's growl intensified, rumbling through the walls like a distant, restless animal.

The Fish and Wildlife lobby was dim, the old fluorescent lights buzzing faintly as they fought against the natural darkness pressing in from outside.

Huck waited in the far corner of the room, leaning against the wall with his arms folded across his chest. Abigail stood a few paces away, her posture graceful and loose, her gaze fixed on something far beyond the peeling paint and faded wildlife posters.

Both of them were silent. Too silent.

Walter and Nester had left after delivering their reports—brusque, tired exchanges with little patience for pleasantries. The entire place felt hollow, stripped of its usual bustling life by the severity of the storm and the sheer audacity of the attack.

Laurel's gaze went first to Huck. His jaw was clenched so hard she half expected his molars to crack. His shoulders were locked under the gray shirt, muscles bunched tight, fists pressed to his biceps like it was the only thing stopping him from breaking something—or someone.

"Rivers," Laurel said, her voice cutting through the silence.

His gaze snapped to her, eyes dark and fierce. "You all right?"

"I'm fine." She met his gaze, refusing to let the storm of his emotions throw her off-balance. "Just finished with the deputy director and Agent Norrs."

"Good. I secured your window upstairs with a couple of boards we had in the basement. This guy is getting reckless and desperate." Huck's voice was low and rough, threaded with an anger he barely bothered to hide.

Good. That just meant the shooter would make a mistake. Soon.

Abigail Caine turned down the heated seat in Wayne's truck and settled back, her body sinking into the rich leather. The warmth seeped through her coat, chasing away the chill from the storm outside. Rain pummeled the truck's roof, and the windshield wipers slapped in frantic rhythm, struggling to clear the rain that sheeted down the glass.

Wayne drove with both hands firm on the wheel, his gaze fixed forward, his jaw clenched in that determined way she found so amusing. It was a long drive back to her high-end subdivision, and he was taking the winding roads with far more care than necessary. She supposed it was his nature to play things safe. It probably had something to do with his job. He had to be serious and cautious as if he thought the entire world was one wrong move away from crumbling beneath his feet.

They'd been driving in silence for miles. Wayne's fingers drummed on the steering wheel—offbeat and restless. Abigail watched tension climb up his spine, the way his shoulders locked and his throat moved like he was choking on words. Any minute now. She could feel it. He'd grow a fucking pair and spit it out.

Finally, he cleared his throat. "Abby, don't get mad at me, but I think you should stay away from your sister for a while."

There it was. Exactly what she'd been expecting. Abigail opened her eyes wide, feigning surprise. "Wayne, how can I do that? She's my sister. Someone's trying to kill her. I can't leave her alone. She's my *younger* sister." Her voice cracked perfectly with just the right blend of anguish and conviction. She enjoyed baiting him, enjoyed watching him try to console her with all the finesse of a lumbering bear. He could be so damn predictable.

"I know, honey." His voice was rough, strained. "But she's in danger, and it would just kill me if anything happened to you."

She'd expected him to call her sweetheart, not honey. The mistake pricked at her like a splinter beneath the skin. Was she losing her edge? That wouldn't do. She forced a tremor into her voice. "I appreciate your concern, but family is what matters, right?"

He flushed under the pale light from the dashboard, the ruddy color creeping up his neck. He made the turn toward her gated community, tires splashing through fresh puddles. "Yes, I know. I'm sorry." His voice dropped lower, thick with guilt. "I didn't catch the guy tonight, but I will. I promise you. I'm not going to let anything happen to your sister. Or to you."

She bit back a smile. Laurel could take care of herself. Abigail had no doubt about that, and she'd never forget the way Laurel tackled her to protect her. She did feel sisterly toward Abigail but just couldn't admit it. But Wayne was so determined to prove his worth, so desperate to be the one who saved the day. She could almost taste his insecurity, sweet and sharp on the back of her tongue.

Every once in a while, Norrs became so predictable that Abigail thought about slitting his throat as he slept, just to relieve the tedium. But he still had his uses. So, for now, he lived. She reached over and took his hand, sliding her fingers over his calloused palm. "I always feel safe with you."

He coughed, the sound awkward and embarrassed, then nodded, his hand warm and solid around hers. "You should. I'll keep you safe, Abby. Always."

His confidence was misplaced, but she let him have it. It was amazing how easy he was to manipulate. He flicked a glance her way, eyes full of that raw sincerity he wore like armor. It almost made her feel something. Almost. Then he leaned forward and cranked the wipers up as the rain went feral, pounding the truck hard enough to make the frame complain.

"You're not in trouble, are you?" Abigail kept her voice soft. "Since we're, you know . . . engaged. I have been charged with murder."

Wayne shrugged one broad shoulder. "I had a discussion with my boss. Told him it was self-defense. And if it comes down to you or the job? I choose you every time."

She almost fluttered her eyelashes but chose to smile instead, letting him see just enough warmth to keep him hooked. "You are the sweetest." The words were easy, automatic. Inside, she was already calculating the consequences if he truly did leave his job for her. If he did, he was of no use to her. But as long as he remained useful, she'd play the role he wanted. "But you really must keep working for the FBI." She patted his hand, her touch light and reassuring. "We need you keeping us safe."

"I know, baby." He patted her thigh.

*Baby.* She should stab him for that alone. She cleared her throat. "You really do have an important job, and you can't be protecting me all the time. My house has an excellent security system. I think you should go back to the city tonight and keep trying to find the person targeting Laurel. I would never want to interfere with your work."

"Oh, hell no." His response was immediate, forceful. "I'm staying with you tonight, Abby. There's no way I'd leave you alone."

Damn it. That didn't fit in with her plans at all. She couldn't tell him he was smothering her because then he'd want to know why, and that just wouldn't do. "All right," she said softly, her fingers trailing over his knuckles. "But you have to promise me, tomorrow, if I stay home and secure, and away from Laurel, that you'll go do your job. It's imperative you find this maniac. I can't lose my sister, Wayne. I just can't."

"Of course. You have my word." His eyes softened, the fierce determination melting into something achingly genuine. "But I won't leave you uncovered."

She dipped her head. "You're too good to me." Tomorrow, she could get to work and find the shooter long before Wayne ever could.

She leaned over and kissed him on his rough cheek. "I'm so glad we're together." She put just the right amount of purr in her voice this time.

He grinned, his hand squeezing hers. "So am I."

She had to ditch him soon if she was right about what was happening . . . and she was always right.

# Chapter 27

After a fairly sleepless night, Walter Smudgeon listened as the rain hit his wooden roof with dull pings. He stood at his kitchen sink with a chipped coffee mug in one hand, watching steam curl off the surface. Dark roast. No cream. Not now that he was healthy.

He hadn't slept well after the sniper had dared shoot into their office the night before. This guy didn't care who he killed.

Behind Walter, the bedroom was quiet. He didn't need to turn to know Ena was still sprawled across his bed, long legs tangled in the sheet, one arm draped over the pillow. Her dark hair fanned across the white cotton like spilled ink. Who would've thought he'd fall for a younger Fish and Wildlife Officer who somehow liked him back? It was way too early to get serious since they hadn't been dating long. But he was serious.

She always looked peaceful in the morning. Peaceful and, honestly, a little dangerous.

He'd seen her take down a guy twice her size with a collapsible trout net once. Flipped him like she was landing a steelhead.

Walter took another sip, then checked the time. Almost eight in the morning. He needed to be at work by nine to head out and execute a warrant with Laurel and keep her from getting shot. Somehow.

He'd lived out about twenty minutes from Genesis Valley for six months now. One of his favorite things? The damn mail. Every morning, like clockwork, his rural route carrier came rumbling up the gravel road and dropped that day's envelope-shaped pile of junk, bills, or bad news into the black metal box nailed to the post at the end of his drive.

By eight in the morning, he had mail. Rain or shine.

He grabbed his coat, shrugged it on, and spared one last glance at the bedroom. Ena shifted in her sleep, the blanket sliding off one shoulder, baring smooth skin and the thin strap of her cami. He paused.

Damn, she was beautiful. Way prettier, kinder, and smarter than he deserved. She was part Japanese, and he was trying to learn the language. Just so he could someday propose to her in it. When was a good time? Was it too early? His best friend, besides Ena, was Laurel Snow, and she didn't understand relationships any better than he did. But it had to be way too early.

He thought, for the third time that week, about looking for an engagement ring, just in case. Ena didn't exactly scream "diamond solitaire," but he wasn't going to propose with a fishing lure. Even if she might appreciate that kind of practicality.

Let her sleep. It was her day off, and he had a quiet moment before everything inevitably turned to—

He opened the front door and froze. A man stood at his mailbox. The figure hunched low, hoodie up, one hand inside the black box, his box, like it didn't belong to a federal agent with a .40-caliber Glock and a mean hook.

"Hey!" Walter barked.

The guy spun and bolted.

Walter leaped down the porch steps in two strides, boots pounding wet earth, mud splashing up his jeans. The rain picked up. The guy slipped, scrambled, and ran like hell toward the tree line.

Walter gave chase.

His legs were longer. His boots were better. He'd chased men through strip clubs, cornfields, and once through a Mardi Gras parade in full riot gear. This? This was just cardio, and he was finally in the best shape of his life.

Until his mailbox exploded.

A sharp crack behind him split the air like a hammer to concrete. Walter ducked instinctively, pivoting in the mud as shrapnel hissed by like angry bees. His ears rang. Bits of charred paper drifted like snow.

He kept running.

The guy slipped at the creek line, fell hard, scrambled again. Walter tackled him from behind, both of them slamming into wet ground. Fists flew. Elbows. The guy had a knife—cheap, dull—but Walter yanked it away and flung it into the mud. Took a hit to the cheek, gave two to the ribs. Flippped the guy onto his gut.

"You idiot," Walter snarled, planting a knee on the guy's back. "You blew up a federal officer's mailbox. That's a felony in every zip code."

The guy thrashed. Young, maybe twenty. Skinny but wiry. Brown buzzed hair, jittery eyes, twitchy hands. Probably juiced up on something besides caffeine.

"Walt!" Ena's voice came from the porch—sharp, alert.

He looked up in time to see her sprint barefoot across the gravel in a camisole and sleep shorts, rain plastering her black hair to her shoulders. One of his handcuffs flew through the air. He caught it, still pinning the guy.

God, she looked good. Soaked, pissed, and hotter than hell. No makeup. Just raw beauty and a sharp mind that could cut through all the crap the world flung at a guy like a buzz saw.

He snapped the cuff onto one wrist, then the other, yanking the guy upright. "You picked the wrong address today, jackass."

Paper fluttered in the air. Something charred and curled landed at Walter's feet, partially soggy but still legible. He bent and picked it up. A scrap of what used to be an envelope. Inside, a half-burned note, blackened around the edges but clear enough in the center to make his gut tighten.

*They'll kill everyone, I'm afraid.*
*—Tyler*

Walter's fingers clenched around it. "Damn it, Tyler," he muttered.

Ena stepped closer, her focus on the note. "What is that?"

He held it up. "A dead man's warning."

The rest of the mail was toast. Ashes smeared across the driveway and into the grass. Bits of carbon curled in puddles. He could make out part of a bank logo on one scrap and something that might've once been a jury duty summons. The only thing intact was Tyler's note—and only because it had been sealed inside a plastic baggie.

Walter yanked the hoodie off his suspect's head. "Name."

"Screw you."

Walter grabbed a handful of wet sweatshirt and dragged him toward the FBI replacement vehicle he'd requisitioned—an older green SUV parked at the curb. "I can work with that."

The guy kicked, slipped, cursed all the way to the back of the rig. Walter flung open the hatch, shoved him inside, and slammed it shut. It wasn't regulation, but it was effective.

Rain poured down. Walter wiped a hand across his face, mud streaking his jaw. His left knuckle throbbed. Probably bruised. Maybe cracked.

Ena stepped up beside him, arms crossed over her chest, a dark strand of wet hair stuck to her cheek. "You okay?"

He looked at her. Really looked. Wet camisole. Flushed cheeks. Barefoot in the gravel. The woman had just sprinted outside and helped him subdue a suspect without flinching. "Yeah," he said. "I'm good."

She raised an eyebrow, sharp and amused. "You look like you wrestled a pig."

He glanced down at himself covered in mud, bleeding from one knuckle, soaked through. "Better-looking than a pig."

"That's debatable." She smirked.

He glanced back at the ruined mailbox, now a smoking crater with a bent post and scorched weeds. "That was a good mailbox."

"I'll get you another one."

He looked at her again. "*Kekkon shite kurenai*?" The words just burst out of him. Not planned. Probably not the right time.

She blinked. Standing in the rain, soaking wet, her body solid and strong. Her dark eyes studied him, searching for something he wasn't sure he had. Finally, she spoke. *"Hai, yorokonde."*

His mind shut down. What did that mean? He learned only so many of the words. Probably. "Um, that means yes?"

Her smile lightened the entire day. "Yes, Walter. That means yes."

After a morning of having Huck Rivers cover her body from the truck to her own conference room, Laurel was ready to seek out the sniper herself. Sighing, she looked away from her backup laptop at the out-of-place tabletop. In the overhead lights, with all blinds in the office closed, it gleamed an incongruent teal color. The conference room had no windows and only one point of entry. It allowed for uninterrupted focus and eliminated unnecessary risk. She had no reason to believe the sniper would strike again soon, but she also had no reason to ignore the possibility.

She'd just ended a phone call with Agent Norrs. He had asked about three of her prior cases: a corporate fraud investigation out of Boise, a cold case abduction in Reno, and an identity theft operation that had crossed into medical records territory in Portland. None were connected, and none had led to active threats. The man sounded as if he hadn't slept in days.

Laurel had already reexamined those cases when the sniper had first appeared on her radar. She had found no common thread. Either Norrs was grasping at patterns that did not exist, or he had access to information he was not prepared to share.

She made a note in her encrypted case file, flagged the call, and opened the subfolder on Melissa Palmtree. Taking a sip of her latte from Staggers, she dialed Dr. Ortega.

"Ortega," he answered.

She assumed he'd be in the office early. "Good morning. It's Agent Snow. I'm sorry to bother you, but—"

"I finished the autopsy on Melissa Palmtree, and I found suspicious lesions in her brain matter. I've sent samples to the lab in Seattle." He sneezed. "Excuse me. Allergies. I'm emailing you my findings right now."

Her inbox dinged. "Thank you." It was nice to find such a professional and one she trusted.

"You bet. I have to run. I'll call when I hear from the lab." He clicked off.

So, no surprises from Melissa's death. A single slip on the stairs in a crowded bar was plausible, and there had been no reason to question the cause of death initially. Yet those lesions had been found on her brain as well. She'd used the detective as a go-between with Mark Bitterson. Why? If she'd given him money, what had he given her? Did this have anything to do with the yew stand he'd been found dead in, or was that just a bizarre coincidence?

Laurel didn't believe in coincidences.

Nester rushed out of his room, down the hall, and into the conference room. His posture and facial expression indicated urgency. He carried a laptop and placed it directly in front of her without greeting. "Laurel. I have the bar footage from when Melissa Palmtree fell down the stairs."

Laurel moved her notebook to the side and turned her attention to the screen. "Was there difficulty obtaining it?"

"Yes. The system was proprietary and time stamp locked. I finally received clearance through a cooperating tech from the city's cyber unit."

Her breath quickened. "Has it been verified?"

"I ran hash integrity. No alterations. Time stamps align with Melissa Palmtree's time of death. It's legitimate." He opened the video file. Laurel adjusted her chair so the screen sat directly in her line of sight. Nester stepped back but remained behind the chair.

The footage displayed the interior of a moderately crowded bar in Seattle. The time stamp read just after ten at night. Laurel recognized the layout: two exits, and a hallway leading to the rear. The lighting was moderate, but the noise level was high—conversations bounced between tables and spilled out from the bar. Patrons appeared relaxed, and the atmosphere was consistent with a typical weekend night.

At 10:19, Tyler Griggs entered the frame.

Laurel gasped. What in the world was Tyler Griggs doing at the bar where Melissa had died?

Tyler did not scan the room. He walked with direct purpose to the far end of the bar, selected a stool, and checked his watch. He remained seated, made brief eye contact with the bartender, and ordered a drink that the bartender soon slid in front of him. Something with two straws and a lime.

At 10:20, Melissa Palmtree appeared. She paused just inside the entrance, performed a scan of the space, located Griggs, and walked directly to him. There was no hesitation in her approach. She did not look around the room for alternatives. She did not fumble with a bag or her coat. Her body language indicated she was focused and likely under stress, though not disoriented.

"So, that was planned," Nester mused.

Laurel nodded. Finally. The answer that tied Tyler to the lab. When Melissa reached him, she initiated conversation.

Griggs looked up and acknowledged her. His facial expression changed subtly—from drawn brows to open ones. From suspicion to surprise? When Melissa reached into her pocket and handed him something small, he took it without hesitation and concealed it beneath his jacket. The object was too small and dark to be identified on the footage, but was likely a flash drive or small folded document.

Melissa leaned closer to Tyler and spoke rapidly. Her hands began to shake, and she looked behind her twice in less than ten seconds. Griggs did not interrupt her. He absorbed what she said, then shifted slightly in his seat and looked toward the rear hallway.

At 10:23, Melissa touched the underside of her nose. Blood appeared almost instantly. She recoiled from the bar, her expression visibly shifting from urgency to fear. She said something to Tyler, possibly one or two words, and then turned and exited the frame at a fast speed.

Laurel waited.

A second camera picked her up in the rear hallway.

Melissa moved quickly. Her steps were uneven, and she collided with another patron without acknowledging the impact. She reached the top of the stairs, grabbed the railing with one hand, and then lost her footing. She fell forward, hit the first landing, and tumbled the rest of the way down.

The footage froze.

Laurel looked at the time stamp. The total time between her entrance and her death was under five minutes. "She sought Tyler out."

"Yes," Nester replied. "He arrived and checked his watch. They intended to meet."

"Can you zero in on whatever she passed to him?"

Nester grimaced. "Doubtful. The bar is dark and it was quick. He died, what? A night or two later?"

Laurel nodded. "We need to tie all of this together. Obviously she gave Tyler information. He was investigating so many conspiracies, so I don't want to assume anything. Could you conduct research concentrated on dementia treatments and the yew tree?" She thought through Tyler's warnings. "Also look for possible bioweapons that could be made with any extract." Tyler's warning of an attack wouldn't leave her mind.

"Sure. We should get some decent records from the lab when you execute the warrant later as well."

That was Laurel's plan. "Afterward, please go through the footage of that bar and see if anybody took an interest in either Melissa or Tyler. Expand the search to all CCTV in the area. If businesses aren't willing to assist, obtain a warrant."

"I'll try, and hopefully many of the places still have the footage from that night." Nester sneezed. "The warrant for Oakridge should be ready in a couple of hours. Do you want me to keep the Seattle office in the loop?"

Laurel was enjoying working with Agent Norrs. "Yes, please do. Thanks."

Kate called down the hallway. "Hey. Walter is here with a guy in handcuffs. Looks like they rolled in the mud together. They're on the way up."

# Chapter 28

Laurel studied the man across from her while Walter leaned against the doorframe of the conference room, his arms crossed. Mud coated his body, and he bled from a narrow scrape along his jawline.

Tom Foster stared at her, shifting like the chair bothered his muddy body. His hoodie was soaked through and still faintly singed. He smelled of wet leaves, burnt powder, and synthetic fabric that hadn't been washed in a long time. Nester had pulled his record: petty theft, drugs, vandalism, a long list of nothing important. Until now.

"You set off an explosive device in a federal mailbox," Laurel said. "Explain."

Tom blinked fast, then licked his lips. "I wasn't trying to blow anything up. It was just firecrackers. I didn't know the thing would actually go."

"You tampered with mail intended for a federal agent," she said.

He winced. "I didn't know it was his mailbox. Honest."

Walter pushed off the wall, stepping closer. "What exactly were you looking for?"

The suspect hesitated. "A letter. Maybe. The lady wasn't clear."

"What lady?" Walter growled.

"I don't know her name." Foster squirmed, the cuffs clinking faintly.

"She found me outside a bar in Elk Hollow. Said there might be an envelope showing up at a certain box at your address, and it needed to be taken."

Laurel twirled her pen in her hand. How did the woman know about the envelope? "What did she look like?"

He gulped. "I was kinda drunk. She was probably average height, slim, and wore a black hoodie and jeans? Sunglasses covered her eyes. White chick. Probably in her thirties or forties. Maybe fifties. I don't know."

"How did she find you?" Laurel asked.

Foster shrugged. "Hell if I know. I mean, I do have a reputation for getting things done."

Laurel seriously doubted that statement. She looked up, expecting fury on Walter's face. Instead, his eyes glimmered and a smile flashed for a second. He caught her gaze and sobered instantly. "What bar did she find you at?"

Foster picked mud off his chin. "I don't know the name. Neon owl sign. Cheap beer. She walked up while I was smoking."

"Did she tell you what might be in the envelope?" Walter asked, tone low and flat.

"Nope. She said it might show up and that I should watch for two weeks. Just look for the name of Tyler Griggs, or one without a return address. Or anything handwritten. But you didn't get anything like that. You get all junk and bills, man."

Walter snorted.

Laurel paused, looking up at him. He was amused?

He sobered again. "You didn't ask the woman any questions?"

Foster shifted his weight and winced. "She was offering five hundred bucks to grab a letter. Or destroy it if I couldn't. She paid half up front."

Walter took a step back, crossed his arms, then gave the faintest, briefest smile.

Laurel blinked. Noted it. Continued. "All right, Tom. Here's the deal. If you help us, we'll help you. Right now you're looking at a felony."

Foster groaned. "Dude. I was drunk. Didn't see her car, didn't even see her arrive or leave. I want to help. I do."

Walter glowered. "You're a moron."

There was the Walter Laurel adored. What in the world was going on with him?

"Ha," Foster said. "A moron wouldn't have brought firecrackers just in case he got caught, now would he? My job was to steal the info, and I would've, but you saw me. So I destroyed it."

The man *was* a moron.

Walter glowered. "You could've killed somebody."

Laurel shook her head. "So just to make sure I have this correctly. You carried out a potentially lethal act for an unnamed woman, on behalf of an anonymous sender, targeting a letter you weren't sure existed?"

Foster looked up at the ceiling and groaned. Loudly. "I know how it sounds."

"It sounds like conspiracy, tampering with federal property, and destruction of evidence," she said. "Among other probable crimes."

"I didn't mean to hurt anyone," he said, quieter now.

What had been in that box? Laurel glanced at the one remaining piece. *They'll kill everyone, I'm afraid.* It made sense that Tyler had sent his half brother, the FBI agent, information in case of his death. Why hadn't Laurel thought of that? Was her head still on vacation? Or did the sniper have her more concerned than she believed? At least Walter and Ena had tried to collect all of the pieces before the rain ruined them, and right now evidence techs were out at the scene. She wasn't holding out hope for anything substantial, though.

She pushed a notepad toward Foster. "You're going to write everything down. Physical description. Location. Exact time. Verbatim conversation if you can manage it."

Foster nodded and cast a glance over at Walter. "Hey. I'm not sure what happened between you and the tough-looking, dark-haired chick after you tackled me, but I feel like you asked an important question."

Walter glared at him.

Foster's Adam's apple bobbed. "That was in Chinese, right?"

"Japanese," Walter corrected.

"Same thing," Foster said.

Walter pushed away from the doorframe. "Not even close."

Foster glanced back at Laurel, picking up the pen. "Whatever he asked her—I'm pretty sure she said yes."

Laurel finished reading through all of the autopsy reports, part of her mind wondering what Walter had asked Ena, and the other part on the glass boards behind her. Nagging at her. Whispering at her to turn around and find the missing piece. Walter had taken Foster to the local jail for processing and to await bond since the FBI had an agreement with the local police. The U.S. Marshals would take over from there.

Huck walked inside, looking tall and broad in dark jeans, flak boots, a black T-shirt, and a Fish and Wildlife jacket. He carried a ballistic vest with one strong hand. "Hi. What's going on with Ena and Walter?"

Laurel sat back and studied his topaz eyes and rugged jawline. Did he get more good-looking every day, or did she become more enamored? Her continually growing attraction to him could be understood through a biological and evolutionary lens: as emotional bonds deepen, hormones like oxytocin and dopamine reinforce feelings of attachment and reward, subtly enhancing perceived physical attraction. From a biological anthropology standpoint, consistent displays of competence, protection, and emotional stability signal strong mate potential—traits historically linked to survival and reproductive success. Her brain, wired for long-term security, could associate his presence with safety and reliability, causing her perception of his attractiveness to intensify over time.

Or, he was just hot, as Kate would say.

Laurel pushed her laptop to the side. "I noticed Walter smiling at odd moments earlier in the interview. Supposedly he asked Ena a question in the Japanese language, and she might've said yes."

Huck's eyebrows rose. "They're engaged? They haven't been dating long."

"Not at all." She shrugged. "Walter went through a near-death experience and may be trying to get on with life, as my mother would say." She glanced at the vest. "Are you heading into hostile territory today?"

"Not yet. I haven't caught the bear bugging the Finderson Subdivision yet, but we dropped a bunch of doughnuts in the cage earlier today, so we'll get her. I'm coming with you to execute the warrant at that lab, and Officer Tso will be flanking your other side."

Laurel sat back in the chair. "I don't need bodyguards. If I did, I'd request them from the FBI."

"You didn't do so, so we're coming."

Laurel sought out his reasoning and then countered. "I'm a trained FBI agent, as is Walter. We don't need babysitters." It was a mite insulting, really.

"Someone keeps shooting at your head, Laurel." Huck's voice had an interesting manner of lowering quietly in a way that somehow sounded threatening.

She needed to learn that skill. "You're being illogical and overprotective. Our jobs can't interfere with each other's."

"We often work together, and I'm a trained sniper. I'll know if there's a scope on you."

That made zero sense. "You'll just feel it?"

"Yes." His tone sounded dead sure now.

With his experience, he'd probably note all good sniper positions, narrow in on them, and see movement or odd shapes. It wasn't instinct. He had training and field experience. Yet she couldn't allow this. "No. Huck—"

"You're my reason, Laurel." Simple words. Intense eyes. Sharply handsome face.

She blinked. "Your reason for what?"

"Everything." He lounged against the doorframe, appearing as if he could lunge in a second if danger rolled down the hallway. "Growing up, the wilderness was my reason. In the army, protecting this country kept me going. Afterward, I worked tough cases in Portland, lost one, and headed up to the mountains to live with my dog. You took me out of that comfortable and slightly lonely world. Dragged me back into this one. For you."

Her mouth slightly opened but no words emerged.

His grin was quick and then gone, replaced by more intensity. "I love you. I know you'll tell me all about hormones and biological imperatives that make us feel love. I don't care. I feel you in my bones. Deep. I'll kill for you and I'll die for you. Definitely take a bullet aimed at you. Not because of a baby we almost had, not because we're colleagues or even lovers. Because you're it for me. The reason I get up in the morning and double-check my security at night. I need you in this world with me. My reason."

"I love you, too." The words rolled out of her naturally before she could think.

He barked out a laugh. "You look shocked about that."

"I don't understand love like this," she said honestly.

"Don't need to. Just feel it and enjoy. And let me be me while I let you be you."

That appeared to be a fair request. "What if those two realities conflict?"

"Then we'll work it out. And how we're going to do so in this situation is that Tso and I are accompanying you and Walter to the building where somebody shot at you the other day. We'll stay out of the way unless I need to get in the way."

She'd already gotten two people shot, one dead, and she didn't want to lose the captain. "We're parking in the underground garage and going right up to the offices. We'll stay away from windows."

"Good plan. Walter is driving and you're sitting between me and Tso in the back seat on the way there." He glanced down at his watch. "I'll grab Tso. It's time to go."

Laurel watched him walk by the conference room windows to the hallway, a mite nonplussed.

She was *his reason*?

# Chapter 29

The security scanner buzzed with mechanical indifference as Laurel stepped into the marble-and-steel lobby of Oakridge Solutions after the guard had read the warrant and buzzed them up. She noted the scent first. Industrial-grade cleaner, faint traces of ethanol, and something organic. Not unusual for a biotech company.

Walter Smudgeon stood beside her, taller, broader, and already shifting his weight like he wanted to start knocking on doors. "Last time we were here, that sniper nearly got you."

Huck and Officer Tso stood behind them, looking like badass bodyguards. Tso was younger than Huck with angled features and dark hair. He'd moved to Washington State recently from Arizona and appeared to be in good shape.

"I know," she said softly, the skin on her neck prickling. They'd parked in the underground parking area and then taken the elevator to this floor. Even so, she scanned the entire area around them and was well prepared to stay away from windows.

They didn't wait long.

Dr. Bertra Yannish carried an air of importance this time. Wearing a lab coat with a sleek navy blouse beneath, she approached at a controlled pace. High heels, midrange designer. Minimal makeup. Calculated professionalism. "I understand you have a warrant."

Laurel nodded and handed it over. "Federal search warrant for full access to Oakridge Solutions' research labs and all supporting documentation in digital and hard copy." She smiled. "Walter and I are just the first wave. An FBI Evidence Response Team should be arriving within the hour to catalog the specimens and all data. We're here for a quick look and also to interview you as the new acting director, Dr. Yannish." A fact the guard had told Laurel.

"Please call me Bertra. I insist." Bertra skimmed the first few lines, her expression remaining neutral. "I'm more than happy to show you around." Her gaze lifted, and her eyes narrowed as she took in Huck and Tso. "Do you still have a sniper trying to kill you?"

"Yes," Laurel said.

Bertra's nostrils flared. "Then I object to this. Dr. Sandoval was my friend, and now he's dead. I don't want to join him."

Walter stepped in. "Just show us the labs. We don't need to be near any windows."

"The warrant is for the FBI and not Fish and Wildlife." Bertra glanced at Huck's jacket. "You two can stay here, and I promise we'll avoid all windows. I'd very much like to remain alive."

"We'll keep you safe," Walter promised.

Bertra looked him over, a little too slowly to be entirely clinical. "You weren't here last time, were you?"

"I was," Walter said, blinking. "I was the one who tackled Laurel to the floor."

Bertra's lips curled just slightly. "You do seem . . . protective."

Walter opened his mouth and then shut it. "I—uh—well, that's sort of the job."

Bertra's smile widened, but only for a moment. "Lucky Laurel."

Laurel didn't react. She turned and motioned forward. "Let's go."

Bertra turned to lead the way. Instead of taking them to the corporate offices like last time, they walked in silence down a corridor lined with locked doors. Laurel noted the badge scanner on each entry that required the key card plus biometric for the main labs. Clean tech, state-of-the-art. Oakridge Solutions was well-funded.

Inside the primary lab, sterile light reflected off steel countertops and glass storage cases. Laurel counted three fume hoods and two refrigerated storage units in use. The walls held framed posters of chemical maps with one featuring a taxane derivative. She paused. "You're using yew tree extract."

Bertra glanced over. "Yes. We utilize a modified taxane compound in very small doses, which we acquire legally through sustainable harvest partners." She gestured toward a file drawer. "We can provide documentation."

Laurel nodded once. "Taxanes are cytotoxic. What's the purpose here?"

"Tau protein stabilization. It's shown potential in slowing cognitive deterioration—particularly in early-stage Alzheimer's and other tauopathies."

Laurel knew all of this. "Side effects?"

"We're still in early phases. Animal testing and very controlled human trials under IRB."

Walter cleared his throat. "And none of those trials led to lesions on the brain?"

Bertra's expression didn't change. "Not as far as our internal data indicates."

Laurel didn't respond. She turned instead to the nearest workstation, scanning the terminal. "Log us in. I want access to batch records and compound storage logs."

Bertra stepped forward and entered her credentials. "You'll find all entries are time-stamped and validated."

"I expect to," Laurel said.

Walter moved toward the refrigeration units. "Any reason your inventory logs are two weeks behind?"

Bertra blinked. "They shouldn't be."

Laurel walked to the storage drawers along the back wall—custom stainless steel, magnet-sealed, temperature-controlled. She opened one to find vials labeled with both batch codes and shorthand compound names. Most were standard. One wasn't. "'RZ-3' isn't in the compound index," she said.

Bertra moved beside her. "It's a placeholder code from one of our early yew variants."

"Who had access?" Laurel asked.

Bertra hesitated, then said, "Myself. Dr. Liu. Dr. Sandoval before he was murdered."

Laurel didn't push further. Not yet. Instead, she followed Bertra into the next lab.

This one was darker with shades drawn over the windows. It was a more clinical environment involving less chemistry and more neurology. A digital whiteboard on the far wall displayed a time lapse of brain scans, highlighting plaque reduction over successive intervals. The MRI comparisons were impressive. But Laurel noticed something else. The earliest scans—the baseline—belonged to someone identified only as Subject 4C.

"Pull the file on 4C," she said.

Bertra didn't argue. She moved to a computer, typed for a moment, and within seconds, a redacted file appeared on the nearest screen.

"Where's the full name?" Walter asked.

"The trial's double-blind." Bertra squinted and studied the board. "This is of a monkey, as I'm sure you know. A very old one." She turned just slightly toward Walter as she added, "But you're probably used to decoding messy scans. Or maybe you just clean up the messes?"

Walter blinked, clearly not expecting the question. "Uh—I mostly do paperwork these days. Less mess."

Bertra gave him a small smile. "I find that hard to believe."

Was she flirting with Walter? Was that why he was blushing? A door across the lab opened, and a slender teen walked in, balancing a tray of pipettes. She wore an oversized white coat, sleeves rolled up at the wrists, with her hair twisted into a quick, no-nonsense bun. Laurel recognized her immediately. Viv Vuittron. Laurel had expressly told her to stay away from the lab.

Viv paused when she saw Laurel, her tray tilting just a hair before she recovered. She gave the smallest shake of her head, showing no expression, no fear. Just a quiet warning.

Bertra turned. "Oh, this is one of our after-school interns. The local high school runs a STEM pipeline program, and she's helping to catalog historical compound data."

Laurel tilted her head. "How long has that program been running?"

"A few months. We're selective. She's one of four. Mostly observational work," Bertra quickly. "This is Viv, who is working all day today because there's a teacher workday at school. She's a straight A student."

Laurel kept her gaze on Viv. The girl had no idea how dangerous this might be. "Who supervises them?"

"I do," Bertra said. "Our compliance officer signs off on all their hours."

Laurel nodded slowly, careful not to glance too long at Viv. "Four interns?"

"Yes."

"What kind of clearance do they have?"

"No clearance," Bertra said. "They can't access anything proprietary and provide mostly archival assistance and basic lab prep."

Viv didn't look at her again. She kept her head down and moved to a supply shelf, sorting tubes into racks. Efficient. Quiet. She was pretending not to listen, but Laurel had no doubt she was catching every word.

Bertra pointed at the door. "I'll show you one of our clean rooms now."

Viv looked up and gave a small smile. Laurel shot her one final look. They would certainly talk about this. Soon.

They moved to the clean room next to find positive air pressure and sealed cabinets. Two techs inside were suited up, moving vials into insulated trays. Laurel watched them for a full minute before turning to Bertra. "I want a list of every compound those two are handling, and I want the current batch numbers cross-referenced with export logs, and I expect the evidence team to secure samples."

"Your warrant doesn't include samples, and our attorneys will fight you under trade secret law," Bertra said.

Most likely. "Show us the rest of the area, and then let's retire to a conference room. I'd like to interview you," Laurel said.

They continued the walk lab to lab, finding each one more specialized. Clean rooms. Observation bays. Testing suites with treadmills and biometric scanners.

Laurel continued walking. "When did your last internal audit take place?"

"Two months ago."

Laurel couldn't read the woman. "Results?"

"Standard issues. Some chemical waste mislabeling. Nothing unusual."

Walter focused on her. "Please provide the report along with the other requested data. You have one week, according to the warrant."

Bertra gave him a sidelong glance. "One week? That's generous. But I'm sure you're very reasonable . . . when you want to be."

Walter cleared his throat and looked straight ahead.

They returned to the main hallway, where a security guard passed with a clipboard, nodded, and moved on.

Laurel stared at her. "We'll need your full internal calendar for the next ten days. Meetings. Deliveries. Anything marked as restricted access."

"Of course." Bertra gestured them into a high-end conference room outside of the labs. One secure and without windows. "I'll include that with all of the data you wish for me to collect. This is going to take some time."

Laurel drew out a chair as the other two did the same. "Do any of your studies create lesions on the brain?"

"Of course not," Bertra said.

"Interesting." Laurel pulled a folder from her satchel and tossed pictures onto the smooth marble table. "Dr. Miriam Liu. Tyler Griggs. Mark Bitterson. Melissa Palmtree. All of these people had lesions on their brains. We don't know about Larry Scott because he was cremated."

Bertra took a moment too long before responding. "Dr. Liu died in a car accident, and Melissa Palmtree fell down a staircase and broke her neck. I heard that Larry Scott killed himself." She frowned, looking up. "Lesions? What lesions?"

"Melissa's body was exhumed last week," Laurel said. "Toxicology revealed chemical traces not explained by recreational use or prescription medication. There were similarities to taxane derivatives discovered."

"That's—" Bertra stopped herself. "I'd need to see that report." The woman paled.

Was she exhibiting surprise or fear? Laurel wasn't sure. "Tell me about Mark Bitterson and Tyler Griggs."

Bertra shook her head. "I've never heard of either of those people."

"Tyler Griggs was a conspiracy podcaster who met with Melissa Palmtree on the night of her death. My guess is that she had something of import to tell him. How about you avoid the federal death penalty and get out ahead of this?" Walter suggested nicely.

Bertra glanced at her phone. "I've already called in my lawyer. He should be here soon."

"You're not in custody and can leave anytime," Laurel noted. "For now, how about you tell us about Elk Hollow Detective Robertson?"

Bertra blinked and a light pink filtered beneath her cheekbones. "Who?"

"Detective Joshua Robertson. He worked security here and functioned as a courier between Melissa Palmtree and Mark Bitterson, who I believe secured stolen yew tree compounds for you." It was a guess and a bluff, but Laurel needed answers.

"A security guard isn't something I'd be looped in on," Bertra said. "Again—logistics. And as for your accusation, we don't utilize stolen samples of anything. You'll find that to be true once you go through the mountainous amount of documents you've requested."

Her phone buzzed and she read the screen. She smiled, then glanced at Walter. "Excellent. Our attorney is on his way down. I hope he's as charming as your partner here."

Walter coughed lightly. "I—uh—don't usually get mentioned in legal strategy."

Bertra tilted her head. "Maybe you should. You're much easier to look at than your average federal agent."

What was happening with the flirting? "One more question," Laurel said smoothly. "What's going to happen here that got Tyler Griggs killed?"

Bertra looked up. "I have no idea what you're talking about."

Laurel studied her. Her tone hadn't changed. Her posture hadn't shifted. But her breathing and blink rate had accelerated. Barely—but enough.

"You have no plans for an event or a test that might be dangerous?"

Bertra drew back. "No."

Movement sounded and then Henry Vexler strode inside, this time wearing a dark brown and silky-looking suit with a red power tie. "I'm attacking the warrant. This interview is over."

Laurel lifted her head. "What a surprise." She cocked her head. Vexler had discovered the investigation into Detective Robertson from Rachel and Sandra. How in the world had he learned about this? "How long have you represented Oakridge Solutions?"

He smiled perfectly pearly white teeth. "That's none of your concern."

Either the man had a source inside the FBI, or— Wait a minute. Laurel reached for her phone and texted Agent Norrs: Did you tell Abigail about the warrant for Oakridge Solutions Labs? It would behoove Abigail to have her attorney mess with Laurel's head for the next couple of weeks.

Not sure. Might have mentioned it in passing. Why?

In passing? Right. For goodness' sakes. That man was truly lost. Because her lawyer is here messing up my investigation.

Agent Norrs didn't answer again.

Vexler leaned against the doorjamb. "How about we make a deal? I'll let you continue questioning my client, so long as I get to ask questions of you as well."

Laurel stood and smiled at Dr. Yannish. "You're not his focus and should secure alternative representation."

Bertra slowly turned her head to look at Vexler. "Is this true?"

His smile didn't dim. "Not in the slightest. I'm very capable of multitasking." He gave one slow wink. "Agent Snow, you and I are going to become very close. You might as well give in now."

# Chapter 30

The SUV idled in the far corner of Red Rocket Burgers, where the parking lot gravel gave way to dry weeds and empty soda cups. The sun was low and orange behind the hills, casting long shadows and bathing the cracked pavement in gold.

Laurel Snow sat in the back of her own SUV, wedged between Huck Rivers and Officer Tso. Walter was at the wheel, his gaze scanning every car that passed on the two-lane road in front of them. The windows were cracked, as the rain had finally let up.

Laurel picked at a cooling container of fries, more out of habit than hunger.

"Tell us about the labs," Huck said, finishing his burger.

"We found yew tree derivatives in the lab," she said, her voice low. "Mostly alkaloids with neuroprotective potential—early stage compounds. They're testing them for dementia. Legit research, by the looks of it."

Huck glanced at her. "Nothing that would hurt anyone?"

She shook her head. "No sign of human trials. No pathogens, no toxins, and nothing biohazardous was found. We discovered no trace evidence that connects to the deaths. The place was spotless."

Huck chewed a fry like it had personally offended him. "What about the Defense Department contracts?"

"There are random procurement records," Laurel said. "We found nothing to do with the yew compounds, but the evidence response team might find more than we did. They'll have mountains of paperwork to go through." She checked the clock. "She should've passed by now."

"She will," Walter said without turning.

"I shouldn't have left her," Laurel muttered. "I hate this."

Huck looked over. "She's not alone. We're five minutes away."

"She's sixteen," Laurel snapped, then softened her tone. "She thinks she's part of the team. She is. But she shouldn't be out there alone, playing undercover."

Walter looked over his shoulder at her. "Are you going to tell Kate?"

Laurel winced. "I think I'm supposed to, right? Kate is my friend, and she runs our office. Viv is a smart and ambitious girl, but nobody goes undercover without a full backup in place. I'm hoping Viv will tell Kate."

Then Walter straightened a little in his seat. "Subaru. Coming in from the south."

Laurel leaned forward between the seats. A battered Subaru trundled past the burger joint at a steady speed—rear fender held by duct tape, one hubcap missing. Familiar. That was Viv's boyfriend's car. "That's her."

Walter pulled onto the road, moving up on the vehicle and flashing his lights. Viv looked in the rearview mirror and then waved. She drove another half mile before signaling and turning into the gravel lot of a rundown tire shop. Laurel let out a quiet breath as Walter eased the SUV forward and parked behind the Subaru, engine still running.

Huck's voice was quiet. "Stay in the middle. Tso? Go get the keys from Nancy Drew there and follow us back to the office."

Officer Tso stepped gracefully from the vehicle, shut the door, and walked to the Subaru. Laurel nodded, lips pressed together. She watched through the windshield as Viv stepped out of the Subaru, hoodie sleeves pushed up, messy bun lopsided, eyes bright. She wasn't nervous. She looked excited like she had something to tell them.

Officer Tso didn't need to say much and just held out his hand.

Viv placed the keys in his palm without hesitation. Laurel watched her closely. No attitude. No fear. Just energy and purpose showed on her face.

Tso nodded toward the SUV. Viv gave a small smile and jogged over, climbing into the front passenger seat and looking back at Laurel.

Laurel exhaled as relief filled her. The nearby trees swayed in the early evening breeze, skeletal pines casting long shadows across the gravel lot. A minivan rumbled past on the road, its side door held shut with bungee cords.

Laurel focused back on Viv. "What in the world were you thinking?"

Viv grinned, apparently a little breathless from the excitement of it all. "I've been working there for a few months, so me checking things out was easy."

Laurel shook her head slowly. "Viv? There are protocols for going undercover. You broke all of them."

The girl rolled her eyes. "Seriously? Nobody would suspect me. All I did was nose around a little bit more than usual."

Walter started the engine and pulled out into the street.

Huck leaned forward, his voice low and firm. "A sniper shot into those offices just the other day. You will not go back. Call them and say your schedule doesn't allow for the internship and that you're very sorry."

Viv frowned. Most people folded when Huck used that voice. She didn't, not quite, but her energy dipped. "I actually had fun today," she said. "And I think I was helpful."

Laurel watched her carefully. Viv looked so young all of a sudden, despite the sharp mind and fast mouth. Too young to be anywhere near this. Her stomach twisted. This was on her—Laurel was the one who'd encouraged her. Encouraged all three girls to follow their interests, really. Pushed Viv toward law enforcement and criminal justice. Toward this world.

Was that a mistake?

Laurel wasn't accustomed to kids. Never had been one, not really. She'd skipped childhood by being so much younger than everyone else at school. But somewhere along the way, she'd gotten close to this one and her sisters. Close enough that the fear had a name now. It wasn't just worry. It was responsibility.

And the worst part was, she wasn't sure what the right move was anymore. "Does your mom know about your afternoon?" she asked, her voice gentling.

Viv paled.

"That's what I thought," Laurel said. "I appreciate your initiative, but it's too dangerous. I'm sorry, Viv."

The girl nodded, not happy, but not pushing back either. That helped. A little.

Laurel hesitated, trying to shift the weight off her chest. "However . . . did you find out anything interesting today?"

"Yes." Viv hopped in her seat. "Seriously. Nobody pays attention to interns, so I kind of had free run of the place. The techs aren't careful at all about the security panels. I just walked inside after a couple of them. Not the clean rooms, but the rest. It was awesome."

Laurel shook her head. "Viv. Your mother was kidnapped in an earlier case, and it hit the news. You have the same last name. If anybody at the lab really takes a deep look at you, they'll know your mom works for the FBI. You are not going back."

"Fine." Viv groaned. "But for now, guess what? There's a door on the bottom fourth floor, to the side of the clean room, that you can barely see. Did you see it during the tour?"

"No." Laurel took out her phone and typed out a quick text to the evidence team to find the door and go through it. "Did anybody see you down there?"

Viv shrugged. "Sure, but like I said, nobody paid me much attention."

Huck dug into the bag at his feet and handed a cheeseburger to the girl. "What else?"

She unwrapped it, smiling. "I had lunch in the break room, and I'd say that Bertra isn't very well liked. She's running the facility, and most folks don't seem to like her."

"Why not?" Laurel asked.

"She runs everything. Staff rotation, lab access, internal security. She's polite, but everyone acts like she might pull the floor out from under them at any second. People are tense. Real tense."

Huck eyed the bag. They'd bought tons of burgers. "Anyone say it out loud?"

Viv gave a small nod. "One lady named Jane joked that Bertra probably hired the sniper who took out Sandoval. People laughed, then got real quiet."

"And Dr. Liu?" Laurel asked.

"I asked three people about her. One said she didn't know, and the other two just walked away. One of them looked . . . scared. Not annoyed. Scared." Viv pushed her hair away from her eyes. "Everyone believes that Melissa Palmtree died by falling down those stairs, and that Larry died by suicide. There are no whispers about either of them."

Laurel exchanged a glance with Huck.

Viv wasn't finished. "I think I stumbled onto something else, too."

"Go on," Laurel said.

"I went to Bertra's office and the door was cracked. She was talking to a guy named John Fitz. He was wearing a lab coat and his badge showed he had top clearance, but that's the only time I saw him. Bertra was mentioning something about moving the next round to the other lab, but she stopped talking when I stepped in."

Huck's eyes narrowed. "So you are on her radar."

Viv shook her head. "Not at all. I played dumb and said I was ready for my next assignment. She bought it, I think."

As they pulled into their parking lot, Laurel spotted Kate's Volkswagen Bug parked to the right of the doorway. "Let's go up and let your mom know about your afternoon. Then I want you to run me through the entire day again, step by step, with names and faces. I'd also like descriptions if you have them."

Viv exhaled next to her, shoulders slumping a little. "Great," she murmured, and looked away, out the passenger window. Her phone buzzed in her hoodie pocket, and she pulled it out to read the screen. "It's from Oakridge Solutions."

Laurel's eyes snapped to the screen. "Please answer and put it on speaker so we can all hear."

Viv obeyed, swiping to connect and holding the phone between them. "Hello?"

Bertra's voice poured through the speaker, smooth and cultured. "Vivienne, I just wanted to personally tell you what a fantastic job you've been doing lately. The team has been very impressed. You have asked thoughtful questions, you've kept up, and you've showed real initiative. We don't see that very often at your age."

Viv swallowed, glancing back at Laurel, then Huck. Her voice was small. "Thank you."

"I'd like you to come in early tomorrow," Bertra continued. "Very early. There's a special project I want you on. I'd like to brief you myself before the others arrive, and we'll get you to school on time."

Laurel stiffened. Huck's expression visibly darkened.

Viv glowed. "What time? I have class at eight."

"How about six?" Bertra cut in, still sounding chipper. "This is a rare opportunity, and I think you're uniquely suited for it. I could really use your help."

Viv blinked, excitement flushing her face.

Laurel sharply shook her head. What was Bertra up to? Did she know Viv had snooped around?

Viv frowned.

Huck placed a hand on the back of Walter's seat, leaning in to stare at the girl.

Viv sighed. "I'm sorry. I don't think I can make it."

"I must insist," Bertra said. "We need you."

Laurel stared at the screen and then gave a short nod.

A smile burst across Viv's face. "All right. I'll be there at six."

"Excellent." Bertra ended the call.

The line went dead.

Silence filled the SUV.

Huck looked at Laurel. "Well?"

Laurel wasn't going to allow Viv to be in danger again. "I don't like this. Viv? You are absolutely not going back to that lab." She looked at Huck. "I can send them out of town on vacation."

Viv winced. "I have practice after school, Vida has a piano recital tomorrow night, Val has a test on Friday, and then I have a big game this weekend. We can't miss those."

Laurel sighed. "Huck? Can you spare someone to be on her through the weekend?"

Huck nodded. "Tso and Jordan could rotate as cover for Viv."

Viv slapped her hand to her head. "My mom is going to kill me."

Huck handed the bag of food to the girl. "Give her a burger. Maybe she won't be so pissed."

Viv took the bag. "Ha. I wish."

# Chapter 31

After an uneventful night where Huck kept his girlfriend from being shot in the head, he clicked off his cell in his office. Finally. Damn bear. Grabbing his coat, he whistled for Aeneas and strode through the office, reaching Ena at the front desk. "A resident reported in at the subdivision and we have the bear. I'm headed out to get her now."

Ena glowed. "That's wonderful."

Huck couldn't take it any longer. She was practically swinging her hips. "What's going on with you?"

"Walter proposed."

"Ah." Yeah, that was the rumor. They hadn't dated long. At all. "Congrats. When's the date?"

She shrugged. "Haven't set one. We've only been dating for a couple of months. There's no hurry, Huck."

That was good to hear. "I'll be back in a few hours." He considered taking one of the other officers but figured he'd take Laurel instead. He'd found that changing locations often, especially to places not normally frequented, was a good idea. He pushed open his door and moved to the FBI office door, scanning in his ID. Oh, he probably wasn't supposed to have one to the FBI office, but Kate had tired of buzzing him in so often that she'd just given it to him.

He climbed the stairs, walking through the open doorway and finding Laurel in the conference room, her butt on the fifties-style table. She faced the three glass boards: one with her face, an unknown sniper, and several pictures of subjects. The next with the lab and all of the victims with lines connecting them, and the final one of Abigail and her multiple crimes. "See anything?"

"Not yet," Laurel murmured. "They're getting blurred together. It's annoying."

No doubt. "I see you have a few suspects for the sniper finally."

She shrugged one slim shoulder beneath a white sweater she'd paired with dark slacks. "Agent Norrs sent them over. I don't see it, but he's working this constantly while guarding Abigail at all times, so I'm not going to argue."

Man, he bet Abigail hated that. No doubt she'd tried to get rid of Norrs a few times, but the guy was like a bulldog. "You don't think she'd kill him, do you?"

"Only if it served her purposes, whatever those might be." Laurel sighed. "I'm not seeing the pattern."

"How would you like to get out of here and scare a bear this fine morning?"

She looked over her shoulder at him. "A bear?"

"Yep. I'll show you what Aeneas was bred to do." He leaned down and scratched the dog behind his ears. "I've also mapped out several locations around the illegally harvested yew trees for us to search. I was thinking—if you had a hidden and secret lab that used the trees, wouldn't you want it close?"

Her eyes widened. "I truly would. Why didn't I think of that?"

"You can't think of everything. You just found out there was a second lab, maybe, last night." Sometimes she was too hard on herself. "Let's go. I'll cover you to the truck." He'd already checked and there was nobody out there, even behind the building where he now had lights and cameras at the ready. "The sniper, if he's still around, won't think to look for you in bear territory." And Huck knew when he was being followed.

"Okay. I'll get my coat." She hustled out of the room.

He waited until she returned and then escorted her down the stairs, making sure to keep his body between her and any danger. The spring day held a blue sky and a lukewarm sun, but at least the rain had finally stopped. Once in his truck, he drove out onto the main road and then around the river, staying quiet as he let her mull through her thoughts.

Nobody followed him.

He found the bear nicely in the cage with frosting all over its mouth. He thanked the neighbors, hooked the cage to the back of his truck, and rejoined Laurel. "We'll take her about twenty miles up into the mountain and let her go. Be prepared to make some noise." He glanced at her. While she appeared to be all brain, she had a huge heart. "We'll scare her but it's for her own good."

"I know," Laurel murmured, watching the trees fly by outside. "We want to associate people and danger to her so she stays away from homes."

Of course she understood.

He soon reached a good area where the bear could head into the woods where there was plenty of food and a great stream with fish. Huck killed the engine, and an encompassing silence settled, broken only by the distant calls of awakening birds. Turning to Laurel, he instructed, "Stay in the cab until we're ready. Safety first."

He exited the vehicle, and Aeneas leaped down beside him, muscles taut with anticipation. Together, they approached the cage. The bear charged the door and bounced off. She was a good-sized one.

Huck glanced at Aeneas, who responded with a focused stance, ready to do his job.

"Okay, Laurel," he called out. "Go ahead and come out. I want you in the back of the truck, gun out."

She followed his instructions, curiosity glimmering in her stunning eyes. She climbed into the back of the truck. "I'm ready."

"Great. All you need to do is jump up and down and make a lot of noise. I'll shoot into the air." Huck unlatched the cage door and swung it open. The bear hesitated. Seizing the moment, Huck fired a shot into the air, and the sharp crack echoed through the trees. Simultaneously, he and Laurel shouted loudly, their voices merging into a clamor designed to instill fear. Aeneas barked fiercely, sounding happy to be back at work.

Startled into action, the bear lunged from the cage, eyes wide with alarm. It bolted toward the forest, claws tearing into the earth. Aeneas pursued briefly, nipping at the bear's heels, reinforcing the lesson, barking wildly with no fear. After a short chase, Huck called Aeneas back, and the dog returned promptly, mission accomplished.

Laurel laughed. "Textbook execution," she remarked, admiration in her tone.

Huck nodded, scanning the treeline. "It's about reinforcing boundaries," he replied. "With luck, she'll steer clear of human settlements from now on."

Aeneas sat beside Huck, panting lightly, his gaze fixed on the point where the bear had disappeared. The forest gradually returned to its natural rhythm, the brief disturbance fading into the vast expanse of wilderness.

Laurel looked around. "You asked me earlier? What about you? Where would you hide a secret lab?"

"I'm not sure, but I'd search from the air. Why don't we take a look around, enjoy the spring day, and then try from a helicopter tomorrow?" If there was even a hidden lab anywhere close by. The lab could be in Seattle.

She smiled, looking more relaxed than she had in days. "That sounds like a nice day. Well, unless we find the lab." Her brows drew down. "I hope we find it. I don't like Tyler's warning."

"Yeah, me either." Huck walked down the side of the truck, leaned over, and lifted her, allowing her to slide down him until she reached the ground.

She reached over the side for her gun carrier. "If we take everything at face value, we have a lab creating some sort of dementia cure that might have a side effect of creating lesions in the brain that kill people. So it could be a weapon as well."

That's what he thought. His gut turned over. "So an attack would mean . . ."

"They might be trying to test it. On a population." She paled. "This is just conjecture."

But it was the only explanation that made sense. "We have to find that lab."

* * *

The aluminum bat cracked against the ball, sending a line drive straight toward third base. Viv crouched, gloved it clean, and fired to first, the ball popping into the mitt before the runner was halfway down the line.

"Nice one, Viv," Tatum called from shortstop, her red ponytail bouncing as she jogged toward Viv. She was a cute sophomore with a scattering of freckles across her nose and a wicked arm that was deadly on double plays. She leaned in, smirking. "You know the cop watching from the dugout? Kinda hot."

Viv glanced toward the dugout. Officer Tso sat alone on the wooden bench, arms crossed, sunglasses tucked into his collar. He looked fit beneath the Fish and Wildlife jacket. Not exactly "hot," in Viv's opinion, but solid. Steady. The kind of guy who saw more than he let on. He gave a quick nod as her gaze met his, and Viv looked away before he could read too much in her expression.

She wasn't used to being watched. Not like this.

Coach Weaver called, nodding with approval as she tucked her clipboard under her arm. "All right, hustle it in. Batting practice next."

Viv motioned to the school. She needed to use the bathroom.

Tso frowned.

Viv wiped her forehead and gave him a short wave to signal she was fine. Not disappearing. Not running back to the lab. She just needed to hit the restroom.

Coach blew the whistle. "Batting lineup in five!"

Viv jogged past the benches, peeled off toward the locker room, and pushed the door open. The scent inside hit her instantly: a mix of lemon disinfectant, fabric softener, sweat, and someone's too-sweet cherry body spray. Her cleats clicked over the tile as she headed straight to the bathroom.

Her bladder was screaming.

The light in the bathroom flickered once. She ignored it and ducked into the first stall. Quick, no time to mess around. She'd be first up for batting if Tatum volunteered to catch again.

She flushed, stepped out, and walked to the sink. The mirror was cracked along the top edge, warped enough to stretch her reflection. She washed her hands, still half-focused on timing and swing mechanics.

Then she looked up.

John Fitz stood in the doorway.

He looked exactly as she remembered. Short. Round. Hair combed too neatly. Like someone's weird uncle who talked too close. His Oakridge Solutions ID wasn't clipped to his collar now. There was no mask of professionalism. Only purpose.

Her heart hit once, hard. "Wrong room." She'd left her phone in the dugout. She didn't take her eyes off him.

His answer was silence.

And then he moved.

Viv pivoted and bolted for the door. He was faster than he looked. She hit the tile hard when he grabbed her from behind and slammed her against the wall near the showers. Her shoulder cracked the tile. The sting registered distantly.

She twisted and slammed an elbow into his ribs. He grunted but didn't let go. His hand clamped over her mouth as she tried to scream.

The smell of him hit her next. Chemicals. Rubber gloves. Something sharp and acidic beneath the surface.

He shoved her into the corner. She kicked his shin, hard, and tried to scratch his eyes, but he turned at the last second, and slammed her against the bathroom mirror. The glass didn't break, but it shuddered.

Viv struggled harder, muscles burning.

"Should've kept your nose out of it," he muttered, breath hot on her ear. "Little girls don't belong in grown-up places."

Viv bit his palm.

He cursed and jerked her sideways, toward the narrow window above the second sink. It was half open from earlier in the day. She kicked and shoved, but he was stronger than he looked, all solid muscle beneath the round frame.

Her hip hit the sink hard. Her fingers scraped porcelain. Her voice rose in her throat, but he caught her again, slamming her head to the side just enough to daze her.

The last thing she felt before the cold hit was his grip on her sweatshirt collar.

Then they were out the window.

The glass exploded around them as he dragged her through it. Her arm slashed against the frame. Her cleats caught nothing but air. She hit the ground hard, breath punched out of her lungs.

Viv rolled, twisted, tried to crawl. He grabbed her ankle and yanked her back.

She opened her mouth again to scream.

His hand clamped down, and the darkness rushed in. She whimpered once and then was out.

# Chapter 32

The phone buzzed on Huck Rivers's belt as he crossed the hallway outside the evidence room. He checked the caller ID and answered before the second ring. "Hi, Tso," he said.

"She's gone," Officer Tso said, his voice ragged. "Viv—she went into the locker room. I watched the door. I swear I watched it, Huck. I thought I was watching it. Five minutes. Maybe less."

Huck stopped walking. His spine locked. "Slow down," he said, though his body had already gone cold. "What do you mean 'gone'?"

"She didn't come out. I went in after her. The window was blown out. There's blood—small trail outside the frame. Her bag's still here. She didn't leave."

Huck didn't speak for a beat. He just breathed. Then he was moving. "I'm calling it," he said. "Full response. You stay put and lock that field down. Nobody in or out. Understand?"

Tso's breath hitched. "Understood."

Huck ended the call and hit the button on his shoulder mic. "Dispatch, this is Rivers. We've got a confirmed abduction. Victim is Viv Vuittron. Sixteen years old, white female, blond, five-seven, softball gear last seen. Pull up her DMV profile and get it moving to State,

FBI, Highway Patrol. Set up perimeter and drone support now. I want eyes in the sky in five minutes."

He scanned his ID and ran up the stairs, barreling through the opening toward the conference room. Handwritten notes, medical research records, and map printouts fanned out between coffee mugs and energy bar wrappers on the conference table. Laurel stood by a board, arms crossed, scanning names and timelines. Kate sat across the table, typing slowly on her laptop, brow furrowed.

Huck paused in the doorway, struggling for the right words.

Laurel looked up first. Her eyes narrowed at his expression.

Kate kept typing.

He stepped into the room, his voice low. "Kate."

She looked up. "Yeah?"

He walked closer, not rushed, not loud. He crouched slightly to her eye level. "I need you to listen to me carefully. Viv's missing."

Kate blinked once.

He kept his voice steady. "She went into the locker room at softball practice. Tso was on watch. She didn't come out. The window's broken. There's a little blood. We don't know what happened yet, but we're treating it as an abduction."

Kate didn't move for three full seconds. Then she stood up so fast her chair tipped back and clattered to the floor. "No," she said. "No, she wouldn't—she wouldn't just disappear. Not from softball practice."

Laurel moved to her side. "Kate. Stop. Breathe."

"I have to go. I need to be there. Need to see—" Kate's voice cracked and broke, her hands fluttering at her sides like they didn't know what to do.

"You can't help right now," Laurel said softly. "But we will. Huck and I are going. We'll find her."

Kate looked between them, her face crumpling, then dropped into the nearest chair like her strings had been cut.

Laurel turned to Huck. "What do we have?"

"Tso called it in. She went in for the bathroom. Never came out. He checked the locker room. Window's busted. Blood on the frame. Her bag is still there, and she left her phone in the dugout."

"Surveillance?"

Huck kept his tone calm. "None from the field. I've got officers locking down the parking lot, and patrol's canvassing the surrounding businesses."

Laurel pulled her gun from her bag. "We start at the school. I want to talk to every coach, every player, every janitor who's clocked in this week. Someone had to have seen a strange face."

"I've got uniforms securing the scene and a mobile command post setting up in the parking lot," Huck added. "Drone support's airborne by now. K9 en route, and Aeneas and I will also search."

"Good. We'll run parallel," Laurel said, moving fast now. "You coordinate field ops. I'll start with staff interviews. Pull class rosters, visitor logs, lunch vendors, field maintenance. Anyone who had reason to be near that locker room today."

Huck turned. "Traffic cameras?"

"I'm calling cyber on the way. I want every plate that passed the lot in the last two hours." Laurel paused at the door and glanced back at Kate, who sat frozen in the chair, face pale, fingers gripping the armrests like they were the only thing keeping her upright. "I'll bring her back."

Kate leaped up. "I'm coming with you. I have to."

"Understood," Laurel said. "Huck, have Ena get the other two girls and bring them here. Just in case." She pulled her phone out and called the Seattle field office.

Norrs instantly answered, and she gave him the information. "I need you to get Bertra Yannish and John Fitz from Oakridge Solutions and bring them here. They might've figured out Viv was investigating them earlier. This is too much of a coincidence. Take them from their homes. Fast."

The office smelled like burned coffee.

Laurel chugged up the stairs at six a.m., her clothes stiff from dried sweat and mud, her brain thick with exhaustion that had long since turned into something brittle. She hadn't slept. None of them had. She tossed her jacket over the back of Kate's empty chair and took several deep breaths before heading back to the conference room.

They'd been out all night.

Interviews. Field checks. Surveillance footage. They'd talked to every coach, every teammate, two janitors, the vending machine guy, and a substitute teacher who claimed he didn't know practice had been happening at all. Laurel had chased leads through parking lots, crawled under bleachers, and reviewed hours of low-res surveillance from four different school-facing businesses.

One camera, angled badly over a loading dock behind a used bookstore, had caught a man walking past the back of the field around 4:53 p.m.

Hood up. Ball cap low. Face turned from the lens every time.

She'd watched it seven times and still couldn't identify him.

The Seattle FBI Field Office was currently searching Oakridge Solutions, and she trusted that Agent Norrs had sent the right agents to do the job.

She pressed her face with both hands, hard enough to see stars. Her head pounded behind her eyes. Her mouth tasted like metal, and fear made her skin tingle. Where was Viv? They needed to find a lab that might not exist.

Kate was home, locked in with her two remaining girls and a rotating pair of deputies outside the door. Huck had taken over command for the morning, splitting personnel into new search zones. Still nothing. No calls. No demands. No Viv.

Just a sixteen-year-old girl somewhere out there in the dark with a possible attack coming.

Gathering herself, Laurel strode down the hallway and stopped at the conference room, where two broad male Seattle FBI agents with buzz cuts and sharp eyes took point with Dr. Bertra Yannish sitting across the table, scrolling on her phone. Apparently they'd allowed her to get dressed because she wore jeans and a light purple sweater with her blond hair up in a ponytail.

She looked up. "This is an outrage. I was interviewed by a bulldog of an FBI agent for two hours. I shouldn't still be here."

Norrs had questioned her and then headed out to help with the search after hitting a stone wall, as he'd put it over the phone. Laurel pulled out a chair and sat. "Where is your other lab? Speak now, or you'll go to prison for the rest of your life."

Bertra's eyes narrowed. "What lab?"

"Don't lie to me. You know Viv heard you talk about it, and now you've orchestrated her kidnapping. Where is John Fitz, anyway?" Apparently he hadn't been at home or the office, and he lived alone. His phone hadn't pinged a location either. So it must be off.

"I have no idea." Bertra tapped her nails on the glass. Nervousness? Maybe.

"Excuse me." Henry Vexler strode inside, rubbing his hands together as if he'd just washed them. Had he been in the bathroom? "You can't interview my client without me." He didn't sit.

Bertra smiled, her lipstick flawless, her eyes sharp enough to cut through wire. "I called my attorney, of course. I'm not happy I'm paying him nine hundred dollars an hour to sit here." She leaned slightly toward Laurel, voice low and full of weaponized calm. "I have no idea where Viv is, and I'd tell you if I did."

Laurel didn't blink. "Where's Fitz?"

Bertra gave a casual shrug, like she was bored already. "How in the hell would I know? It's after hours and I don't expect to see him until later today. In the office. Where we work."

Beside her, Vexler in his expensive suit, polished shoes, and the constant air of courtroom smugness, sighed with exaggerated patience. "Agent Snow, we're very sorry there's a missing girl, but my client doesn't know anything about the situation. You have zero reason to hold her. She's not a suspect or a witness. So either stop this right now or I'll file a motion, and it'll be public. Very."

Laurel could not care less about public.

"Your client hired Viv as an intern," she said, voice cool but laced with the anger she barely kept in check. "Viv overheard her discussing a secret lab. I believe your client had her kidnapped. I also believe your client is involved in the deaths of people with fatal brain lesions we traced back to compounds developed at Oakridge Solutions. And we have credible intel suggesting a bio-attack will occur soon."

Kind of. Not really. Not enough.

But God, she needed it to be enough.

Vexler gave her a tired smile. "Arrest my client or let her go. You have nothing specific tying her to the abduction. You know it. I know it."

And he was right.

Laurel's chest burned with the truth.

Bertra stood, graceful and smug. She gave Laurel a slight nod, like they were adversaries in some corporate chess match and not standing on the ruins of a missing girl's future.

"You want to get in front of this," Laurel said sharply, rising. "Now."

Vexler smirked. "I do appreciate your tenacity. You remind me of your sister."

Laurel didn't flinch, but anger rushed through her, making her ears heat.

"I wish you luck in finding the girl," he added smoothly, and turned toward the door with Bertra beside him.

Laurel watched them go, fury boiling under her skin. She leaned forward, hands braced on the table, the fight draining out of her legs. She felt raw, cornered, and two steps behind. The only thing worse than not having enough to hold Bertra was knowing she was dirty and having to let her walk anyway.

Laurel's eyes burned. She pressed the heel of her hand against them, once. That was all she'd give it.

Where was Viv?

They had surveillance, yes, but no faces. No license plates. She had officers sweeping the neighborhoods and canvassing every parking lot. The drones hadn't found heat signatures worth chasing.

Laurel turned and looked at the boards filled with names, numbers, possible connections, and none of it giving her what she needed.

Her jaw clenched until her teeth ached.

She wasn't losing this girl.

Shaking herself, she stood and walked down the hallway and stairs, intending to go into the Fish and Wildlife offices, which had become a central hub for the investigation since it had more square footage. She stepped into the vestibule and ran right into Tim Kohnex. His dog sat over by the door, yawning. "I don't have time for you."

His blue eyes widened. "The wind is talking. About spinning tires and the missing girl."

Laurel breathed deep. "Bullshit." She rarely uttered profanity. Her brain wasn't using all its power as she hadn't slept. "I know the news got ahold of this." She'd seen Rachel at the school and had stayed away from her.

Kohnex grasped her arm. "It's the wind. I heard it with the cars near the church. Whispering that she's lost. Why don't you come to the Spring Worship Day with me tomorrow at the church? The wind will whisper to you at that holy place." He stood nearly six foot seven, his body fit and slender. "Let me help you."

Laurel jerked free. The man wanted to write a book about being psychic, and he'd told her so. "You're trespassing. Leave or I'll have you arrested." She pushed through the door to the Fish and Wildlife offices, where the bustle of agents and officers desperately trying to find a missing teenager sounded like a busy city at lunchtime.

Where could Viv be?

# Chapter 33

Tim Kohnex muttered all the way home as he drove away from Genesis Valley toward the unincorporated area. "She thinks she knows everything. That woman's brain is too big for her own good."

Buster, his border collie, let out a soft whuff from the back seat as if in agreement. Or boredom. Probably both. The wind was gusting again, tugging at the side mirrors of his rusted truck as he passed the glorious Genesis Valley Community Church. What a beacon of hope and goodness. Why wouldn't Laurel Snow believe him? He should be preparing for the worship day, but no, he had to be out here doing her job.

"She won't listen. I told her I heard them. Heard tires on gravel, late last night. I told her I could feel the girl was still alive."

The dog stared out the window, tongue lolling, unconcerned.

Tim gritted his teeth. "Fine. She doesn't believe me, fine. I'll follow the damn wind myself."

He turned right where the mountain road split, letting the tires crunch over the loose gravel. Higher ground. That's where he'd heard them. And if the wind had a direction, this was it. It always whispered down the mountainside before dark, like breath curling through a keyhole.

As the road narrowed, he slowed, his gaze flicking between the trees and the steep drop to the right. No headlights shone behind him. No sign of Laurel Snow or her army of feds. Good. They'd just talk him out of following the wind's directions.

Another gust hit the windshield, and Tim felt the pull—stronger this time. Not metaphorical. Not spiritual. Physical.

He pulled off onto the gravel shoulder, brakes squeaking, and let the truck idle as Buster pushed up between the seats and gave a sharp bark.

"I know, boy. You feel it, too."

They both jumped out.

The wind tugged at his flannel, and the smell of damp moss and pine needles thickened as they walked toward a trailhead—no signage, just an indentation in the brush like something had passed through often. Deer maybe. Or trucks.

Tim followed the path, winding upward through thick trees. It wasn't long before he saw something that didn't belong.

Stone. Concrete.

The building was half-hidden by the slope, built directly into the cliffside. It was nicer than it should've been, with steel-reinforced windows and polished wood siding. The facility was tucked behind rock and pine like someone had gone out of their way to bury it.

"I had no clue this was here," Tim whispered.

Buster didn't bark and just stared.

There was no driveway, no path down from the road. Whoever used this place had to be getting in another way.

A hundred feet away sat a low outbuilding. Utility shed? Generator shack? It had the right kind of loneliness about it. Tim crouched as he approached, boots soft in the moss, hand lightly resting on the handle of the small knife he always kept at his belt.

The windows were grimy, thick with dust and dead flies. He had to cup his hands against the glass to see. And there she was. The pretty blond girl.

Tied to a chair. Pale. Blood on her temple. Eyes wide and wild—until they locked on his.

Tim's heart slammed into his ribs. "I knew you were here," he breathed.

She shook her head quickly, frantically, as Buster gave a sharp bark and darted around the shed to the side door. It was unlocked.

Of course it was unlocked.

Tim pushed it open.

The girl gasped as the light shifted inside. Her eyes filled instantly with tears, but she didn't sob. She didn't scream. Her voice came out cracked and dry. "Please."

Buster reached her first, levering up to put his paws on her legs.

Tim stepped inside, crouching to untie her. "It's okay now. We've got you." But he never finished releasing the knot.

Something whistled through the air behind him.

Viv's face twisted in a silent scream, but the sound was drowned by the wet crack that followed.

Tim dropped instantly, his body folding like a paper doll, blood arcing against the concrete wall.

He hit the floor face-first and couldn't move.

Buster let out a sharp, high-pitched whine.

Then the darkness took him. Where was the wind now?

Abigail Caine stared out at the blustery rain from her seat in Wayne's truck.

More damn rain. Washington had a way of pressing the damp into human bones. The narrow road twisted through the dense forest, flanked by towering pines that loomed like silent sentinels, always watching, never judging. She rather liked them for that.

The storm beat fully now as they drove away from picking up pizzas to take back to the Fish and Wildlife offices for lunch. Most of the officers, including Wayne, hadn't slept. But Viv was nowhere to be found. Abigail should probably do something about that, but she couldn't decide what.

The truck's headlights carved twin tunnels through the murky day, and Wayne—sweet, predictable Wayne—hummed some tough guy country song.

She folded her arms, watching the rivulets of water chase each other down the window.

Rain covered everything. Mistakes. Blood. Tracks. It was practically a gift.

He thought she needed protecting. From what, exactly? Consequences? Other people? Herself? She had survived more dangerous things than lovestruck federal agents. She'd orchestrated them.

Wayne existed in a world of rules and rightness, of protect-and-serve delusions and tender affections he hadn't realized he'd aimed at a weapon. It would be almost sweet if it weren't so insufferably naive.

She had plans. Big, sharp, elegant plans, and every moment he hovered, every time he reached for her elbow like she might fall apart, he became a liability. Even though she had no intention of actually going to trial next week, it was good to keep him around. Just in case. She glanced at him, smiling faintly.

He looked like a tough bulldog. Strong muscles, wide face, fairly handsome. Plus, he was unusually good in bed, which had saved his life more than once. Not that she had a decent reason to kill him.

"You know," Wayne began, his voice gentle, "I think it's so nice of you to help with the search. You're a kind one, Abby. After all this is over, after we find that girl, the sniper after your sister, and you survive your trial, let's go away together. Somewhere warm."

Abigail forced a smile, turning to face him. "That sounds lovely," she lied.

"I'm close to finding the sniper. Very."

Abigail perked up. "How so?"

Before Wayne could respond, the world erupted into chaos.

A battered pickup truck, its rusted frame barely holding together, burst from a concealed side path. The driver, face obscured by a blue ski mask, showed no hesitation. The battered old truck slammed into Wayne's truck with bone-jarring force, sending it skidding off the road and into the dense underbrush.

The impact was disorienting. Abigail's head struck the window, and a sharp pain blossomed at her temple. Wayne reacted instinctively, his training kicking in. He reached for his sidearm, a Glock 22, standard FBI issue, and shouted, "Abigail, stay down!"

But she was already moving, opening her door and stumbling out toward the trees. They were sitting ducks in the mangled truck. The world around her had narrowed to a singular focus. She needed to neutralize threats. Fear was a foreign concept, and only cold calculation remained.

The assailant emerged from the truck, a figure clad in jeans and a flannel shirt, moving gracefully. Without hesitation, he raised a handgun toward them. The muted thuds of suppressed gunfire punctuated the air as bullets tore through the foliage.

Wayne returned fire, his shots echoing loudly through the trees. He moved to shield Abigail, placing his body between her and the attacker. "We need cover," he hissed.

She didn't argue. At least the stormy weather darkened the day. Her hair matted against her head and she swiped it off her face.

They ran, boots slamming through moss and fallen needles, weaving through trees slick with rain. The forest was thick, uneven, full of shadows and potential cover, but the shooter, calm and relentless, was gaining ground. Abigail didn't need to see his face to read his control. He moved like someone used to hunting prey.

A bullet smacked into the trunk of a tree just inches from her head, bark exploding against her cheek. She didn't flinch but adjusted her path and kept going.

Wayne grunted behind her, stumbling, then recovering. She glanced back. He was still moving, still firing in bursts, but there was blood now. Dark and spreading across his chest. A hit. Likely not a kill shot yet, but enough to slow him. Maybe enough to end him.

They crashed through a thicket of fern and low pine, and Wayne faltered. This time, he didn't recover. He dropped to one knee, then the other, his gun slipping from his grasp into the wet brush.

Abigail turned.

Her heart didn't race. Her breath didn't catch.

This was an opportunity. One she hadn't counted on so soon, but she knew how to adapt. With Wayne down, she was unencumbered. Free to finish what she'd started. But not yet. The shooter was still coming. He wouldn't expect her to fight back. Probably.

She crouched and plucked Wayne's Glock from the forest floor, finding the weapon to be both cool and familiar in her grip. Then she turned, remaining fluid and calm. Rain slashed down, hindering her vision.

The assailant saw her and hesitated. Just for a second.

It was enough.

Abigail raised the gun, aimed cleanly, and fired.

The first shot missed, embedding itself in a tree trunk. The second found its mark, striking the assailant's leg. A guttural cry escaped him as he stumbled backward, retreating toward his vehicle.

Abigail advanced, not feeling anything. She could hear Wayne behind her, grunting as he must've stood, crashing through branches.

She fired again, and the bullet grazed the attacker's shoulder. He ran faster and so did she, firing again. Missing. She could barely see through the branches and punishing rain. He scrambled into the truck, and the engine roared to life. The tires spun, kicking up mud and debris as he sped away, disappearing into the murk.

Silence enveloped the forest once more, broken only by Wayne's labored breathing. Abigail turned to see him falling onto his back, the rain pummeling him, his eyes closed. She observed his pallor, the sheen of sweat on his brow.

She walked to him slowly. Deliberately. Stood over him. She could leave and let the mud soak him in. Let the bullet do the job.

But not now. Sighing, she strode back to his hissing truck and fetched his radio. Then she clicked the button and shoved the right kind of panic into her voice. "Help! Agent down! FBI Agent Wayne Norrs is down. We need medevac and backup now. I don't know if the shooter's still in the area. Just get someone out here, please!"

Static crackled, then a voice replied, sharp and immediate. "Copy that. Agent down. Transmit location. Stay put."

She returned into the trees and planted her hands over Wayne's chest to stem the blood. Was he still alive? He couldn't die yet. She might still need his visible support at the trial, if she had one.

If he died, she'd have to come up with another plan.

# Chapter 34

Laurel pushed through the hospital's automatic doors as rain slid off her jacket. The fluorescent lights were nearly blinding after the murky day outside. Abigail sat in a plastic chair with dried blood smeared on her hands. Wet strands of hair curled just slightly where they clung to her collarbone, and she appeared pale beneath the fluorescent lights.

Laurel reached her quickly. "How is he?"

Abigail looked up. Her eyes were red-rimmed, not from crying. Laurel had seen that look before. It was adrenaline tapering off a high. "He's in surgery. Penetrating trauma to the right hemithorax. Entry wound just medial to the midclavicular line. The projectile missed the heart but collapsed the lung. They're concerned about internal hemorrhaging and vascular involvement."

Laurel sat beside her. The chair squeaked, cheap vinyl protesting her presence. She liked Agent Norrs. He appeared to be a trustworthy and conscientious agent. "What happened?"

Abigail arched a brow. "Why are you here without bodyguards? There's a shooter out there."

"I have two on the outside door right now." Laurel couldn't shake them. "Now talk, please."

Abigail took a deep breath. "Are you taking my official statement?" Her eyeliner had bled slightly beneath her eyes. Not perfect. That was new.

"Yes. Everyone else is still searching for Viv. You'll give a formal statement later, but I want your raw account. Now."

Abigail flicked her hand like she was batting away something unworthy of her time. "We went to pick up pizzas for the joint task force at Fish and Wildlife. Just a favor run. A truck came out of nowhere and T-boned us hard."

Laurel cut her a look. "You have an eidetic memory. I want detail for detail."

Abigail's nod was sharp. "He was masked and his movements were surprisingly graceful. He fired first and followed us into the trees. His shots were aimed at center mass, and he maintained a textbook tactical stance. He seemed genuinely surprised when I grabbed Wayne's Glock from the ground and returned fire."

"You sure you hit him?"

"Positive. Twice. Lower extremity—right thigh—and lateral aspect of the upper arm. He flinched both times. But he kept moving."

Laurel nodded once, her mind already ten steps ahead of the moment. "We've issued BOLOs and then called clinics, hospitals, and even veterinary offices within two hours of here to provide warning. They'll call us if he seeks help."

Abigail leaned back, eyes calculating. "I barely slowed him down."

Laurel resisted the urge to pat Abigail's hand. "Yes, but he's hurt." She thought through the scenario. "Are you certain he aimed for Wayne and not you?"

Abigail focused on her. "Why? Because I look like you? You think maybe he got us mixed up?"

Laurel exhaled slowly, a long stream of breath through her nose. "I have no idea, but we can't assume anything."

Abigail arched an eyebrow. "Wayne was just telling me he had a break in your sniper investigation."

Laurel's spine stiffened. "What was it?"

"He didn't say. We didn't have time. But he was . . . confident. He said he was closing in."

Perhaps he'd left notes in his Seattle office. Laurel would call them and find out. "Is there anything you can point to that would help me identify this attacker?"

"No." Abigail scratched dried blood off her hand. "Do you think Wayne tipped off the sniper somehow? Accidentally?"

"Maybe," Laurel said. "Like I said, we'll start a broad investigation and narrow in, but since there's a sniper out there, it's likely the same perpetrator. We'll pull every case Agent Norrs ever worked, but I don't believe in coincidences."

Abigail tilted her head. "Nietzsche didn't either. 'There are no facts, only interpretations.' And patterns."

Laurel shot her a look. "And in those patterns, 'coincidences are just crimes in costume.' Foucault."

Abigail smirked. "Touché." Then her head went back against the sterile hospital wall, and her eyelids shut. She was trembling.

Laurel frowned. "I should've brought you something warm to wear. I didn't even think of it."

"Why would you?" Abigail murmured. "We're rarely on the same page. All I've ever wanted is to be your sister."

Laurel doubted that. Abigail's desires were layered, twisted, and often tactical. But maybe, beneath the machinery, there was something that approximated need. "I'm sorry that Wayne was shot. You do care for him. Don't you?"

Abigail didn't move. "Of course I do. We're engaged."

That wasn't an answer. "Is he your reason?"

Abigail cracked open one pale blue eye. "My reason for what?"

Exactly. She wouldn't understand. "Are you really planning to go through with it? Marry him?"

"I don't know." A beat. "We're engaged."

Laurel let that hang. "What about after your trial if you don't go to prison?"

"I'm not going to prison, Laurel. We both know it." Abigail's voice had a cool certainty, like she'd already read the verdict.

"You can try for self-defense, sure. But it's not a slam dunk. The prosecuting attorney is sharp, and you didn't exactly have a sanctioned reason for going to that motel alone."

"Sure I did." Abigail folded her arms, the dried blood on her sleeves cracking slightly. "What about Joley, that poor girl Zeke said he had stashed somewhere?"

Laurel had to refrain from rolling her eyes. "The only evidence that Zeke had anything to do with that missing teenager is your word. That's it."

Abigail hummed softly. "Interesting." That tone. It told Laurel that somewhere, in the folds of Abigail's mind, wheels were turning. Not in panic. Abigail never panicked. She strategized. She designed. If corroboration didn't exist, she'd manufacture it, bend the narrative, and make truth pliable.

"Why did you really kill your father?" Laurel asked.

"*Our* father." A small smile played on Abigail's mouth. Just a quick flash before it disappeared. "Are you asking as my sister or as an FBI agent?"

"I'm always both."

"That's what I figured." Abigail turned those dual-colored eyes on Laurel. "I killed him because he came at me. It was self-defense."

That was highly doubtful. Zeke wanted money to get out of town, and Abigail had plenty. She could've been his bank for decades. "What else?"

"Talk to me after the trial," Abigail said dryly. "Double jeopardy and all that."

So the bastard did have something on her. Laurel knew it. Whatever it was, if there had ever been real evidence, it was almost certainly dust and ash by now. "When I testify, I'll tell the truth."

"You weren't there, Laurel, and have nothing to say. Your testimony will include the fact that Zeke raped your mother and created you. She spent her life making sure he didn't know you existed. Then he tried to kill you the night I killed him." Abigail spoke softly. "My attorney is excellent, and by the time he's done with you, the jury will want to throw me a party. You can't help yourself. The truth is the truth, and you'll give it."

Laurel's stomach cramped. "I think you had an ulterior motive in killing him. I know you did." Yet Abigail had been furious that the baby had died. Truly livid.

"Your opinion doesn't hold the weight of evidence. Period."

Before Laurel could answer, a doctor stepped into the waiting room. She was tall and angular with storm-gray hair and steady brown eyes.

"Abigail Caine?" The doctor looked at them both, her eyebrows raising. Yeah, their brown-red hair and heterochromatic eyes always caused interest, especially when they sat together.

"Yes," Abigail said, rising with the grace of someone who'd been waiting for a cue.

The doctor turned her attention to her. "Agent Norrs is out of surgery. He's stable. Conscious. Asking for you."

"So he's alive." Abigail exhaled. "How is he?"

The doctor smoothed down her pink scrubs. "Agent Norrs sustained two projectile injuries to the right thoracic region—one anterior, one lateral. Fortunately, there was no penetration to the pericardium or major vasculature. He did experience significant blood loss and a partial pneumothorax, but both wounds were managed surgically. He's expected to recover with supportive care and time."

"Oh, thank God," Abigail said, voice almost cracking. But Laurel knew the trick of that—Abigail could fake warmth so well it looked real even to herself.

Laurel stood. "I'm glad he's going to be okay. When can I interview him?"

"Not right now," the doctor said, her voice firm but not unkind. "Give him a few hours. He's lucid but exhausted. He specifically asked for his fiancée to sit with him."

Abigail hesitated. "Oh. Well, I thought I'd go help with the search for the missing teenager by taking over Wayne's field responsibilities."

Laurel didn't even pretend to entertain that idea. "No. You stay with him. That'll help him more than anything right now." And keep her out of the way.

The last thing Laurel needed was Abigail loose in the middle of an active investigation, leaving her signature chaos just because she could. Of course, her brain was impressive, and if she truly wanted to help, she'd be an asset. It was unfortunate she didn't use her high intelligence to actually do some good in the world.

Abigail put a hand on Laurel's arm. "Are you sure? I could help."

"I'm positive. I'll have an agent bring you dry clothing," Laurel added. "Let me know when he's clear for an interview."

Abigail stepped forward and, without warning, leaned in for a hug. Her arms were wet but her grip tight. Even after her ordeal in the forest, with blood and mud on her, she smelled like an expensive citrus perfume. Laurel patted her back once.

"You're a good sister," Abigail said, just loud enough for the doctor to hear.

"Thanks," Laurel replied. She leaned back, once again wondering if there was any way to reach humanity in her. She looked at her sister's very familiar eyes. "You probably saved his life when you returned fire at the sniper."

Abigail winked. "I had to save my sweet Wayne, didn't I?"

Now Agent Norrs would be in deeper than ever. Abigail could've run. She might've been able to hide. But she seemed like a hero now. "Were you frightened? At all?" Laurel asked. Whatever psychopathy Abigail held, and it would take years of testing to truly determine that, it was doubtful she felt true fear.

Abigail studied her back, an unidentified light in her eyes. As if wondering what to tell her? "No."

The truth caught Laurel off guard. For a brief and very unexpected moment.

The outside door opened and Rachel Raprenzi hustled inside with her cameraman behind her. "Dr. Caine? Do you have time for an interview? I have a source that says you shot back at an assassin today. How is the agent who went down?"

Laurel turned toward her. "You're trespassing, Rachel. Get out."

The cameraman kept filming, and Rachel stepped to the side to give him a better line of sight. "We're here with Special Agent Laurel Snow and her sister, Dr. Abigail Caine, after the shooting of an FBI agent earlier today. My, don't they look alike?"

"Out," Laurel ordered.

Abigail lifted a hand, her eyes gleaming. "I'd be happy to give you an interview, Ms. Raprenzi. First, I need to go see for myself that my fiancé is all right."

"Your fiancé is the FBI agent?" Rachel's tone turned salacious.

"Yes. I'll be back in about fifteen minutes." Abigail brushed a strand of hair away from her face, her hand shaking. She went from assertive with Laurel to looking fragile and lost in an instant. How did she do that? "All right, Doctor." Abigail turned with a flourish, following the physician toward the double doors at the end of the hallway. At the threshold, she paused and looked back. "I hope you find the girl, Laurel. I can't imagine what Kate is going through right now."

Neither could Laurel. "We'll find her."

Abigail disappeared around the corner with the doctor.

Rachel moved in with her microphone. "Agent Snow? While we wait for Dr. Caine to return, please give us an update on the kidnapping of Vivienne Vuittron."

"No comment." Laurel turned and strode back into the storm. She had to find Viv and soon. Would there be a biochemical attack? If so, where?

# Chapter 35

It had been a long and useless day. After dark, alone in her office, Laurel sat on her conference table and stared at the boards. Huck was downstairs in his, arranging for another helicopter search first thing in the morning. The storm was making surveillance difficult, and they'd had to stop for the day. What if the lab was nowhere to be found?

What if Viv wasn't even in some hidden lab?

Laurel reached for her phone and called Huck. "We have to get Dr. Yannish back in here but I'm coming up short. So far, the evidence teams haven't found anything from the lab that will give me probable cause. No records of another lab." Her mind spun confusion around. "I forgot to tell you that Tim Kohnex was here earlier saying the wind is whispering about Viv. It's a long shot, but if we don't find anything else, I guess we should interview him." He lived in the far opposite direction of the yew trees, but he had mentioned tires in the wind.

Unless Laurel was wrong. What if Tyler had been warning Walter about something else? Why wasn't this case coming together?

"Okay. We haven't searched that direction yet," Huck said. "I'm still on the phone with aviation and will be up in a few. You haven't eaten all day. Ena picked up sandwiches from the deli and I'll bring one up to you."

"Thanks." Laurel clicked off absently. She cocked her head. Then she swung her legs onto the table and stood, looking down at all the pictures from a different angle. She'd placed one of Agent Norrs on the sniper case board where he looked tall and formidable. Abigail had kept her updated all day, and he was no longer in critical condition and would make a full recovery.

The board morphed in front of Laurel's eyes.

Wait a minute. Fascinating. She jumped down and approached the boards, taking Abigail's photo off her board and putting it on the sniper board next to the one of Norrs. The sniper had hit Abigail the first time. Could Abigail have been the actual target?

Then Laurel took Dr. Matteo Sandoval's picture off the lab board and taped it onto the sniper's board.

What if the sniper had hit who he wanted? What if he hadn't actually missed? What if Laurel wasn't even the target?

Abigail and Sandoval. Plus, Abigail had been in Laurel's office during the third shooting. Why would somebody want both Abigail and Dr. Sandoval dead?

"Hello there," Abigail said smoothly from behind her.

Laurel jumped and spun around, her heart racing. "How did you get up here?"

Abigail snorted. "Please. I secured a badge the first week you installed it. Did you really think you could keep me out?"

Laurel glanced to her right to see Henry Vexler, his gaze on the boards. "You brought your attorney."

"I did." Abigail smiled, moving her painted red lips. "I thought we might reach an agreement."

Laurel glanced back at the sniper board. "You have degrees in biochemistry and neuroscience," she said slowly.

"I do." Abigail read the board. "I see what you're doing here."

Vexler frowned. "I don't. Also, if you don't have access to this floor, we shouldn't be here. It's a federal building, Abigail."

Abigail barely looked at him. "Don't be a dumbass, Henry. You're here to make me a deal. Well, the beginning of one. We need to meet with the county prosecutor about my case after we secure my sister's assistance. Time truly is of the essence."

Heat flushed down Laurel's torso. "The sniper meant to hit you at the courthouse that first day."

"Yep," Abigail chirped. "Chalk one up for Wayne. That vest saved my life."

Laurel breathed out. She couldn't believe she'd missed this. "You work for Oakridge Solutions."

Abigail sighed. "Really, Laurel? You're slow sometimes. I merely consulted with the offshoot of the labs. For a nice sum of money, actually."

The hidden lab? "Where's the lab?"

Abigail's tongue darted out to lick her bottom lip. "That information is going to cost you. Cost the county, really."

Fire shot through Laurel. She didn't lose her temper, ever, unless Abigail was around. It was frightening, really. "Tyler Griggs warned Walter via a letter about some sort of attack."

Abigail's eyes widened. "No. They're really going to do it? Really try out a bioweapon? I didn't even know for sure they'd created it. Oh, no. We'd better get a deal in place fast." She looked at Vexler. "I think you should call the county prosecutor right now, and we'll hammer it all out here in the conference room. Time is of the essence if they're going to test that concoction."

"Tell me about the concoction," Laurel hissed.

"I don't think so." Henry Vexler drew a handgun from the inside pocket of his jacket with a slow, practiced motion—showing no urgency, no panic, just the chilling efficiency of someone who'd done this before. The weapon was matte black, thick-barreled, and unnervingly quiet in its presence alone. A suppressor was already threaded onto the front, giving the gun an elongated, ghostly silhouette. He raised it, casual but certain, leveling it between Abigail and Laurel. "I'm way too close to miss this time, ladies."

Laurel recognized it instantly as an HK USP Tactical, built for special operations. It was a professional's weapon with a threaded barrel, high-profile sights, match trigger. Wait a minute. How was this even possible? "*You?* You're the sniper?" The high-priced lawyer?

Abigail stepped away from him and toward Laurel, true shock on her face. "I did *not* see that coming."

Laurel didn't take her eyes off the gun. Vexler's expression hadn't shifted. No flash of gloating, no twitch of adrenaline. Just calm malice.

He grabbed Abigail's arm and yanked her toward him, shoving the weapon into her rib cage. "You'd run, Abigail." He stared at Laurel. "But you'll follow nicely so I won't shoot your sister."

That fast, finally, Laurel put it all together. "You wanted Abigail dead. She has knowledge about the lab. You're more than Bertha's lawyer. Right?" He hadn't told her when he was retained and she'd wrongly assumed it just happened because he was dogging her. Laurel had nothing to do with him representing Oakridge Solutions.

"Yeah. I was aiming at Abigail each time." He shrugged. "Was a sniper years ago and I might've lost my touch a little bit. I'm hell in a courtroom, though." His gaze hardened. "You, move. In front of us. And if you cause any sort of scene downstairs, I'll shoot you both, aim inside the Fish and Wildlife office, and kill everyone." He turned, wincing.

Abigail pushed against him. "How's the leg, Henry?"

Red spiraled beneath his cheekbones. "Flesh wound. Same as the arm. But you will pay for shooting me, bitch."

Abigail actually rolled her eyes. "How pedantic."

"Where is Viv?" Laurel stepped forward, subtly shifting her weight, mapping exits, calculating angles, but the odds were not good.

"I'll take you right to her," Vexler said, visibly tightening his grip on Abigail. "It's the only way you'll even find her."

Laurel swallowed. "Is she alive?"

"For now." He motioned for her to move. "You first. Now."

Laurel led the way down the hallway and then stairwell, her mind spinning. The damn lawyer was the sniper? This was her only chance to get to Viv. A buzz of activity came from the Fish and Wildlife office, but nobody looked outside as they walked past and out the main exit.

The relentless rain hit them like a wall as they stepped outside into the night. It was the kind of storm that blurred vision and erased sound.

Vexler marched them to a battered maroon Chevy Caprice, its

trunk already popped like it had been waiting for them. The car screamed of neglect and anonymity, rust curling around its fenders like rot. It was a throwaway vehicle and the kind used for one-way errands.

"Get in," he said.

Abigail hesitated. Laurel didn't. She guided her sister to the trunk and climbed in first. The carpet instantly scratched her wrists. There was no emergency latch, and the taillights were old. Strong and sturdy.

Vexler shoved Abigail inside, and she rolled into Laurel. Then he slammed the trunk shut. Seconds later, they were bouncing out of the parking lot with rain beating against the metal.

"I can't believe you wanted to get in this old car trunk," Abigail muttered, rolling over onto her back, her knees up.

"I have to find Viv." Laurel turned on her side, facing Abigail, her butt against the back of the rear seat. Darkness enveloped them. The carpet had that unmistakable odor of old glue and mildew, like someone tried to clean a spill years ago and just gave up. Beneath that, the synthetic fibers were steeped in decades of smoke, motor oil, and something vaguely organic. Maybe food, maybe blood, maybe both. It was the smell of neglect.

Laurel could practically taste it.

The car groaned over uneven asphalt, then pitched as it left the road entirely. Laurel's spine thudded against the cold back of the rear seat. She shifted, pulling her knees in tighter to brace for the terrain ahead. Gravel sprayed up into the wheel wells—sporadic, loud. They were climbing now, the incline constant, the turns sharp. It wasn't freeway driving. This was mountain. Rural. Off-grid.

She let her mind mark the changes: fifteen minutes of inner-city grid, six turns, then the long curve upward, a sharp right onto dirt. The pavement had been gone for five, maybe six minutes. The engine strained against the slope, old suspension creaking like bone on bone. Had they headed outside of town toward the Genesis Valley Community Church? It felt like they were driving east that way.

Beside her, Abigail breathed evenly. Of course she did.

Laurel angled her head toward her. "Tell me about the lab."

A pause. Then a lazy, almost amused response. "You're going to have to be more specific."

Laurel resisted the urge to elbow her. "I don't have time for this. Are you an employee?"

"Of course not. I contracted with them a year or so ago to work on the dementia project and received both a stipend and stock options. I'm quite good with biochemistry, you know."

This was unbelievable. Abigail's ace up her sleeve was her ties to a biomedical company? She'd known of a bioweapon in the works and had stored that just in case she needed leverage someday? Seriously? "Who in the world thinks that far ahead?"

Abigail chuckled. "Me. It's always good to have backup information in one's pocket just in case. For leverage or blackmail."

Laurel breathed out. "Obviously the compound can be weaponized and has been."

"Apparently," Abigail agreed. "I didn't have anything to do with that. Financially, I make out if they go public with their dementia treatment, or if the government purchases it as a weapon. But the lab going rogue does not help me financially."

"No, but you're planning to use your knowledge to get an immunity agreement, right?"

Abigail chuckled. "Wayne mentioned a possible attack coming soon, which means I need that agreement tonight, and right now, we're headed to our deaths. So this might not have worked out the way I planned."

Laurel couldn't help but figure out the entire situation. "Your case is a state one, not federal. A possible biomedical attack would be federal. The feds can't give you immunity for a state homicide charge."

"True, but they can sure pressure the county prosecutor to do so. It's my understanding that she holds strong political ambitions. I believe she can be brought around to look like a hero in all of this. I mean, if we get out of this alive. There's a good chance both of our brains will end up with lesions on them. How sad is that? We do have the best brains."

Laurel flashed back to Walter whispering to her: *That chick is batshit crazy.* Man, he was right. Dangerous, too. "Since we're about to die, how about you tell me why you really killed our father. I mean, Zeke." Her voice trembled on the last. They hit a pothole and Laurel rolled against Abigail before trying to move back.

"I truly was upset about losing the baby. But for any other reason, like I said, you'll have to wait until double jeopardy becomes applicable."

"Will you really tell me?" The rain beat harder against the metal hood.

Abigail remained silent for a bit. "Most likely, no."

So Zeke had had proof of one of Abigail's crimes. If she confessed, Laurel could pursue that case, so she'd never tell the truth. "I will get you."

"Perhaps. For now, tell me why we're in this stupid trunk. Kate has three girls. Is it such a bad thing if she loses one? She'll still have two left." Abigail shifted her weight, elbowing Laurel in the ribs.

Bile rose in Laurel's throat. "Stop talking now."

The road pitched again, going upward. Steeper. Wind slithered through gaps in the trunk seal, sharp and cold, carrying the scent of pine, wet stone, and altitude. They were deep in the mountains now. No city noise, no other cars. Just the crunch of gravel, the whine of tires on dirt, and the low, steady rumble of a plan Laurel wasn't in on.

Finally, she had to ask another question. "Where is the attack? Is there one?"

Abigail was quiet long enough that Laurel thought she wouldn't answer. "I can only guess. But it sounds like there might be an attack as an example? It'd be a small one, nothing huge like Seattle. But that's all I can surmise, and it's really more of a guess."

They finally rolled to a stop. A door opened and shut, and then the trunk popped open. Rain slashed down at them, and Laurel naturally ducked.

"Out," Vexler said, gun trained on them.

Abigail held out a hand and allowed him to assist her out. "I'm quite irritated I missed this part of you, Henry. Most people don't fool me."

Laurel climbed out without assistance.

Vexler jerked the gun toward a steel building set into the hillside. They had to be, what? Maybe twenty or so miles from the church? Far away from the yew stands, damn it. Laurel walked across muddy ground and into the structure, noting the sleek lines with wooden accents.

"This is interesting," Abigail said. "My guess is misappropriated governmental defense funds?"

Vexler opened a door and pointed down the stairs.

"No elevator?" Abigail asked. "I do hate half-assed projects."

Vexler swung the gun on her.

"Shut up," Laurel said. Where was Viv? She began to climb down, found a wide hallway, and followed it past a clean room and then a lab. Apparently the place was well equipped, but most of the research must've been performed at the main lab. They just hadn't found the right requisition records yet.

"Open the door," Vexler muttered.

Laurel did so and walked inside another lab, this one humming with machinery. Viv sat on the floor against the far wall, her hands tied and a bruise on her jaw. Her eyes lit. "Laurel."

Next to her sat a dazed-looking Tim Kohnex, blood down the side of his face. He swayed and then focused on her. "The wind told me you were coming. Did you see my dog?"

# Chapter 36

Rain battered the roof of the Fish and Wildlife building, drowning out the sound of anything human. Huck leaned over the table with a dozen maps spread out, water-stained and marked with routes in red and black ink. Elevation lines, forest roads, decommissioned firebreaks—every inch mattered. Viv was still missing, and they were almost out of reasonable guesses.

Walter Smudgeon stood across from him, pointing at a trail that cut north past Deadman's Hollow. "That was cleared within the last three months. Old satellite feed showed it washed out. This one's recent. Maintained. Someone's running through it."

Huck narrowed his eyes. "That's privately owned land by some corporation back east. I haven't noticed any construction, but they're far enough out, they could've come from the east and not through Genesis Valley." The desk phone rang. Huck grabbed it, expecting a call from Norrs in the hospital. "Rivers."

"Huck, this is Pastor John." The voice was steady but off. "I'm here working late preparing for the Spring Worship Day tomorrow. Tim Kohnex's dog just showed up at the church covered in mud with blood on his ear. The blood isn't the dog's."

Huck straightened. "Is Tim there with him?"

"No. I went out to his place and saw no sign of him. His truck is gone, and his house is locked up with no lights showing. But the dog was soaked and shaking from cold. That man wouldn't go anywhere without that dog."

Huck stopped breathing. Maybe Kohnex hadn't been full of crap earlier. "Thanks, Pastor. I'll handle it." He dropped the receiver and grabbed his jacket. "Kohnex is missing. His dog showed up at the church, with somebody's blood on him."

Walter raised an eyebrow. "You think this is related?"

"Who the hell knows. I'll go ask Laurel exactly what he said earlier." Huck was already out the door before Walter could ask more. He cut across the door and jogged up the FBI steps before realizing it was quiet. Too quiet.

"Laurel?" Nothing. No answer. He ran down to the conference room, which was vacant. No sign of her. She wouldn't just leave without telling him.

Warning heated down his torso. He ran back down to his office and brought up the security feed. Skipped back. Found her. She and Abigail were walking outside to an older Caprice, Abigail's attorney holding her close. Was that a gun?

Huck watched, jaw tight, as Laurel went with him. No hesitation. Eyes locked. Abigail's mouth moved, but the audio was down. Didn't matter. They both got into a trunk and allowed the man to shut it.

What the fuck?

Laurel hadn't fought or gone for the gun. Or even tried to let anybody in Fish and Wildlife know what was going on. Why? He smacked his head. Viv. She thought she could get to Viv.

Huck turned. "I need a chopper in the air now. I don't give a damn about the storm. We have an abduction, and it just went operational."

Walter yanked on his coat. "What happened?"

"Vexler took Laurel. And Abigail. From inside the building."

Walter stopped moving. "The lawyer?"

Huck didn't slow. "Get his background. I want everything, and I want it on the way to the field."

They ran outside and hit the vehicle, heading wildly toward the helipad. Wind shook the windshield, but Huck kept the speed high.

The rain made it worse. Visibility was down to nothing, but they weren't waiting for it to clear. Panic rushed through him, and he forced himself to calm. Laurel had just purposefully put herself in the hands of people he believed had a chemical weapon. It was the only thing that made sense. She'd done it to find Viv.

Hopefully, they were both still alive. He had to get to them.

Walter worked fast on the tablet, tapping into files. "Henry Vexler. Officially licensed out of Washington. Attorney with high-profile clients."

"Military?"

"None, but he has an impressive list of weapons registered to him. Nothing sniper based, but . . ."

But he'd have those off the books. "So we have a sniper who's also a lawyer," Huck muttered.

"Now, that's a combo."

"The kill of Dr. Sandoval. So he was the target?" Did that mean the sniper wasn't after Laurel? Who was the other target? Abigail? "Why would a sniper want Abigail dead?"

"Don't we all?" Walter asked grimly.

Good point. They reached the pad. The helicopter was already prepped, blades turning, storm be damned. The pilot gave them a nod, barely more than a glance. No questions asked.

Huck climbed in, headset on, gaze scanning the ridgeline as they lifted off. "Head toward Genesis Valley Community Church and then east from there. We're looking for an older Toyota Tacoma owned by Tim Kohnex, or a burgundy colored Chevy Caprice. Also search for any type of buildings once we hit the outskirts of the county."

God, they had to be okay.

Laurel sat on the cold metal floor, her spine tight, every inch of her body coiled despite the stillness. She wrapped an arm around Viv's narrow shoulders, pulling the girl close. Viv trembled once, then stilled. The girl was breathing, warm, and alive. That was enough. For now.

Vexler stood near the door with his weapon trained on them.

Abigail sat on her other side, next to Kohnex, with her legs extended and her body far too relaxed for the situation. Her eyes were half-lidded. "Well," she murmured. "Can we fight back now?"

"Absolutely," Laurel said.

The door opened.

Two people stepped inside. Dr. Bertra Yannish and a man with dark hair.

"That's John Fitz," Viv muttered. "He kidnapped me. Asshole."

The air shifted with them, sharp with chemicals and damp wool.

"Nicely done," Bertra purred to Vexler. She wore brown jeans, a fitted white shirt, and a brown leather jacket that looked smart against the shirt. Her hair was tied back, and her eyes were heavily lined in black, deliberate, and cold. She crossed the room without hesitation and leaned in to kiss Vexler, her fingers brushing his collar. "I was a little worried about your sniper proficiency," she murmured, lips against his. "But your kidnapping technique? Two solid stars."

Fitz folded his arms, face still, tone flat. "I got the girl."

"You know I'm a federal agent," Laurel said. "You're staring down the death penalty."

Vexler gave her a brief glance. "That assumes any of this ends in a courtroom."

"Tell me about the attack. When is it?" Laurel asked.

"Saturday," Fitz said. "I need another half an hour with the last canister tonight."

"Make me a smaller one, too," Bertra said. She smiled at Laurel.

Laurel's stomach dropped.

Fitz winked at Laurel and then turned back to the door and exited quietly.

Laurel shifted, sliding her arm off Viv's shoulder, but the girl leaned back into her.

Laurel kept her eyes on Bertra. "So what's the plan? I take it you've gone rogue with this yew tree compound."

"'Rogue' is a bit dramatic," Bertra said, already moving toward the storage locker across the room. "Let's say we're operating outside traditional constraints."

"You're going to kill civilians."

"Not many," Vexler said. "Just enough to make the message clear."

Laurel's jaw locked. "There are buyers?"

"Several organizations from many countries," Bertra said. "Saturday is just the prototype run."

Laurel's pulse kicked, but she didn't show it. "What exactly does the compound do?"

"It attacks the brain," Bertra said, her voice clinical, almost bored. "Originally, it showed promise for treating certain forms of dementia. Neuro-regeneration, receptor reactivation, even brief moments of lucidity. But when concentrated with an enhanced binder, the compound triggers acute cortical lesions. Subcortical areas first, then it spreads. The subject becomes erratic. Manic. And then, very quickly, dead."

Laurel didn't move. Her muscles had gone still in a way she recognized, right before everything in her wanted to fight.

"We've been trying to refine it," Bertra continued. "Ideally, we'd be able to modulate reactions. Induce calm. Even create obedience. Willing subjects. But as of now . . . the death curve is the only reliable result." Her gaze slid over to Abigail. "You could've been useful in that phase. But with your sister being FBI, I couldn't exactly reach out, could I?"

Abigail's smile didn't touch her eyes. "We started working together a year or so ago."

Bertra shrugged. "I wasn't told about this application until recently. Why, do you want in now?"

Abigail looked at her. "Sure."

"I don't believe you," Bertra said.

"I don't either," Vexler muttered.

"You're a shitty lawyer," Abigail said, flat and unimpressed.

Vexler turned his head slowly. "I'm an excellent lawyer, and I'm really going to miss the law," he said, like it had been a fond memory.

Abigail cocked her head. "Where are you going?"

Vexler glanced at Bertra. "Somewhere without an extradition treaty. Somewhere warm. Expensive."

Laurel cut in. "Where's the attack?" She already knew.

No one answered.

Laurel's jaw clicked once before she spoke. "It's Genesis Valley

Community Church, right? They're having some Spring Worship Day Saturday. We're close by, and it's a closed environment."

Bertra smiled faintly.

"Of course," Laurel continued. "You can't really want to do this."

"I'm attending the celebration," Bertra said, glancing down at her clothes. "Though I may change my boots."

Bile rose in Laurel's throat. How could the woman even contemplate such a thing? "Is the compound liquid?"

"No," Bertra said. "Aerosol."

Laurel's stomach dropped. That changed everything. "What's the viability window?"

"About fifteen minutes," Bertra said. "If the subject doesn't inhale it, they live. If they do, that's it."

Laurel ran the numbers in her head. Crowd size. Airflow. Exposure time. It didn't matter. Everyone was going to breathe it in.

Bertra gave a small nod toward the door. "Fitz is making you a special little canister with your name on it. I can't wait to see your brain fry."

Viv whimpered and drew closer to Laurel.

Kohnex leaned across Abigail to stare at her. "Don't fret, little one. I have the universe on my side."

Laurel cut him a look. Did he actually believe what he was saying? The detached, self-justifying delusion of it? She couldn't parse whether he was lying or had fully subscribed to his own warped narrative.

Viv's eyes filled. A single tear slid down her cheek, cutting through the grime. "I'm sorry about this, Laurel. This is my fault."

"This isn't your fault," she said tightly. "I didn't know Abigail's lawyer was a war criminal in a leather jacket."

Abigail leaned forward to look past her. "But you got in that trunk because of the girl." Her eyes locked on Viv. "It is your fault we're here."

Laurel shoved her back, hard enough to snap Abigail's head around. "Shut up. I'm done with this."

Bertra's voice cut across the tension. "All of you, shut up."

Viv sniffed. "This is because I snooped, isn't it? I'm sorry."

Bertra focused on her. "I knew who you were the second I hired you. We sought you out, remember?"

Laurel frowned. "You hired her because of me?"

Abigail chuckled. "You're smarter than you look, Bertra." She shrugged. "Bertra knew I had information and would use it if necessary, so she looked for any leverage. I'm tied to you, Laurel, and you're tied to Viv." Her chin lowered. "But you really didn't need to have a sniper aim at me."

"I wish he'd killed you," Bertra snapped. "Henry? Lock them in the storage closet. We'll spray the canister under the door."

Vexler adjusted his stance and raised the gun—aiming it directly at Viv's face. "Everybody get up and move."

"No," Abigail said.

He cocked his head. "I'll just shoot you."

She exhaled. "Good point." She stood and yanked Kohnex to his feet. Laurel followed suit, pulling Viv up and shielding her with her body.

"This way," Vexler said, gesturing with the gun. "I'm tired of you people. I wish we could skip to the end."

"The canister will be ready in just a few minutes," Bertra added, her voice too casual. "We can perform a quick experiment on them, film it, and send it off to the bidders. Then hit them hard tomorrow with the church carnage."

Laurel kept her body between them and the girl as they walked down the sterile hallway. Every second bought was worth it. "Why did you kill Dr. Sandoval?"

Bertra shrugged. "He was sleeping with Melissa Palmtree. She's the one who told Tyler Griggs about our plans."

"And?"

"She was in until she heard how many people were going to die. Then she tried to back out and gave that moronic Tyler Griggs evidence of our trials and upcoming plans. So we slipped a canister into her car, and it went off before she headed into that bar to speak with him. We got to him the next day. Took him out to the forest to watch, and he jumped off a cliff."

Poor Tyler. "So Dr. Sandoval was killed—why?" Laurel asked.

Bertra glanced at her watch. "He was acting off. Paranoid. Pissed off that we ended Melissa. I was concerned that he'd turn into a whistleblower. So, when you visited the lab, and everyone seemed to think you were the target for the first sniper attack, it made sense for Vexler to shoot him through the window. You still thought you were the target."

Abigail looked at Vexler. "You're one for four. You suck as a sniper."

Laurel elbowed her hard. "Would you shut up?"

Abigail rolled her eyes. "Fine."

Laurel tried to attach the dots. "Why send Mark Bitterson in his black truck to shoot at us?"

"Agent Smudgeon. We figured Tyler might've gotten word to him, so we had to take a risk." Bertra snorted. "Then we had to kill Bitterson, that moron. He was illegally harvesting the yew trees for us, as you probably know. He'd pass the pickup information to Melissa Palmtree through the good Detective Robertson, and she'd send money back to Bitterson the same way."

Viv whimpered but kept moving.

"What about Larry Scott?" Laurel asked, trying to find a way out of this mess.

Bertra's lip rose in contempt. "He was a tech who got too nosy. Fitz killed him and staged the suicide."

Viv gave a soft sound of distress.

Bertra ignored her. "As for Dr. Liu? That was an accident. Can you believe it? She helped make the concoction, and she sprayed herself. Dumbass."

They reached the end of the hall. A metal door stood half-open—supplies stacked along the shelves. Cleaning fluid. Paper rolls. Sealed boxes.

Vexler jerked the gun toward the closet. "Inside. Now."

Viv went in first. Abigail followed. Kohnex stepped in without a word, followed by Laurel. The room smelled like bleach and old dust. Everything inside was quiet.

Vexler stepped back, grinning faintly. "I'll be back," he said. "Or rather, the spray will." He slammed the door. The lock turned with a loud rattle.

Laurel cataloged the entire room in a second. "Tim? I need your jacket."

He shrugged out of it and handed it over. She ducked down and shoved it between the door and floor.

"You think that will work?" Abigail asked.

"Can't hurt." Laurel turned to study the supply shelf. Nothing too dangerous there.

Viv sank to the floor to sit, and Kohnex followed suit, looking dazed again.

Laurel grabbed three bottles off the shelf—one labeled DESCALER, another PEROXIDE CLEANER, and the third marked AMMONIA-BASED DEGREASER. It was all cheap and generic industrial stock.

She set them down. "We mix the peroxide and descaler first. That'll give us heat, gas expansion, and the exothermic reaction we need. Then we'll add ammonia for vapor pressure."

"We need pressure *and* direction," Abigail said, stepping in close.

Laurel nodded. "We're going to make a directional blast. Controlled. Somewhat." She reached for a mop bucket that was lightweight plastic, warped slightly from age, and tore off the handle. Then she grabbed a roll of foil and a box of steel wool pads. She shredded the foil and packed it into the base with the wool, pouring in a shallow layer of descaler. The chemical stench bit immediately into the air.

Viv coughed once and covered her nose with her sleeve.

"Aluminum and acid. Unstable gas production," Laurel explained, working fast. "It'll heat and build. When we add the peroxide, the whole thing kicks."

Kohnex stared. "How do you know this stuff?"

"I read." Laurel didn't look up. "Now give me that bottle."

He handed her the peroxide. She poured half of it over the mixture. It hissed, immediately bubbling. Foam climbed over the aluminum, slow at first, then racing.

"Ammonia is last," Abigail said.

Laurel had to hurry. "Seal it up."

They slammed the lid on the bucket and duct-taped it shut with a roll from the shelf. Laurel tilted it sideways, pressed the taped spout directly against the bottom edge of the door, and lined it up with the lock assembly.

"Everybody go to the back far corner and cover your ears," Laurel said quietly.

They obeyed.

Laurel twisted the spray cap off the ammonia and dumped it through a small cut she'd made in the lid with a rusted paint scraper. She sealed the hole with pressure from her palm, counted to five, then scrambled back.

The bucket swelled with its plastic creaking and deforming.

Then it blew.

# Chapter 37

The bucket detonated with a wet, concussive crack. It wasn't quite an explosion, not quite a chemical rupture, but something messier and louder than it should have been in a space that small. The air recoiled. The door shuddered violently in its frame, its metal at the base flaring outward in a warped curl. Smoke hissed out in thick gray ribbons, sharp and acidic.

Laurel's ears rang, her equilibrium listing sideways, but she didn't wait for the world to steady.

She surged forward, grabbed the handle, and tore the door open. It resisted, metal warped just enough to fight her, but she forced it. The hallway beyond glowed sickly under flickering fluorescents. "Viv, behind me. Tim, follow her. Abigail, rear guard with your eyes open."

She kept her tone controlled, clipped, and cold. There was no time for comfort. No time for fear. They fell into formation. No alarms blared, and there was no sound beyond their footsteps and the low hum of fluorescent lights. Either the explosion hadn't registered outside the storage room, or the entire lab had been built to hide noise.

Probably the latter.

Laurel led them fast down the corridor, past sealed labs and clean rooms, her boots echoing on the concrete. They climbed the stairs two at a time, reached the main vestibule, and ran outside into the rain.

Laurel turned to Abigail. "Go. I'm sure you can hotwire a car. Take Vexler's Chevy and get help." She nudged Viv toward the car and met Abigail's gaze, making sure she had her sister's full attention. "Keep them safe."

"I'll stay and help you," Kohnex panted. Rain streaked the blood on his face.

"No. Go protect them," Laurel said, pushing him off balance just enough to send him moving. "Get help."

She pivoted and ran back inside, hustled to the emergency cabinet bolted into the corridor wall, and ripped the fire ax free from its brackets. The metal protested with a sharp screech, as if warning her this was a one-way decision. Her hand adjusted on the handle until the grip locked into her palm like it belonged there.

She couldn't let them finish filling the canisters and possibly escape.

Running down the stairs, her boots struck the concrete in hard, purposeful strides. Hitting the bottom, she turned left and advanced down the hallway.

Her fingers tightened around the ax.

The door to the secondary lab hung slightly open. She didn't stop to listen or wait for backup that wasn't coming.

She stepped in.

Fitz stood inside near the center table, hunched over something. The harsh ceiling lights cast jagged angles across his back and shoulders. His hands worked quickly, fingers twitching over a small black box in front of him that appeared slick, mechanical, and humming with silent energy. Not the canister. Wires ran from it to something on the counter behind him. A detonator? A secondary device?

"Hey," she said.

He turned fast, just beginning to register the threat when she closed the distance.

She swung the ax handle and hit his skull with a blunt, sickening crack, just above the temple, careful not to cut him with the blade. His body dropped straight down, knees buckling, arms falling limp at his sides. He collapsed in a heap, his head smacking the floor once more on impact.

She didn't watch him fall.

Didn't check for breath.

Her eyes were already on the workspace.

The canister wasn't there.

Her stomach tightened.

Damn it.

She turned, scanning every surface and clocked the metal table, the open drawers, and the black box blinking slowly on the bench. Had he been preparing a bomb for the facility? If so, he hadn't had enough time to arm it. Her thoughts sharpened again, pushing through the ringing in her ears, through the rising thrum of tension in her spine.

The canister was gone.

She pivoted fast, her boots sliding on the slick floor. Her vision blurred at the edges—adrenaline pushing blood too hard, her body catching up to what her mind already knew. The weapon was still close by, and Vexler had a gun. Gun usually beat ax.

The lab buzzed with the low hum of active equipment. Oscillating lights on the far wall blinked in no discernible pattern. She could feel her pulse pounding behind her eyes. Her grip on the ax tightened.

She forced her breathing to slow, but her heart wouldn't cooperate as she sprinted back into the hallway, cutting right and toward what looked like offices. She could hear typing. Her boots pounded down concrete. Alarm klaxons started to whine behind the walls. Fitz had triggered something before she dropped him. Great.

She slammed through the first door.

Vexler stood over a workstation, typing with one hand, the other holding a small, sleek silver canister. Viv's name had been written on it in marker.

"Laurel," he said, voice calm, his gun on the table. "You're faster than I expected."

Laurel lunged.

He turned and raised the canister like a weapon, but she drove into his chest with her shoulder. The canister clattered across the floor and rolled under the desk.

Vexler swung with his fist and connected with the side of her face. Pain lit up her temple. She didn't stop fighting, going on pure adrenaline.

They went down hard. He scrambled for the desk chair, but she caught his ankle and yanked. He kicked at her, but she was already on him. She reached for the ax and used it again—swinging the blade this time, slicing it across his ribs. Once. Twice. He stopped moving. Blood spread across his shirt in a dark, blooming smear.

Laurel stood, breath coming in broken shards, ribs aching from the hit she'd taken in the fight. Her whole body hummed with exhaustion, the kind that didn't wait for rest. It clawed at the edges of consciousness, pulling her toward collapse. But she wasn't done.

Not yet.

Where the hell was Bertra?

Laurel turned in a slow circle, the ax still clutched in her hand. She scanned the room and studied low counters, overturned metal chairs, and shattered screens. Vexler lay crumpled on the floor, blood seeping across the tile, face slack.

"Henry?" Bertra called from somewhere upstairs. "Hurry up. I'll meet you in the van."

Laurel bolted into the hallway and ran, holding the ax handle with two hands. Every breath burned. Her legs carried her forward on instinct, not energy, up the stairwell toward the main exit. She burst across the main room and slammed into the final door with her shoulder, stumbling out into the open.

The storm had broken.

The night was a chaos of wind and driving rain, and for a moment she was blinded as the rain and noise crashed into her at once.

Then—

Bertra.

She stood in the open, just outside the exit. Her jacket was half-zipped, and her hair was slicked back and plastered to her skull. She held a larger canister in her right hand, her arm extended toward Laurel with the calm steadiness of someone pointing a cigarette, not a weapon.

"This is not the test I wanted," Bertra said. Her voice was quiet and almost casual with the storm muffling it. "I guess I'll try again after you." She shrugged, and her thumb twitched toward the release valve.

Laurel didn't breathe.

Then the sky opened.

A mechanical roar split the air—heavy blades cutting through the storm, steady and close. Wind pushed down from above, flattening the grass and pelting them with rain. The helicopter came into view just above the tree line, searchlight piercing through the downpour. The beam swept across the compound and locked onto them.

Laurel flinched from the brightness, raising her hand instinctively to block the light.

Bertra turned her head.

That's when Laurel saw him.

Huck.

Half his body leaning out of the open door of the chopper, headset on, rifle braced against the edge. He didn't shout. He didn't give a warning.

Muzzle flash.

The shot cracked through the storm, sharp and final.

Bertra's eyes widened a fraction as a hole appeared in the center of her forehead. The canister slipped from her hand, her mouth opening as if to speak. She dropped straight back, her body folding like someone had cut a string.

Laurel surged forward, slipping on the wet concrete. Her knee hit hard, but she didn't stop. The canister bounced once, dangerously close to the edge of the stairwell.

She caught it midroll and tightened her hands around it.

The wind from the helicopter blasted against her skin. Laurel didn't know if it was rain or tears on her face. Didn't care. Her pulse thundered in her skull. Every muscle screamed, but she stood, gripping the canister.

The helicopter circled lower. Laurel saw Huck again, leaning out, scanning the ground, rifle still in hand. His gaze met hers. No words passed between them. He gave a small nod.

She was *his reason*.

# Chapter 38

"This might possibly be my worst nightmare," Huck said, placing the bowl of popcorn beside the bottle of wine.

The wineglasses were already half-full, sweating a little under the soft glow of the old floor lamp. His coffee table bore the scars of time, such as rings from forgotten mugs, the ghost of a fishing lure project gone rogue, and a deep gouge that may have involved a screwdriver and a bet. Laurel didn't say anything right away. She made a small sound, something between a sigh and a hum, and reached for her wine. One foot tucked under her, she leaned into the cushions, shoulders relaxed, a blanket bunched at her side with an ice pack next to it.

She held bruises from her fights at the lab.

The fire crackled gently in the corner, warm enough to make the windows fog just slightly. Even the thermostat had given up trying to compete. The dog had commandeered his bed and allowed the cat to share it, which in itself was something worth writing down. They were nose to nose, both deep in the kind of nap that only came after a long day of doing nothing.

Huck sank into the couch with a sigh. He extended his legs onto the table, clinking his ankle against a coaster, and slid his arm over Laurel's shoulder.

"As nightmares go, you're not wrong." Laurel took a long sip and stared at the screen. "It's the smirk," she said. "I want to slap the smirk right off her face."

The podcast ran on the plasma screen, where three women sat under overly flattering lighting. Journalist Rachel Raprenzi, whose blond braid appeared tight and elegant at the same time, her eyebrows up and her face open. Prosecuting Attorney Tamera Hornhart, all jawline and controlled breath, who already looked like a politician ready for state office. And Dr. Abigail Caine, who appeared like a brave and wounded heroine in a pink dress just a little too large.

"I just cannot believe everything you went through," Rachel said, blinking slowly, as if the weight of it might take her under.

Abigail lifted a hand, two fingers raised. "As soon as I knew what was happening, I had to act and tell the truth. I can't believe that my lawyer, my successful and rather well-known lawyer, was working with this lab group that had created a bio-weapon and thought himself a sniper."

"Of course not," Huck muttered, rolling his eyes.

Laurel snorted. "Can someone please tell her this isn't a silly movie?"

"She probably already wrote the script."

Onscreen, Rachel zeroed down. "Abigail, it's my understanding that the charges against you have been dropped. The charges for the murder of Zeke Caine, your father?"

"Yes," Abigail said smoothly. "They have."

Rachel put on her serious face. "Did you reach some sort of immunity agreement with the feds?"

"Of course not," Abigail said. "My case wasn't federal. I was charged by the state of Washington."

Tamera nodded. "Yes. In looking at all the evidence that we have, and in speaking with witnesses, Dr. Caine has a clear case of self-defense. We believe very strongly that she is innocent of the murder of Zeke Caine because she was defending herself."

Huck tucked Laurel in closer to his body. A log popped on the fire. The cat lifted its head, gave one unimpressed blink, and settled back down onto the dog's flank.

"The feds convinced her to drop the case," Laurel admitted. "So Abigail would tell them more about the compound. Where the other canisters were hidden in the main lab."

"She knew?" Huck asked, voice flat.

"Yeah. She knew." Laurel had just been filled in by the Seattle office. Agent Norrs was still in the hospital but should be released in a day or so. Laurel stared at the screen. Abigail's face filled the frame now, calm, poised, well-practiced. "It makes you wonder what else she has up her sleeve, doesn't it?"

Huck swallowed some of his cabernet. "This gives Tamera a higher profile, too. She's the one who 'cleared' Abigail. It looks good from every angle. Right here, we have a real bipartisan redemption arc."

"It worked out for everybody," Laurel said. "Except for Zeke Caine. Not that he deserved to die, but he did deserve to go to prison."

"Double jeopardy attaches," Huck muttered. "Abigail can't be tried for murdering Zeke again."

"Not for the death of Zeke Caine," Laurel agreed. "But we still have two or three other cases open against her. She's not going to win in the end, Huck. She can't."

He didn't respond.

On the screen, Abigail looked directly at the camera. There was the hint of a smile that wasn't quite smug. It was more like she'd already read the last page of the entire story and knew the rest of them hadn't caught up yet. "I would also like to thank and note the bravery of my sister, FBI Special Agent in Charge Laurel Snow."

Laurel didn't blink. Didn't move. Huck didn't either. The silence in the room stretched, brittle and tight. Even the fire seemed to lean in.

"After we escaped that hideous lab," Abigail said, her voice silky,

"Laurel went back in by herself and took on people who had guns and explosives and a deadly pathogen that would've fried her brain. She is truly, truly brave and should be commended."

Rachel lost her smile. It disappeared slowly, like a camera lens pulling out of focus. "Oh. I totally agree," she said. "Such bravery is . . . impressive."

"Then there's the handsome Huck Rivers," Abigail added, winking. "Talk about a crack shot."

Huck winced. "Sometimes I just don't know what we're going to do about her."

"I don't either." Laurel reached for the remote and clicked the screen off. Just like that, Abigail was gone. The fire still burned. The cat blinked. The dog snored. "Enough of that. There's nothing we can do right now. We'll pursue the other cases against her as soon as we can."

Huck chuckled and leaned back against the couch. "Who the hell knows what else is out there? If she was tied up in this, she could be tied up in anything."

"Yes. Abigail is cocky and arrogant and likes attention. That makes her reckless." Laurel snuggled closer into Huck's side. She felt the weight of him, warm and real and exactly where he should be. "I think I should speak with Walter about taking his time with Ena. They just started dating."

Huck chuckled. "That's totally up to you. I'm staying out of it."

Laurel exhaled. She'd worry about that talk at another date. "Also, I invited Kate and the girls over for a barbecue tomorrow. Same with Walter and Ena. I hope it's okay."

He was quiet for a moment. "Of course it's okay."

She caught something in his tone. Something unspoken. Not quite doubt. More like . . . waiting. She turned and looked at him, really looked at him. Took in those ridiculous honey bourbon eyes that always felt like they could look right through her.

"Yes," she said. "I accept your proposal to live together."

His eyes widened slightly, then softened.

"I would still like to build that barndominium over on my mom's property," Laurel continued, "but we could build it to your specifications, if you like. And then we can decide where to live."

"That sounds like a plan, Special Agent Laurel Snow."

He leaned in and kissed her. Not polite. Not tentative. Deep. Certain.

She kissed him back and let herself feel those emotions she usually kept locked down in a steel box under ten layers of rationality. She let them move. For once, she didn't care if they made sense. She didn't have to.

They were going to live together. Plan a future together. She filled with warmth. "I do love you, Huck Rivers."

"I know." He kissed the top of her head. "I love you, too. It's not chemical, anthropological, or biological. It's the real kind."

She didn't understand it, but she believed him.

The fire crackled. The rain fell. Somewhere in the background, the cat rolled over and kicked the dog in its sleep. Huck's hand slid to her waist, and Laurel let her head rest on his shoulder.

She had no idea what the future held. Had no clue what Abigail would do next, or what cases would land on her desk next week. But she knew Huck Rivers would be a solid force in that future with her.

For right now, that was more than enough.

He just might be *her reason* as well.

***Obsession takes center stage in this steamy, neon-lit, dark romantasy twist on* Snow White and the Huntsman, *set in a seductive world of money, power, billionaires, and the dangerous desires that drive them.***

*Mirror, Mirror . . . on the wall. Will desire make them fall?*

ALEXEI

I've spent the last seven years in the hell of a maximum-security prison, every moment consumed by the need for revenge—revenge against the bastards who framed me, and revenge against the family who stole everything I owned.

Now that I'm finally free, nothing will stand in my way.

Not even her—my hot-as-sin new lawyer. Maybe she's another weapon sent by my enemies to break me, or maybe she's the key to my freedom. Either way, once she's mine, I'm never letting her go.

ROSALIE

When I took this case, I thought I had it under control.

But Alexei is no typical convicted killer—he's a dangerously seductive force of nature. Perhaps it's the lingering power from his days as heir to a global social media empire.

Innocent or not, he's dangerous in the worst and best ways.

I secure Alexei's release as we prepare for a new trial, but he wastes no time turning against his traitorous relatives and plotting his return to power. Amidst the chaos, our explosive chemistry ignites, putting us—and everyone I care about—in the crosshairs of ruthless enemies. If we can't stop them, Alexei plans to burn the whole world down.

And if anything, he's a man of his word.

## Grimm Bargains: Tales of Power and Dark Deals

Ancient cultures first used crystals in rituals, medicine, and adornment. The smartest of these people quickly learned that gems hold a vibrating energy that can be captured and exchanged with human beings. This exchange grants health and clear thinking, which in ancient times, when a cold could kill, quickly led to power and wealth.

As the world turned away from natural medicine and philosophy, four powerful families continued exploring their connection to certain stones. They began to hide their ability to exchange energy and thus exploited this extra health and strength to become leaders throughout the centuries without fear of pandemics, most diseases, and nonlethal injuries.

In the modern age, these families are no longer kings and queens, but modern moguls, true billionaires who have learned how to utilize the energy of crystals in business systems. Today, with social media and AI infiltrating every aspect of our lives, these four families have created social media companies by harnessing and using the power from these precious stones.

Now, not only do the families control social media companies, but they run mafia-like organizations where members obey their every command. In the social media world, the more follower interactions, the more the stone powering the system draws. The families with their companies have jockeyed for position, and currently, as of the writing of this book, here is the ranking when it comes to number of followers and financial assets:

*MALICE MEDIA*, powered by the energy harnessed from garnets, is a next-generation platform that uses neural interface technology to share thoughts, emotions, and experiences directly. It offers glimpses into a user's mental and emotional state. Thorn Beathach charges and exchanges energy with the garnets. Its call to action is: MINDMELD NOW.

*AQUARIUS SOCIAL,* powered by the energy harnessed from aquamarines, is an emotional intelligence platform that uses AI to analyze a user's emotional state. There are real-time updates of connections where people can share emotions over long distances. Alana Beaumont charges and exchanges energy with the aquamarines, and she's trying to teach her cousin, Scarlett Winter, to do the same. The call to action is: EMOTE NOW.

*HOLOGRID HUB*, powered by the energy harnessed from amethysts, is a 3D holographic social media platform where people can share experiences together at any location, including Mars or the Moon or Ancient Rome. Hendrix Sokolov and Alexei Sokolov charge the amethysts. Its call to action is: PROJECT NOW.

*TIMEGEM MOMENTS*, powered by the energy harnessed by citrines and/or diamonds, uses advanced temporal technology to record, save, and replay moments in real time, so people share memories with each other. Sylveria Rendale can charge diamonds, and Ella Rendale can charge citrines. Its call to action is: CAPTURE NOW.

There have been hints of a fifth social media company making moves, but nobody knows if this is just a rumor or if there is a new player on the board.

# One Dark Kiss

*Rosalie*

Alone, I cross my legs again beneath the intimidating metal table secured to the floor, feeling as out of place as a raven in a nursery rhyme. The heat clunks and whispers from a grate in the ceiling but fails to warm the interview room, and when the door finally opens, the heavy frame scrapes against the grimy cement floor.

My spine naturally straightens, and my chin lifts as my client stalks inside, his hands cuffed to a chain secured around his narrow waist. He doesn't shuffle. Or walk. Or saunter.

No. This man . . . stalks.

His gaze rakes me, and I mean, *rakes* me. Black eyes—deep and dark—glint with more than one threat of violence in their depths. He kicks back the lone metal chair opposite me and sits in one fluid motion. The scent of motor oil in fresh rain, something all male, wafts toward me.

I swallow.

The guard, a burly man with gray hair, stares at me, concern in his eyes.

"Please remove his cuffs," I say, my focus not leaving my client.

*My client*. I don't practice criminal law. Never have and don't want to.

The guard hesitates. "Miss, I—"

"I appreciate it." I make my voice as authoritative as possible, considering I'm about to crap my pants. Or rather, my best navy-blue pencil skirt bought on clearance at the Women's Center Thrift Store. I don't live there, but I'm happy to shop there. Rich people give away good items.

In a jangle of metal, the guard hitches toward us, releases the cuffs, and turns on his scuffed boot toward the door. "Want me to stay inside?"

"No, thank you." I wait until he shrugs, exits, and shuts the door. "Mr. Sokolov? I'm Rosalie Mooncrest, your new attorney from Cage and Lion."

"What happened to my old attorney?" His voice is the rasp of a blade on a sharpening stone.

I clear my throat and focus only on his eyes and not the tattoo of a panther prowling across the side of his neck, amethyst eyes glittering. "Mr. Molasses died in a car accident a month ago." Molasses was a partner in the firm, and he represented Alexei in the criminal trial that had led to a guilty verdict. "I take it he wasn't in touch with you often?"

"No." Alexei leans back and finishes removing the cuffs from his wrists to slap onto the table. "You're responsible for my being brought to this minimum-security section of this prison?"

Actually, my firm has juice and a named partner had made this happen. "Yes, and it's temporary. You're back to your normal cell block after this meeting."

His chin lifts. "So this plush locale for our conference is for you, princess? The prestigious law firm doesn't want you dirtied by the bowels of this place?"

Probably true. "I'm here to help you, Mr. Sokolov."

His eyes glitter sharper than the panther's on his neck. "Don't call me that name again."

I frown. "Sokolov?"

"Yes. It's Alexei. No mister."

Fair enough. I can't help but study him. Unruly black hair, unfathomable dark eyes, golden-brown skin, and bone structure chipped out of a mountain with a finely sharpened tool. Brutally rugged, the angles of his face reveal a primal strength that's ominously beautiful. The deadliest predators in life usually are.

Awareness filters through me. I don't like it.

Worse yet, he's studying me right back, as if he has Superman's X-ray vision and no problem using it. He lingers inappropriately on my breasts beneath my crisp white blouse before sliding to my face, his gaze a rough scrape I can feel. "You fuck your way through law school?"

My mouth drops open for the smallest of seconds. "Are you insane?"

"Insanity is relative. It depends on who has who locked in what cage," he drawls.

Did he just quote Ray Bradbury? "You might want to remember that I'm here to help you."

"Hence my question. Not that I'm judging. If you want to do the entire parole board to get me out, then don't hold back. If that isn't your plan, then I'd like to know that you understand the law."

It's official. Alexei Sokolov is an asshole. "Listen, Mr. Sokolov—"

"That name. You don't want me to tell you again." His threat is softly spoken.

A shiver tries to take me, so I shift my weight, hiding my reaction. I stare him directly in the eyes, as one does with any bully. "Why? What are you going to do?" I jerk my head toward the door, where no doubt the guard awaits on the other side.

Alexei leans toward me and metal clangs. "Peaflower? I can have you over this table, your skirt hiked up, and spank your ass raw before the dumbass guard can find his keys, much less gather the backup he'd need to get you free. You won't sit for a week. Maybe two." His gaze warms. "Now that's a very pretty blush."

"That's my planning-a-murder expression," I retort instantly, my cheeks flaming hot.

His lip curls for the briefest of moments in almost a smile. "Women who look like you don't usually have a brain."

My eyebrows shoot up so quickly it's a shock a migraine doesn't follow. He did not just say that. "You are one backassward son of a bitch," I blurt out, completely forgetting any sense of professionalism.

That smile tries to take hold and almost makes it. Not quite, though. "Fuck, you're a contradiction." He flattens a hand on the table. A large, tattooed, dangerous-looking hand. "As a rule, a beautiful woman is a terrible disappointment."

Now he's quoting freakin' Carl Jung? "You must've had a lot of time to read here in prison . . . the last seven years."

"I have." A hardness invades his eyes. "You any good at your job?"

The most inappropriate humor takes me, and I look around the room. "Does it matter? I don't see a plenitude of counselors in here trying to help you."

"Big word. Plenitude. I would've gone with cornucopia. Has a better sound to it."

I need to regain control of this situation. "Listen, Mr.—"

He stiffens and I stop. Cold.

We look at each other, and I swear, the room itself has a heartbeat that rebounds around us. I don't want to back down. But also, I know in every cell of my being, he isn't issuing idle threats. A man like him never bluffs.

Surprisingly, triumph that I refrained from using his last name doesn't light his eyes. Instead, contemplation and approval?

I *really* don't like that.

My legs tremble like I've run ten miles, and my lungs are failing to catch up. I suppose anybody would feel like this if trapped with a hell beast in a small cage. There's more than fear to my reaction. Adrenaline has that effect on people. That must be it. I reach into my briefcase and retrieve several pieces of paper. "If you want me as your attorney, you need to sign this retainer agreement so I can file a Notice of Appearance with the court."

"And if I don't?"

I place the papers on the cold table. "Then have a nice life." I meet his stare evenly.

"My funds are low. I don't suppose you'll take cigarettes or sex in trade?"

Is that amusement in his eyes? That had better not be amusement. I examine his broad shoulders and, no doubt, impressive chest, beneath the orange jumpsuit. How can he look sexy in orange? Plus, the man hasn't been with a woman in seven years—he'd be on fire. A little part of me, one I'll never admit to, considers the offer just for the—no doubt—multiple and wild orgasms. "I don't smoke and you're not my type. But no worries. My firm is taking your case pro bono until we unbind your trust fund."

He latches onto the wrong part of the statement. "What's your type?"

I inhale through my nose, trying to keep a handle on my temper.

"Don't tell me," he continues, his gaze probing deep. "Three-piece suit, Armani, luxury vehicles?"

"Actually, that's my best friend's type," I drawl. Well, if you add in guns, the Irish mafia, and a frightening willingness to kill.

Alexei scratches the whiskers across his cut jaw. "Right. When was the last time you were with an actual man? You know, somebody who doesn't ask for guidance every step of the way?"

That fact that I don't remember is not one I'll share. My thighs heat, and my temper sparks. "Was this approach charming seven years ago?"

"Not really. Though I didn't need to be charming back then."

True. He was the heir to one of the four most powerful social media companies in the world before he went to prison. Apparently, his family had deserted him immediately. "You might want to give it a try now."

His eyes warm to dark embers, rendering me temporarily speechless. "You don't think I can charm the panties off you?"

"All right. You need to dial it down." I hold out a hand and press down on imaginary air. "A lot."

Heat swells from him. Somehow. "Dial what down?"

"You," I hiss. "All of this. The obnoxious, rudely sexist, prowling panther routine. Use your brain, if you have one. It's our first meeting, and you're driving me crazy. You want me on your side."

"I'd rather have you under me."

I shut my eyes and slam both index fingers to the corners, pressing in. This is unbelievable.

"Getting a headache? I know a remedy for that."

I make the sound of a strangled cat.

His laugh is warm. Rich. Deep.

Jolting, I open my eyes. The laugh doesn't fit with the criminal vibe. It's enthralling.

He stops.

I miss the sound immediately. Maybe I need a vacation.

Using one finger, he draws the paper across the table. "Pen."

I fumble in my briefcase for a blue pen and hand it over.

He signs the retainer quickly and shoves it back at me. "What's the plan?"

The switch in topics gives me whiplash. Even so, I step on firm ground again. "The prosecuting attorney in your case was just arrested for blackmail, peddling influence, and extortion . . . along with the judge, his co-conspirator, who presided over your trial and sentenced you."

His expression doesn't alter. "You can secure my freedom?"

That's my plan, but I don't want to raise his hopes. "I don't know. My best guess is that I can secure you a new trial."

"Will I be free for the duration?"

"I'll make a motion to the court the second I leave here but can't guarantee the outcome." I tilt my head. "Your family's influence would be helpful."

His chin lowers in an intimidating move. "I don't have a family. Don't mention them again."

I blink. "One more comment."

"Go ahead."

"I'm sorry about your brother's death." His younger brother, rather his half brother, was killed a month ago, possibly by my friend's boyfriend, if one could call Thorn Beathach a boyfriend.

Alexei just stares at me.

I feel like a puzzle being solved. "There's a chance his death was part of some sort of social media turf war against Thorn Beathach, who owns Malice Media." Alexei's family owns a rival social media platform, and from what I understand, it's war between them all.

"So?"

This is a mite awkward. "Thorn is currently dating my best friend, so if there's a conflict of interest, I want you to know about it." Not that anybody would ever catch Thorn, if he had killed Alexei's brother after the man had injured Alana. I'm still not sure he was the killer, anyway.

"Are you finished mentioning my family?" Alexei's tone strongly suggests that I am.

"Yes," I whisper.

He cocks his head. "How many criminal trials have you won?"

"None," I say instantly. It's crucial to be honest with clients. "I haven't lost any either."

His head tips up and he watches me from half-closed lids. "You're in charge of the pro bono arm of the firm?"

"No."

"Why you, then?"

It's a fair question as well as a smart one. "I've never lost in a civil trial, so the partners assigned me your case, even though this is criminal procedure."

"Why?"

"Because I'm good and they want you free." I shrug. "This is positive exposure for the firm." Which is what my boss, Jacqueline Lion, told me when assigning me to the docket. "We have several verdicts being overturned because of the judge's corruption, and yours came up, being the most high profile. Losing your case harmed the firm seven years ago."

His nostrils flare. "The firm? The loss hurt *the firm*?"

"Yes." Damn, he's intimidating. Do I want him free to roam the streets? "This is a chance to fix the damage caused."

"And promote you to partner?" he guesses.

My life is none of his business. "I'm good at my job, Alexei." Yeah, I don't use his last name. "You can go with outside counsel. I'll rip up your retainer agreement if you want."

"I want you."

I hear the double entendre and ignore it. "Then it's my way and you'll follow my directives."

Now he smiles. Full on, straight teeth, shocking dimple in his right cheek.

Everything inside me short-circuits and flashes electricity into places sparks don't belong.

He taps his fingers on the table. "I signed the agreement, and this means you work for me. Correct?"

"Yes." But I call the shots.

He moves so suddenly to plant his hand over mine, that I freeze. "You need to learn now that I'm in charge of every situation. Do you understand?"

I try to free myself and fail. His large palm is warm, heavy, and scarred over my skin, with the hard metal table beneath it a shockingly cold contrast. My lungs stutter and hot air fills them. "Whatever game you're playing, stop it right now."

His hand easily covers mine, and his fingers keep me trapped in sizzling heat. "I don't play games, Peaflower. Learn that now."

"Peaflower?" I choke out, leaving my hand beneath his because I have no choice.

"Your eyes," he murmurs. "The blue dissolves into violet like the Butterfly Pea Flower. A man could find solace from everlasting torment just staring into those velvety depths."

I have no words for him. Are there words? Scarred, barely uncuffed, and intense, he just whispered the most romantic words imaginable. And he's a killer. Just because the judge was corrupt doesn't mean Alexei hadn't committed cold-blooded murder. Two things can be true at once. "We need to keep this professional, if you want me to help you."

He releases me and stands. "Guard," he calls out.

My hand feels chilled and lonely.

Keys jangle on the other side of the door.

"Rosalie, this is your out. If you tear up the retainer, I'll find another lawyer. If you stay, if you decide to represent me, there's no quitting. You're in this for the duration. Tell me you get me." Fire burns in his eyes now.

I stand, even though my knees are knocking together. "I'm doing my job."

"Just so we understand each other."

The door opens, and the same guard from before moves inside, pauses, and visibly finds his balls before securing the cuffs on Alexei, who watches me the entire time. He allows the guard to lead him to the door.

Once there, he looks over his shoulder. "I hope you stick with me in this. Also, you might want to conduct a background check on Miles Molasses from your firm. He was a co-conspirator to the judge and prosecutor." His teeth flash. "How convenient that he just died in an accident. Right?"